Missing Mercy

Other Books by Stephenia H. McGee

Ironwood Plantation
The Whistle Walk
Heir of Hope
Missing Mercy
*Ironwood Series Set
*Get the entire series at a discounted price

The Accidental Spy Series
*Previously published as The Liberator Series
An Accidental Spy
A Dangerous Performance
A Daring Pursuit
*Accidental Spy Series Set
*Get the entire series at a discounted price

Stand Alone Titles
In His Eyes
Eternity Between Us

Time Travel
Her Place in Time
(Stand alone, but ties to Rosswood from The Accidental Spy Series)
The Hope of Christmas Past
(Stand alone, but ties to Belmont from In His Eyes)

Novellas
The Heart of Home
The Hope of Christmas Past

www.StepheniaMcGee.com
Sign up for my newsletter to be the first to see new cover reveals and
be notified of release dates
New newsletter subscribers receive a free book!
Get yours here
bookhip.com/QCZVKZ

Missing Mercy

Ironwood Plantation Family Saga Book Three

Stephenia H. McGee

Cover Design: Ravven
Cover Models: Ciera LadieCe Smith and Elizabeth Eaves Eubanks

Library Cataloging Data
Names: McGee, Stephenia H. (Stephenia H. McGee) 1983 –
Title: Missing Mercy; Ironwood Plantation Family Saga Book 3/ Stephenia H. McGee
376p. 5.5 in. × 8.5 in. (13.97 cm × 21.59 cm)
Description: By The Vine Press digital eBook edition | By The Vine Press Trade paperback edition | Mississippi: By The Vine Press, 2019
Summary: Mercy is missing. Faith is floundering. Only truth can lead them to freedom.
Identifiers: LCCN: 2019949559| ISBN-13: 978-1-63564-041-0 (trade) | 978-1-63564-042-7 (POD) | 978-1-63564-040-3 (ebk.)
1. Christian Historical 2. Historical 3. Coming of Age 4. Clean and Wholesome 5. Action & Adventure 6. Religious Historical 7. Friendship

So shall my word be that goeth forth out of my mouth: it shall not return unto me void, but it shall accomplish that which I please, and it shall prosper in the thing whereto I sent it.
Isaiah 55:11

For the one who feels plain, ordinary, or forgotten.
He has great plans for you, and His plans always prosper.

Prologue

The dust motes swirled in the land of discarded treasures, rising from where they had collected for generations to find flight once more around what had once been a grand ballroom. Emily pushed up from the floor where she'd been sitting, the rounded bump of her belly making her feel unstable. She breathed in the familiar scent of the forgotten and used an antique coatrack to steady her unbalanced form.

Pressing her hands into her back, she contemplated leaving the last of the box for another day, but not being one to leave things unfinished, reached down to pull up the final stack of yellowed magazines out of a deteriorating cardboard box to store in a new plastic bin. They teetered in her hands, the stack uneven.

She shifted the magazines and discovered a small leather book tucked between them. The copies of *Good Housekeeping* and *Southern Living* tumbled to the floor.

Could it be?

Emily clutched the book, a thrill running through her. It looked so much like Lydia's diary that her palms began to sweat.

Excitement skittered down her spine as she brushed her hands down her jeans. This could be the key to unlocking the next chapters of Ironwood's history! Untying the fragile string, she gently released it and pulled back the cracked cover.

Her eyes devoured the first few lines of perfect script and she let out a squeal. Wait until Luke saw this! Cradling the treasure in the crook of her arm, Emily hurried down the stairs as quickly as her rounded form would allow. To think, Luke had wanted to throw that box out!

Ah, but she'd known better. Ironwood held far too many secrets for such rash actions. If her discovery of Lydia's diary and the hidden treasures under the floorboards hadn't taught Luke that fact, then Emily didn't know what would.

She held firm to the worn handrail that still tingled with the caress of her ancestors and did her best to watch her step, though she couldn't see much past her belly.

The smell of roasting meat tickled her nose and made her stomach rumble. She rubbed her palm over the baby and smiled as she stepped around one of Luke's latest projects at the bottom of the stairs. "Eating for two" hardly covered it. More like eating for an elephant. She tucked a stray hair behind her ear and stepped into the kitchen, relishing the anticipation of a surprise.

"You won't believe what I found!"

Luke closed the oven and draped a hand towel over his broad shoulder. "Shall I venture a guess?" He propped a hand on the island. "Another treasure hidden up there in all that dust?"

So far she'd uncovered pictures, trinkets, and even old letters in her aunt's attic storage, but none of them compared to this. "Best thing since Lydia's diary."

His blue eyes widened, his amusement replaced with curiosity. "Really?" He skirted the island and came closer. "Fodder for another book?"

Emily held up the small journal. The novel she'd written based on her ancestor Lydia's diary had been picked up by a publishing house. The editor had loved the story and had offered a contract better than Emily could have ever hoped for. Not that Emily could take much credit for the series of events she'd woven into a tale of love, loss, and discovery. That had been Ruth and Lydia's story. Emily had simply retold the events.

Then there had been her own story, the one she'd never intended to write, but her editor had loved that one too.

"So?" Luke asked, drawing her out of her thoughts.

She ran her finger over the cracked leather cover. "Another journal. I think this one belongs to Lydia's daughter."

Luke took the book and turned it over. "Family tradition continues, I see." His eyes sparkled. "Should I even ask if you have already read it?"

Emily laughed and plucked the book from his hands. "See? You don't know me at all."

Luke grinned. "You mean you actually waited for me?"

"Waited. Starving. Lost feeling in my toes from sitting too long…" She gave him a wink.

Luke laughed as he pulled her against his side and kissed her temple.

After giving him a squeeze, she moved to the table so she could sit and try to keep seven months' worth of pregnancy from making her feet swell. As she propped her puffy ankles up on a chair, however, she realized it was already too late.

Emily opened the cover and cleared her throat, then let a pause linger in the air. She was more anxious than her husband to know the contents of the journal, but enjoyed teasing him too much to let the moment pass without plumping the anticipation.

"Well?" Luke chuckled.

She ran a finger over the small, perfect script. "May twelfth, eighteen eighty-seven. Mercy has gone missing."

One

Ironwood Plantation
Oakville, Mississippi
May 1887

*H*er life would begin as soon as that preacher stopped talking. Lord forgive her, but the news burning in her chest and squirming its way out of her fluttering fingers brought with it far more hope than the drone of the second Sunday sermon. And the Lord knew better than anyone that Mercy Carpenter yearned for the kind of life that happened for everyone outside the beautiful prison of Ironwood.

Heat swarmed through the open chapel windows like the Mississippi mosquitos, making her feel sticky and all the more ready to move. No one else seemed to notice. Women lazily swished paper fans in front of dark, glistening faces but kept their focus on the message.

Mercy's feet wouldn't be still. They'd tapped during the singing, they'd shuffled during the preaching, and now they shifted around so much during the prayer that she received an elbow to the ribs from Mama.

"Stop it," Mama whispered through clenched teeth. "You about to wear a hole in the floor."

Mercy forced her feet to settle, but then her knees started

bouncing. She'd never wanted so much for a preaching service to end. Not that she minded Mr. Dawson's way of doing it. He made good points, and his thoughts were clear and intelligent. He just wasn't as passionate in his delivery as Mr. John, who had a way of preaching that made the people shout out agreements and praise the Lord. If John had been preaching, no one would've noticed her fidgeting.

Mama pinched her arm.

"Ouch!"

Mama leaned so close that the feather on her straw hat tickled Mercy's cheek. "Listen!" she said loudly enough that Mercy's two younger sisters snickered. Mama leaned back into Papa's side, casting Mercy one final warning glance.

Mercy shifted her attention to Mr. Dawson, whose blue eyes were now fixed upon her. He kept talking, but the flush in his pink cheeks told her he'd been agitated with her interruption. She'd always found it interesting how white folk's skin changed color so much. Especially when they were irritated. She glanced at Faith, who sat calmly across the center aisle with her parents. As much a sister as the two born to her own parents, Faith was in many ways Mercy's opposite.

Where Mercy's complexion was tawny brown, Faith's was milky. Mercy loved people, Faith held back in social gatherings. And Mercy fidgeted while Faith could settle into a statuesque picture of serenity.

Faith caught her eye and smiled, then nodded ever so slightly back toward the preacher. Leave it to her to try to keep Mercy out of trouble.

After Mercy had learned that most other churches had only one preacher, she'd asked Papa why Ironwood had two. Papa had said Ironwood chose to let men of two different shades of God's color pallet share the pulpit, so every second Sunday, Mr. Dawson brought the word. At the time she hadn't questioned it. Today she did. Mr. John wouldn't be glowering at her like that.

When the service finally ended, Mercy popped up, wove through the small community of colored families that populated the seven hundred acres of Ironwood, and avoided looking at Mr. Dawson on her way out of the chapel.

She'd taken no more than two steps outside when Faith gripped her elbow. "You have to help me."

Her friend's voice held so much urgency that Mercy jerked to a halt. "Why? What's wrong?"

"It's Mr. Watson." Faith threw a narrowed gaze to her left, where her father stood with another man under the shade of a wizened oak.

Mercy shifted and glanced at Mr. Charles Harper, Faith's father, who listened intently to whatever Mr. Watson seemed to be excited about. He didn't look displeased by the younger man's company. "What about him?"

Faith made a sour face, puckering her pink lips. Her pale cheeks were red, though from anger or heat, Mercy couldn't tell.

"He's here, that's what."

Dressed in a fine linen suit with a neatly knotted blue cravat at his neck and his sandy yellow hair combed back from his sturdy features, Mr. Watson looked like any of the other suitors who'd shown up at Ironwood since Faith's sixteenth year. A nice-looking white gentleman, she supposed. Not that she'd seen all that many for comparison. She turned back to Faith. "You still don't like him?"

"Even less so than I did last week."

"Why's that?"

Faith tugged at her gloves. "You won't believe what he said in the parlor the other day. I don't know why Daddy keeps letting him in the house."

Mercy blinked at the venom in her friend's tone. Whatever the man had said, it must have been dastardly to receive such a bite. Faith was usually much more reserved, even when alone with Mercy. Intrigued, she leaned closer. "What did he say?"

"He had the audacity to imply that once I wed, I would be able to take my proper place in serving as a wife and mother and would no longer have to worry about my brain decaying from reading." She finally sucked in a breath. "Can you imagine?"

Mercy wanted to laugh, but Faith was serious. She drew her eyebrows low. "And you're sure he said exactly that?"

Faith picked at the cuff of her sleeve. "Mother says it's a common thought. Doctors are saying women only have so much room in their smaller brains, and that if she fills her head with sensationalized novels, she may well slip into madness."

This time, Mercy did laugh. "That's preposterous."

"Precisely. I have come to the conclusion that not only will I insist I not be made to endure Mr. Watson's company any further, but also that I have no intentions of entertaining any other gentlemen's attentions either. I simply will not be affected by their mental malady."

Mercy's forehead wrinkled. "What are you talking about?"

Faith lifted her chin. "I may never marry."

"What? Why?" Mercy glanced to her parents, who stood closely together as they chatted with Aunt Bridget and Bridget's eldest daughter, Sarah. Marriage was a good thing. Her parents were proof. For that matter, so were Faith's parents. Lydia and

Charles Harper seemed to hold a very deep love for one another. Surely Faith had merely worked herself into a tizzy over one misinformed fellow. They weren't all of the same mindset.

"Well." Faith crossed her arms. "When I got the impression Daddy considered Mr. Watson as a felicitous suitor for me and after he made such a boorish statement, I went into Daddy's study and pulled down some of my grandfather's law books."

Only Faith would think to do such a thing. Mercy should end this nonsense now, but as the topic of women and reading played some part in her own news, Mercy followed the thread. She leaned closer to speak into Faith's ear, though no one paid their furtive conversation any attention. "What do law books have to do with Mr. Watson?"

Faith narrowed her eyes, looking far more riled than Mercy had ever seen her. "Do you know that when a woman marries, everything that's hers becomes her husband's?"

Mercy laughed. "Of course. And his becomes hers. That's what Papa said. The good book teaches us that a man and woman join together. They share life and all that's in it."

"That's not what I mean!" Faith glanced around and then lowered her voice. "The law says that she *belongs* to him. Anything she owns, anything she does, belongs to them as a single entity."

"That's what a marriage—"

"An entity in which *he* is the sole head and can do as he chooses. She has absolutely no control over anything." Her light brown eyes blinked rapidly, and more color reddened her cheeks. "Not even her own person."

Mercy opened her mouth, but she wasn't sure what to say. There seemed to be something deeper to Faith's concern than the sharing of property. Like with anything else Mercy needed to understand, she would have to do a little research. Perhaps Mr. Charles would fetch her a few more books on the suffragette movement. Or bring in more newspapers on his next trip to Memphis. She'd also need to read that law ruling.

"I'll not marry some brainless oaf so that he can rule over me." Faith clenched her fists.

Mercy stared. This line of thinking wasn't at all healthy. Perhaps she should go get Mama. "Now, Faith...."

"Shh." Faith stiffened. "They're coming this way."

Mercy's gaze darted up to Mr. Charles and then to the face of the unwelcome suitor. His gaze fell down the length of Mercy, and his forehead crinkled. It smoothed an instant later, however, and he smiled.

She'd seen that look before. White folks, even the most tolerant of them, never understood the Harpers and the community of Ironwood. They couldn't quite grasp the harmony of the people living equally on the thriving cotton plantation rather than slaving over it.

"Ladies," Mr. Charles said, pulling a watch from his pocket. "We will soon be moving back to the house for the meal."

Mercy glanced at Faith, who had become rigid at her side.

"Daddy, I would—"

"And Mr. Watson has asked you ride in his carriage with him."

Faith glanced at Mercy. "Ride? That's rather unnecessary, don't you think?"

Mercy and Faith always walked from the village chapel the half mile back to Faith's house on Sunday afternoons. The former slaves, freed by Miss Lydia even while Mississippi waged war to keep her people as property, had built a church, a blacksmith shop, a medical clinic, and a market area where they traded goods on Saturdays.

On the opposite side of the property from the old slave cabins, Ironwood village was their own little hidden community kept separate from the hostile world beyond the confines of the Harper land.

And Mr. Watson was the first of the suitors to be allowed this deep into the property. Mercy glanced at the families giving them a wide berth as they dispersed from the church lawn. The four of them stood in awkward silence while Mercy fidgeted.

Finally, Mr. Charles glanced at the other man, looking uncomfortable, before turning his gaze onto Faith again. "Just because something may not be necessary, dear, doesn't mean it can't be pleasurable." The soft correction in his tone made Faith wither just a little. She would crumble soon enough, and she'd be all the more angry for it later.

Mercy slipped her hand in the crook of Faith's elbow. "It does grow rather warm, Miss Harper. Don't you agree? Why, sooner returning to the house would give us time to refresh ourselves before the picnic, wouldn't it?"

She turned her gaze back to Mr. Charles and smiled sweetly at him. As she expected, his eyes twinkled with gratitude. He looked expectantly at Mr. Watson, who seemed to have lost his ability to speak.

Mr. Charles clasped the other man on the shoulder. "We'll see you at the house, then."

Before any of them could respond, Mr. Charles turned on his heel and strode away.

Mr. Watson cleared his throat and offered his arm to Faith.

"If you will come with me, Miss Harper, the carriage is this way."

Faith glanced at Mercy, who slightly lifted her shoulders. Faith hesitated.

Mercy cast her a mischievous grin and looped her fingers around Mr. Watson's other elbow, enjoying the way the flabbergasted man sputtered. He'd likely never had a colored woman be bold enough to take his arm.

Faith pressed her lips together to suppress a smile and placed her hand lightly on his proffered arm. "Why, thank you, Mr. Watson. It's rather kind of you to offer to escort my dearest friend and me to your carriage. I do believe it is getting rather warm after all."

Mr. Watson said nothing as he walked away from the church, his long stride causing Mercy to have to lengthen her own as they hurried to the market grounds where a few wagons waited on the families who lived on the back acres. When they were still a few paces from the large barouche carriage pulled by two matching black horses, he snaked his arm free of Mercy's grasp.

The fancy rig seemed as out of place as Mr. Watson. Dust clung to the skirts of brown skinned women as they lifted children into buckboard wagons. Mercy nodded to them as they cast glances her way. The people were always curious—or suspicious—of any unknown white men who came onto the property. It had been years since the last incident, but some things were impossible to forget. And having one intrude on Sunday services was sure to stir memories.

Where had he been during the preaching? Had he come after?

Mr. Watson pulled open the small door, which Mercy found rather unnecessary for an open-top conveyance. Why not leave the side open as well? A half-door was as frivolous as Mr. Watson's fancy suit and two pawing horses. Her eyes drifted past the horses. He even had a white driver. Novelty, indeed.

"Why, thank you, sir. You are most kind." Mercy scrambled into the carriage ahead of Faith and settled onto the forward-facing leather seat. She winked at Mrs. Smith, who stared at her with astonishment. The woman ducked her head and joined her elderly mother on their wagon. Abe, her husband and the town blacksmith, refused to look at the strange white men in their midst.

Faith gathered the folds of her bustled dress and plopped down next to Mercy, giving Mr. Watson no option but to sit opposite them on the rear-facing bench. Mercy withheld the smile Faith could not.

Mr. Watson seemed not to notice the reason for Faith's pleasant expression and returned the smile with a friendly one of his own. The fellow may be backward in some of his thinking, but he appeared good-natured.

He straightened the cloth tied around his neck. "It is a pleasant day, is it not?" He nodded to the driver perched behind him on the box seat.

It was no wonder children gaped at them. Had that poor man been sitting out in the heat the entire time, blistering his pasty skin? She hadn't noticed them in church today. Perhaps he and Mr. Watson had sat in the rear of the church. They'd not been on the Harpers' pew.

The reedy driver snapped the reins, startling the horses.

"Indeed it is, Mr. Watson," Faith said as the carriage jerked into motion. "A perfect day for reading in the garden."

Mercy ducked her chin to hide her smile. In doing so, however, she missed the man's expression.

"Perhaps painting, instead?" he suggested.

They meandered down the tree-lined road, following the dust of other wagons headed to the big house. Mercy swatted at a fly as it buzzed around her bonnet.

"Oh, I think not," Faith said, her voice dripping with sweetness. "I'm no good with a paintbrush. But I did find some books in Daddy's library that are fascinating. I'm eager to continue my study of them. Did you know that in 1839 Mississippi was the first state to grant women the right to hold property in their own name?"

Mr. Watson tilted his head. "Only with her husband's permission."

Mercy lifted her eyebrows but remained silent as Faith batted her eyelashes. "Surely any good husband would allow his wife such a freedom. Wouldn't you agree?"

He offered another smile. "I'm sure there are special circumstances where that may be necessary."

The carriage swayed and bumped over the rutted ground, and Mercy had to grip the side of the conveyance. She hardly ever rode in a wagon, and never in one with padded seats. The cushions did little to ease the jostling, however. She made a mental note to ask Faith more questions about carriage travel. It would be yet another bit of information that could prove useful in the near future. If she ever got a chance to share her news.

"I do find it enthralling." Faith snapped open her fan and fluttered it around her face. "Perhaps I shall study law."

Mercy nearly rolled her eyes. Last year Faith had declared

she wanted to be a nurse. Before that, it had been a governess. Perhaps she should tell Faith about Florence Cushman. She'd recently read an article in the *Boston Globe* about the female astronomer who'd started working at the Harvard College Observatory.

Mr. Watson's eyes widened. "Women cannot be solicitors."

"Oh? And why is that?"

Mercy grinned, amused by her friend's boldness. Mr. Watson had sorely underestimated Faith. No doubt he would soon become frustrated and give up any notions of wooing her.

He laced his fingers, seeming confused. "Why, because of the Supreme Court ruling, of course."

Faith recoiled. "What ruling?"

"You didn't read about the recent Illinois case that specifically excludes women from practicing law?"

Mercy felt, rather than saw, Faith wither beside her. "I saw no such ruling."

"Perhaps your father's books are out of date."

Faith brightened. "Perhaps they are." She fluttered her fan. "I shall endeavor to acquire newer editions."

Mr. Watson studied her, his expression a mixture of confusion and surprise.

"Oh, look. We're here," Mercy said, drawing the two from their staring match. "Shall we exit?"

Mr. Watson turned his gaze on her as though he had forgotten she occupied his carriage. "Oh. Of course." He opened the door and stepped out, offering his hand to assist Faith down.

Not waiting on Mercy, Faith hurried up the walk to the grand front porch of the big house of Ironwood. Mr. Watson made a noise in his throat as he watched her hurry away.

"Thank you for the ride, sir," Mercy said, drawing the man's attention as she stepped down and closed the little door behind her.

Mr. Watson tugged on the hem of his coat, mumbling. "And here I didn't believe them."

"Pardon?"

Mr. Watson turned his gaze back to the big house as Faith slipped inside. "They all told me this place was odd and that Miss Harper would give any gentleman trouble." He shook his head. "I didn't believe them." His shoulders lifted in a sigh, and he dipped his chin. "Good afternoon, Miss...?"

"Carpenter."

"Good afternoon, Miss Carpenter." He gave her a nod and tugged his black bowler down on his golden hair, then turned to walk around the side of the house to where the people gathered for the picnic. At least Faith's rudeness hadn't caused him to leave altogether.

Mercy watched him go. He didn't seem all that bad. But then, perhaps the man just didn't have enough wit in his head to balance the good looks God gave him. She started up the walk.

The carriage reins snapped, and the silent driver moved the conveyance to the barn. What was it like to drive people around and just wait on their leisure? Is that what people generally expected out of drivers? She hadn't recalled reading about etiquette for interactions with carriage drivers in Walter R. Houghton's *American Etiquette and Rules of Politeness*. She'd need to look into that.

Other carriages passed the curved drive at the front of the big house and plodded straight toward the barn, where Johnny would see the animals watered and tied for the afternoon while the people enjoyed their fellowship.

Voices swelled and children's laughter pierced the air as nearly all of Ironwood's three hundred residents gathered for Miss Lydia's tradition of eating on the lawn. Mama had once told her the picnic had started back during the war, right before Mama and Papa had married. When Mercy was a girl, they'd gathered several Sundays during the spring and summer months to enjoy food and fellowship. However, in the years since, they'd pared it down to only once a year.

She'd made it to the front door and was reaching for the knob when Mama's stern call stilled her. Mercy clenched her teeth. With the excitement over Mr. Watson, she still hadn't had a chance to tell Faith her news. Maybe if she hurried inside, she could pretend she hadn't heard.

"Mercy Carpenter, I know you heard me call you. Don't you dash into that house and ignore me!"

Ugh. Stalled again!

Faith pinched her lips together as she hooked the top button of her high-necked bodice, then fixed her face into a scowl. Yes, that would do nicely. Such an expression coupled with the most unsightly dress she owned might be enough to persuade one haughty Mr. Watson to seek his female company elsewhere. If she couldn't deter him with intelligence or a fiery wit, then one thing was sure to work. A man wanted an attractive woman. Take away that, and he'd no longer feel compelled to put up with other annoyances like intellect and self-respect.

Reminding herself once again she possessed those qualities, she examined herself in the mirror. With her plain but smooth features, she was pleasing enough, she supposed. She'd never been a beauty, but neither had she been unsightly enough to turn fortune-seeking suitors aside.

Faith breathed deeply and looked down at the light green dress. Mother had warned the color was unflattering against Faith's pale skin and mahogany hair, and looking at herself now, it seemed Mother had once again been correct. When Faith had chosen the fabric, she'd hoped it would bring out the green in her hazel eyes, but it made her skin look sickly instead. Her lips curved. Perfect for today's undertaking.

She pulled a comb through her mass of wavy hair. A knock came at her door. She crossed the thick rug spread over the plank floors and edged past her four-poster bed, already set with the mosquito netting for the warmer months. Before she could reach it, however, Mother opened the door and bustled inside. She took one glance at Faith and started shaking mahogany curls loose from the pile on the top of her head.

"Why did you change your gown?"

Faith bit her lip.

"I already told you not to wear that ghastly thing. Why put it on now?"

"You don't like it?"

Mother tilted her chin. "Why don't you give it to Mercy? The color would look far better on her."

Faith returned to her dressing table. "That's no longer an option. I've worn it now. Mercy doesn't want my castoffs."

Mother grumbled something Faith didn't decipher and

plucked the comb from Faith's fingers. She gathered Faith's long locks in one hand and started working the comb through the bottom section of already tangled hair. "I've given her dresses before."

"Which she never wears."

Mother opened her mouth and then closed it, considering. "I gave her mother dresses all the time. She always liked them."

Faith lifted her eyebrows and tried to study Mother's eyes in the mirror, but she couldn't read them. It wasn't the first time she wondered if she might require spectacles. "That was before, when Miss Ruth was your maid. Mercy isn't my maid, and I'm rather certain she would find offense in the offer."

Mother pursed her lips and yanked on another tangle. "Perhaps you're right. She is rather different than Ruth in that regard." She gathered Faith's thick hair. "Did it slide out of the pins already? I used extra this time."

"No..." Faith plucked at a fingernail. "I wanted a...different style."

Mother flew through the task, distracted. "Your father said Mr. Watson seems agitated. Is all well?"

Faith groaned. "He's terribly boorish, Mother. Daddy shouldn't encourage him."

Mother feigned ignorance. "Whatever do you mean? He's rather handsome, and he's the object of many a young woman's attention. Besides, your father likes him. He says these past months of employment have proved Mr. Watson a fine young man."

Faith slouched into her chair, the mask of refinement momentarily forgotten. "Did you know he said reading is one of the most pernicious habits a young lady can be devoted to?"

Mother twisted a lock of her hair. "Surely he didn't say that."

Faith rolled her eyes and slipped back into practiced fastidiousness. "Of course not. He never sounds that intelligent. Let me see. I believe the exact phrase he used was, 'women shouldn't be reading when there are so many other things to occupy them.'"

"Like what?"

"He meant rearing children and tending house, of course. What else would he mean?"

"Did you ask?"

"No."

"Then you don't know for certain what he meant, do you?" Mother turned her slim finger around a curl and pulled it forward to drape over Faith's shoulder.

"Just a simple knot, please."

She hesitated, then dropped the curl and brushed it back toward Faith's nape. "Don't think less of him for such a statement."

Faith swiveled around in her seat. "You cannot be serious."

Mother squeezed her shoulder. "Your father and I allowed you and Mercy to read many things that are deemed unsuitable for women. I assured your father many years ago that I would be diligent in training you in your feminine pursuits, and he agreed that as long as I did, he would allow for you to also expand your education into other areas. However, such a thing is rather uncommon. Don't judge Mr. Watson too harshly because he is surprised by the way you think. Not many young women are like you."

Faith swallowed a burning in the back of her throat. She

knew that well enough already.

Mercy finally escaped Mama's endless instructions and lifted her skirt to climb the rear steps to the big house. Why did Mama always want to tell her about every detail of organizing events like this? It wasn't as if she'd ever be doing it. She opened the back door without bothering to knock.

She'd been reared in this house as much as she had her own. Mama spent most of her time here, doing things with Miss Lydia and caring for the needs of the plantation. Mercy had been allowed to accompany her from six years of age. However, her training soon took a different turn. Upon Miss Lydia's insistence, Mercy started taking lessons with Faith from the various governesses who'd spent time at Ironwood. Coupled with her voracious reading of every outside material she could get her hands on, Mercy knew too much of the world to let fear keep her safely at Ironwood. She would never take over her mother's position, no matter how much Mama wanted it.

Mercy ran her ungloved fingers up the banister and made her way directly to Faith's room. She didn't knock on this door, either. As she expected, she found Faith sitting at her dressing table staring into the mirror.

She looked terrible. The light green dress did little to flatter her figure and even less to complement her peach-colored skin tone. "What are you doing?"

"Sitting here. Obviously."

Mercy crossed her arms. "Because you're too embarrassed to go out in that gown?"

Faith gave her a flat look. "I chose to change into this dress specifically for Mr. Watson."

And from the looks of her, she was trying a new tactic for undermining the man's interest in her. "You gave that fellow quite a time."

"No less than he deserved."

Mercy regarded her friend, concerned with this sudden bitterness. "Are you seeking to gain a reputation as a contentious woman?"

Faith lifted her chin. "No." She sniffed. "Not that I care if I do, mind you."

"It's a good plan. Then even the desirable gentlemen will want to avoid you." Mercy laughed, trying to draw Faith out of her mood.

It garnered the opposite response. Faith turned up her pert little nose. "Maybe I'll do just that."

"That's nonsense." Mercy turned serious. "You're just annoyed with Mr. Watson's opinions. You're taking this entire thing too far. If he bothers you that much, you simply need to inform your father you don't wish to entertain the man. There are other gentlemen you'll find more to your liking." She bounced on her toes. "Now, I have something I need to tell—"

"Have you spent much time with gentlemen, Mercy?" Faith narrowed her eyes, and her tone quelled more of Mercy's excitement. "I have. You haven't had the unfortunate displeasure of attending parties and balls away from Ironwood. You only know colored men born on Ironwood, and they are not at all the same. You just don't realize how different things are away from here."

Mercy's feet stilled. "You know that wasn't by my choice. They won't ever let me leave. Not since…" She waved a hand. "You know."

"And you're the better for it."

Frustration flared. "I find that rather doubtful. You've no idea what it's like. All those things we dreamed about as girls, *you* have all the opportunities you could want to experience them. My parents will scarcely let me away from the house."

"Well, that's for your own—"

"But that's about to change."

Faith pursed her lips. "What are you talking about?"

"I've been trying to tell you all day!" She grinned. "I had an article printed!"

Faith blinked. "You what?"

"Can you believe it?" She twirled like a little girl in a new dress, laughing.

Leaping to her feet, Faith scrambled to Mercy's side. "How in the world…?"

Mercy grinned. She'd been keeping it secret for weeks, and the revelation was just as sweet as she'd imagined. "I wrote an article. I used plenty of sources and gleaned information from the papers your father brings us. I worked until I got it perfect. Then I had Johnny slip it in with the mail and send it off." She bounced on her toes. "This morning before service he brought me a reply. They printed it!"

Faith's brow furrowed. "Where?"

Mercy grabbed Faith's hands. "The *Boston Globe!*"

Faith stared at Mercy in shocked silence for several painstaking heartbeats, then let out a giggle. "I'm so proud of you!"

She pulled her into an embrace.

Mercy wiggled free, too excited to be contained. "I'll finally be starting a real life!"

Faith's smile faltered. "But you'll keep writing from here, right?"

"Why would I want to do that?" She grabbed Faith's hand and pulled her toward the door. Her heart fluttered with the possibilities. Maybe Faith would want to take classes at Harvard College. "Imagine it! We are now ladies of a certain age. We can finally go on an adventure!"

Mercy savored the moment, anticipating the look on Faith's face when she told her the rest of the news.

But Faith's feet slowed, and she arrested Mercy's progress toward the door. Her face held none of the excitement it should. "That's…well, it would be lovely, wouldn't it, but…"

Was she still worried about leaving home? They were women now! "Don't be nervous. It would do you good to spend some time away from here. Lord knows it would be good for me."

Faith put forth one of those smiles Mercy knew she used when she just wanted someone to be happy. Mercy hesitated. Faith wasn't reacting like she'd expected.

"No matter what, I'm proud of you."

Mercy shook off the odd compliment. Faith didn't understand. Maybe telling her friend about the plan that had been swirling in her head all day wasn't a good idea after all. She would have to think on it some more. She squared her shoulders. "Come on, we better get downstairs."

Faith turned up her nose. "You go. I find I no longer have an appetite."

"Ugh." Mercy tugged on Faith's hand. "Listen to you! You sound like a petulant child."

Faith's eyes widened. "What?"

"You sound like Gracie." She gestured toward the door, too annoyed to placate Faith's mood.

"You're comparing me to your whiny little sister? Because I don't wish to entertain a bull-headed man?"

Mercy shrugged. "That's the way she acts when something doesn't go her way. So do you."

Tears glistened in Faith's eyes, and Mercy sighed. She shouldn't have been so harsh. She knew better than anyone how fragile Faith's confidence truly was.

She softened her tone. "Do you really think your father is going to respond to you acting this way? He's only going to believe you need a husband even more if you don't show him you are capable of presenting a logical argument instead of having a tantrum and embarrassing him."

Faith deflated and she swiped her cheeks. "I suppose you're right." She drew a deep breath and composed herself, slipping back into the carefully crafted persona she wore whenever the two of them weren't alone.

Mercy snagged a simple straw hat with white feathers and handed it to her friend. She squeezed her shoulders. "Now come on." There was too much excitement for Faith to be this sour. She would soon see.

Their lives were finally about to change.

Faith struggled through the afternoon meal, Mercy's words constantly nagging at her. She wasn't being childish. Was she? Did it not make her a *woman* to know her own mind? To be strong and intelligent? Had she been working toward the wrong end?

Oh, Lord. Help me keep myself together.

The warm afternoon sun warranted a fan, but she used it as much to hide the boredom from her face as she did to cool it. Her plate of barely touched chicken and roasted potatoes sat on the low garden table next to her, attracting flies. Really, what was Mother thinking? Just because they had eaten outside after the war didn't mean they still needed to do so now. The drone of Mr. Watson's voice carried on the breeze, buzzing around her like the bees seeking their nectar from the surrounding roses.

For Daddy's sake, Faith tried her best to smile at Mr. Watson as he prattled on about some business matters, though she suspected she accomplished little more than stretching her lips across her clenched teeth. He didn't seem to notice.

She watched him talk. He had an interesting way of speaking. His words were usually evenly spaced and lacked the drawl of most of the men she knew. But now that he seemed excited over something, some of his words were spoken with odd accentuation. Strange how she'd never noticed it before now. With an accent normally so bland, had he tried to cover up a different one? Why?

"So I told him that either he bought the entire shipment, or we didn't have a deal." The sunlight filtering through the leaves overhead gave Mr. Watson's face a dappled appearance, sort of like Mother's favorite mare. The thought brought on a more genuine smile, which he enthusiastically returned. Overhead, a squirrel chattered as though it had read her thoughts and shared in her amusement. After a moment, she realized Mr. Watson had stopped speaking.

He stared at her expectantly.

Faith tried to recall his words, but found herself at a loss. "I'm sure," she said, hoping he would take that in whatever way suited him.

Her response seemed to please him, and his face brightened. Faith inwardly groaned. She really shouldn't be encouraging him. She'd have words with Mother for putting her in this predicament. She'd left Faith with no options but to accept the man's request to sit with her at meal or embarrass them all.

Mr. Watson leaned closer, and the smell of his shaving oil tickled her nose. "That's how I earned a place in your father's shipping enterprise. I've much more to learn, mind you, but I find the work excites me. I hope to see the company grow into all Mr. Harper hopes it to be."

Faith dismissed the comment with a wave. "Daddy's primary business is this plantation, sir. He merely dabbles in shipping."

Mr. Watson sat back in his woven chair. "I do believe you are mistaken, Miss Harper. Are you not aware that your father's shipping business now runs the length of the Mississippi?"

"Of course. Though it's simply a means of moving our cotton to various ports and bringing in the supplies the people need."

Mr. Watson stroked his hairless chin, then offered a placating expression. "Forgive me. I should not expect for a young lady to worry herself with the details of business."

Had she been a dog, Faith suspected her hackles would have

risen and a low growl would have emanated from her throat. Being her beloved father's daughter, however, all she could do was clench her fists in her lap. Well, and perhaps snarl a little. "Why, sir, must you insist that women are dull of wit?"

His brows drew together in what appeared to be genuine confusion. "I've never stated such a boorish thing. What would give you that idea?"

Faith stared at him. Perhaps he was so deeply disillusioned that he didn't even notice his own foolishness. She spoke slowly, as though to a child. "Mr. Watson, during our conversation on your previous visit, you stated women had smaller brains that should only be filled with mundane feminine pursuits or else they would be destined for the asylum. During the conversation we are presently holding, you *just* stated that you would not expect a woman to understand business because she lacks a man's ability to think and reason."

Mr. Watson smoothed his already styled hair. "I find you a great mystery, Miss Harper. I must apologize. I don't recall speaking those words, but if I did, please know it was never my intention to say you were in any way a dullard."

The heat in her face dissipated. Had she misjudged him? He seemed so utterly confused that she began to wonder if she had read more into his statements than he'd intended.

"My father taught that women are precious, fragile creatures," he said, lacing his fingers together. "We men are to shield them from life's more unpleasant matters and provide them with our protection and care. A woman should be allowed to embrace her God-given talents for nurturing and home-making and not be burdened with the heavier concerns of men." He stared into her face with earnestness. "Though it is far too forward to do so, I feel that under these circumstances I must speak plainly of my intentions, lest you miss my affections for you and misunderstand my words."

Faith's mouth went dry, and she found herself entirely unable to ward off what he would say next.

"My intentions go beyond mere companionship, Miss Harper."

Faith caught her breath. Was he asking her to court? Or had they somehow already skipped that part?

"Your father has graciously offered to let me help him grow his business, and if you don't mind my saying so, has indicated he approves of my interest in you. I find you remarkable and your family kind, despite their odd tendencies." He smiled brightly, revealing perfect teeth. "To be frank, Miss Harper, I have found myself captivated by the daughter of a man I greatly respect."

Faith's jaw unhinged, and she had to snap it closed. *Odd tendencies?* Despite everything else he'd said, she hung on that one phrase. What odd tendencies? That they allowed their daughter to think beyond a sewing needle? She let that jab slide, however, focusing on the more important aspect of his statement. "I'm not part of a business transaction, a mere way of gaining your way into my father's company."

Mr. Watson's eyes widened, and he lowered his head and rubbed his temples. "Lord, forgive me."

A good start, but shouldn't he be asking for her forgiveness as well? Perhaps he was surprised she'd had enough insight in her tiny brain to recognize his manipulative intents. Faith rose and ran her hands down her gown. "If you will kindly excuse me, I believe I'm feeling a bit unwell."

Mr. Watson rose with her. "Allow me to escort you to the house."

"No, that will not be necessary, thank you." She swallowed the bile churning in her stomach. "I just need to move around for a few moments. Please, enjoy your refreshments."

Without waiting for his response and ignoring the concern etched on his admittedly handsome features, Faith made her way down the garden path and to the tables set out near the rear porch. Mercy stood near the edge of the yard. When their gazes locked, Faith hurried over.

"What's wrong?" she asked.

Mercy's eyes glistened, but she blinked away the moisture. "Nothing."

"Then why are you teary?"

Mercy glanced to where the community had gathered around the tables spread out on the lawn. "Mama's upset with me again."

"Why? Did you tell her about the article?"

Mercy rolled her eyes. "I didn't even get the chance. I made a statement about not needing to learn to organize gatherings because I had ideas beyond Ironwood and she got angry with me."

Faith grew serious. "Such statements are hard for them, Mercy. You know that. Consider how that must make them feel."

Mercy sighed. "But they have to know I want something more out of life."

"They will." She patted Mercy's arm. "One day you'll be the most famous writer in all of Mississippi."

"You believe so?"

Faith's lips curved. "Of course I do." She winked. "Have a little faith, Mercy."

Mercy laughed at their childhood quip and brushed a lingering tear from her eye. "Oh, have mercy, Faith."

They laughed. Their mothers, having had daughters only months apart, decided to name them both for spiritual aspects. Ruth had continued the tradition with her next two daughters, Grace and Joy, but Faith's mother had not been able to carry more children. She'd said God had given her a miracle with the birth of both a son and a daughter, and she was more than pleased with His generosity.

Mercy smiled. "Maybe you're right. Once I tell them about the article, they will see things differently. They'll know I can handle leaving someday."

Faith doubted that, but didn't want to quell Mercy's spirits. She was just overly excited and not thinking clearly. Mercy had been restless lately, and this article would give her the connection with the outside world she craved. Mercy didn't really want to leave home. She just wanted some freedoms.

She would speak to Mother about it. Mother had a way with Miss Ruth. Surely Mother could convince Mercy's parents that allowing Mercy to send off more articles would be a good thing.

Faith offered her friend the encouraging smile she knew Mercy needed. "I can't believe you didn't even show it to me before you sent it off! It isn't fair to leave your sister of the heart in the dark."

Mercy shrugged, but the endearment sparked light in her eyes.

"Come, we shall tell our parents all about your article."

"Now?"

"Why not?"

Mercy planted her feet. "Perhaps I should wait until another time." She drew her lip through her teeth. "A time when all of Ironwood is not present."

"Why?"

Mercy huffed. "It's better I tell them at home. That way"— she lowered her voice—"when Mama has a conniption, no one will see it."

Faith tugged on Mercy's hand. "*Now* who is being childish and ridiculous?"

Mercy glowered. "Still just you." She turned her nose up, but the humor in her tone belied her expression.

"Ha! Then we two muddled, immature females shall just have to keep the news to ourselves and enjoy the afternoon on our own." She winked. "While also avoiding one befuddled Mr. Watson."

Two

It truly was impressive. They would see. Mercy's eyes danced over the words of her article, squinting to judge their clarity. If she angled the page right, she didn't even need the lamp to read it. Mercy blinked, realizing what the light she'd been using to read meant.

The door flew open, startling her and causing traitorous fingers to drop her prize. Yelping, she scooped it off the floor and tried to shake off any dust particles.

"Mercy! What you doin' out here in the potato shed? Ain't hardly dawn yet."

She smiled sweetly at Papa, and his frown melted. "I have something to show you, Papa. It's very important."

He regarded her for a moment, then his broad shoulders drooped. "All right, hummingbird, let me see." Papa plucked the page from her fingers and turned his wide frame toward the first rays of a new day. He squinted and pulled it closer to his face. "The Balance of Views," he read slowly. He glanced back at her. "You write this?"

Mercy nodded, her stomach churning. "Do you like it?"

Something Mercy couldn't quite place sparked in his deep brown eyes. Pride with a mixture of...worry? "Looks mighty fine, hummingbird." He scratched his chin. "But I don't think your mama is going to like you stayin' out in this shed all night writing."

Mercy winced but didn't bother to correct him. She'd been rereading her letter and article out here in secret, in case one of her sisters discovered her. But she wouldn't tell anyone about the letter. Not yet. Not until her parents could first accept her article. "I know."

He handed the paper back to her. "I reckon you best be getting to your chores." He wiggled his thick eyebrows. "Mama ain't quite up yet. If you hurry, she might not even know."

"Yes, sir."

As she scurried back to the house, she thought she heard Papa chuckle. She bounded up the brick steps, slipped quietly through the front door, and made it upstairs without being caught. She hurried past her parents' bedroom door and ducked into the room she shared with her two younger sisters.

As soon as the latch clicked, Joy popped upright in her bed, headscarf askew. "Where you been, Mercy?" she asked with the exuberance only a seven-year-old could muster this early in the morning.

"Where *have* I been," Mercy corrected.

Joy unwrapped her braids and ran her slim fingers over them to see if they'd stayed smooth during the night. They hadn't, and as soon as she discovered it, she'd beg for Mercy to do them again. Hoping her sister wouldn't notice before she could get back downstairs, Mercy stepped over to the wardrobe to find her egg apron.

"It's too early for you to be correcting me," Joy said, her full lower lip protruding.

Mercy threw a glance at the other bed, the heaps of blankets shielding her fourteen-year-old sister from the world. How the girl slept with that many quilts this time of year was baffling. "Best you go on and get Gracie up."

"Ain't my turn."

Mercy resisted the urge to roll her eyes. She wouldn't be sucked into another argument. She was nineteen years old. Far too old to keep getting into childish squabbles with her sisters. She strode over to the softly snoring bundle.

She put her hands on what she thought was Gracie's shoulder and shook. "Come on, time to get up."

Gracie groaned and tried to bury herself further under the covers. Though since Mercy couldn't see a single hair on her closely braided head, she didn't see how that was possible.

"Gracie, you know you have to get up. Why do you do this every morning?"

Gracie grunted. "'Cause every mornin' one of you two starts poking me."

Joy giggled, but Mercy ignored it. "Well, you're awake. If you're late starting your chores, I'll not be the one to blame for it."

Gracie grunted her response, and Mercy narrowed her eyes. She meant it this time. She spun around and stalked back to the wardrobe. It was time these two started learning to do things without her. In a couple of moments, she'd donned her egg apron and pulled on her work boots. Then Joy found the mirror.

"Mercy," she whined, "they look all nappy."

Mercy smiled. "They look fine. You're just too sensitive about it."

Joy crossed her arms over her thin chest and stuck out her tongue. "You say that 'cause you don't ever have to worry 'bout your hair. It always looks perfect."

"That's probably because I don't fuss with mine the way you do yours. If you'd keep your hands off of it, it would stay smooth."

Joy puckered her lips.

"I have to go. Maybe Gracie will help you with it."

"But, Mercy—"

She gave the girl a squeeze and rushed out of the room before she lost any more time. The old cow in the milk barn was a bit more ornery than usual, but Mercy still managed to collect all the day's eggs, fill a bucket with fresh milk, and even pour a batch of separated whey for Gracie to churn by the time Mama came into the kitchen.

Mercy fidgeted as Mama looked her over, arching her brows. "You think I don't know, don't you?"

"I'm sure I don't know what you're talking about." Mercy pushed a chair Papa had finished last spring under their dining table and avoided Mama's gaze.

"Mm-hm. You're forgetting that I know you too well, child."

Dash it all. She squared her shoulders. "I got all my chores done."

To her surprise, Mama laughed. "I see you did. And I suppose you'll be the only one who'll be suffering for lack of sleep."

"Yes, ma'am." Mercy removed the eggs from her apron and placed them in a basket on the wooden counter. They continued the kitchen work in silence. All the while the folded paper in Mercy's dress pocket screamed out to be seen.

Finally, she could stand it no longer. She set down the milk pitcher with a thud. "I have something I want to show you."

"Hmm?" Mama stirred the gravy slowly, seeming entirely uninterested in Mercy's declaration.

Mercy bit back her annoyance. "Would you stop a moment and look?"

Mama raised her eyebrows.

"Please?"

Mama put down her spoon, removed the finished gravy from the flame, then wiped her hands on her apron.

"Now, I want you to read it before you say anything." Mercy fished the paper out and gently unfolded a handwritten copy of her article.

Mama accepted it and scanned the page. Mercy waited until she'd read the entire thing, then drew up her courage.

"It's an article I wrote. Do you like it?"

Mama placed her fingers on her lips and closed her eyes. When she opened them, Mercy didn't like what she saw. "What're you planning on doing with this?"

Tears gathered. "You don't like it?"

Mama sighed. "It's not that I don't like it. I always prayed that my children would grow up different. And, land's sakes, you sure enough has." She handed the paper back. "But now I worry what trouble it's going to cause you."

Mercy tilted her head. "Different?" She knew a few things from some of the other families about the old times when her people were slaves, but her parents didn't talk much about them. Maybe Mama meant Mercy was able to read and write well. When Mama had been a girl, it wasn't allowed.

Mama patted her cheek. "It's a fine article." She turned back to the stove and muttered, "Seems like you learned a lot of things from all those books and papers the Harpers let you read."

Mercy twisted her fingers together. "And I want to write other things. Events, opinions, politics. Whatever I can investigate."

Mama's eyes widened. "Investigate?"

"What's that mean?" Joy interjected, bounding into the kitchen.

"It means to study, to look into," Mercy replied as the girl settled onto the stool at the churn without being asked. "Means I try to find out all the details of a subject so I can write about it."

"Hmm." Joy pumped the handle. "Sounds boring to me."

Mama's forehead crinkled as she regarded her youngest child. "Where's Grace?"

Joy lifted her thin shoulders. "She was still sleeping." She shot them a grin. "But don't worry. I'm big enough to churn." She heaved on the handle. "See?"

Mama turned quizzical eyes on Mercy.

"It's time she starts learning to be responsible for herself, Mama. What's she going to do after I'm gone and she's the oldest?"

Mama pressed her full lips into a line as though she had no intention of answering that question. "I reckon if she misses breakfast and her stomach grumbles all morning, it'll be her own fault."

Mercy shifted from one foot to the other. "Mama, about that article…?"

Mama rummaged in the cabinet and pulled down some

plates. "We'll talk more about that later." Mama stacked the plates on the table for Mercy to set out and nodded toward Joy. "Thank you for doing Grace's work while she's being lazy. Because of that, you can stay up tonight while she has to be the one who goes to bed first."

Joy's face split into a toothy grin. "Really?"

Mama grinned at Mercy. "Seems like Grace needs that extra rest."

Mercy began to set the table. Gracie would sure enough have a fit when she found out she lost her nearly-grown-up privilege of getting to sit up late with the adults. Not that anything important happened then either.

Mercy finished setting the table, her mind running with ways to tell her parents she'd not only written that article, but had already sent it to a newspaper. And received a response.

They wouldn't be happy.

Joy ran out to find Papa in the barn to let him know it was time to eat.

When they were alone, Mama's heavy gaze settled on Mercy. "I'm glad you're enjoying writing. Was a time when I liked it too. Course, in those days, it had to be secret."

Mercy fiddled with the hem of her sleeve, sensing there was more to the statement than another declaration that things were now different for Mercy. "But?"

Worry danced behind Mama's eyes, and she seemed to struggle for words. Whatever she might have said was lost when Papa opened the door and his presence filled the kitchen. Papa had a way of doing that. Not only because he was as thick as a horse and nearly as strong, but also because he had so much life in him that it simply couldn't be contained. It spilled over into every place he went.

He flashed a smile at her and then scooted around her to wrap Mama in his arms. He gathered her up and placed a long kiss on her lips. Joy, who'd followed Papa in, groaned, but Mercy had come to appreciate this show of affection from her parents. The fact that they openly loved one another told Mercy such things weren't just for story books.

He took his place at the head of the table, casting a sideways glance at Gracie's empty chair. But when he spoke, it was about Mercy. "Did our little hummingbird show you her writing?"

Mama placed a tray of biscuits next to a platter of sausage. "She did."

Papa rubbed his chin, and Mama didn't say anything as she settled into her chair and folded her hands in front of her on the table. Taking her cue, Papa bowed his head to pray over their day, their family, and their meal.

And before she said her "amen" Mercy added, *and please let me find my place beyond Ironwood.*

The day was spent as every other mundane day at Ironwood, working in the garden, tending the animals, and hanging laundry on the line. Mercy moved through each task without devoting her mind to any of them. Instead, she mulled over every possible way to make her case to her parents. When the day's work was finished, she was no closer to crafting a suitable argument than she had this morning.

The world is dangerous. She knew that. *People are unkind.* She knew that as well. *It's safe at Ironwood.* She knew everything they would say. And they were right.

It didn't matter. Because among all the other things she knew, she knew what she wanted, and if God alone was the only one that supported her, then so be it.

When she sat down that evening for supper, Mercy had made her choice.

Mama ladled potatoes onto her plate and pinned Grace with a glare. She'd been in a petulant mood all day. "Grace, you will be going to bed at dark tonight. Be sure to wash up as soon as we are finished and the table is cleared."

Gracie dropped her fork onto her plate with a clatter. "What?"

Papa cleared his throat. "Tone, daughter."

"I...uh..." Gracie stammered. "Sorry, Mama. I'm confused." She picked up her fork again. "What did you say?"

"I said you would be going to bed at dark tonight and not staying up."

Gracie worked her mouth a moment before any words came out. "I'm going to bed with Joy? But why? I need to work on my dress."

Gracie liked her needlework in the evenings, but this preoccupation with that dress was becoming concerning. Last Christmas Miss Lydia had gifted each of Mama's girls with bolts of fine silk and delicate lace. She'd said it was for each of them to fashion a wedding gown for when their time came. Mama had carefully packed away Joy's, and Mercy had set hers aside until such a time as she might use it, but Gracie had taken to hers with gusto. Already she'd fashioned an elaborate skirt, which she had now begun embroidering with pink flowers and vines. Mama wouldn't allow her to work on the bodice, saying that by the time she had need of the dress, it would no longer fit. Yet somehow, Gracie seemed to think she would soon enough be getting in that gown, even though she was just now beginning to show signs of womanhood.

"You're not going to bed at the same time as Joy," Mama said, ignoring the comment about the gown, though Mama's eyes mirrored Mercy's concerns. "You'll be taking her place."

As a look of pure angst washed over her sister's features, Mercy almost felt sorry for her, but not quite. The girl needed to learn. If she was in such a hurry to be grown, she needed to act like an adult.

Gracie turned a scowl toward Joy, who kept her focus on her plate. "I don't understand."

Mama lifted her cup to her lips, and Joy continued to feign fascination with her meal. When Gracie's frustrated gaze swept to Mercy, Mercy slowly shook her head. She should take her reprimand and move on.

Gracie smoothed her scowl and turned wide eyes on their father. "Papa?"

Papa shook his head. "Sorry, Grace. You done brought this down on yourself."

Mama put her cup down a bit too forcefully, and it landed with a *thud* on the plank table. "Since you seem to be so tired *every* morning, then you must need extra rest."

"But I just—"

"And," Mama interjected, "since Joy took the responsibility of your chores, then she has earned your privileges as well."

"But...but..."

Mama held up a hand. "I've spoken my piece."

Gracie grumbled, "Yes, Mama," and pushed peas around on her plate in defeat.

"You must learn responsibility," Mercy ventured. "You'll soon be the oldest."

Gracie made a face. "Ain't nobody looking to marry *you*. You'll be here long after I get a man."

"Grace!" Papa rarely raised his voice, but when he did, silence fell heavy afterward. All eyes turned to him. He lowered his eyebrows at his middle daughter. "You'll not talk with that kind of disrespect and meanness to your sister. You treat your family with kindness."

"Yes, Papa." Gracie shot Mercy a cold glance.

"You owe your sister an apology," Mama said.

"Sorry, Mercy," Gracie mumbled, not bothering to look up from her plate. Even still, Mercy could nearly feel the anger radiating off of her.

"For?" Papa barked.

Gracie snapped her head up, eyes wide. She took one glance at Papa's stern face and turned to Mercy. Resentment glazed her eyes. "I'm sorry for disrespecting you, Mercy. Will you forgive me?"

Ah, poor Gracie. Ever she chafed at humility. "Yes, sister. I forgive you."

"Now, no more of that talk," Papa said, stabbing a slab of salted ham.

Mercy must speak now or lose this opportunity. Mercy set down her fork and placed her hands in her lap. "I may not be wed any time soon, but that doesn't mean I'll still be living here. I'm old enough to go out on my own."

"Go where?" Mama frowned. "What are you talkin' about?"

Mercy fidgeted. She hesitated and then let the words break free in a gush. "I want to be a real writer. A journalist. I can't do that here."

Her parents stared at her and then exchanged a look.

The words settled on the table like heavy fog, and it took several nervous heartbeats before either of her parents spoke.

"Oh, Mercy." Mama sighed. "You know you can't be doing that."

"You don't think I can write?"

Papa rubbed the back of his thick neck. "Ain't that we don't know you have talent, hummingbird."

"Did you know they have colleges for Negros now?" Mercy's fingers drummed along the edge of the table. "I could take classes with our own people. It would be safe."

Her sisters stared at her. Her parents said nothing.

"It's different up north," she pressed. "They don't have to hide up there."

Mama narrowed her eyes. "Who told you 'bout colleges? Faith?"

"No. I read about it." She glanced at Papa, the only one of them to have ever gone north. "It's true, right? Things are much different up north."

Papa still rubbed the back of his neck. "I wouldn't listen to that kind of talk."

She tried not to let her frustration show. "Then ask Aunt Bridgett. She told me once about what it was like going with the Union Army. The white people up north are more like the Harpers."

Mama let out a long breath. "Mercy, you don't know nothing about that."

Because they wouldn't let her know about anything! She held back the words. The heat in her chest grew. They would never let her leave. They thought the entire world was here at Ironwood, in their self-made, self-sufficient community that had shunned all contact with the outside world for a decade.

Papa patted Mama's hand to calm her but kept his eyes on Mercy. "Don't you remember what it was like?"

She cut a glance to her sisters, who were now listening intently. They were too little to remember the raids on Ironwood. The smoke and fire in the night. People dragged from their homes. They didn't remember Mr. Harper having to set watchmen throughout Ironwood to protect the people from roving bands of monsters dressed in white robes and claiming they were cleansing the land.

Mercy bit her lip. "That was a long time ago. Things are different now."

Papa squared his shoulders. "You'll get no better life than the one you have here. Now, I'll hear no more about it."

They returned to their supper, though Mercy hardly tasted her food. They didn't understand. And they would never let her go.

Three

Faith squinted in the darkness. "Why can't we talk in the house? The bugs are awful out here." She swatted a mosquito that sought to treat her as its supper.

"Don't want anyone to hear," Mercy whispered, tugging Faith deeper into the rose garden to Mother's stone bench. "We need a plan first."

"Plan?" Faith sat down with a plop. "What plan?"

Mercy sat next to her but kept shuffling her feet. "About going to Boston."

Faith's heart stumbled. "Boston?"

"I want to be a journalist. You want to do…" She waved her hand. "Something."

"Well, now—"

"We can't accomplish anything here." Mercy hurried on before Faith could say what they both knew. "And who cares what our parents have to say about it? We're grown women."

Faith twisted her fingers in the folds of her dressing gown and listened to the crickets. The rich scent of roses hung in the air, draping them with spring's sweetness. She drew in a long breath of it as she watched her friend jump off the bench and anxiously pace.

"Where's your sense of adventure?" Mercy's words came out in a strained whisper. "Don't you want to do more with your life?"

Faith closed her eyes, the warm breeze tickling the back of her neck. "The world isn't a nice place."

"We'll be fine."

Ever the optimist. "So you've told your parents about this?"

"Of course I did." Mercy shifted again. "Well, maybe not exactly. But I did tell them I wanted to leave Ironwood and go be a journalist. Maybe even take some writing courses at one of the Negro colleges."

"And?"

Mercy glared at her. "I'm grown. I can have my own say."

Faith considered her words. "Mercy, you don't—"

"I know what you're going to say." Mercy crossed her arms. "You're going to say I haven't been away from Ironwood. I don't know anything about the world." She groaned. "But that's exactly it. I want to finally *see* the world I've only ever read about. Can't you understand?"

Faith looked up at the stars. "Don't you remember what happened?"

Mercy stared at her.

Of course Mercy remembered. How could any of them forget? Faith reminded her anyway. "We thought we would lose you that night. All of you. If it hadn't been for your father..." She shook off the cold memory of the flames racing toward the Carpenters' house and the chants of men with raging eyes intent on hanging innocent people for merely walking around town on their own. She shuddered. "It's safer here."

"That was ten years ago!" Mercy flung out her arms. "No

one has trespassed here in years. No one has even bothered Johnny when he goes to town." She pointed a finger at Faith. "He told me so himself. It's not like it once was. Things are better."

"How could you possibly know that?"

"I'm as educated as you are."

Faith kept her tone calm, hoping Mercy could see reason. "You've never been off this land."

Mercy huffed and resumed her pacing. "Exactly. The other families have a choice. They choose to stay or go. My parents deny me that option." She fixed hard eyes on Faith. "I won't be a prisoner my entire life."

Faith sucked a sharp breath. "You can't be serious."

"Of course I am!" She knelt and grabbed Faith's hand. "You don't know what it's like. You get to go places and do things. All I ever get to do is stay here and do chores. When's it going to be my turn to have a life?"

"Oh, Mercy, it's not that simple."

She dropped Faith's hand. "Why not?"

The words burned her throat. She pushed them out anyway. "No one will hire a Negro journalist, even if you do go to a college."

Mercy glared at her. "The *Boston Globe* printing my article proves I have talent."

Faith tried to pick her words as carefully as possible. But doing so seemed as pointless as choosing which one of a skunk's toes to pull. No matter what she said, this was going to stink. "It doesn't matter. Places like that don't hire your people. Not for the real jobs. They printed it because they didn't know."

Something flickered in Mercy's eyes. She drew a long breath

and moved to stand at the edge of the small clearing. She was quiet for several moments, stiller than Faith ever remembered seeing her.

Finally, she turned on her heel, the fire in her eyes evident even in the deepening night. "That's ridiculous." Mercy started pacing again. "Maybe they don't do things like that down here. But they have *colleges* up there, Faith. The North is different."

"Not that different. It won't be what you hope."

Mercy looked up at the twinkling stars.

Faith pressed, "Why would you want to subject yourself to needless scorn and rejection?"

Mercy paced again, her voice quivering. "So I can't do anything? Ever?"

"I'm sorry, but that's—"

"How would you feel!" She stomped her foot. "How would you feel if someone wouldn't let you go to law school or be an accountant, or whatever you decide you want to do next, just because your hair was brown instead of yellow?" Mercy threw up her hands. "That would be just as foolish as this!"

Faith remained silent, her heart aching. It truly wasn't fair. But what could they do about it?

"You're always talking about how women should have more rights. What about *this*? Where are *my* rights?"

"I wish I could change it." She rose and tried to place her hand on Mercy's arm, but her friend moved away. Faith let her hand drop. "I don't know how."

Moisture gathered in Mercy's luminous eyes. "I'm just supposed to hide here forever? I can't." Mercy stepped farther away, her posture stiffening and sparks of lightning chasing away the lingering glisten in her deep brown eyes. "You don't understand." She pointed a finger. "But why should I expect anything different? You're white, so *you* always get *everything*."

Faith nibbled on her bottom lip.

"Your family thinks you have made everyone equal here. Really? Which of us gets up every morning and milks a cow? Which of us hoes a garden?" Venom laced her tone, and Faith's heart sank. "And which of us sleeps past dawn and goes to balls and teas? Seems to me there's always been some injustice in that as well. Shame on me for not noticing the ways of the world were always right in front of my face."

"Mercy, it's not my fault that—"

"Of course not. Nothing is ever your fault."

Heat rose in her ears. "Will you let me finish a sentence?"

"Of course, Lady Harper." Mercy's voice thickened. "I wouldn't want to insult my betters."

Faith drew her head back as though the words had physically slapped her. Instead, they had only opened a wound that bled anger. "Now, just a moment." She pointed a finger at her friend, irritation stealing any attempt to remain gentle. "That's not fair and you know it."

"Fair?" Mercy nearly choked on the word. "What do you know of fair?"

Without giving Faith a chance to respond, Mercy whirled around and dashed through the garden and into the darkness.

The firelight danced over the paper in Mercy's trembling hand.

She didn't need to read the words. She'd memorized them already. She ran her finger over her secret. The part she hadn't told a soul.

She turned the wick on the lamp down low, creating shadows over her faded nightdress. The sounds of the night sang to her secrecy, sharing in stolen moments of hidden contemplation.

A federal dollar. She'd never had one of her own. Mercy ran her finger over its crisp edge. If they paid that much for one article, how much would they supply a journalist? She'd never have to milk a cow again.

Something scurried in the corner of the potato shed, stirring up bits of dust that drifted in the air as aimlessly as her scattered thoughts. She paused, wishing she'd grabbed a pair of shoes.

She'd stayed awake to be certain her family slept, and then she'd tucked her small hope chest under her arm and crept silently through her home and out to the cool privacy of the shed to plot her betrayal.

Mercy sank to the floor and propped her back on the hewn wall, gently lowering the chest to the floor. When had it come to this? Hiding in a shed to avoid her family's prying eyes? Stealing the small box that was meant to contain a very different future than the one she now conspired?

After the printing, the newspaper had received wave after wave of positive responses. The *Boston Globe* wanted more from Mr. Fredric Mercy, and they wanted to meet with him to discuss his coverage of the various women's rallies happening around the country.

What would they think if they knew *Mr. Fredrick Mercy* was really just a timid girl hiding in a potato shed in Mississippi?

They didn't know the article they loved had been written by a colored girl who had never left her farm, much less attended a rally. She rubbed her fingers over the page. But if she could get that kind of response based on her research and thoughts alone, what kind of responses could she get once she was able to learn, see, and experience more?

Weeks ago, Mercy had begged Johnny to send her article. It had taken quite a bit of pleading, but he'd finally agreed to do his best to find an address. Johnny was one of the few of her people who left Ironwood, and only because he drove the Harpers and occasionally fetched things for them from Oakville. And he'd always been kind to her. Sympathetic to all her questions about town, and in later years, her requests for any publications he could bring her. He was always willing to trade for her apple tarts and a hearty thanks.

She'd wanted to prove to herself she had what it took to do something with her life. To prove the education she'd gained at Faith's side truly was enough to earn a life other than farm work. It was possible. Frederick Douglass and Harriet Tubman were proof her people could be heard.

Her eyes landed on the page once more.

Dear Mr. Mercy....

She wrapped her arms around her waist, shivering despite the mild temperature. Could she? Did she dare?

She stared at the contents of an envelope that would change her life. The printed article. She'd told Faith about that. The money that came with it. She'd kept that to herself, though she wasn't sure why. And finally, the letter that meant everything. The part she'd told no one. Not even Faith.

And now she was glad she hadn't.

The letter said Mr. Mercy had a keen insight into the social and political implications of the women's suffrage movement. It suggested Mr. Mercy presented logical ideas that women appreciated and men understood. He, they said, was the perfect balance. He would go far in journalism, they promised.

Come to Boston, they said, and accept the position.

Papa would be saddened by her deception. He wouldn't understand that she'd *had* to use a man's name or else they would have never even read the article they so enthusiastically supported now.

She'd poured her heart into that article. She'd scoured the papers. She'd listened keenly to Faith as her disgust with society's treatment of women grew, and she'd applied that to her own words...tempered with a good dose of Papa's perspective.

God means for the man to be the head of the family, hummingbird. Just as Christ is head of the church. And just like our Lord did for us, a man is supposed to sacrifice hisself for his woman. That's the way it's supposed to be, and when we follow that way, we are blessed with a good marriage. Look at your mama. She's smart and strong and does a good bit of leading around this plantation. But she still looks to me, and we're a team. Now, not all men treat they wives like God told, so I agree there needs to be some laws that protect them. But I'm wondering, Mercy, if some of these women be seeing things in the wrong light.

Papa's words had stuck to her, and she'd woven them into Faith's opinions, trying to create a balance of the two. She must have rewritten that article twenty times until she had it perfect. Then she'd signed it with a man's name and sent it to the first major Northern paper she could think of. An act of defiance. A far-flung hope. A desperate attempt to prove herself.

She plucked the letter up again and smoothed her fingers

over the fine paper. The *Boston Globe* recognized her talent. Without the option of knowing anything about her physical person, they'd focused on what really mattered. Her mind.

A job already awaited her. All she had to do was accept it. But did she dare? Could she leave and not tell a soul?

She'd told Faith everything since childhood. But she wouldn't tell her this. Faith didn't understand. But how could Mercy expect her to? Faith didn't know what it was like to have to hide.

No, she was entirely on her own.

Mercy clenched her fist and stared at her small hope chest sitting in the dust next to her and a bulging sack of sweet potatoes. Tears stung the back of her throat, but she swallowed them down. She would prove them all wrong. They would see.

Faith railed about the injustices women suffered. Carried on about how they were treated as second-class citizens. Well, what of the injustice for Mercy? Did Faith not see? How could she not? Faith thought Mercy couldn't accomplish anything because of the color of her skin. That made her no better than Mr. Watson, who thought Faith couldn't think because she was a woman.

Did her friend not understand the double standard? Or did she simply not see it as equal? Worse, how had Mercy been so blind all of these years to something that should have been obvious?

The more Mercy pondered it, the more furious she became. Her parents had tried to shield her from the pain they had suffered in the world. She couldn't begrudge her family for wanting her to live in blissful ignorance.

But Faith had lied. They were not like sisters. Faith didn't see them as equals.

As she'd planned for a life beyond the confines of home, she'd known Mercy could never do the same. And she didn't care. Perhaps she was nothing more than a convenient companion. Someone to be left behind as Faith moved forward in her life.

Faith believed the paper would never hire her because of her brown skin. But Faith only knew about things in Mississippi. Down here, white people had fought to keep her people slaves. But the North was different. Those states had fought for the end of slavery. Had given their own lives in order to see her people free. Yes, the North would be entirely different. If she ever had a hope of making a way for herself, it had to be out of Mississippi.

Mercy had been educated the same as Faith. She was just as intelligent. Just as capable.

She smeared the tears off her face and set her jaw. She didn't need Faith. She didn't need anyone. She had all she needed on her own.

She looked at the paper one final time and made up her mind. Maybe Faith didn't see. But the *Boston Globe* would. They were people from the North, clear thinkers who cared so much about her article that they wanted her to work for them. Even if they made her continue to write under a man's name to appease the less educated masses, *they* saw her value.

Mercy folded the paper and placed it in her nightdress pocket and then caressed the top of the small chest beside her. Polished cedar with metal banding and a spring latch, it was as beautiful as all the things her father crafted. Papa had meant for this to be hers upon her wedding. A help starting a new life.

She opened the lid and peered inside. Shadows scurried from the lamplight, dancing over the embroidered tablecloth Mama had prepared, sliding over tiny knitted socks meant for her first child, and then bouncing off the shimmer of the coins inside.

Coins her father had worked hard to procure. Mercy touched the cold metal, hesitated, and then gathered them all in her hand. Papa had meant for them to aid her as she stepped into her next stage of life.

And that's exactly what she was about to do.

Four

aith stood next to the carriage and fiddled with her gloves. Clouds gathered, and a persistent breeze sought to pluck her hat from her head. A fitting setting, if you asked her. The weather seemed as uncertain as she. This morning marked eight days, and she'd not seen Mercy. Her friend hadn't even come to church yesterday. Miss Ruth had said she'd not been well.

She thought if she'd give Mercy time to think things through, once she had, their friendship could go back to normal.

Miss Ruth bustled out of the house and handed Mother her reticule.

"Oh, gracious. How could I have forgotten that?"

Ruth chuckled. "Have a good time in Memphis."

The women embraced. "I'll bring you back some apples." Mother squeezed her friend. "We can make tarts."

Faith watched them, wondering what would have happened if their friendship had had to endure the circumstances of hers and Mercy's. Would it have survived this well? They chatted as Faith stood there in the breeze, feeling out of place. But that wasn't unusual.

Daddy came and took Faith's elbow. "If we don't hurry,

we'll miss the train."

Faith turned to Miss Ruth, gushing out the question she should have already asked. "How's Mercy?"

The older woman's brow wrinkled. "She finished her chores early again today and then disappeared."

"Disappeared?"

"She's been doing that a lot this week. Just needs time to herself." Ruth smiled, but it was tight. "Been takin' one book after another with her. You know how she likes to slip off into the woods."

Faith did. She and Mercy had often gone to a meadow of wildflowers behind the fields. They'd called it their secret magic place—a place where, as small children, they'd pretended fairies lived among the wildflowers. As they aged, Faith had stopped going there, but Mercy never had. She said it was a good place for thinking.

Faith allowed Daddy to help her into the carriage. Her parents sat on the bench across from her, and Daddy tapped the roof to signal Johnny to move the horses out. Daddy stretched his legs and massaged his left knee, something that had troubled him since he'd returned from the war. Mother had once revealed he also had a terrible scar from where a wooden stake had impaled him in the shoulder when enemy troops had nearly destroyed Corinth. But he never said anything about that.

Neither of her parents spoke much about the time before her brother Robert was born. They were hard times, Mother had said, and there would be no use souring peaceful days with thoughts of war. Robert had pestered them often to tell him about the battles, restless boy that he was.

Thinking of him, and desiring to turn her thoughts from

Mercy lest she succumb to either unfruitful anger or the weakness of tears, she said, "Daddy, have you heard any news from Robert?"

Daddy turned his gaze from the passing trees. "Not since his last letter, which I have already shared with you. He's rather determined he will strike a fortune out west."

Mother made a sour face. "I do wish he would desist with that foolishness." She eyed Daddy. "If you'd stop sending him funds, then he'd have to return home."

Daddy shook his head. "You know that wouldn't bring him home, it would only cause him to get himself into trouble."

Mother crossed her arms. "When the prodigal son ran out of funds he returned to his father's house. So, too, will Robert."

Daddy sighed, and Faith regretted bringing it up. Mother, seeming to think the same, changed the subject. She turned to Faith. "You and I will enjoy the shopping in Memphis while your father conducts his business. You need some new gowns for the turn of the season, and there are some fabulous millinery shops in the city."

"If we have the time." Faith waived a hand, having already had this talk with Daddy. "I'm going to learn shipping, which I cannot do if we spend all our time shopping."

Mother's face fell.

"There will be plenty of time for both," Daddy said, squeezing Mother's hand. "As well as time for you to get to know Mr. Watson better."

Faith withheld a sigh. That again. She'd have to find a stronger argument to dissuade Daddy than she'd thus far proffered. Couldn't he see the world was changing? Just because she neared twenty and had no husband on the horizon didn't mean she was destined to be an old maid with nothing to show for her life. Though men wanted to fight it, women were becoming more independent. Why, before long they would even be able to vote!

Trying a conversation that would be safer than the two precarious topics she'd thus far trod upon, Faith clasped her hands in her lap. "Do you think Mercy's parents will ever let her leave Ironwood?"

Mother drew a long breath and took a moment before speaking. "Why would she want to?"

Faith relayed their last conversation in the garden, and when she'd finished, Mother sighed.

"Mercy might be upset now, but she'll eventually understand her parents only want what's best for her. She'll learn to accept it, and, someday, appreciate it."

"I'm not so sure she will." Faith adjusted the annoyingly fashionable hat perched on her mass of hair. "When I tried to explain it to her, she became furious with me. I fear this is something that will cause lasting animosity if they don't find a way to give her some kind of freedom."

Daddy grunted. "I told Noah and Ruth years ago that child has too much of a restless spirit."

Mother cut her eyes at him.

He wouldn't be cowed. "We all should have expected something like this. Had Noah better prepared her, she wouldn't have her head filled with things that can never be possible."

The carriage bounced down the road, and the heavy cloud cover made it seem far later in the day than mid-morning. Faith poked at her hat again. "Perhaps she could attend school or something up north, where people are more reasonable than they are in Mississippi."

Daddy leaned forward. "I've dealt with many people on the issues of racial relations in our country. The North is not as progressive as you would like to believe."

Faith scowled. "That hardly seems right."

Daddy rubbed the back of his neck. "As you've no doubt noticed, your mother and I have made Ironwood into something very different than what exists beyond it."

"Well, yes, but—"

"The attacks on Ironwood may have stopped, but that doesn't mean anything has changed. We simply used enough prayer and gunpowder to persuade them to forget about us."

Faith pressed her lips together. She wasn't as oblivious as her parents thought. She knew all too well how people disapproved of her family and Ironwood. She'd not once attended a ball that hadn't subjected her to clandestine glances and haughty whispers. Even still, she knew Mercy could never be happy living out a copy of Miss Ruth's life at Ironwood. "There must be something she can do to still accomplish her desires."

"Well," Daddy said, "Mercy's parents don't want their daughters to suffer the life that exists for their people away from Ironwood, and I—"

"That's not fair!"

"Faith." Mother's clipped use of her name brought her words to a halt. "You will not interrupt your father."

Faith lowered her chin. "Forgive me."

The sides of Daddy's eyes crinkled with a sympathetic smile. "It's their decision, and I cannot say I disagree with it."

Faith slouched back in her seat. "But she isn't letting this go.

She has a yearning for adventure, and she's always wanted to experience the world. I fear what she may do."

Mother huffed. "The world is not a good place to experience. If I had my way, neither of my own children would be stepping foot in it. I, for one, agree with Ruth."

Daddy wrapped his arm around Mother's shoulders and pulled her close. "That's not the way things are meant to be, my love. God designed children to grow and leave their parents for lives of their own, just as we did." He smiled at Faith. "And our little one is hardly a child any longer. It's past time she start moving in the direction we agreed upon."

Mother drew her lower lip through her teeth. Even with gray now shading her temples and the scowl upon her face, Mother was still a beautiful woman. "They could make lives of their own at Ironwood. There's plenty of room."

Daddy squeezed her again. "This is not the time for this discussion."

Mother nodded and tried to smile at Faith, but the attempt did nothing to abate the fluttering in Faith's stomach. What were they talking about? Had they made plans for her future without discussing it with her?

"Have you two been plotting something I should be aware of?"

Her parents exchanged a glance, both looking uncomfortable. But before either responded, the carriage conveniently rolled to a stop at the train station, halting all further discussion on the topic. Faith disembarked and waited with Mother while Daddy saw to the unloading of their luggage.

Faith scanned the people waiting on the platform, and a sense of excitement bubbled within. On the precipice of this journey, she glimpsed the hope for adventure Mercy always spoke of...the desires to *go* and *see* and *do*. The thrill of seeing Daddy's new shipping port in Memphis and the adventure of experiencing the bustling city life had her heart fluttering.

Poor Mercy. Her guilt felt so heavy that she clasped the fabric on her bodice as though to stem the burning in her heart. *She should be here embarking on an adventure with me.*

If Ironwood could be a place of radical aberration from social normalcy, then perhaps Ironwood Shipping could be as well. And why not? Her thoughts began to churn. She'd just have to convince Mercy's parents it would be a safe place for Mercy to taste the freedom she longed for while at the same time staying connected to the family and Ironwood. Mercy could make occasional trips to port towns along the river and could help Faith draft necessary letters for trades. It was perfect! She only needed to work out the proper argument, and, as soon as she returned home, she would have a plan ready.

Her eyes roamed over the faces of the people milling along the platform, wondering where they were going and what business took them away from home. A tall figure caught her eye. Something about the way the woman moved seemed familiar. Black hair was piled at the woman's nape, but all of her other features were hidden beneath an elaborate gown that seemed slightly familiar.

Faith squinted, wishing again that her eyesight were stronger. The woman glanced over her shoulder, giving Faith the tiniest glimpse of a smooth brown cheek.

Was that Mercy?

No! It couldn't be. Faith shook her head. Her mind must be playing tricks on her. She turned to Mother.

"Did you see that woman?"

Mother followed her gaze across the crowd. "Who?"

Faith searched the platform for the woman in the camel-colored bodice and small feathered hat, but she had disappeared.

"Nothing, Mother. I was probably just mistaken."

Mercy clutched her copy of *True Politeness, A Hand-Book of Etiquette for Ladies* to her chest and tried not to cough. The smells coming off the locomotive mingled with the thick smoke clinging to the air. She'd seen drawings of trains but hadn't expected this one to be so large...or so dirty.

Be calm. Hold your head high. Don't flirt with men.

Rules. So many rules to remember. But she was determined to adhere to them all, and thus present herself a lady.

She looked down at her dress. Miss Lydia had given it to her. Faith's mother didn't mean to offend anyone with her cast-offs, so Mama had made Mercy accept it with grace. At the time, she'd wondered what the woman had thought Mercy would ever do with such a silly fashion. Now, she was glad she had it.

The light brown fabric complemented her coloring, and the reds and gold in the fashionable bustle made her look like a lady of means. And that was certainly better for her first trip up north than a faded farm gown. She must look the part.

But...all the other women at the station had dressed in muted colors and sturdy fabrics. Rather than blending in, Mercy stood out.

The plainest dress is always the most genteel, the book stated, *and a lady that dresses plainly will never be dressed unfashionably. Next to plainness, in every well-dressed lady, is neatness of dress and taste in the selection of colors.*

She straightened her shoulders. Nothing she could do about the dress now. She ran a hand down the side of the soft skirt as she scanned the locomotive. She'd figured out how to purchase the right ticket. Now she just needed to board a passenger car.

Even if she didn't fit in at the train station, she would soon be on her way to the newspaper offices. Surely they'd help her find an inn for the evening and, eventually, a suitable boarding house. People were willing to help a lady in any circumstance, so long as she executed her request with politeness.

Excitement buzzed in her veins. Imagine it! Her own room!

She was getting ahead of herself. First, she must find a passenger car so she could get to Boston, accept her position at the paper, and find lodging for the evening. Then, first thing in the morning, she would send a telegram home. It would only be a day. Her parents wouldn't have to worry too much.

She hoped. Her research into proper train travel had revealed much about how to dress, speak, and interact with passengers. It had not, however, given much information about the more technical details of procuring the correct ticket and finding the correct traveling car. Nor had it told her much about travel times. Her calculations based on distances and recorded train speeds meant it couldn't take more than a day of travel.

But she couldn't be certain.

Mercy pushed the doubts out of her mind. She'd thus far made it off Ironwood, into Oakville, and to the train station. She had managed to purchase a ticket. For a girl who had never left her own village, she'd already accomplished quite the feat. She could do this.

She finally located the passenger car and placed her foot on the loading step.

This is it. No turning back now.

Mercy held her head high and stepped into the car. Plush carpeting cushioned her feet, and ornate decorative carvings curved across the domed ceiling. She paused. Who would have thought the greasy exterior hid such a lovely traveling compartment? This, too, was far beyond what she'd expected. Something pricked at the back of her mind, warning her that so many surprises weren't good, but she ignored it. Her gaze drifted down from the ceiling to land upon several white women who occupied the car. They stared at her, whispering to one another behind gloved hands.

Mercy held her head high and refused to look at them.

She plopped down in the nearest seat, scooting close to the window. Perhaps sitting, no one would notice her attire, which she now realized was far too ostentatious. She needed to keep quiet, keep her head down, and enjoy the trip in peace.

Her father's teaching warred with that from the book. *Keep your eyes down when addressing any white folk. Stay out of they way, and they won't bother you.* The advice had been meant for her interactions with friends of the Harper family whenever Mercy had been at the big house and people had visited. Perhaps it would work for the unfriendly faces on the train as well.

She tucked her bag under her feet. She'd packed her two best church dresses and her necessities. That would do for now. She could purchase everything else once she began her assignments for the newspaper.

Smiling to herself, Mercy looked out the window and watched the people on the platform. They milled about as colored porters loaded bags and assisted ladies. She tried to watch the white women carefully. They moved slowly, gracefully, and kept their eyes downturned under veils that shielded at least part of their faces. But she didn't see any women who looked like her.

She'd been right, though. Things must be different now, or at least not as bad as her parents believed. Not a single person at the train station had tried to harm her. These were civilized people. The madmen who had come in white robes weren't what all white people were like.

Mercy touched her hat. It had a bit of a veil, but not enough to pull over her face. She despised the feeling of needing to hide and yet sought its comfort anyway. She gathered the ruffles around her throat. She'd never seen so many white folks, and the mere fact that she sat on a rumbling hunk of iron had her nerves in a titter. There was so much she didn't know!

Some journalist she would make. Why hadn't she taken more time for research? Surely she could have found some information on trains, or traveling, or proper women's attire. But she was afraid if she'd taken too long, the paper wouldn't honor their offer.

She'd prepared as best she could. The rest she'd have to learn by paying close attention and experience. If she wanted people to take her seriously, she'd have to be diligent in presenting herself as a lady, not an uneducated farm girl. A balance of remaining unobtrusive while also adhering to proper etiquette.

Mercy tapped her feet in a nervous rhythm. What else had

she neglected? The wrong dress and an incorrect hat, apparently, but had she made any other gaffes?

Someone to her left made a harsh, loud noise of irritation. Mercy turned her head slightly and looked at the other woman through her lashes. The lady was plump with a flushed complexion, and the heavy scowl upon her face made her rather unattractive. Mercy's stomach tightened. That mean scowl was focused right at her!

"Where's your mistress?" The ugly woman glared at her.

Her heartbeat quickened. These were just women. Not men with torches and—

"Did you hear me, girl? I asked you about your mistress."

Mercy set her teeth and dipped her chin as politely as she could. "At home," she lied. The falsehood pinched her conscience, but Mercy sensed that if she'd said she didn't have a mistress, it would cause an incident.

She lowered her eyes and held her breath.

The woman made a rude comment unbefitting a lady that Mercy chose to ignore, but then said nothing more. Mercy slowly let out the breath and tried to sink deeper into the plush seat. She clasped her hands tightly and turned back to the window. She'd have to try to remain as still as possible. Maybe they would forget about her.

It would be a difficult challenge. Papa called her humming-bird because he'd said even from the time she'd been cradled in her mother's womb, she'd never been still. She fluttered about like a tiny bird whose wings moved too fast to be seen.

"No one wants you here. Your kind isn't welcome."

Another voice, different from the ugly woman's, hurtled through the train car. Sweat trickled down her temples. Mercy sank lower.

Her parents had been right. The world wasn't nice. But she wouldn't let it stop her. Once the train took her north, she could leave such self-righteous bigots behind.

Thinking of Papa tightened her throat and caused an uneasy feeling in her empty stomach. Would he be terribly angry with her? Mercy squeezed her hands. Surely he'd forgive her. He wished to protect her, and she loved him all the more for it, but like the little bird, she needed to test her wings. She needed to fly away from the nest and see the world on her own. She must prove herself.

He would see. He would have to.

She blinked back tears that tried to form against her will and returned her focus to studying the crowd on the platform. *Remain quiet. Make them forget you're here.*

The upturned face of a white man with a waxed mustache hovered directly below. She leaned closer to the window. Next to him, a thin white woman waved her hands about, gesturing wildly. The man scowled, tugged down on the hem of his vest, and then stalked down the platform.

Mercy crossed her ankles and pulled her feet under her seat. She'd already gone to shuffling again. This would be even harder than she'd thought. She tried to peek over the seats at the other passengers. As she feared, they all stared at her. Some with wide eyes, others with confusion, and still others with unfriendly frowns.

She ducked her head. *Remain hidden long enough, and they will forget.* The repeated thought did nothing to calm her nerves. If the train would just hurry up and move, perhaps they would be resigned to her presence. She just needed to wait a little longer and—

"Excuse me."

A man's voice drew her regard, and she turned to find the mustached man from the platform staring at her. Her throat tightened.

She tilted her head down in an attempt to get the wisp of the veil on her hat to cover more of her face than a portion of forehead. She kept her gaze pointed at his boots.

"Yes?"

"You will need to vacate immediately."

Her gaze shot up to his splotchy face. The ticket had taken most of her money! Despite the fear writhing in her stomach, she could not miss the train. "I-I have my ticket, sir." She plucked it from her lap, dismayed to find it had been crinkled by her nervous fingers. She held it out to him, keeping her eyes downcast.

He snatched it from her as though he feared touching her gloves and studied it for a moment. Then, to her great relief, shoved it in his pocket.

Still, he did not leave. His eyes bore down on her. "You're on the wrong car."

"I'll say," the ugly woman snapped. "Really. What nerve."

Mercy ignored her. "I'm sorry, sir, but what do you mean?"

He narrowed his eyes. "We will not have one of your kind making your ridiculous equality displays on this train. You sit in the proper car or you do not ride."

Mercy's mouth fell open. Displays? What was he talking about? Deciding that the look on his face meant it was better she didn't ask, she focused on the other part of his statement.

"I'm sorry, sir." *Deep breath.* "I mean no disrespect. But is this not a passenger car on the train to Boston…the one for which I was allowed to purchase a ticket?"

"It is."

Mercy blinked. "But, then, why—"

"The *Negro* car is further down the train."

Oh. She should have known.

The man snorted. "Remove yourself, or I'll have you ejected."

The woman with the pink flush and weighty scowl leaned around him to pierce Mercy with her stabbing gaze. "Disgraceful, it is. Unable to stay in their proper place." She shook her head. "This girl in her mistress's flamboyant dress thinks that just because she put on a bustle she can ride with us." She clicked her tongue.

Mercy looked to the other passengers only to see them nodding along. Fire burned in her belly, and she rose to her feet. The train man seemed to relax and held out his hand to gesture toward the door.

Humiliation pricked her as one of the ladies called her a name she'd never heard but was quite certain was disgraceful. She grabbed her bag from the floor and stepped into the aisle. She held her head high, refusing to let their scorn make her cower. It didn't matter which car she rode in as long as she made it to Boston.

She disembarked and stood on the platform, looking down the line of cars. The man left without the courtesy of giving her further directions, not that she expected anything different.

Which way? She was running out of time. She scanned the faces, and then, blessedly, saw an elderly man with stark white hair and an ebony face approach one of the cars.

She hurried forward only to be immediately snatched backward. She yelped as the sound of ripping fabric mingled with a man's groan. Her dress! Someone had stepped on the short length of fabric trailing from the elaborate bustle. Regaining her balance, Mercy looked behind her and into the glower of a middle-aged man. The woman on his arm regarded the fabric beneath her button-up boot with a look of contempt.

The man sniffed and turned up his bulbous nose, and the couple turned away to continue down the platform without a word of apology. Trying to tamp down the fear and frustration fluttering in her chest, Mercy reached behind her and snatched up the fabric. She sighed at the trodden bundle of beautiful material in her hand, finally understanding why none of the other ladies dressed as she had. There were too many feet moving around for piles of fabric to be trailing behind her.

Well, she could solve that problem. She raised her hem to clear her feet. There. That should do it. Now she could walk freely.

A woman gasped, and Mercy turned to look at the incredulous expressions of two women in large hats. One shook her head while the other began fanning her face.

What now? Had she committed some other heinous sin? Heavens, at this rate she—

A shrill whistle pierced the air and nearly made Mercy's heart leap from her chest. People on the platform scurried, and the porters called out to one another over the commotion.

Terrified, Mercy lurched forward and stretched her legs out into what she knew would be a most inappropriate and unladylike stride. But better she had the scowls of the people at the station than she miss her only chance to get to Boston.

She hurried to the car she'd seen the elderly man board and prayed it would be the right one. She hadn't known there would be so many rules about trains.

Her hand grasped the cold handle, and she swung up onto the step. A terrible screeching sounded down the line. Mercy scrambled the rest of the way into the car, nearly losing her valise as she snatched it through the doorway. Whatever car she was on now, it would have to be the one that took her to Boston. What were they going to do? Throw her off of a moving train?

The thought that someone may well attempt just that made her blood run cold. Drawing heavy breaths, she looked up to judge the passengers. The elderly man and other men, women, and children who looked like her gathered on plain wooden benches next to the open windows of the car.

Mercy gulped. This was the difference between the mansion at Ironwood and the stable behind her house. There were no plush carpets, no carved ceilings, and goodness, not even glass windows to stay the wind!

But at least there were people who looked like her. And they were all going to Boston.

Several of them turned her way, their dark eyes roaming her dress. Mercy held her head high. Let them think what they would. Some of the women's eyebrows rose, and one young man had the audacity to jab his fellow in the ribs and nod at her.

Mercy's chest fluttered. She didn't care for the way that young man looked at her, and she began to understand why Mr. Charles had so often told Faith a lady did not go about without an escort. These young men didn't know Papa the way the young men at Ironwood did.

Suddenly, the car lurched, and Mercy lost her balance. She stumbled, dropping her bag, and had to grip the back of a bench to keep from falling. Her face warmed, and she retrieved her belongings from the floor and then lowered herself onto the nearest bench with as much dignity as she could muster.

As the train pulled away from the station, tears blurred her vision. Papa had been right all along.

Five

Faith settled next to Mother in the Pullman parlor car on the Memphis line. The whistle for another train on the other side of the station called a warning for passengers to board. Daddy had insisted they arrive early so as to be boarded and settled long before the whistle. Mother didn't like to be rushed.

Couples filled the traveling parlor, settling in as though they were gathering to have a nice visit. The Pullman Company had made every effort to ensure their passengers felt at home, but Faith felt anything but.

Daddy spoke to the porter about their trunks, though both she and Mother had decided to keep their smaller valises with them. Faith watched as men pulled out decks of cards, and women settled down to chat.

Mother squeezed her hand. "It'll still be a time before we depart."

"I'm content to wait. I brought a novel."

From Mother's other side, Daddy chuckled. "Of course you did."

"It's *Jane Eyre*, Daddy." She smiled broadly. "Written by a woman. I picked it up at the bookstore when Mother and I went shopping."

Mother scrunched her nose. "She was supposed to be looking for new dress fabrics, but I couldn't keep her attention away from books."

"And just think how much better the bookstores will be in a city like Memphis!" Faith said. "Why, I bet I'll even be able to find some newer law books."

The shadow that passed over Mother's eyes wrenched Faith with the familiar feeling of guilt. She shifted. "But I still hope you and I will enjoy one another's company even if we are not dress shopping?"

Oddly, Mother's eyes moistened, and she blinked rapidly. "Of course." A smile warmed her features. She studied Faith for a moment, thoughts churning behind her eyes as though she could see straight through all Faith said and instead look into her anxious heart.

Faith looked away.

"I'd thought to wait until…" Mother trailed off and then shook her head. "Well, never mind." She offered a sweeping smile, but only part of its light reached her eyes. "I have a gift for you."

"A gift? For what occasion?"

Mother reached into her valise and plucked out a small object wrapped in brown paper. She extended it to Faith without explanation.

Faith pulled away the wrapping, revealing a small leather-bound book inside. She looked to her mother, who watched her rather intently. Faith fanned the pages, then sent a questioning glance back to Mother. "It's blank."

Daddy laughed. "That's because you've yet to fill it."

Mother squeezed her hand. "Just before I wed, my father gifted me with a journal in which to record my thoughts and experiences."

Faith had no memory of her grandparents. Both of her mother's parents had died when she was very young, and Daddy's parents had passed before he and Mother wed.

Her eyes bore into Faith's. "I found it to be very helpful to my overcrowded heart to get my thoughts onto paper. It helped me find clarity."

Faith plucked at the button on her sleeve, scrambling for a suitable response but finding none.

"That journal was very dear to me," Mother continued, "I thought, as you are moving into the next stage of your own life, you may wish to do the same."

Faith clutched the little book. "That's most kind of you, Mother. Thank you."

Mother took the wrapping paper and shoved it down in her valise. Faith suspected the movement had less to do with disposing of the discarded paper and more to do with hiding her face while she did so.

Something Mother had said plucked her curiosity. "I don't ever remember seeing you write in a journal."

Daddy laughed. "That's because after your brother and you were born, she didn't have a spare moment."

Mother looked away, but not before Faith noticed something strange in her eyes. The train whistle cut through the air, causing Mother to startle.

Faith smoothed her bodice. "Where is this journal Granddaddy gave you? I should like to see it and know what kind of things you wrote about at my age." Had Mother's thoughts been just as tangled?

"As you will soon discover," Daddy replied instead, "the journal will become a private thing. Something you can record your most intimate thoughts in. It isn't really for anyone else to read."

Heat touched her cheeks. "Of course."

What kind of things had Mother written about? Faith tried to judge the woman she'd known all her life from the corner of her eye, wondering if Mother had hidden something from her.

She tucked the journal into her bag. "Thank you for the gift."

The car lurched, sending Faith's thoughts tumbling to the uncertainty of her future. The wheels outside churned, making a rhythmic sound that could be heard even inside the elaborately padded and decorated parlor car. The engine gained speed.

Mother grabbed Faith's fingers and held them. In silence, they watched the train pull away from the station. As it puffed down the line, the passengers settled into conversations and men dealt cards to their companions. Mother and Daddy soon began a discussion about which families they would need to visit once they reached the city.

Faith opened her novel and stared at words she couldn't focus on enough on to read. Her thoughts instead swirled around the shipping company and what position she could fill.

She knew far too little of the industry. All she knew for sure was that she would have to find a way. If she didn't, she sensed Mercy's deep disquiet would soon sour into bitterness, or worse, recklessness. And she couldn't lose her. Mercy had always been the steady one. A refuge of safety who never judged her.

Until last week.

Faith drew a long, slow breath and exhaled as much of her apprehension as she could. She needed to think. If she could find a way to get Daddy to give her a permanent position at Ironwood Shipping, then her next step would be to ask to remain in Memphis. To do that, of course, she would need a living companion. And who better than Mercy?

Her hope lifted, only to immediately fall. She'd forgotten something important. Such an arrangement would cause one unavoidable inconvenience.

It put her directly in the path of Mr. Watson.

The thought brought a piece of conversation from the carriage ride back to her mind. Her mother and father had been discussing her future. Faith cut her eyes to where her parents conversed, pieces falling into place. They were taking her to Memphis. Where Daddy intended to ask Mr. Watson to head the offices there. Why had Daddy brought her this time when he hadn't before?

And, more than that, he'd been entirely too quick to accept her requests to spend time at his office. She squeezed her novel so hard the pages crinkled.

What a ninny she'd been! They weren't bringing her to Memphis to learn the shipping business. They weren't even taking her for company as Mother shopped.

She narrowed her eyes at her parents. No, they had a far more dastardly plan in mind.

They were plotting a marriage.

She should have known.

Mercy jolted awake. She'd dozed off again, and her chin had dropped to her chest. She shifted and rubbed her eyes. She stretched her head from side to side. It had been a terrible night trying to keep herself upright on the bench. Her neck, back, and shoulders ached, and she was certain she looked frightful.

Her fingers reached up to touch the skewed hat perched on her head. It took constant fiddling to keep the thing properly pinned with the incessant wind. She narrowed her eyes at the window as though her dour expression could warn away the gusts. Outside, the gray of early morning gave birth to pink and red swaths of color, ushering in a new day. A second day in which she was *still* on the train. Who knew it would make so many stops on the way to Boston?

Someone plopped down beside her, and Mercy bit her lip to hold back an ungracious order to go away. She didn't feel inclined to entertain company.

Expecting the scoundrel who'd kept eyeing her, Mercy had to suck back her breath when she was instead greeted by the bright eyes of an adorable little girl. Tension drained, and she couldn't help but smile at the child whose pale yellow dress overlapped Mercy's skirt.

The little girl flashed white teeth at her. "Hello, Miss fancy lady. Ma said I could come up here and sit wit you."

Mercy glanced behind her, looking for a flustered mother searching for her child. "Is that so?"

"Yup. She say you look like you could use some company,

and so after I asked her 'bout"—the little girl counted her fingers, then held out all five to Mercy—"this many times, she finally say I could come up here wit you."

Mercy stared at the child, unsure what to say. The girl returned her gaze with bright brown eyes, and they looked at one another for a moment while the wind tugged at their hair and the steady clack of the train wheels pounded a relentless rhythm.

"We're goin' north to look for work. Is that what you doin', Miss Fancy?"

"My name is Mercy, not Fancy."

The child bobbed her head. "My pa says he can work at one of them factories up there or get work on one of the boats, or maybe even on the railroad." Her eyes sparkled. "He says railroad men get a dollar every Sunday!"

Mercy smiled. "That's nice." How much would the paper pay? Another thing she'd not properly researched. They hardly used money at Ironwood. The people mostly bartered. She wasn't ignorant of the use of money, merely inexperienced in the daily necessity of it. She would figure it out. It would be fine.

"What's it like on one of those big boats?"

Mercy tilted her head at the little girl's question. "I don't know. I've never been on a boat."

The girl's eyes filled with disappointment. "I figured a fancy lady like you has been lots of places."

"I'm afraid not. This is my first time on a train."

The girl brightened again. "That so? Me, too." Then her eyes widened and she straightened herself. "Oh! I forgot. Ma says I'm always forgettin' my manners. I'm Miss Magnolia Peters. Named after the big pretty flower trees and the place where both my parents came from before the war."

Mercy opened her mouth to respond but the girl hurried on.

"The Peters family owned Magnolia Hill. Both my ma and pa was born there. After they got they freedom, they moved away."

Mercy studied the girl, who looked to be no more than about seven years of age. Papa had said most people didn't have second names in the old days, so they came up with ones that suited them. Some took names based on where they were from, and others took names they liked or fit their work. Papa took Carpenter because that's what he did. And, Papa had said, since Jesus was a carpenter, they couldn't ask for a better name anyhow.

Remembering her own manners, Mercy dipped her chin at Magnolia. "I'm Miss Mercy Carpenter."

The girl giggled. "I like Miss Fancy better." She tentatively reached out and then rubbed a bit of Mercy's torn bustle between her little fingers.

Mercy couldn't help but smile. At least *someone* saw her as a fancy lady.

"Don't you go calling her that," a woman's voice said from behind.

Mercy looked up to find a woman with her hands on her hips. "I know you don't know no better, but a fancy lady is one who does things that ain't proper, things no Christian woman would do." She eyed Mercy. "You ain't that kind, are you?"

Mercy gulped. "I wore this dress to look nice for a perspective employment position." She grimaced. "I didn't know it wouldn't be suitable for the train."

The other woman sat on the seat across from Mercy. She looked to be in her mid-thirties, with a wide nose and smooth features. She wore a simple green dress, similar to the ones Mercy had left at home, and had tied a tightly wound piece of matching cloth around her hair. Apparently, she'd understood the windy conditions of the train better than Mercy.

The woman folded her hands in her lap and looked at the girl. "I'm sorry if Maggie's caused you any problems, but she insisted on coming up here to talk to you. Once she gets something in her head, there ain't no turning her from it."

Mercy hid her smile. That particular quality sounded a touch familiar. "Not at all. She makes fine company."

The little girl beamed. "See, Ma? I told you she was a fan...uh, fine lady."

A bitter laugh bubbled up from Mercy's chest. "I'm afraid not. It would seem my efforts to appear better off than the farm girl I really am have not been sufficient." She waved her hand at the open window. "Or appropriate, for that matter. My attempt to blend in only made me stand out like a peacock in a pen of chickens."

Magnolia leaned forward with wide eyes. "What's a peacock?"

"It's a big bird with lots of bright blue and green feathers. Nothing at all like a chicken."

The little girl smirked. "Yup. Seems right, you being that pretty bird and the rest of us plain ol' chickens."

Mercy couldn't believe she'd not caught her mistake. "No! I didn't mean that." She shot an apologetic look at the woman. "I'm sorry, I didn't mean to imply that everyone else was as plain as chickens. I...oh, what a mess I am!"

The other woman leaned back and laughed so hard she had to dab her eyes. "I've thought those prissy white women strut about like roosters many times."

Despite herself, Mercy let her discomfort dissolve under laughter. "They kind of do, don't they?" Mercy giggled again and pressed her hand to her lips.

When they'd regained their composure, Magnolia's mother pursed her lips. "You sure don't sound like no girl from a farm. I figured you must have been brought up by one of those wealthy colored gentleman up north we always hear about."

Mercy wasn't sure what the woman meant. "I'm from Mississippi. My father makes furniture and my mother helps manage the farmlands."

The woman's eyebrows rose nearly to her hairline. "Isn't that interesting." She shrugged. "Still don't sound like a farm girl."

Mercy gave an apologetic turn of her palms, not sure what she could say. She'd noticed she spoke differently than the older generation, but she'd never given it much thought. Apparently that made her stand out as much as her dress did. But perhaps it would be a good thing. It may help her when she approached the men at the newspaper.

"Anyway," the woman said, "Benny—that's my husband—said we could ask you if you want to come back and eat with us. We don't have much, but it didn't look like you've had nothing at all."

Mercy's shoulders relaxed and she grinned. "That is exceptionally kind of you, Mrs. Peters. I would be most pleased to join you, and thank you for your generosity." Her stomach, as though to confer, grumbled.

For the remainder of her trip, Mercy's anxieties waned under the acceptance of the Peters family, who shared their meal without hesitation and treated her with kind regard. By the time they pulled into the station in Boston later in the afternoon, she was tired and dirty, but she hadn't starved—for lack of food or company. Feeling rejuvenated, Mercy exited the train in Boston with newfound hope.

She could do this.

She couldn't do this.

Faith clutched her hands so tightly in front of her that her fingers were turning numb. Mr. Watson strode down the platform, a smile too pleasant and—perish the thought!—too attractive gracing the face of a fellow whom she could not seem to escape. Catching her stare, his grin broadened, and she had to look away.

"Good afternoon, Mr. and Mrs. Harper." He offered a slight bow. "And you, Miss Harper. You look lovely today."

Lovely. Ha. Years of experience told her otherwise. "Thank you, sir." Faith lowered her eyes, though the gesture was not born of a lady's demure shyness in the presence of a handsome gentleman as he likely thought. Rather, she simply couldn't stand to look at him. And it had nothing to do with the heat rising in her cheeks, either.

Daddy gestured off the platform. "Come, let's get away from the dust of the station, shall we?"

"I have a carriage ready, sir, if you will follow me." Mr. Watson turned toward the line of carriages situated not far from the tracks and the horses pawing at the grass.

Faith trailed behind, her mind whirling. When Faith made her request, Daddy would eventually give in. He always did. Mother would be more of a challenge, but surely she would see that Faith having a profession of some kind was a good thing and that Mercy coming with her only made sense.

She glared at the back of Mr. Watson's perfectly combed head and seethed. No, *he* would be the unwelcome piece on her chessboard that would cause her the most trouble. Mr. Watson had Daddy's ear too much as it was, and he would not be happy when she asserted her plans to take part in the company. He'd made it clear he didn't think women were meant for business. Would his opinions sway Daddy?

Clearly her father thought Mr. Watson a suitable prospect. But Faith knew better. She could see right through Mr. Watson's façade. His feigned interest in her was nothing more than a ruse. A calculated plan to woo a witless female into marriage in order to use her for his financial gain.

A smile of her own pulled at her lips. Well, if it was a battle of wits he wished to play, then he had sorely underestimated his opponent.

Nolan Watson straightened his cravat. Why did it feel so tight around his neck? The afternoon air, while thick with smoke from the trains, was not overly warm.

He could nearly feel Miss Harper's eyes on him, and it made

the hairs on the back of his neck stand on end. Her scrutiny must be the cause of the uncomfortable itch. *Daft fool.* He knew he shouldn't have been so open with his intentions when last he saw the lady. Father had always advised a man should carefully woo a woman, and he'd gone and made a fool of himself instead. What woman was going to respect that? Now he'd taken two steps backward.

Clearly his employer's daughter had taken a distinct dislike to him. Not that he could truly blame her. He often found himself at a loss in the company of women, and this woman only exasperated the condition further. No matter what he said, it offended.

Perhaps he should give up thoughts on courting her. Miss Harper had no interest in him. The thought brought disappointment, but he shoved it aside. He'd been far too quick to imagine a life grafted into this family. Probably better he set aside such thoughts and focus on his work. Despite the way Miss Harper fascinated him, such an unconventional woman would likely prove to be more trouble than a man could handle.

Mr. Harper slapped a hand on his shoulder as they approached the waiting carriage. "Good of you to come meet us, Nolan."

"Certainly, sir." He nodded to the driver. "We have several things we need to discuss during your visit."

"Of course." He glanced back at the ladies as the driver opened the carriage door. "But there will be time for that later."

Mr. Harper offered his hand to assist his wife inside the enclosed conveyance, a tender smile passing between them. Nolan darted a glance to their quarrelsome daughter, surprised to see her lift her hand in expectance of his assistance.

He took her gloved fingers and silently handed her into the carriage. She took a seat on the plush padding across from her parents. He hopped in and rapped on the roof to signal the driver.

The scent of her delicate perfume wafted through his senses, tangling them. She sat primly at his side and, after a few moments, the silence unnerved him.

He grappled for a topic of conversation appropriate in the company of ladies but could think of little more than the pressing business issues he needed to discuss with Mr. Harper. Finally, it was Mrs. Harper who spoke.

"How do you find Memphis? Still thinking of making it a permanent residence?"

"I find it quite to my liking, ma'am." He'd toyed with the idea of asking to move to the Mississippi office instead, where he could more easily ask Miss Harper to court, but he'd thrived on the work in Memphis.

He dared a glance at Miss Harper's pinched expression. *Too complicated*, he reminded himself. "If your offer still stands, Mr. Harper, I would like to accept the position here."

"Was there another position you were interested in, Mr. Watson?" Miss Harper's warm eyes coolly swept over him, making him feel like a child on the verge of a reprimand.

He tugged his cravat. "Your father graciously asked if I would prefer to work from the Mississippi office or the Tennessee office, and while I briefly considered the other, I believe Memphis is the better choice."

She arched her brows. "Oh? You don't wish to stay closer to the main office?"

Was she disappointed he would be farther away? He opened

his mouth, then closed it again, lest more words that had not been carefully considered seeped out.

"Nothing to say?" she quipped.

His face heated. He glanced at Mr. Harper, catching the man's scowl. No wonder he'd been so open to the idea of Nolan's suit. The more time he spent in the woman's company, the more he understood the reason one so lovely had not yet wed.

Six

Mercy tried to shake the dust from her skirt but found she only stirred it and created more rumples in the fabric. She should have worn her regular clothes and found a place to change into this gown prior to stepping into the newspaper offices.

But how was she to know it would take more than a day and a half to reach Boston? Or that she'd have to ride in an open train car?

A shame she hadn't better appropriated her funds so that she might have secured a boarding house first, but she hadn't known the train ticket would cost so much. Too many things she didn't know. The nagging worry niggled at her mind again, but she brushed it away. No matter. She was learning. Like the bird, she'd drift along with the breeze rather than fight it.

Besides, the newspaper was hiring her based on her merit, not her appearance. With that in mind, Mercy gripped her bag and stepped down from the station platform. People dispersed in different directions, many stepping into conveyances or greeting friends and loved ones who'd come to retrieve them. Hopefully, it wouldn't be too long of a walk to her destination.

"Mercy!"

She turned to find Mrs. Peters hurrying after her. She smiled at her traveling companion and waited for the woman to approach.

"We got a wagon that's taking us out to my cousin's house. You want to come with us?"

Mercy hesitated. A chance to clean herself up would be worth a delay of a few hours. "Where does your cousin live?"

"Out from the city a few miles in one of the smaller towns."

Mercy shook her head. "I'm afraid that would require me imposing on someone overnight." She wouldn't become a burden on their kindness and ask for them to return her to the city tomorrow. She'd simply have to make do today. "I'm most grateful for the offer, but I need to get into the city as soon as possible."

Mrs. Peters took her arm and looked at Mercy with worried eyes. "You be careful in that city. There's a lot of things that can go wrong in a place like that."

Mercy tamped down her anxiety. "I'll be careful."

The other woman didn't appear convinced. "You get into any trouble, you come up to Medford and ask after the Negro blacksmith by the name of John Elm, you hear?"

Mercy couldn't help but smile. "I will. Thank you again. And once your husband finds work, you be sure to come by the *Boston Globe* and see me."

Mrs. Peters looked confused, but her husband called to her, and she gave Mercy one last squeeze. "The blacksmith in Medford. Don't forget."

Mercy watched her go, her heart hammering. She lifted her hand to wave at little Magnolia, then started her journey once more. Once she cleared the bustle of the train depot, she paused along the side of the road under a shade tree and pulled out the rumpled envelope from her skirt pocket to look at the address.

A map would have been helpful, but she'd make do. Someone would point her in the right direction. It took but a few moments for the train station to blend into the rest of the town. The city abounded with more people than Mercy had ever laid eyes upon. She attempted to recall how the governesses had instructed Faith to act during outings. She tried to keep her gaze properly downcast but found that the jarring noises and sights warring for her attention made it impossible to do so.

She drew a deep breath of air that tasted both salty and somewhat smoky and turned her head to the left. A wharf teeming with ships of all kinds extended past the nearest row of buildings, and even from here she could hear dock men calling out to one another. Curious, she passed through a very narrow strip of road between two buildings to draw closer. A few moments to see the harbor would not delay her much.

Mercy paused and drank in the exotic scene. The sun glimmered off the pristine water, its bright blue color more vibrant than any she'd ever seen. Above, large white birds swooped along the water's edge and cawed to one another. Ships bobbed in the harbor, their massive sails and curved edges testaments to excitement and adventure. She'd seen drawings of these great ships, but hadn't been prepared for their immense size. How many people would fit on one of those contraptions?

She stepped out from between the two buildings and looked around, pulse thrumming. What a wonder! She would have to make time to explore the city once she got settled. Perhaps there would be a boarding house near the water. Mercy gripped her bag tighter and let a smile form on her lips. No harm in looking for a living space while she attempted to locate the newspaper.

The cobbled street continued a great distance in either direction. Signs hung from the front of each of the shops facing the water, giving an indication of some kind of business within. None of them seemed to be rooming houses. Maybe those were located farther away from the docking area. Mercy stared up the long walkway, trying to decipher which establishment would be the best place in which to inquire about her destination.

She studied the signs hanging above her. They depicted mugs, animals, and boats and left her confused as to exactly what types of establishments were housed within. Why were there no words?

"Hey, there. You lost, girl?" A voice leapt out of the shadows and tugged Mercy's attention away from her scrutiny of one particularly odd sign depicting a barely clothed woman with the tail of a fish in place of her legs.

She swung around to see a large man with bulging forearms and a soiled shirt leering at her. She took a step back as his gaze swept down the front of her dress.

He ran his tongue over his lips. "If you're lookin' for the Pink Parrot, I can show you where it is." He lifted burly eyebrows, and her stomach knotted.

Mercy shook her head and took another step back. "I'm not. Thank you."

He laughed, though Mercy found no humor in it. Sudden terror erupted in her chest, and with no further thoughts about appearing ladylike, she grabbed her skirt and whirled around, hurrying away from the man as quickly as she could. His laughter followed her down the street, but thankfully, his booted feet did not.

She scrambled past three establishments that, upon passing, she figured out must be ale houses. Four more unidentifiable shops later, she dared a glance over her shoulder. The unscrupulous man had disappeared, though the others who milled about didn't seem any better. She'd been too occupied with the shops and scenery to notice that the people here seemed of a different sort than the ones at the train depot.

Mrs. Peters's words came back to her, stirring worry like a hornets' nest. She must hurry and find the paper. They would direct her to a proper boarding establishment for an unmarried lady. Mercy returned her gaze to deciphering the signs and casting furtive glances in murky windows. The further she continued up the street, the cleaner the stores seemed to become, but Mercy didn't dare step into any without knowing their purpose. The unscrupulous man's insinuation about the establishment called the Pink Parrot left a bad feeling in her middle.

She began to think she'd never find somewhere decent to make inquiries when a sign up ahead offered hope. This one boasted a map and compass. Relief settled over her like one of Mama's hand-stitched quilts. Certainly that would have to be better than a tavern. She quickened her steps.

Mercy grabbed the knob almost desperately and ducked inside, causing a little bell above her head to jingle.

"Be right with you!" a man's voice called from the rear of the store.

Rolled scrolls, books, and all kinds of instruments lined the shelves crammed into the small space. She breathed deeply, her nose tingling with the familiar smells of parchment and ink. The sensation was enough to ease her shoulders down from where they'd tensed up nearly to her ears.

A balding head popped out from behind one of the shelves. "How can I help...oh."

Mercy resisted the urge to smooth her dress. She clasped her hands in front of her and met the elderly man's gaze. "Pardon me, sir. I'm sorry to disturb your business, but I fear I'm in need of some assistance."

The man stiffened and glanced behind her as though searching for someone. "What do you want?"

Mercy tried to smile. "I'm looking for the offices of the *Boston Globe*."

"That's on the other side of town." The man rubbed the back of his neck. "On Washington Street."

"Oh." Her shoulders slumped. "Is it a very long way?"

The man shrugged. "Be better to get a hansom cab." His gaze raked down her. "If you could."

Mercy gave a small nod, though she didn't have the funds to do so. "If I may inconvenience you a moment more, may I ask how one might get from here to Washington Street by foot?"

The man glanced behind her again, seeming annoyed, and Mercy had to resist the urge to turn around and see what he was looking at.

"Sure, sure." He gestured her toward the door. "Go to the end of this street and turn right. Go down seven more streets until you get to Commercial Street. From there, take Hanover to Congress. Then you can hit Washington and Newspaper Row."

Mercy pursed her lips, hoping there was not a great distance between streets. The man looked at her expectantly and waved to the door again. She fixed a pleasant smile on her lips. "Thank you, sir. Good day to you."

She was in desperate need of a fresh dress, and now she would need to walk quite a distance further. She should have gone with Mrs. Peters, cleaned herself up, and come up with a new plan. Charging headlong into this harebrained scheme wasn't going well. Not well at all. Her lip quivered, and moisture pricked her eyes, but she clamped down her emotions and squared her shoulders.

She had but one direction to go. Forward. That thought kept her trudging through Boston with her head high though her stomach gnawed, her back ached, and she was rather certain the blisters she'd gained on her feet were now beginning to bleed. Time seemed to lose meaning as the sun lowered further in the sky and she doggedly focused ahead.

People scowled at her as she passed. Some mumbled rude remarks. Mercy kept her head down and dodged out of their way. She wasn't sure how much time had passed since she'd left the map shop. She tried not to think on it too much lest her withering resolve crumble further. Then, when she feared her feet would take her no farther, the sign for Washington Street glimmered like a halo of hope.

Feeling bolstered, she fixed her gaze ahead, moving past people on the busy streets with new resolve. Mercy stepped off the boardwalk for another unfriendly white woman, too tired to lift her trailing skirts from dragging in the mud. She'd ruined the gown. Guilt bit at her and blurred her vision.

What a terrible waste. Not only had she ruined Miss Lydia's gown, but she'd made a mess of this entire thing and was squandering her article payment—and worse—the money Papa had worked so hard to earn.

She blinked back tears and stepped back onto the sidewalk.

It would be worth it. It had to be. She would replace what she'd taken. Papa would be proud. Once she made it as a journalist. She scanned the façade of the buildings, admiring the craftsmanship of their structures.

Papa would like it here…..so many carvings.

The thought scurried into her head and darted out again like a timid mouse. Mercy blinked quickly and tried to clear the fog beginning to settle. She had enough wherewithal to realize her mind didn't seem to be functioning normally, but it wouldn't be anything a good night's rest and a large glass of water wouldn't fix.

First, though, she had to find the—

There! Her heart beat faster, gifting a bit of energy she didn't know she possessed into her tired legs.

A building shone in the late afternoon light. Its polished stone gleamed like a beacon. Mercy drifted toward it like an insect to the fire.

The *Boston Globe*. She'd found it!

She shifted the valise she'd carried all through the city to her other hand and reached for the door. Her trembling fingers glided over the metal handle, and the large wooden door swung easily. Her shoes clicked across the smooth floor as she stepped inside, and cool air brushed her face. The building nearly dripped with finery. Why, working in a place like this, in no time at all she would have a wardrobe full of fashionable dresses! Yes, she would make Papa proud.

Her fingers reached to smooth her hair, and her gaze traveled upward. Huge columns, like the ones on the front porch of the mansion at Ironwood rose to the ceiling, which went all the way up to a second story, where a banister guarded a line of doors. And she'd thought Faith's house grand.

Ironwood was nothing like this. She scanned the doors, imagining offices behind them where great minds penned words to stir the masses.

If she worked hard, would one of those doors be hers someday?

Excitement welled up and flooded her exhausted body. Things were changing, and she would be on the front lines. Mercy's gaze drifted from the upper floor down to where desks stood in neat rows, ready to bear the weight of the ideas that would change the world. She would likely start out here, on the lower floor, where...

"Excuse me?" A nasally voice plucked her from her contemplations.

Mercy turned to where the voice called to her from behind a large marble counter. She summoned her best smile and stepped to where a man of about middle age with yellow hair and a thin nose waited.

"Hello, sir. I'm here to speak with Mr. Marcus Johnson, please."

The man's face scrunched in confusion. "What?"

Mercy leaned forward and spoke a bit louder. "I'm here to see Mr. Johnson."

His face pinched as if he'd eaten a persimmon. "I heard you the first time. You'll need to speak with one of the boys on the floor if you have anything to report."

"Report?"

"You have some kind of information to supply the paper?"

"Oh! Well..." She hesitated. She didn't want to explain herself to this stranger. She studied him. Was he a reporter? She darted a quick glance back at the men who were writing at their desks and decided it would be better to convey her need to speak with the editor to one of them. "Yes, sir. I have information I need to share." Still the truth.

He nodded to the area behind her. "Then take it there quickly and be on your way. We don't like your kind lingering."

Her kind? The words nearly stilled her heart. This was the *North*. People were supposed to be different! Sudden fear threatened to rob her of the determination she needed.

No. She wouldn't let him demean her. She had rights.

Mercy squared her shoulders and scowled at the man. When surprise flickered over his pinched features, Mercy curved her lips.

Well, she might have to deal with people like him even in Boston, but people like him would soon have to learn to deal with *her*.

Before the gaping man could regain his composure and demand she leave, Mercy walked over to the first young man seated at a sparse desk. She waited for him to finish tallying a set of figures.

He looked up at her, then gave a small groan and glanced at two of his fellows, who seemed too engrossed in their work to notice him.

"Good day, sir. I'm sorry to interrupt your work, but I'll just be a second. I need to speak to Mr. Johnson. Would you kindly direct me to him?"

The man leaned back in his chair and let out a hardy laugh. "Do you now?"

Mercy paused, not sure how to respond. She kept her features passive as she took note of him. He wore a white shirt and vest with no jacket, and the face above his stiff collar had a sparse covering of light brown whiskers. Was he anyone with any authority in this place? This man who did not even wear a jacket?

He lifted one eyebrow at her assessment of him, and she realized she had been inappropriately staring. She dropped her gaze.

"If you'll but give me a moment," Mercy said, setting down her valise and fishing in her pocket. "Ah. Here it is." She plucked the letter free and handed it across the desk, still keeping her eyes downcast. "As you can see, Mr. Johnson has asked for me to come."

The man leaned forward, and she glanced up to see the humor on his face disappearing. Good. Perhaps now he would take her more seriously.

He opened the letter and scanned the contents, then looked back at her. "This letter is address to Mr. Mercy, who"—he gestured down the length of her person—"clearly, you are not."

"I am, sir. I submitted the article under a pseudonym. I don't believe that's an uncommon practice for a lady."

At his incredulous stare, she added, "It *is* done, is it not?"

The man's eyes widened, and his gaze bore into her for several heartbeats. Finally, he rose from his chair. "Nelson!"

She flinched from his sudden outburst and had to resist taking a step back.

A man from a few rows of desks deeper into the building leaned back in his chair. "Yes?"

The man holding her letter lifted it higher. "Come here."

The fellow called Nelson ambled over, giving Mercy one quick glance before turning his attention to the proffered paper.

He scanned the page. "I remember that article. Johnson sent for him, huh?" The man shook his head. "Can't say that surprises me."

"Except," the first man said, snatching his chin toward Mercy. "This one here says *she* is the man in question."

Nelson made a derisive noise in his throat. "Preposterous."

Mercy clenched her hands. "It is not," she snapped, then checked her tone and tried to remain calm under a growing sense of unease. "I wrote the article under a man's name so it would not immediately be discarded without even being read."

The two men eyed one another but said nothing.

"I sent in the article and received the reply you are now holding. How else would I have come by the letter?"

"Stolen it," Nelson retorted.

She would not let them raise her ire. Mercy shook her head and kept her voice gentle but firm. "Gentlemen, I know you may chafe at the idea of a woman writing an article, but I'm sure it's not the first time it's been done. I can continue to write under a man's name, but I would like to speak with Mr. Johnson on the matter, seeing as he is the one who wrote me the letter."

The men looked at one another again, and then Nelson shrugged. "You tell him."

The other hesitated.

"Jim, you know he's going to want to know about this," Nelson said low, though Mercy had no trouble hearing him.

The one called Jim gave him a flat look. "Very well."

He eyed Mercy, looking just as sour as Gracie when Mercy tried to rouse her for morning chores. "He's not going to like some darkie claiming one of his articles."

Darkie? Mercy blinked at him, her frayed sense of hope

raveling with every bigot she encountered. Had Papa been right? Were these people who'd fought for the freedom of slaves really no better than those in the South? Anger warred with her fear. Would she have to fight against not only being a woman but being one of color as well?

Setting her teeth lest words that wouldn't help her cause slipped through, Mercy simply left her valise by his desk and followed the man called Jim to a staircase leading to the upper floor. Once above, he rapped on one of the doors and slipped inside, leaving her to stand at the railing and look down at the men working below.

Remain hidden. Papa's words returned with more force, coaxing her to find a way not to raise white men's ire that could lead her into all kinds of trouble. It could work for a time. She could be unobtrusive. At least until she proved herself.

She would just have to promise the editor not to use her own name and not tell anyone her true position here. She would work in secret. It wouldn't be ideal, but perhaps after she completed a few assignments they would be willing to let her reveal her identity.

One thing at a time.

The door unlatched with a click, and Mercy turned back around. Jim stuck his head out of the door and regarded her with a peculiar expression. "Mr. Johnson will speak to you." He took in her appearance and shook his head.

She must look a mess. Oh! How had she not thought more of that? In her determination to adhere to the plan she'd put in place, she'd lost her senses. This was going terribly wrong.

Mercy took a step back. "Perhaps I should call upon him tomorrow."

That's what she needed to do. Find a room. Or go to Medford…somehow. She needed to start over before she ruined everything.

"He wants to see you now." Jim gestured toward the door.

Mercy shook her head. "Please tell him I'll return when I've had a chance to freshen up. It was a long trip you see, and—"

Her words cut short when he grabbed her arm. "He wants to know who you took the letter from." The words slithered into her ear and brought sourness to the back of her throat. Jim shoved her through the opening. "Best tell him the truth."

Mercy stumbled forward, nearly tripping on her now ragged hem. Sucking in a gasp, she straightened herself and straightened her hat. She could not—would not!—crumble in this world of white men. To do so would only reinforce their ideas that she was too weak or too unworthy for the work. Shoulders back, she stepped farther into the large office with shelves lining the walls. The faint scent of cigar smoke lingered in the air, and a sour-looking man with a balding head sat behind a desk as large as their dining table at home.

Sensing she best wait until spoken to, Mercy clenched her hands and willed them not to tremble. She held the man's gaze for a moment, her heart beating rapidly. Now wasn't the time to hide. Bold. She must be bold.

"Who are you?" His voice, deep and thick, bounced off the walls and nearly made her jump.

"Mr. Johnson, I am Miss Mercy Carpenter, known to you as Mr. Fredric Mercy."

His scowl deepened.

She hurried on. "But I can continue to write under the assumed name if you'd like." She held up the letter. "I've come to accept your offer."

The man rose from his chair, the growl in his throat and the hunch of his shoulders reminding Mercy of a bear. A mean bear with fangs. She longed to bolt but dared not. She couldn't let him intimidate her. She held her gaze steady.

"You lie."

Despite the dryness in her mouth from thirst and fear, she managed to form words. "I do not, sir. *I* wrote the article you published."

"That's utterly absurd. You cannot have done such a thing." He glared at her. "Come now, tell me the truth. Where is the master you stole it from?"

Mercy blinked. "Master?"

His gaze went down her dress, and his eyes narrowed. "Ah. I see. A leman by the looks of you." The corners of his mouth turned down in disgust. "Why some men find that more exotic, I'll never know. Just plain filthy if you ask me."

Mercy's jaw unhinged. Filthy? Her dress or her person?

Before she could move, he rounded the desk and snatched the letter from her hand. "Now, enough of these games. How did you come by this letter?"

She took a step back, not caring for how he invaded the space around her. "It came by way of the postmaster in Oakville, Mississippi."

He glared at her, but she refused to be cowed. "I tell you the truth, sir. It's my article."

Silence.

Desperation gathered in her chest. "But no one ever need know my identity. I can stay hidden. I promise."

He barked a laugh.

She stared at him, fear and determination warring to take over and send her fleeing from the room. But without employment, she had nowhere to go and no way home. "I just want to be a journalist." Her voice quivered, and she fought to strengthen it. "No one will ever see me."

He whirled around, seeming incredulous. "Some Negro night flower has the gall to call herself a *journalist?*"

She wasn't entirely sure what he meant, but she didn't care for what his tone indicated. "The color of my skin doesn't change my abilities, sir."

He stared at her as though contemplating the merit of her claim.

"I tell you I wrote the article myself."

At the bite in her tone, the man straightened, and he looked even more the snarling bear than before. "No *griffe* is going to come in here and act all highfalutin just because some man keeps her in his left hand."

She had no idea what the word meant, but it didn't sound good. "Sir," she tried again. "Allow me to apologize if I have offended you in some way."

He sniffed and pointed his nose in the air.

How to proceed? She was making a fine mess of this. "I don't know how to prove to you that I am indeed the one who wrote the article you admired. Perhaps I could have a chance to show my merit by writing another?"

"Ha!" He waved his hand at her and started back around his desk. "Be gone with you."

Mercy planted her feet. She couldn't leave here with nothing. "I will not, sir. You extended the offer of employment, and I would like the chance to prove I'm worthy."

"You are thick-headed. Nothing you could write could change my mind."

Mercy gaped at him. "But why? I've said I can continue to write under a man's name."

He scoffed. "I don't hire darkies." He narrowed his gaze and something slithered into his eyes that made Mercy squirm.

She put her hand to her throat. She was a fool. Looking at this man now, she felt more of a pain in her stomach than when she and Faith had argued. Faith had told her she wouldn't be hired, and she'd been right. Where were the gallant people of the North who had fought to end slavery? Why had she been treated with disdain when she was now supposed to be equal?

Anger clawed its way out from beneath her fear and unsheathed words as sharp as daggers. "So I suppose it will never matter how well I write or how much your readers like my work." Her voice gained steam as she went, and she pulled herself to her full height. "Even though they will never see more of me than my words on the page, you still won't allow it."

He waved his hand. "I'm finished with you. Be gone."

Furious, Mercy whirled around on her heel and stalked out, praying the tears gathering in her eyes wouldn't hinder her from snatching up her valise and finding the front door.

Seven

arkness crept in on spindly shadows that plucked at Mercy's skirts and made her feel as though hidden monsters would haul her away to unknown horrors. She began to tremble. Only two of Papa's coins remained tucked away in her bodice pocket. She ran her finger over their keeping place. Would it be enough for her to fill her stomach and find a safe place for the night?

She pressed her back into the rough brick of a bank building only a few paces removed from the newspaper offices. She hadn't been able to bring herself to go any farther, so she'd hidden in this alley among rotting dreams and soiled expectations until the sun had set. The scent of something putrid had long ago singed her senses and then left her numb to it.

Foolish. She had been impertinent and foolish! Now what was she to do? Standing here in the deepening shadows was getting her nowhere, and she didn't wish to remain on the street come full nightfall. Despite it being late spring, once the sun had dipped behind the buildings, it had gotten much colder in Boston than she'd expected. Mercy shivered.

The blacksmith in Medford. Don't you forget it.

Mercy ran her fingers down her skirt, the worried words of

her traveling companion thrumming in her heart. Why had she been so impatient? Oh, how she wished she could be in a safe home somewhere among kind people. But she'd been so sure the paper would...

Tears burned, but she blinked them away. Further wallowing in self-pity would do her no good. Setting her jaw, she stepped out onto the street. People hurried to and fro and paid her little heed other than a couple of disapproving glances. Whether those came because of her swollen eyes, rumpled dress, windswept hair, or the shade of her complexion, she couldn't tell. Nor did it matter. Looking in both directions, she chose to follow this street away from the paper's offices rather than have to pass back in front of them. She'd not seen any restaurants or boarding houses from that direction anyway.

Best she keep moving forward rather than retracing where she'd already been.

She'd gone but a few steps when just in front of her a boy no more than Gracie's age propped a ladder against one of the poles spaced at even intervals along the street and scrambled up it. He opened a small door and stuck a match inside the glistening glass encasement at the top of the tall pole. Fascinated, Mercy paused in her shameful trudge to watch him. Soon a light flickered to life, and the boy closed the door and scrambled down again. A pool of light gathered below this lifted lantern, scaring away the shadows nipping at her skirts. Mercy turned to see lights winking on all along the street like tiny stars held captive.

She turned her face to the sky. *Thank you, Lord, for light.* Her heart burned. *And I am so sorry for what I've done. Help me, please.*

Struck by a thought, Mercy hefted her skirts and hurried

after the boy as he tucked the ladder under his arm and rushed down the street. "Excuse me!"

He hesitated and looked over his shoulder, his feet slowing. He waited for her to approach, eying her with suspicion. Pained to garner such a look, Mercy stopped a few paces from him and tried to offer her best smile. "I'm sorry to bother you, young man, but I fear I have become…lost in a strange city. Do you know where I might be able to find respectable lodging for the evening?"

The fellow shrugged and straightened himself, and Mercy realized he was as tall as she with hair and eyebrows nearly as light as his pale face. Perhaps less a boy and more a youngster on the cuff of manhood. He stood at the edge of the elevated lamp's light and narrowed his eyes. "My Da told me about women like you. Says it right there in Proverbs." He rubbed his chin. "I figured he was just a foolin' with me."

The strange sound to his words took Mercy aback. She'd never heard someone speak with such a melody. The language was the same, but he accentuated his words in different places and delivered them with an unusual cadence. Perhaps he'd traveled here from a distant country.

Then, her mind settled on the meaning of his words rather than the sound. Proverbs? The book of wisdom. Some of the tension drained from her. He was of a Christian family and would not hesitate to lend her aid.

"You are a Christian, then?" Her smile widened. "Would you direct me to your church?" A sudden wave of relief washed over her. Of course. Why hadn't she thought of it? The preacher at the church would give her aid.

The boy took a step back from her and shook his head. "Pa

said the immoral woman has lips like honey."

Mercy's jaw slackened. "What did you call me?"

"I'm real sorry, but I don't think Da would want you tempting the good reverend. His wife just died and all." The boy glanced behind him as another, larger figure emerged from the shadowed alleys snaking away from the main road. "You best get on back to the docks."

Fear stole her words, and Mercy clasped her trembling fingers. Before she could rein in her emotions, the young man jogged down the street to join the other figure, their forms melding into the deepening night.

Confusion and anger stirred enough to sour her empty stomach. Why would he think her an immoral woman? She glanced around at the trickle of people leaving the streets, noticing a few couples and lone men, but not a woman on her own. Perhaps that was it. Not that her disheveled appearance helped.

Mercy clenched her teeth. No wonder the editor had thought she lied. After all her grand thoughts of presenting herself a lady.

She wrapped her arms around herself. She would not return to the docks. That place had made her nervous in the daylight. A church might be her only hope, and she didn't remember seeing one as she'd come down this street. Not that she had been looking for one. Would she have noticed it earlier in her dogged determination to get to the newspaper?

She turned in a slow circle. She'd not gone far from the paper's office. Perhaps only a couple of city blocks. She didn't see any chapel spires.

Placing one aching foot in front of the other, Mercy made

her way farther south away from the *Boston Globe*, ducking her head when a carriage rolled by. The horse's hooves clacked down the cobbled road, swaying the lamps on the sides of the polished vehicle. She lifted her head to scan the cramped rooftops dipped in shadow.

There.

A tower rose above the other structures, reaching toward the sky. Mercy dropped her hands from around her middle. In her studies, she'd seen the images of tall spires and towers of churches from around the world. Surely this had to be one of them. She'd taken two determined strides and stumbled to a halt.

Her bag!

How had she forgotten it when she'd finally stepped out of that alley? She turned back, but the street seemed a great long tunnel with its encroaching buildings and spaced lamps. She shuddered. Should she retrace her steps? To her left, a cat yowled, and Mercy startled so hard her teeth jarred.

No. She'd have to come back with the first rays of morning and hope it had not been disturbed in the alley where she must have left it. Ducking her head, she dashed down the street, aiming for the hope she'd seen rising in the distance.

She neared a massive structure, its fortitude like that of an ancient castle. Thick stone walls were cut only with leaded windows set deep into the side, and more towers rose to the sky. The structure stood so tall it needed extra support along the walls. The curved columns held the building together like a ribcage. If there was safety to be had, surely she would find it here. Mercy pushed herself to move faster, rounding the side of the building and coming to a halt in front of huge wooden doors.

She craned her neck to look up the face of the building, noting a large round window set high above her. Her heart hammered. It looked like a church. It had to be. Gathering her courage, Mercy climbed the steps and placed her hand on the handle of one of the two grand doors. Gulping in a breath, she grabbed the latch and pushed.

It didn't budge. Horrified, Mercy shoved harder but was met with the same result. She stepped back and tried the other door. Also locked. Panic rose in her chest. Who would lock a church? There must be another way in. Had to be.

She rounded the other side of the structure, trying another door on a smaller tower near the larger one at the front only to find it also held fast. She ignored her swollen feet and dashed around the giant building but found not a single door that would yield to her. She rounded the building once more and tried pounding on the front door, but not a soul responded from within.

Somewhere in the distance a dog howled. The cold wind bit at her neck and she shivered. No one was going to open the door. They must have returned to their homes for the evening. Would the pastor live nearby? How would she know? She couldn't just start knocking on strangers' doors. Heart hammering, she ducked into a nook created by one of the small support walls on the side of the building. She needed to think.

Tears spilled down her cheeks and her exhausted legs collapsed. She slid down the wall and drew her knees into her chest, pushing herself as deep into the crevice as she could. For the first time in her life, it seemed she would be spending the night out of doors.

She rested her forehead on her knees and closed her eyes, preferring the darkness of her choosing to that which surrounded her. In the distance, more carriages rattled down the street, taking people to warm homes.

What was her family doing now? Had they sat down to the evening meal, or had she sent their lives into upheaval? Mercy bit her lip until it stung. Papa might even now be out in the woods, searching for her and fearing the worst. In her foolish pride, she'd not even left a letter of explanation.

Some journalist she would have made. She hadn't even researched how long train travel would take! No, Mercy had up and left her family and plunged headlong into her whim without so much as a workable plan. Now, two full days had passed. Mama must be sick with worry.

She'd thought she would travel for a day, sweep into the newspaper offices and be handed royal treatment, and then be unpacking her things in a fine boarding house that same evening. She'd thought by the next morning she would send a telegram home and let her parents know where she'd gone and then wait for their excited response. Sure, they would be sore at her for not telling them first, but they would be so proud of her that it would be forgotten.

How proud would they be to see her now, in a soiled gown with nary enough money to get her back to the train station, let alone home? Why hadn't she researched? At the very least, she should have known how long the trip would take. She should have found the newspaper's location and a boarding house before leaving Ironwood.

Why hadn't she?

The ugly answer crawled across her brain. Because then she

would have needed someone's help. She would have had to rely on someone else to supply the information and help her secure passage and lodging. She'd wanted to do this on her own. She'd wanted to prove herself capable.

All she'd proved was that she was childish, impatient, and foolish. There had been better ways to go about this. Ways that wouldn't have had her huddling against the side of a building and shivering in the cool breeze tugging at her collar.

She could have sent a response to the newspaper and introduced her true self, giving them a chance to warm to the idea and let her produce more articles. But instead, she'd tried to rush ahead and snatch the offer before it expired just so she could prove Faith and her parents wrong. She hadn't been humble. She'd been filled with pride.

And as it always followed, she'd taken a fall.

I'm sorry, Lord. Please don't let my family worry too much.

She shivered again and then let exhaustion carry her away.

Mercy woke with a start, sucking in a sharp breath and knocking her head into the hard wall behind her. *What was that?* A scuffling sound and shuffling. She held her breath and tried to bring her legs tighter against her. Had she dreamed it?

The moon had risen high above her, giving silvery light to her surroundings. How long had she slept? It had to be at least midnight or somewhere into the wee hours of morning.

"I knew it," a voice spat into the darkness. "Every one o' them is locked."

The man's words carried on the breeze and danced over her ears. Another soul in need of the compassion of the church?

She leaned forward, allowing one eye to see past the stone of her protective nook. Two figures stood in the shadows.

"Then we bust the lock."

Mercy swallowed and ducked back again, straining her ears to catch their next words.

"You said it would be open."

"It usually is."

Silence settled, and Mercy wondered if the two had moved on. After a few more moments, she dared another peek and saw them inspecting the door. The shadows were too thick for her to make out anything more than the forms of two men, one of lithe build and the other of more girth. The larger one grunted.

"I say it's not worth it, lad. This door's too thick. We won't be gettin' in there without making too much noise." The man's accent mirrored that of the young man she had met on the street.

"If we don' get it tonight, then they're goin' ta move it tomorrow. I told you that bishop was coming and he's goin' ta take it all back with 'im."

The nefarious nature of the strangers settled on her and stoked her fear. Did they think to steal something from the Lord's house?

One of them said something disturbing with the use of God's name. Mercy snatched her head back, banging her head and causing a muffled cry to escape.

There was a grunt and the shuffling of feet. "You hear that?"

Mercy pressed her hand to her lips and tried to slow her breathing. She pressed herself harder against the wall. Silence returned, hampered only by the chirp of a lonely cricket. She strained to listen but couldn't hear much beyond the pulsing of blood in her ears. Her head began to ache and she blinked against a strange feeling of dizziness. Perhaps if she didn't move, they would dismiss the sound and move on.

Mercy waited, keeping her breathing shallow. Slowly, she filled her lungs and let it back out again, but the dizziness that had taken up residence in her head remained. When silence ruled for a few minutes longer, she relaxed her rigid spine and sank back against the wall. Perhaps the miscreants had thought better of their ill-conceived notions and had fled the sanctity of holy ground.

She leaned her head against the cold stone. The dizziness swelled into a throb, a steady rhythm that felt as though someone had taken one of Papa's hammers to the base of her skull. She'd felt this kind of ache once before, when she'd spent all afternoon working in the garden and hadn't stopped to drink. Likely, her lack of food and water since leaving the train, coupled with banging her head on stone, and the stress of her day was going to give her a sizable headache. She squeezed her eyes tight, willing away the feeling that was also causing her stomach to flounder.

Oh, how she wished daylight would soon arrive! How late into the night was it? Something scurried inside her skirt, and she felt the brush of tiny legs against her stocking. Mercy yelped, lurching to her feet. She grabbed the skirts and shook them violently, trying to dislodge the insect seeking shelter there. The movement caused her head to swim, and she placed a hand to her forehead. Heat welled up from her center and spread along the back of her neck and down her arms.

Oh, no. Was she going to be sick? She stumbled a few steps away from her hiding place, sweat pricking her forehead. Her stomach convulsed and she leaned forward.

There was a sudden grunt, and then a thick arm of corded muscle snagged her around her waist before she could step away. Terrified, Mercy loosed a scream that was immediately smothered under a clammy hand.

Bile rose in her throat, burning its way into her mouth. She struggled against her attacker, but he merely clamped her against his chest, using his hip and one leg to keep her from kicking out at him.

Mercy tried to breathe, but her ribs couldn't expand sufficiently enough. Pain pulsed behind her eyes, and her vision blurred.

Another figure stepped in front of her and leaned close. "Now, what're we goin' ta do with you?" he said, his thick accent making the words seem almost foreign. His sinister laugh hung in the air. "Looks like we still found us a way to get paid after all. Luck, it is."

Mercy tried to concentrate. She shook her head, but the beast restraining her would not loosen his grip. Her stomach heaved, and despite the fingers that tried to contain it, Mercy lost what little her stomach contained.

The man swore and tore his hand from her face. The other man laughed.

Mercy heaved again, turning her head to the side.

"Looks like we found us a lady o' the night who had too much o' her customer's ale," the big one groused. He smeared his hand down the back of Mercy's gown. "Disgusting."

The smaller man laughed as Mercy ran her sleeve over her mouth and tried to regain herself.

"You got to be thinkin' now, Angus. Remember what old Charlie said?"

The bigger man growled but didn't release his hold around Mercy's waist despite her weak struggling. Her stomach rolled again, and the pain in her head increased. Her knees sagged, and the vice around her tightened.

"You mean them fellows that's been payin' for girls?"

The words drifted into her ears and lodged like an ant in sap. Amid the fog settling in thick waves, she tried to decipher his meaning. What were they paying for? A night of services? Mercy squirmed. Mama had told her of the secret things that went on between husband and wife when she'd come of age, and Mercy had no intentions of sharing that intimacy with anyone for his money. She would walk back to Mississippi before she did that.

"Please…" she mumbled.

"He's got a collection of 'em," the thin one said. "Somewhere at the wharf."

Mercy tried to twist again, and dark spots clouded what little of her vision she still had. The big man said something, but the rolling of her stomach and the throbbing in the back of her head robbed her of understanding his meaning.

The man started to move away from the side of the church, hauling her against his side. Her feet slid against the ground. With a surge of raw panic, Mercy planted her heels in the grass and lurched backward. She stumbled out of the man's grasp and hit the ground. Sucking in a deep breath, she let out a piercing scream.

"Grab her!"

Before Mercy could roll to her side and try to scramble away, the smaller man was on top of her. She struggled against his weight, but he pinned her with his knees.

She opened her mouth to scream again, only to have her lips and nose covered with a smelly palm. The man leaned closer. "Retch all you want, girl. You'll only choke on it."

Mercy struggled, her need for air causing her lungs to ignite in fire. She couldn't breathe! Couldn't move!

Her head swam, and the throbbing increased. Her body grew slack. Then, when she thought her lungs would burst within her, everything faded away, leaving her in the icy grips of nothingness.

Eight

Faith drummed her fingers on the velvet seat and ignored her father's stare. The heavy conveyance bumped along the road, causing her to sway and brush against the wall. She wished they had sent for an open carriage to return them to Ironwood. She felt too confined as it was, and the need for fresh air caused a flurry in her chest.

During their three-day stay in Memphis, Mr. Watson had seemed to lose interest in her. It was what she'd wanted, so why did it chafe? And worse, when he lessened his interest, why had that piqued her own? She pursed her lips, the confounding puzzle an annoyance she wished would leave her be. Despite the obvious turn of events, her father seemed more intent than ever to arrange more time for them to become better acquainted. Mr. Watson would be arriving on tomorrow's train. Daddy claimed it was for business, but Faith suspected otherwise.

It had been bad enough to suffer his attentions when he'd been interested. Now she felt like unwanted chattel.

"Do you truly like him so much?" She spoke to her father, though she did not turn her face from the carriage window.

There was a pause, a hesitation that said more than his words. "I do. But you know your mother and I are never going to force a suitor on you."

No, they'd never done that. And despite the fact that most ladies her age now had babes of their own, they had not insisted she wed.

"You'll create permanent creases on your forehead if you continue to scowl," Mother said a few moments later. Her words were light and teasing, but Faith found no humor in them.

Daddy leaned across the carriage and cupped Faith's chin, forcing her to look away from the passing trees and into his troubled gaze. "Faith, you are far more distressed than the situation warrants. I sense there is more to this than one gentleman."

She allowed the creases marring her face to relax. Daddy always had a knack for reading her thoughts. She lowered her gaze before he read them further. "I just..." She shrugged, at a loss for the proper words to describe the feelings that gnawed at her.

"If you want, we'll discuss the idea of the townhome," Daddy said, his tender voice a balm to her frayed nerves.

As she had hoped, he'd listened to her idea and considered it. In the end, Daddy always gave her what she wanted. She offered him a warm smile of thanks.

"You can always stay with me at Ironwood," Mother interjected. "Even if you never wed. Perhaps Ruth and I could start letting you and Mercy take over some of our tasks. That would give you something productive to do."

Faith considered Mother's offer, which had been meant in deepest affection, but felt no desire for it. She loved Ironwood but held little interest in the daily duties of managing their pantries and settling the occasional disputes among those who farmed the land. Even her mother's role of caring for sicknesses that didn't require the midwife or surgeon held no intrigue for her.

"I believe she's more interested in shipping than farming," Daddy said. "At least for now."

Mother toyed with her lower lip between her teeth. "It's one thing for women to conduct business from home. It's quite another to attempt to do so in the public realm."

He chuckled. "What's one more deviation from the acceptable norms?"

Faith tilted her head, unsure of his meaning. "I don't wish to cause you any trouble. I'll be content to observe and learn. And you know I'm quick with figures," she said as the thoughts popped into her mind. She smiled. "Perhaps I could start on ledgers. If you have need of it, that is."

Her parents exchanged a look she did not understand, and then Daddy grinned underneath his trimmed beard. "I'm sure we'll be able to find something for you. We have a shipment due any time now, and you can help me assess our newest river captain."

Excitement stirred, pushing away some of her anxiety. "Have you thought more about opening more offices along the river? Mr. Watson was right. It will expand our influences."

Mother rolled her eyes. "You know, your father never planned to go into shipping."

Daddy shrugged. "I did what I had to. We needed to make sure Ironwood survived."

Faith took the opportunity to ask something she'd been wondering about. "Daddy, at the picnic Mr. Watson made it seem as though the shipping company's income outweighed the farming at Ironwood. Is that true?"

Her parents exchanged another look, and Faith withheld a sigh. Why did they always seem to conduct their own silent conversations in the midst of spoken ones?

"After the war, we began sharing crops with the people who worked the land," Mother said. "At that time, forced government reconstruction was difficult for our neighbors, and most of the men who moved cotton up river didn't want to do business with your father."

She knew but wanted to hear Mother's response. "Why?"

Mother lifted her eyebrows. "It's improper to ask another question before you have received the answer to the first."

Faith compressed her lips.

Daddy patted Mother's gloved hand. "They didn't care for the way we treated the people of Ironwood. I began my own shipping ventures to make sure I could still trade the cotton. After years of war, it was in high demand, and despite the economic conditions we endured, the company survived. In the past few years, it's begun to thrive, and, much to my surprise, is becoming a higher revenue generator than the crops."

So again, Mr. Watson had been right. The frequency at which he was so was a disconcerting discovery. She brushed the thought aside. She knew nothing about ships and shipping, and he did. It was only logical. "So since you wished for the shipping industry to continue to grow," Faith said, thinking aloud, "then you had to maintain a presence in Memphis. To keep a more constant eye on the goings on."

Something sparked in his gaze. "That's why I'd been looking for someone I trusted to run the offices and report back to me."

"Mr. Watson." What position could she take with him running that office? He would fight against her at every turn.

"Regardless of your personal thoughts on him, Faith, he has an eye for the business."

Had he been reading her thoughts?

However, the thought of how Mr. Watson would respond to seeing her working in her father's offices lifted her mood. Perhaps he would soon see her mind was capable of reading *and* doing figures without turning to mush. The thought made her smile. It quickly vanished, however, at the thought of how he'd all but dismissed her presence in Memphis.

Her parents settled into another conversation about her brother and whether or not Daddy should continue to aid his foolish hope of finding gold in the West. Faith lost interest in the predictable discussion and let her mind drift to her own troubles. Robert would do as he pleased. Surely Mother must know that by now. It was a luxury afforded to men that they usually took advantage of.

Faith fiddled with the trim on her sleeve. What would Mercy think of her new idea? She returned her attention to the window and watched as the familiar landscape around Ironwood returned. Miss Ruth had once told her Federal troops had camped in these very fields during the war. Looking over the rich dirt now, Faith couldn't picture what that must have been like. All those men gathering and staking their tents, and the officers as unwelcome guests in the house.

Mercy's mother was more willing to speak of those times than her own mother. Each time Faith brought it up, something odd and distant entered Mother's eyes, and so Faith had stopped asking. She didn't want to burden Mother with painful memories.

The fields gave way to the lawn, and in a moment the carriage rolled to a stop. Johnny, a man about a dozen years her senior, opened the door with a sudden yank.

"Suh!"

"Good afternoon, Johnny," Daddy said, smiling at the man's enthusiastic response to their return. He stepped down from the carriage. "Would you see the horses get a good drink before brushing them down?"

As Faith accepted Daddy's assistance from the carriage, she smiled at the dark-skinned man who ran the barns and cared for all their horses. His wide brow creased as he shook his head.

Unease settled on her. Johnny had never balked at one of Daddy's requests, and something in his eyes sent a cold pang down her spine. Daddy must have noticed it as well because he stepped closer, releasing Mother's hand. "Has one of the horses gone lame?"

Johnny glanced at Faith and lowered his voice. "I got news for you, suh. But be best if I tell it on the porch."

Mother stepped forward, her blue silk gown ruffling in the breeze. "What news?"

Johnny glanced at Daddy again, and Mother huffed. "I wish to know what's going on. In case you have forgotten, I—"

Her words were cut off by a shout as Miss Ruth came running out of the house, her skirts flying behind her. Mother gasped and turned away from the men, leaving them to whisper harsh words too low for Faith to understand. Figuring she would learn more from Miss Ruth than Johnny, she scrambled after Mother.

"She gone!" Miss Ruth wailed, twisting her hands into her

gingham skirt.

"What?" Mother gripped her friend's shoulders. "Who's gone?"

"My baby!" She sobbed and Mother pulled her into a tight embrace.

"Get your wits." Mother eased the other woman back to arm's length. "Come now, you're frightening us. What are you talking about?"

Faith stepped closer to the older women, but she darted glances back to where Daddy and Johnny had been joined by the towering figure of Mercy's father. Dread settled in Faith's stomach, and she put a hand to her throat.

"Where's Mercy?" she choked out, her words dissipating to a mere whisper as they struggled past the lump in her throat. She swallowed and lifted her chin. "Where's Mercy!"

Miss Ruth wailed again, and fear swam in Mother's eyes.

Faith clutched her bodice as though clawing at the material over her heart would slow its drumming.

Daddy appeared at her side and placed a heavy hand on her shoulder. "She's missing."

Faith stared at him, the meaning of his words refusing to take hold. "What?"

Missing.

Miss Ruth dabbed her eyes, regained her composure, and once again became the formidable woman Faith had known all her life. "We ain't seen her since the night before you left. When she didn't do her chores that morning, I thought she got up early, or done stayed up all night, and was hiding in that shed reading again and forgettin' she had chores. But, she wasn't there."

Faith twisted her hands. "The meadow. She goes out there when she's upset about something."

Miss Ruth slid her gaze past Faith and let it settle on her husband as Mr. Noah approached.

The big man rubbed the back of his neck. "I went looking for her there. Didn't find her nowhere. Then I figured she just needed some time to herself. But when she didn't come in for supper…" His voice thickened, and he looked away.

Mother looped her arm through Miss Ruth's and squeezed. "May I assume, then, that you've searched the woods in case she fell and sprained her ankle or something?"

Mr. Noah nodded. "Yes'um. Did that. Been doin' it all day every day. Was headed to the barn to get a fresh horse when we saw you coming."

"Did Mercy take a horse?" Faith interjected.

"None are missing," Miss Ruth said. "Why?"

Faith looked at the ground. "I thought maybe she'd gone to town."

"She wouldn't have no cause to go to town on her own," Mr. Noah said.

Faith held her tongue. What if she had gone to the postmaster to submit another article and came across trouble on the road? "Was a horse out of its stall?"

Daddy seemed to follow her line of thought and shouted for Johnny.

He jogged over to them. "Yes, suh?"

"Were any of the horses out of their paddocks or loose in the barn?"

Johnny shook his head. "No, suh. I done thought of that, but I don't think any of the horses was taken and then returned back on its own. They was all where they was supposed to be."

Daddy dismissed him back to his duties and let his gaze drift over the women. "Why don't you three go into the house? Noah and I will discuss his efforts, and you can find some refreshment."

Mother nodded, dragging Miss Ruth to the front door. Faith followed, knowing they would discuss the matter on their own. This was no time for tea. She hurried through the foyer and crossed the dogwood rug on the parlor floor, finding a place on one of the settees.

Mother took a seat and arranged her traveling skirts, then pulled her hat pins from her head.

Miss Ruth paced the floor. "Don't make no sense, Lydia." Miss Ruth flung her hands wide. "Where could that girl have gone? We ain't seen any trespassers in years."

Mother pulled the hat off, placed it on a side table, and then pulled more pins from her head. Did she mean to undo her hair in the middle of the day?

"Do you think she walked to town?" Faith asked, removing her gaze from Mother's odd behavior and turning it back to Miss Ruth.

The older woman stopped and narrowed her eyes. "What do you know? You keep asking about her going to town."

Now was not the time for secrets. "Mercy wrote an article and sent it to a newspaper."

Miss Ruth stared at her. "She what?"

Faith glanced at Mother, who had indeed freed her hair and was now running her fingers over her scalp.

Miss Ruth came closer. "When?"

Faith returned her attention to Mercy's mother. "Before the

picnic." She shifted under Miss Ruth's steady gaze. "They printed her article."

Miss Ruth groaned.

"I thought maybe if she went to the postmaster to send another article, then maybe she got lost on the way to town or...something."

Miss Ruth and Mother exchanged a loaded look. Then Miss Ruth dashed toward the door. Faith guessed she would go tell Mr. Noah to start looking in the woods along the road to Oakville. Mother sighed and leaned back in her chair, her regard for posture forgotten. She rubbed her temples.

"Mother?"

Mother opened her eyes, and the pools of sadness in their blue-green depths sent another ribbon of fear through Faith's stomach.

"It's my fault."

Mother rose and came to sit next to her on the settee, her mahogany hair flowing all the way past her lower back in thick waves. "How?"

Faith sniffled. "We didn't leave things very well. *I'm* the reason Mercy was upset enough to do something foolish."

Mother rubbed Faith's back in small comforting circles. "Argument or not, you're not responsible for where Mercy chooses to go. She's always been flighty. I can't truly say I'm surprised."

Faith had never heard her mother utter such a thing. Couldn't believe she'd done so now.

"A young woman will do strange things when she feels trapped."

Faith scowled. "Do you really think she decided to run

away?"

Mother gathered her hair and began working it into a braid. "I think it's possible."

"Without leaving a note for her parents?" Faith fingered her cuff. "I don't think she would do that."

Mother twisted her hair into a roll at the back of her head and rose to recover her pins. "You're probably right. Still, it seems a more favorable explanation than…"

Miss Ruth stalked back into the room. "Noah will organize men to go out looking along the roads, and Mista Charles will be going into town to talk with the postman." She crossed the room and stood in front of Faith. "You know anything else that can help us find her?"

Faith hesitated, a dangerous thought churning.

"She could be in danger. If you know anything, you got to tell us." Miss Ruth's eyes were liquid pools of intensity. "Now."

Faith gulped. "She was really excited about having an article published in the paper. I don't know." Faith's eyes widened. Mercy wouldn't dare…would she?

"What?" Mother said, coming to stand beside Miss Ruth.

"Boston," she whispered.

"What!" Miss Ruth gripped Faith's elbow. "What're you talking about?"

Faith's voice pinched, and she had to force her words free. "Mercy sent that article to a newspaper in Boston." As they gained momentum, the thoughts tumbled out faster. "She wrote it under a man's name, but they published it." Faith bit her lip. "Do you think… I don't know… Do you think she would dare to try to go to Boston? To go to the newspaper?"

Miss Ruth stared at her, her mouth agape. "Boston! That's

days from here. Mercy ain't never been off Ironwood!" She shook her head so adamantly that her braids quivered. "She would never be able to do something like that on her own."

Faith exchanged a glance with Mother before focusing again on Miss Ruth. "Is anything missing? Clothes? Money?"

Her eyes widened, and she leapt to her feet. In a heartbeat, she was dashing out the door, leaving it to bang into the foyer shelves.

Faith and Mother grabbed up their skirts and rushed after her.

They passed the startled men, who still stood in the front yard, and rounded the back of the house. Miss Ruth's skirts flopped behind her. Daddy called out to Mother, and she must have stopped to answer him. Faith couldn't be sure, because she didn't look back and she didn't slow.

Panting, she ran along the path she'd traveled all her life, rounded a bend, and stumbled into Mercy's yard, amazed the older woman had so easily outrun her.

She paused, her lungs heaving. The brick house Mr. Noah had built stood proud, surrounded by a few small outbuildings and a couple of dogs. One of them sniffed Faith's skirts, but she didn't have time to rub its ears today.

Gaining her breath, she bounded up the steps and through the gaping front door and paused. Where had Miss Ruth gone? A loud bang sounded above, and Faith lifted her skirts to the top of her boots and rushed up the stairs.

In Mercy's room, she found Miss Ruth leaning over a small box, crying.

After Mother and the men arrived and Mercy's mother spouted a half-discernable explanation about some coins, the five of them convened in the kitchen below.

Mercy's father gripped the edge of the Carpenter family's table so tightly Faith wondered if the wood might splinter. He hung his head between his wide shoulders, and, for the first time, she noticed the white hairs mixing with the dark ones covering his head.

Miss Ruth placed a hand on her husband's shoulder, giving it a squeeze and pinning Mother with a pained look.

"We will, of course, all be leaving for Boston in the morning," Mother said, the stiffness in her spine the only indication of distress.

Noah shrugged off his wife's touch and rolled his shoulders. "Ain't been out of Mississippi since I married Ruth."

Faith wondered where he'd gone before, but now wasn't the time to ask.

"Ain't got no choice," Ruth said, her tone resolute. "You know that."

Noah gave his wife's hand a squeeze. "But who's going to look after the girls?"

"They could go as well," Faith said.

Everyone, including Daddy, who had thus far remained silent, looked at her, then they all exchanged glances as though they had forgotten her presence.

Faith clenched her hands. "Why is it that every time I say something, you all look at each other like that?"

As though to prove her point, they exchanged loaded glances once more. Finally, Mother took her hand. "Long ago, we four decided we would make Ironwood a special place, separated from the ways of the rest of the world. We were war weary, and, at the time, it was the best thing we could have done. But now—"

"But now," Mr. Noah interjected, "we got a bunch of children that don't have no idea what the world really be like, and they ain't prepared for it."

"Well," Faith said, "I don't think that's entirely true, Mr. Noah."

He grunted and waved his hand. "See? That right there is proof enough. No young white ladies call no Negro *mister*."

He spat the word and Faith recoiled. She'd never called Mercy's parents anything different.

Daddy ran a hand through his hair. "Our children are the better for it. They see people for their God-given souls and not for their skin tone. I don't think we did wrong there."

"Maybe you're right," Mr. Noah said, "but what we gonna do now? My Mercy has taken her hope chest money and run off into a world that she don't know is going to try to grind her to bits." He clenched his big hands and glared at Faith's father. "You know exactly what they gonna do with an uppity Negro who needs to be taught her place."

Silence fell on the room, and Faith's stomach churned.

Miss Ruth pressed her lips together, and Faith couldn't tell if she agreed with her husband's words or not. Mother seemed to be unusually interested in the toes of her boots, which peeked out from beneath the fringed hem of her skirt. She noticed Faith's scrutiny and looped her hand around Faith's elbow.

"Perhaps," Daddy said at length, "It would be best if I go after her."

Noah looked to Ruth, and the indecision in the older woman's eyes was clear even from where Faith stood across the cozy kitchen.

Finally, Ruth nodded and looked back to Daddy. "Much as I want to be there when you find her, I don't think we would be much help. And we got the other girls to look after." She pinned Daddy with a steely gaze. "But you promise me you're going to bring my baby back."

"I'll do everything in my power to make it so."

"I'm going, too." Faith squared her shoulders, pulling her arm from Mother's too tight grasp.

Mother shook her head. "I don't think—"

"This is my fault." Faith set her jaw and pinned Mother with a glare. "I *am* going."

The four parents exchanged glances again, and Faith wanted to scream.

Mother scowled at her, but she didn't care. Impertinent or not, she would make herself clear.

"I'll take her," Daddy finally said.

They spent another few moments arguing before Daddy finally convinced the others Faith going would be for the best, as she could both help him if his knee troubled him and for propriety's sake, it would be important to have another young lady traveling with him when he brought Mercy home.

After Mr. Noah led them in a prayer for Mercy's safety, Faith and her parents left the Carpenter's house and returned home to prepare. Her mind fluttered with questions, worries, and scattered prayers.

Mother followed her to her room, giving a string of advice Faith barely heard. They paused at her door. "Try to get some rest," Mother said, planting a soft kiss on Faith's forehead. "You begin a difficult journey tomorrow."

"I doubt rest will be possible under the circumstances."

Mother nodded and then tilted her head. "Do you have the journal I gave you?"

"It's still in my valise."

Mother gave her a long look. "It seems the time has come for you to start it."

Nine

*P*oor luck, it was. Nolan checked his timepiece once more. He'd left far too early. It wouldn't be proper to knock on the door at this hour. Served him right for dashing out without even a crust of bread. As if in accordance with his thoughts, his stomach growled.

He tied the horse to the hitching post outside the grand house of Ironwood and contemplated the transaction he needed to discuss with Mr. Harper—the very thing that had kept him running figures through his head all night and had him up well before dawn.

Because it had to be the transaction and nothing else. His tossing and turning couldn't have had anything to do with the way a particular lady kept slipping into his thoughts. He had made his decision to keep things polite and nothing more. Which had proven difficult during the Harper's visit to Memphis.

But something bothered him. If Miss Harper didn't care for his attentions, then why had she seemed dismayed by his feigned lack of interest in Memphis? Had she come to think differently?

He glanced up at the house. Pursuing Miss Harper would lead to disappointment, he reminded himself.

The front door swung open, and Mr. Harper stepped out. His eyes widened when he saw Nolan. "What a surprise."

"My apologies, sir."

Mr. Harper stepped down from the porch and gestured toward the barn. "Walk with me?"

"I apologize for calling at this hour, but I'm concerned about Tuesday's shipment."

Mr. Harper nodded along, his gait not slowing.

Nolan scrambled to gain the man's side. "I've been going over the numbers on the Chamberlin account," he said, falling into step, "and something doesn't seem to be adding up."

"Unfortunately, we'll need to look into that another day."

Nolan studied his employer's tense profile. "Is something wrong, sir?"

They stepped into the barn, where the fresh scent of hay mingled with the earthy tones of horseflesh.

"An urgent personal matter. You understand."

"Of course, sir."

His employer seemed distracted, looking around in the barn for something. Probably the stable hands.

"May I be of any assistance?"

"No, I must..." Mr. Harper turned suddenly, as though something had just occurred to him. "Do you still have family in Boston?"

Breath lodged in his chest, and it took a moment to force it back out. "In a manner of speaking."

"Splendid." He slapped Nolan on the shoulder. "I should have thought of it sooner."

"Thought of what, sir?"

"I would like for you to accompany my daughter and me to

Boston. We can discuss business on the way, and you can introduce me to your uncle once we arrive." He walked away, the matter apparently settled.

Nolan shook his head, but Mr. Harper was already out the barn door. He hurried after him. "Sir!"

"Johnny!" Mr. Harper stalked around the side of the barn, the tails of his linen suit fluttering out behind him. "Where is that man?"

"Suh?" A voice called from behind the barn only a breath before a Negro man of good stature rounded the edge of the structure.

Dressed in sturdy trousers with a clean blue cotton shirt tucked under his bracers, the fellow greeted Mr. Harper with a pleasant smile. "Thought you might be hankering to head out early today. I done got the mares fed and brushed down. Was just fixing a buckle on Powder's harness b'foe I hitched them up."

Mr. Harper slapped the fellow on the shoulder in the same way he'd done a moment ago with Nolan. "Always a step ahead of me, Johnny. Don't know how we'd get on without you."

The man's easy smile split his face, and Nolan couldn't help but admire his employer even more. He seemed to always have a word of encouragement and a way of inspiring the best out of the people around him.

"Nolan, you'll need to head back and pack your trunk. We'll meet you for the ten o'clock train."

"Uh, sir, about Boston—"

"Splendid luck. I need someone who is connected in the city." He offered a smile that caused all protest to die on Nolan's tongue. "And since this is a matter of grave importance,

I'm most grateful."

Moments later, Nolan was back in the saddle, dread in his gut. How would he keep his past a secret now?

Faith's stomach was in such turmoil that she'd not been able to take breakfast, and it continued to knot as she stood on the train platform while Daddy purchased their tickets. She scanned the faces of the people waiting to board and remembered something.

"If I may ask," Mr. Watson said, drawing her attention, "what thoughts keep your brow so furrowed?"

She smoothed her features as she regarded the man at her side. To her surprise, Mr. Watson had met them at the train station and had not seemed offended by her father's very brief explanation that they were traveling to Boston in order to recover Mercy. If anything, he'd seemed genuinely concerned.

Faith offered a smile. "When I was last here, I saw a woman who looked familiar. She had black hair piled across her nape, and though I didn't get a look at her face, she had the same build as Mercy."

"Maybe one of the ticket masters or porters remembers seeing her," he said with a nod.

Exactly what she'd been thinking. She looked up at him, and his gaze lingered on her face. She looked away.

He stepped back, clearing his throat. "It could confirm her destination." He grinned. "It certainly wouldn't be good for us to go to Boston if she bought a ticket to someplace else."

"I'm rather certain she didn't." Faith made a move to step around him. "But I'd like to know."

"I'll make inquiries." He slipped around her, throwing over his shoulder, "You wait here."

Before she could release a retort, he was gone. She groaned. She shouldn't have told him. She didn't need him swooping in and doing everything for her.

Annoyed, she waited where he'd left her, presumably to stand idly by and look fetching, as that was all a lady was meant to do. Faith pursed her lips. Though, to be honest, that seemed the very idea her mother must have had in mind when she'd insisted on dictating Faith's clothing this morning.

She'd chosen a brown traveling dress with a new hat featuring a massive plume. Faith had tried to tell Mother when they'd bought it that the feather was too large. Mother had insisted large feathers were the latest fashion. Looking at the other women on the platform, Mother had been correct. Actually, by the looks of it, her hat was decidedly less pompous than any of the others floating about like large birds hovering over the crowd.

Faith squinted to look closer at one young blond woman. She actually had a multicolored stuffed fowl perched upon her wide brimmed hat.

"You were correct."

Mr. Watson appeared back at her side, startling her from an uncharacteristically vapid train of thought.

"The man in the ticket booth remembered a young colored woman several days ago. She caught his attention because she was dressed in a fine gown. From his description, it could very well have been Mercy."

Faith pressed her fingers into his sleeve. "And?"

He looked down at where she touched him, and she snatched her hand away. Furrows shadowed his brow. From her touch? Did she now offend him that much?

"The young woman purchased a ticket to Boston and departed on the ten-thirty."

Her heart fluttered. "I knew it!" Faith scanned the crowd looking for a porter. "Perhaps someone remembers something else that might help us."

She stepped away, and Mr. Watson grumbled something, then gripped her elbow and eased her behind him. He worked his way through the throng of travelers, opening a clear path for her. She hated to admit it, but allowing him to lead her through the crowd was easier than having people bump into her.

Faith listened closely as he asked various men, both white and of color, about Mercy. But none had any recollection of her.

Daddy met them in the traveling compartment a few moments later, rubbing his knee.

"Are you well?" she asked as he took a seat next to her.

"I took a wrong step on the platform. I'm sure it'll be fine after some rest."

Faith nodded, her thoughts already moving ahead. "We'll start with the newspaper office, of course, just as soon as we arrive." She tapped her fan against her palm, thinking aloud. "Perhaps Mercy was right."

Mr. Watson secured their small traveling bags in the storage area. The trunks had been delivered to their sleeping cars. "Right about what?"

"She said her words would be the only thing that mattered

to the paper. Maybe they really will let her keep writing for them."

Tension flickered in Mr. Watson's jaw.

"Let's not speculate," Daddy said. "One thing at a time."

Mr. Watson turned to her, his eyes earnest. "We'll find her, Faith. We'll do everything we can."

The use of her given name without her permission startled her, but the sincerity in his eyes doused the anger she expected to erupt. Tears burned in her eyes. *Please, God. Let that be true.*

She glanced at her father, who seemed to hide a smile behind the paper he'd flicked open. She summoned Mother's astute sense of propriety.

"As you have decided to call me by my Christian name, may I have permission to use yours as well?"

His eyes widened a fraction as though he'd not realized he'd made such a gaffe, but he quickly composed himself and gave a small dip of his chin. "I would be honored."

Behind his paper, Daddy chuckled.

Ten

The world swayed, careening back and forth in an unnatural undulation. Somewhere in the distance, voices shouted, and a low rumble drummed. Mercy pulled in a lungful of air, tasting brine. She turned her head and coughed. Her cracked lips stung, and as she ran her tongue over them realized they too tasted salty.

She groaned, and the voices grew louder. Urgent. As though calling her away from the land of swaying shadows with fervent pleas.

Something brushed her lips, and she jerked her head away, causing a wave of nausea.

"Come on, you got to chew the ginger," a feminine voice said. "It helps."

Mercy tried to open her eyes but found them crusted together. It took a couple of tries before the blurry face of a woman swam into her vision.

"It helps," she repeated.

The ground lurched again, and Mercy grabbed onto the side of a bed beneath her. "Where?" she croaked.

"Shh. Don't talk. It makes the sickness worse. You can't afford to lose no more."

Something moist brushed her lips again, and Mercy opened her mouth. The woman dropped something that had the texture of bark between Mercy's lips.

"Chew it."

Mercy closed her eyes. She ground her teeth on the spicy bark several times before her mouth responded and produced moisture.

"Good now. That will help you."

"Where?" Mercy asked again, too weak to do more than chew and croak out the single word.

"I best let Jed answer that for you," the woman said. She patted Mercy's arm. "I'll go get you some water."

The ground jolted again, and the woman stumbled back, nearly dropping on top of Mercy. She righted herself and moved across a wooden floor to a barrel in the corner. Mercy blinked, trying to get her eyes to discern her surroundings. Thick beams held up a wooden ceiling, and she was in a narrow cot with what she assumed to be another just like it right above her. On the other side of the barrel the woman pried open was a solid wall with no windows. The room was dim, and Mercy had no way of knowing the hour.

The small woman carefully ladled water from the sloshing barrel into a tin cup and made her way across the careening floor back to Mercy. She was short, elderly, and of the same soft brown complexion as Mercy. Had this woman taken her in? What had happened to the two men?

As though remembering them brought back the pain of their rough hands, her body ached, and she groaned.

"Easy now. You safe." The woman grabbed the upper portion of the bed, lowered herself to her knees, and then put her arm behind Mercy's head, tilting it up.

Pain exploded, causing little dots to erupt in her vision.

"I know you hurt, but you must drink. Hold the ginger in your teeth and swallow a little bit for me."

The woman tipped the cup to Mercy's lips, and tepid water flowed into her mouth. She swallowed twice, and the woman pulled it away.

Suddenly aware of her desperate thirst, Mercy reached for the cup. "More."

"That's all you need. Give it a moment 'fore we try more." A smile brightened her careworn face. "Keep chewing the ginger."

Mercy had forgotten about the woody substance in her mouth and was surprised she hadn't actually swallowed it. She mashed her jaws together and eyed the woman, who watched her just as closely. She produced a small rag, poured some of the water on it, and then applied it to Mercy's forehead.

The coolness felt wonderful, and Mercy closed her eyes. Memories took shadowy form and clawed their way into her mind, but she was too tired to examine them. In a few moments, she drifted off.

The next time she awoke, she was alone. The throbbing in her head had eased significantly, and she pushed up on her elbows. A flat, hard-looking piece of bread sat on a plate next to her alongside a cup of water. The room no longer swayed, though she still felt an unnatural movement beneath her. Mercy slowly gained a sitting position and took the cup in both hands. The cool liquid flooded her mouth, and she gulped it down. She replaced the cup and eyed the bread.

She picked it up, turned it over, and then returned it to the plate. Tossing a thin, ragged blanket off of her, she swung her feet to the floor. Bare toes grazed rough wood. Where were her shoes? Worse, her dress? She wore a clean but thread-worn nightdress, its sturdy construction and simple lines reminding her of the gowns Mama wore to bed. Thoughts of home pushed the lingering fog from her brain, and she leapt to her feet. She steadied herself with one hand on the cot until her head cleared, then looked around.

A quick search of the tiny room yielded no answers as to the whereabouts of her clothing. She glanced at the door. Mama would scold her for the very thought of stepping out of her room in such a state of undress, but what was she to do?

Footsteps sounded from the other side of a plank door, and before Mercy had time to conjure a plan should the owner of those feet mean her harm, the door swung open.

"Good! You're up." The elderly woman shuffled in, her white and ebony hair pulled into a tight knot behind her head. Her work dress skimmed the floor as she placed her hands on her hips. "I was starting to wonder how long the Lord was planning on taking to answer my prayers."

Mercy stared at the woman. "Who are you?"

"Hephzibah. But you can call me Hezzie."

Mercy blinked. "What?"

"*Hephzibah*. It's a bit of a working for the tongue, I know. But my Papa, he had a dream one night before I was born that we would be freed from our chains. I was born a slave." Her hands danced around as she spoke, and light sparkled in her eyes. "But Papa had that dream, and he insisted that was the name he was supposed to give me. Mama settled on Hezzie." She bustled around the tiny room, frowning at the piece of uneaten bread and looking Mercy over.

"My Papa got a vision from God, he did. No other way to explain it."

Mercy glanced toward the door. Had Hezzie taken her clothes to wash?

"See, he couldn't read. So he had no way of knowing that name was in the Bible. No way of guessing that one day I would be able to read myself and find my name in the Word." She grinned, showing uneven teeth that were surprisingly white against her rich brown face. "Or that a Rabbi from a far off land would tell me what it meant. God, He works like that, you see."

"I'm sorry, but—"

"It's from the sixty-second book of Isaiah." She pulled the blanket back over the cot, making the bed Mercy had exited. "God says, 'people ain't going to call you deserted no more. No longer will they call your lands desolate. But you will be called Hephzibah. And the Lord will take delight in you.'" She grinned, the wrinkles on her cheeks gathering into joyful folds that seemed out of place with Mercy's circumstances.

"Um, that's nice."

"He was talking about Israel, of course, but to my Papa, he was also using those same words for our people here. Calling out in our slavery. So my name was a sign. It means *my delight is in her.*" She smoothed the blanket of any remaining wrinkles. "Fits, see, because my God delights in me like I delight in Him. And He delights in all His peoples."

Mercy nodded. "Would you mind telling me where I am?"

The woman shrugged thin shoulders. "We're always right where God wants us to be."

Mercy couldn't help the bitter laugh that swelled from her

chest. "Well, I doubt that."

"Nothing to doubt, girl." Hezzie pointed a bony finger at Mercy. "There's only One who's in control, and it ain't you."

She sank back against the bed. "You're right. I certainly haven't been in control of anything." Tears stung her eyes, and she let them slide down her cheeks. "But why would God do this to me?"

"Do what? Save you from a couple of bad men who meant you harm and give you into my keeping instead?" She rubbed her chin, seeming genuinely confused. "Why, He did that 'cause He loves you, of course."

"Bad men?" As soon as the words left her mouth, the memory of hands grabbing her brought on a new wealth of tears. "How did I get here?"

Compassion flooded Hezzie's ebony eyes. "It's better on this ship."

Suddenly, the strange swaying made sense. "I can't be on a ship! I have to get home."

Hezzie pulled Mercy down to sit on the cot she'd just smoothed. "Jed will see to that once we get to Georgia." She patted Mercy's hand. "Unless, of course, God gives us different plans."

"Who is Jed?" Feeling like her youngest sister when the child was filled to the brim with endless questions, Mercy nonetheless asked, "And we're going to *Georgia*?"

"Jed's helping with a school and new church there," Hezzie supplied, though it was hardly the answer Mercy sought. "We were going to go by wagon after our visit in Boston, but then God gave us a free passage on this ship, which was much faster and easier." She eyed Mercy. "Guess now I know why."

Mercy rubbed her temples. "None of this makes sense." She took a deep breath. "Where are my clothes?"

Something flickered in the old woman's eyes. She squeezed Mercy's fingers. "I got plenty of dresses you can wear."

Did the woman never answer a question? The weight of Mercy's strange circumstances felt like cold iron in her stomach. Nothing was going like it was supposed to. At every turn, things only got worse. "None of this is what I wanted."

The ship swayed to the side, and Hezzie gently drifted with it. "And what did you want?"

Mercy let loose a heavy sigh laden with the weight of both guilt and frustration. "Not this."

"The plans we make ain't always the ones God wants for us. Sometimes He has something else He wants doin', and we just have to accept that."

Mercy clenched her teeth. "He wanted me degraded, then attacked, and then"—she flung her arm wide—"then here?"

"He don't ever want the sin, no. But the rest of it... He puts us where we are supposed to be. Often times, the thorn is a gift."

Mercy didn't feel like listening to a sermon. Her foot started twitching. She needed to find the captain of this boat and get him to let her off. First, though, she needed some clothes. Then, she'd need to come up with the right thing to say to get the captain to take her to the next port. And she'd need money to get home. Mr. Charles would... She stopped herself. No. She wouldn't ask the Harpers for anything.

"Already making plans, ain't you?"

Her thoughts tumbled to a halt. "What?"

"You." Hezzie shook her head. "You ain't listened to nothing I said. You ever listen to anything anybody says, or you just go right on with your own plans?"

"Um..." Mercy stared into the perceptive eyes across from her. She lowered her gaze and stilled her fidgeting hands.

"You ever think that God tries to give you some direction in the form of wise words from those around you before you walk off into trouble?"

"I..." Her shoulders slumped. "No."

"I know the plans I have, God says." Hezzie patted her hand again. "Take it from an old woman. His plans be better than yours." She bounced up off the bed, too spry for one of her years. "I'm going to get Jed."

"But—"

"First a dress," she said with a grin, "then Jed."

Hezzie was out of the door before Mercy could respond. Mercy hung her head, letting the weight of it pull on the tight muscles in her neck. No doubt she'd made her own plans and barreled off in the direction she'd wanted to go. She hadn't thought it through, hadn't prayed about it, and hadn't sought wisdom. And where had that gotten her?

But it didn't make any sense. Why would God give her a passion, and ability, and a dream, and then not allow her a way to fulfill it? Why give her opportunities she could never grasp and torture her with a hope that could never be realized?

She lifted her head and straightened her spine. There had to be a purpose. And she was determined to find it.

First, she would go home. Apologize to her parents. Then, she would fight against the injustice she'd seen in Boston. Somehow.

A knock sounded at the door, then Hezzie scuttled back in.

"Blue. Thought it would look nice with your pretty coloring." She twisted her lips. "Sorry I couldn't find no shoes that looked like they would fit."

Mercy accepted the frock and allowed Hezzie's grandmotherly hands to help her sore arms pull the nightdress over her head. Dark stains the size of men's fingers discolored the skin that had been hidden underneath. She stared at the bruises.

What all had they done to her? She couldn't remember. She splayed her fingers, trying to cover an angry purple splotch across her thigh. She probed at it, the injury blackening nearly as much as the one from the time she'd been kicked by the milk cow.

"All hurts heal, if you take them to the Healer." Hezzie eased a shift over Mercy's head, and the cotton fabric fell over the offensive places.

Mercy looked at her, and the compassion and kindness in her eyes cracked something within her. Hot tears fell down her face. Immediately, she was pulled tight into the old woman's embrace.

"There now, child. Don't you worry. It's all going to work out fine. You'll see. Lord got big plans for you." She stroked Mercy's hair, the words both soothing and achingly bitter for the abhorrent untruth of them.

Finally, Mercy stepped back and swiped the heels of her palms over her eyes. Bruises would heal. No sense in mourning over them. "Enough of that." She sniffled. "Let's go, shall we?"

Hezzie lifted her eyebrows but thankfully said nothing. She helped Mercy into underpinnings and the simple dress and then waited as Mercy's trembling fingers worked the buttons down the front.

With an approving nod, she pulled open the door. "Now, we'll just go on up to the deck and find Jed."

Mercy swept past Hezzie and into a hallway that was little more than an elongated wooden box. A few paces away stood a steep set of stairs. The light at the top of it beckoned to her, an escape from the confines of the tiny room and coffin-like hallway. Mercy rushed ahead, the sudden need for fresh air like a raging thirst.

"Lord, there she go again. Running off like You say she always do. What You want me to do with that?"

Mercy ignored the old woman's mutterings and lifted the borrowed dress. The raw blisters on her feet made her glad she didn't have shoes.

At the top of the stairs, she burst out onto a shifting deck and saw a sky teeming with high clouds. Mercy blinked against the briny wind. It immediately took hold of her hair and whipped at her dress, as though summoning her to come and frolic with it. She steadied herself. The salty scent it carried assailed her senses. She needed to adjust to it as much as to the bright light.

She squinted, eager to see her surroundings. Immediately beneath her feet, more of the same smoothed wood bobbed with unsteady movement. At its edges was a type of fence, a railing to keep tottering persons from tumbling off. And past the rails of the lilting wooden floor was nothing but an endless expanse of churning blue, broken only by dots of land off in the distance. She looked straight up. White birds called and swooped overhead, their caw like what Mercy had heard from the docks in Boston.

Suddenly, the ship shifted again, throwing her off balance

and forcing her to look back down as she regained her footing. Across the ship's deck, men toiled at a vast array of ropes, tugging here and there. Their broad shoulders fought against the wind as they maneuvered the bright white sails that snapped over her head. She let her gaze roam freely, watching as the men with coloring nothing like hers or even Faith's labored. Theirs was a warm color, not as deep as her own, but certainly not pale. It had more of a golden quality to it.

One man called to another, and a melodious language she'd never heard glided from his lips. Perplexed, Mercy could only stare.

A huff came from behind her, and Hezzie gained her side. "Lordy be. What you in such a rush for?"

Mercy didn't answer. She couldn't draw her eyes away from the strange adventure unfolding before her. Why, it was like something from a book! Everything was unfamiliar. From the tilt of the ship, to the look of the sailors, to the exotic words that cascaded from their animated lips.

A man emerged from a door at the rear of the ship's deck. Dressed in trousers and an opened neck shirt, he stalked forward with the air of one who had confidence in who he was and what he meant to do. His black hair was a sea of thick waves with shining locks swinging around his ears as unruly as the ocean surrounding her.

Muscled forearms lifted as he called to the sailors in the same melodious language they'd used. She watched him, transfixed. Never had she seen a people such as this. They seemed…she struggled to put a name to it. Free? In a deep sense that must surely be brought on by the lack of confinement out here on the water.

Suddenly, the man's dark eyes landed on her, and he changed his course for her direction. He stared at her, and Mercy couldn't drop her eyes. His bronzed face drew closer, eyes hooded by dark brows that drifted lower as he neared.

She ran her hands down the borrowed dress. This must be the captain.

The man came to a stop a couple of paces from where Mercy nervously stood twisting her hands. She had to choose her words wisely. But how could she do that when he spoke a different language? She'd learned a few French words, but this was something else. Spanish, perhaps?

"I see you are looking better," the man said. "Has the pain in your head eased?"

His smooth English startled her, and Mercy found herself at a loss.

Hezzie, however, didn't seem the type to ever have such a problem. "She's already up and moving around like she ain't never had no episode."

The captain smiled at the old woman, unaffected by her lack of propriety.

Hezzie bobbed her head. "You wouldn't know how bad off she was, looking at her now." She pointed a finger at the captain. "What did I tell you? Lord answered just like I asked."

"He indeed is good. When I found you on the docks…" The captain's tight mouth relaxed. "I'm pleased you've recovered."

Had the captain saved her from the men who had taken her from the church in Boston? Maybe he had some better answers than Hezzie.

"This here is Jedidiah," Hezzie interrupted, pride thick in her voice as she gestured at the captain. "My son."

Eleven

*N*ever had she been more annoyed with having been born a female than in that moment. Faith forced her fingers to relax from where they were clenched together. Getting emotional would only undermine her protest against the misogynistic ramblings of the editor of the *Boston Globe*. His office might have been lined with books, but the boar before her couldn't possibly have been a man of education.

"So you insist she must have been lying merely because she was a woman?" Faith clarified. "Do you think a female so incapable of coherent thought that she couldn't have possibly written the article you yourself professed to have found admirable?"

His thick jowls reddened. "It's impossible. The girl that came into my office was a Negro. The letter was stolen."

Nolan cleared his throat. "Excuse me, but how do you know the letter was stolen?"

"Because it's the only explanation he can fathom," Faith said with disgust, "as he refuses to see that a woman wrote the article. A colored woman."

Mr. Johnson had the audacity to appear amused as he addressed Nolan. "You see my point, of course."

Faith opened her mouth to let forth a stinging retort, but Nolan raised his hand. She paused. The twitch in Nolan's jaw and the set to his shoulders made him a formidable opponent, even if he was the smaller man. Not that she needed a man to speak for her. She'd told Daddy as much when he'd insisted Nolan accompany her to the newspaper while he rested his knee.

After a tense moment, Mr. Johnson flicked his gaze back to Faith. He cleared his throat. "Perhaps the young lady would like to wait outside?"

"I most certainly would not."

Mr. Johnson tugged the collar of his shirt, clearly uncomfortable with a female who spoke her own mind and had no intention of leaving such important matters to a man.

"Then I have nothing more to say on the matter." He flipped open a wooden box on his desk and drew out a cigar. "Regardless of who you say wrote the article, I extended my offer to the *man* whose name was printed with it. If that man doesn't exist, then neither does my offer." He clipped the end of the cigar. "I have no idea where your girl went. Now, if you will kindly excuse me, I have business to attend."

"But…"

Nolan gripped her elbow and gave a terse nod to the editor. "Good day."

He turned her around and steered her through the office door before she could protest, then closed it behind him with enough force to make Faith jump.

She whirled around, breaking his hold on her arm. "I had more to ask him."

"And he wouldn't have told you anything else."

She glared at him. "You don't know that."

The muscle in his jaw convulsed again, a movement she'd come to notice occurred whenever she said things he thought she shouldn't. Which was often.

"We know Mercy was here. We know he sent her away." He lowered his voice. "Do you really think that man cared to see where she went when she left his office?"

Her shoulders slumped with the implications of his words. "No." She balled her hands. "Mercy would have been crushed. Or furious. Probably both. I hate to think what he said to her."

"'Scuse me."

A boy of no more than eight or nine years with big eyes and a broom in one hand emerged from the shadow of the alcove. "You talking about that Negro girl that came in here telling everybody she wrote an article in this paper?"

"You saw her?"

The boy stepped closer, glancing at the door to Mr. Johnson's office. "Sure did. The whole place was talkin' about that for days. You know her?"

"She's my friend," Faith said. "We need to find her."

The boy glanced at the closed door again. "She left out of here awful upset."

Faith could imagine. "Did you happen to see where she went when she left? Or hear her say anything about where she might have gone?"

The boy shook his head. "Sorry, Miss. I was just sweeping outside around the walkway when she came runnin' out."

"Which direction?" Mr. Watson asked.

The boy thought a moment. "I was standing with my back to the building." He turned around and then lifted his left arm.

"So she would have gone that way."

It wasn't much, but it was something. "Thank you." Faith tried to summon a smile. "We appreciate your help."

Mr. Watson fished a coin from his pocket and pressed it into the boy's dirty palm. "Good work, lad."

The boy grinned and scurried off.

"Shall we go?" Nolan gestured toward the grand stairway.

She inclined her head. "Mr. Watson—"

"Nolan."

Heat crept up her neck, and she turned away. "I should thank you for accompanying me, especially after my father was indisposed this morning. As much as it annoys me to say so, I doubt they would have even let me talk to him on my own."

He chuckled. "My pleasure. And here I feared you resented my presence."

She descended the stairs, her hand trailing along the railing. "Not yours in particular. I merely resent the fact that a woman is thought incapable."

He offered his arm. "I've never thought you incapable of anything."

She slipped her fingers over his sleeve, unsure how to respond. "Why did you come to Boston with us?"

"Your father asked me."

The polished floor clicked beneath her heels as they made their way through the neat rows of desks, where men poured over newssheets. Of course. He would want to serve as her escort to better position himself with her father. Why had she even bothered to ask? For one who considered herself of better than average intellect, she seemed to keep forgetting that Mr. Nolan Watson had his own agenda.

"And, truth be told," he said, holding open the door for her, "I was concerned if you came to the paper on your own, you would work yourself into a tizzy and find yourself in trouble. I thought perhaps I could help if you did."

The bright sunlight caused her to tip her chin in order to shield her eyes underneath the brim of her Gainsborough hat. "And you felt the need to protect me from my female bouts of histrionics?"

He groaned. "Why must you be so contentious?"

Faith paused, the bustle of the streets of Boston flowing around her. "Pardon?"

That muscle in his jaw ticked again. "Don't spout indelicate words one moment and then be appalled in the next when I don't respond with the proper deference to a lady's sensibilities."

She stared at him.

"Forgive me." He drew a long breath. "I've forgotten myself."

"On the contrary, Nolan, I believe you've finally remembered yourself."

"Pardon?"

She laughed, rather enjoying the look of confusion splayed over his features. "I often bristle toward you because I dislike the way you want to treat me like I'm too delicate and"—she searched for the right word—"vacuous."

"I've never thought of you as empty." He scratched the back of his head. "Baffling, certainly, but never lacking in wit or wiles."

"You, sir, are the baffling one."

He shook his head, looking over the people bustling on the

street. She followed his gaze, wanting to prompt a reply but not sure how. Why did it always seem to take him so long to respond?

Nolan continued to look down the street, then up at the towering building lining it. "I apologize if I have confused you in some way. It's never been my intention."

The breeze ruffled her hair, sending a strand across her nose. She brushed it away and followed his line of sight. "I suppose you and I are..." Her eyes snagged on a grand tower reaching toward the heavens.

"We are what?"

Faith grabbed his arm. "Come on! I know which way to go."

Mercy stared at the old woman, then looked back to the captain. The salty air played through his hair. The soft ebony strands matched his mother's only in color. No other features were shared. Where her nose was wide, his was thin. Where her skin was dark, his was golden.

Hezzie laughed. "You seem surprised. Happens all the time. Don't know why it bothers folks so to see that a colored woman adopted a Spanish boy as her own."

Mercy schooled her features. "Forgive me." She inclined her head. "It's a pleasure to meet you, Captain."

The man blinked, then a hearty laugh shook his broad shoulders. "Captain? Who told you I was the Captain?"

Heat crept up her neck. "I, um, I just assumed…"

"That's the captain over there," Jed said, gesturing toward a man in a faded shirt pulling a rope along with the rest of the men. The man seemed agitated. "I'll introduce you in a moment."

Mercy pressed her lips together and nodded. Perhaps it was best if she just stopped talking altogether. Seemed it gained her nothing but trouble. She waited, Jed's steady gaze unusual but not disconcerting.

"I would like to ask you a question," he said, "but don't wish to offend you."

She braced herself, offering only a slight nod.

"Did those men hurt you?"

Why would that be offensive? "I have some bruising."

He shifted his feet. "Is that all?"

Understanding dawned, and she dropped her gaze to the smooth wood of the ship's deck. "I'm afraid I don't remember much after they grabbed me at the church, but I don't believe they…defiled me."

He released a breath of what Mercy assumed to be relief and then stiffened again. "They took you from a church?" Anger slithered through his words, and a vein appeared on the side of his neck.

"From outside of it, yes. They were trying to break in to steal something. They heard me nearby, and I suppose they thought I would foil their plans." She lifted her shoulders in a feeble attempt at indifference. "After they grabbed me, I lost consciousness. Probably from not eating and all that walking and…"

He watched her, the sea wind tugging at his collar and the

steady sway of the boat tipping the floor beneath them. He waited as though he didn't plan on saying more until she finished.

Mercy twisted her fingers. "I was hoping you would be able to tell me more." She flicked a gaze toward the elderly woman. "Hezzie has said very little, and I would like to know how I ended up here—and how I can get home."

"My mother... Well, she has her ways." His lips curved, and a dimple appeared on his right cheek.

Hezzie grunted and turned her gaze out over the ocean.

"We were on our way to the ship to accept the offer of passage the fine captain had extended us," Jed continued. "We'd been delayed when the wagon axel broke and didn't arrive at the Boston harbor until late into the night. I'd wanted to find lodging and board the ship in the morning before it set sail, but Mamá insisted we needed to go straight to the ship, even though the hour had grown late."

Mercy's stomach tightened as eyes the rich color of pecan studied her. She blinked, unable to look away. She both wanted and feared what words might come next.

"When we got to the docks, we saw two men in the shadows, one with something slung over his shoulder." His jaw tightened. "It wasn't until we were closer that I realized what was slung there wasn't a sack but a woman."

A wave rocked the boat, and Mercy lost her balance, stumbling forward. He took her elbow, steadying her. He smelled of ocean and leather, a strange combination that felt as foreign to her senses as the unusual fluttering in her stomach.

Once she'd gathered herself, he released her, stepping back. He and his mother must have been used to... Mercy glanced around. Where was Hezzie? Had Mercy been so engrossed in her conversation with Jed that she'd not even noticed the woman leave?

"The brute propped you against a lamppost," Jed continued as though her clumsiness had not been an interruption, "while he and his companion argued."

She remembered none of that. What else could have happened without her being aware?

"Mamá said we had to get you out of there immediately." He looked uncomfortable. "So, when they were otherwise engaged, I took you."

"Why would you do that?"

His gaze held firm. "I knew their intentions could not have been good."

She should be thankful that a good man had taken her rather than the ones who'd meant her harm, but the notion of so many hands doing with her what they willed without her consent soured her stomach.

"Mamá insisted you come with us. I told her we should have taken you to an inn, but she would not be persuaded." He scratched the back of his head. "I'm glad you're safe, but you're still on a boat bound for Georgia, which I'm sure isn't where you'd like to be."

Mercy wrapped her hands around her waist. "My parents must be beside themselves with worry."

Jed gave a small nod. "I must apologize. I really shouldn't have let my fatigue and my mother's stubbornness take you from your home. It was entirely irresponsible."

Mercy shook her head. "Boston is not my home. I live in Mississippi."

He stared at her, waiting further explanation, but embarrassment over the foolishness of her actions kept her tongue held firm. She didn't want this kind stranger to know that she'd all but asked for the calamities that had befallen her.

She looked out over the ocean, holding her eyes wide in hopes that the wind would dry tears wanting to gather before he could notice them.

"I'll do what I can to see you safely returned to your home, if that is your wish."

"Thank you, Mister..." She paused. Had Hezzie given a surname?

"You may call me Jed. Jedidiah Abisha can get heavy on the tongue." He laughed, and little creases appeared at the edges of his eyes.

She extended her hand. "Mercy Carpenter."

He lightly grasped her fingers, then quickly released her. "I'll take you to—"

One of the men shouted, and the crew yelled out. Then the ship lurched again, this time thoroughly dislodging her feet and sending her careening. Behind her, the crew bellowed as a great snap of the sails split the air. Mercy slammed into the railing, pain searing across her middle. She sucked in a breath and dug her nails into the wood as the floor dipped. Lord, help her!

The ocean rose up as though to greet her, it's salty spray licking at her face. She tried to scramble away from it, and splinters tore into her hands as an invisible force kept her pinned to the railing.

Men shouted.

Hands reached for her sleeve but didn't grab hold.

The deck rose.

The wood slipped beneath her fingers. She rose into the air, and then, suddenly, there was nothing at all beneath her.

Twelve

The cathedral's tower rose to the heavens, a beacon of hope calling Faith forward. She hurried down the street, leaving Nolan to scurry after her through the bustle of pedestrians.

If Mercy had come out of the *Boston Globe*, then perhaps she'd seen the church. And if she'd seen the church, then maybe she'd gone there. Mercy always did like the elaborate designs of cathedrals. And maybe she sought it for shelter.

Faith let out a breath. Her thoughts were running rampant. This entire experience, from leaving Ironwood to arriving in Boston to the conversation at the newspaper, had her thinking in strange circles and—

Someone snatched her arm. She lurched to a halt just as a horse and hackney trotted over the pavers she'd been about to cross. She gasped.

"You really should look before crossing the street, Miss Harper," Nolan said, a touch of humor laced through the concern in his tone.

Her heart hammered as the carriage rumbled past, its gleaming black sides dulled by the coat of gray clouds smothering most of the sunlight. She absently gave a small nod in response, then looped her hand through Nolan's elbow and stayed a safe half-step behind him as he crossed the street. She kept his arm even as they took the sidewalk on the opposite side, the fluttering of her heart causing a temporary need for a steadying presence.

He said nothing, guiding her with ease through the throng. Even Memphis hadn't teemed with so many people clogging the walks. With the leaden clouds, it wasn't as if it were the type of day to be out for a stroll. What were so many people doing meandering about?

Gentlemen nodded politely as they passed. More than a couple of women demurely turned up their lips and lowered their eyes, but not before Faith noticed their appreciative glances at her escort. Faith looked up at Nolan, for the first time trying to study him without the veil of her own frustrations.

He'd smoothed back his golden hair into fashionable waves, and the planes of his face were admittedly appealing. She could see why women would look at him in such a manner. The fact that they did so while another lady was on his arm, however, caused a sudden irrational tightness in her chest that could not be explained by her near accident. Or her anxiety over finding Mercy.

Nolan caught her eye. His gaze slid down to where she clutched at his arm like a ninny, but he didn't comment. No, he was too polite for that. Faith set her teeth and removed her hand, freeing him of the discomfort of having to escort a horse-faced termagant.

She immediately chided herself. Where had that thought come from? She'd not allowed those long-buried words to torment her in years. She pushed the troubling thought aside as they approached wide steps leading to double sets of doors nestled underneath a sweeping arch. They paused, Nolan tilting his head back in the same manner as she. Gray limestone stacked upon itself, reaching toward the matching palette of the heavens as though to join the dreary ranks of pewter clouds above.

"Impressive," Nolan said, his voice holding more awe than she would have expected.

Indeed. It sat like a castle in the middle of the bustling city, impressive in its size and steady in its call to needy souls. Perhaps one of them had been Mercy.

"Let's see if anyone has seen her."

He followed her up the front stairs and grumbled something as she pulled open one of the doors. She swept inside only to immediately stop once more. Nolan grumbled again, coming to stand next to her as she gawked at the two-story arches and carved wood beams overhead. The sanctuary was like a massive cavern bursting with splendor. And nothing at all like their chapel at home. She'd seen photographs of the great European cathedrals, of course, but none of them did justice to the vibrancy of seeing such a place in person. Muted sunlight filtered through stained glass windows, creating tiny shards of color on the floor. The pillars were washed in white and the floors were—

"May I help you?"

Faith startled, turning to find a petite woman dressed in a nun's habit. "Oh. I'm sorry. I'm looking for my friend." She shifted, feeling out of place. "She's lost, you see, and I thought she may have come here."

Concern flashed in the nun's blue eyes, and she glanced to

Nolan. "Another missing girl? Oh, dear."

Unease clawed through Faith's veins. "Another?"

"Perhaps you should come with me." The nun turned and gestured for them to follow her down the length of the grand room, past the most elaborate altar Faith had ever seen, and through another doorway at the rear. Several turns later, they came to a carved door.

"One moment, please, while I see if the archbishop is available." Without waiting for their response, she disappeared.

Nolan put his hands in his trouser pockets only to immediately remove them to check his timepiece. "Once we speak with the priest, we should probably check in with your father before continuing further."

"Why?"

He shifted his stance. "It's been a couple of hours."

Faith pressed her lips together. Had she made Nolan so uncomfortable that he was ready to deliver her back to her father already? She straightened her already stiff spine. "You can be rid of me once I find the information I need."

"Why do you always think...?"

The door swung open, and a man dressed in long robes with a golden cross hanging from his neck stepped out. Kind eyes looked them over from an unassuming, clean-shaven face.

"Sister Mary tells me you're looking for a lost girl."

Nolan gave a small bow. "We are, sir. She's of African descent and is far from home. We have come to find her."

The man's eyes narrowed. "Are you sure she wishes to be found?"

Faith stepped forward. "Her name is Mercy Carpenter, and she's my dearest friend. She wrote an article, and it was published in the *Boston Globe*." The man's eyes softened, and she quickly continued. "She came up here hoping they would hire her to write for the paper, but"—her voice cracked, and she had to swallow her emotions before she could continue—"but Mercy...well, she just doesn't understand. We were reared by parents who believe God created all people equally." She twisted her hands.

The priest studied her, letting the silence hang in the air.

"She came up here all on her own and..."

The archbishop patted her arm. "We keep a door in the rear where the sisters receive those in need. But no new young women have come to us recently. How long has your friend been missing?"

Faith's shoulders slumped. "She would have arrived only a couple of days ago." How would they ever find Mercy in this city? It was too large, too overwhelming.

"I'm quite concerned," the archbishop continued, "about all the girls being taken."

Nolan frowned. "Taken?"

"There're rumors of girls disappearing from the streets. The poor or fallen ones that most people ignore." He sighed. "If the girl you're looking for is out on the streets alone at night, then she could well be in danger."

"What happens to these girls?"

The archbishop looked to Faith before responding to Nolan. "We don't know. We've heard a few disturbing tales of girls being loaded onto boats at the dock, but the authorities haven't confirmed any of it." He paused a moment, as though considering. "There may also be something going on with the Pink Parrot."

Faith didn't like the sound of that. While Nolan got directions to the establishment, she tried to keep herself from imagining all manner of terrible things that could have happened to Mercy.

They left the church, silent as they passed through the massive doors and down the front steps. Faith didn't take Nolan's arm, and he seemed engrossed in his own thoughts. It wasn't until they climbed into a rental hackney that he spoke again.

"I'm uncomfortable with you traveling into what is likely an undesirable part of town. I don't think your father would be pleased."

She held the side of the narrow conveyance as it jerked over a rough section of cobblestone. "I'm sorry you're uncomfortable. But *I'm* uncomfortable with the fact that Mercy may be in any *undesirable* places all alone."

Nolan held her gaze. "You two have a very close friendship."

Faith blinked back sudden tears. His tone held no condemnation, annoyance, or judgment. It held only concern and understanding toward how she must feel. "She's been like a sister to me. When I was a girl, Mercy was…" Her voice wavered. "She never called me hateful things behind her hands or shamed me in front of anyone. I could always be myself with her."

Nolan watched her, concern evident in his eyes. Why was she telling him any of this? But then, it felt good to let it out. She was tired of having to maintain social standards when she didn't care for any of it in the first place. And as she wasn't trying to lure this man into marriage by pretending to be a lady of a constantly pleasant disposition with nary a troubling thought, what did it matter if she let him know her true feelings?

"Children were not nice to me."

He waited in that way that often annoyed her. At the moment, however, the pause gave her the opportunity to gather and compose her thoughts. He never seemed to rush anyone into words, and he took his time with his own.

She straightened her shoulders to the proper posture Mother always taught. "Girls would whisper about me behind their fans and make up tales about me and Ironwood to amuse themselves. None of it had any bearing in truth, of course."

At his nod of acceptance, she continued. "Boys hated that I could learn numbers and figures faster than they could, and they would call me horse-face and say it was a good thing my father had enough money or no one would ever want to marry such a goat."

The muscle in his jaw twitched again. Had she hit a nerve? Had she touched on Nolan's own designs on her father's favors? She pushed the thought aside. Even if he did harbor such thoughts, they would never come to fruition.

"That must have been difficult," he said. "I know how unkind children can be."

Faith watched the scenery pass by. Stately buildings and whitewashed walls gave way to humbler structures made of hewn wood. "When I was twelve, my parents took my brother and me to visit friends of theirs. The two brothers and one of their friends found me reading in the garden." She met his gaze. "They took my book and laughed as they tore the pages out. They laughed more when I cried, taunting me and saying girls were only meant for kitchens and the bedroom, and it was better I learned that now."

Nolan's eyes widened, and his face reddened, but he didn't speak.

"My mother found me and went into hysterics. She thought they'd done worse to me than they had. I didn't know what she meant until we were back home, when she explained to me that a girl had to keep her wits about her and protect herself to be sure a man didn't hurt her." She lifted her shoulders. "I've tried to do that ever since."

Nolan sat back against the cracked leather seat and rubbed his forehead. "Is that why you hate men?"

A defensive retort rose, but she squelched it. Nolan had listened politely. His question seemed genuine. "I don't hate men. I merely refuse to be dominated by them."

He was quiet for some time, and she'd begun to think the conversation finished when he finally spoke again. "Do you think I've tried to dominate you?"

She laced her fingers on her lap, taking a moment to consider how she might answer. "Your comments that a woman shouldn't read and doesn't need to concern herself with men's business suggests that you follow a common way of thinking that is prevalent among males."

Nolan considered this, then nodded. "My father taught me to honor a woman by treating her as something precious."

She tilted her head. Telling a lady her brain would turn to mush if she read a book was treating her as precious?

Nolan sighed. "My mother died when I was young, and I think he always regretted that he'd spent so much time away from her. From the time I was a boy, he tutored me in the ways I was to treat any lady I met, and then one day, my own wife."

"And in what way is that?" She hadn't meant for the remark

to come out as condescending as it sounded, and she immediately regretted her tone.

Nolan, however, seemed not to notice. He held up a hand and started counting on his fingers. "A man is to treat a lady with dignity, respect, and reverence. A lady, and especially a wife, is to be shielded from all that could harm her, and it is a man's duty to be certain that any of life's blows must first pass through him before ever reaching the woman he cares for."

Faith stared at him. Not quite what she'd been expecting, and not quite what the suffragettes touted were every man's views—the archaic nonsense that a woman is to be treated as a less intelligent being of no use beyond housework and childrearing.

Nolan tugged at his collar. "He always said the Word teaches that a husband is to give himself up for his wife."

Mercy's words about marriage surfaced. But what Mercy had believed wasn't normal for a marriage in the real world. Just like everything else at Ironwood, the relationships of the Carpenters and her own parents were not commonplace. She would never find a man who believed like her father.

Would she?

Nolan caught her eyes and held her gaze. Her heart hammered. The sincerity she saw there caused her stomach to knot. In all of his worrying, and pestering, and grumbling over her actions, had he thought himself protecting her? Would letting him do so really have been so terrible?

"I always strived to please my father," he continued, still holding her gaze. "When he passed when I was fourteen, I vowed then to keep all of his commands close." He looked away, and his voice hardened. "Especially when I saw the way my uncle treated my aunt. His neglect and harsh words made an otherwise lovely woman sour. She eventually succumbed to wasting disease."

Faith slid her lower lip through her teeth, contemplating his words. On one hand, his chivalry was commendable…desirable, even. But on the other hand, seeking to shelter a woman by not allowing her to have any freedom wasn't really shelter. It was prison. She tried to choose her words carefully. "If your father taught you to honor a lady and treat her as precious, then should that not include allowing her to express herself and pursue things she enjoys?"

He hesitated. "It does."

"Then why tell me reading would turn my tiny brain to mush?"

He shook his head. "You have a quick wit and, truth be told, I rather admire the fact that you care so deeply about the world and the people in it."

She offered a smile of gratitude and waited to see if he would answer her question.

He shifted on his seat. "At the time of that conversation, I'd just recently heard there'd been studies on women and reading." He lifted his shoulders, appearing almost sheepish but too confident to truly accomplish it. "I suppose I simply didn't wish to see you come to any type of harm."

That's what he'd been thinking? Heavens, he certainly hadn't made that clear!

He smiled, and it was so bright that she couldn't help but return it. "I must admit," he continued, seeming almost surprised, "that it's nice to be in the company of a lady who has more to talk about than hats and fashions."

Faith laughed. "So, are you becoming a progressive man now?"

He crinkled his brow. "Well, now that I think on it, reading gains a person knowledge and…" He lifted his hands. "I apologize. I thought only to protect you from harm."

A warm feeling spread through her heart, only to be doused a moment later by his next words.

"I see now you're much more like a man."

Like a man? What did that mean? Did he see her as more of a boyish companion than a lady? She clenched her teeth. Vexatious thoughts! What did she want? His attentions or not? To be treated as a man or a lady?

Frustrated, she heaved a sigh. "So then does a woman *acting as a man*, as you say, by reading, drawing up figures, and having thoughts on politics and other areas she's not supposed to have a care for mean she is, then, no longer considered a lady?"

He sat in that infuriating way he had, considering. She stifled her impatience. Perhaps a well-thought answer was better than letting loose the first one that came to one's tongue. As she often did.

Maybe she'd not given this man enough credit for his own intellect. The thought stung. Had she made her own assumptions about him while at the same time admonishing him for making conclusions about her?

The carriage swayed to a halt. Nolan opened the door and stepped out, offering his hand for her to descend. She took it, more to appease his needs as a gentleman than because she needed the help.

As he handed her down, he gave her fingers a squeeze that sent a jolt of strange tingles up her arm. "As I believe you have so aptly demonstrated, Miss Harper, a young woman can, indeed, be both intelligent and a lady."

Thirteen

*M*ercy was going to die.

Cold fingers wrapped around her dress, pulling her down to murky depths of swirling chaos. She struggled, her lungs burning. Never had they longed for air so fiercely, yet she dared not take a breath. The waves lapped at her as she kicked furiously, desperate to keep her head above the tumultuous water. She tilted her nose toward the surface, only to have the surface swell away from her once more.

The weight of her dress pulled her down, farther and farther away from the hope of air. She kicked against it, the fabric tangling around her legs like bindings.

Finally, she lurched above the water and greedily sucked in a breath, only to be submerged an instant later. She slipped beneath the waves, saltwater stinging her eyes and filling her mouth. Had God abandoned her? Was this her punishment for leaving home and disobeying her parents?

Her lungs burned, the tiny sip of air she'd managed to find not nearly enough to quench her body's need.

I'm sorry, Papa.

Something snatched at her outstretched arm. Involuntarily, she wanted to scream, but was able to catch herself before her mouth filled with too much water. Her arm wrenched, and she lurched toward the surface. Hands wrapped around her waist, and she was thrust above the water. She sucked in air, coughing up what she'd swallowed and immediately trying to refill her lungs again.

Her rescuer bobbed up beside her, his face streaming water. Still coughing, she grabbed him, wrapping her arms around his neck and clinging to his strength. Jed's powerful legs kept them both above the water, and the comfort of his arm around her back was the only thing keeping her from panic.

"You're safe. I've got you." His words in her ear slowed a little of the rapid beating of her heart, but she dared not loosen her grip.

Above, men threw a rope ladder over the side of the ship, shouting instructions in words she didn't understand. Jed moved his arm, and she yelped, tightening her hold around his neck.

"Easy, Mercy. I'm not going to let you go." When she didn't respond, he brushed wet hair back from her face and lifted her chin to meet his eyes. "I've got you. Understand?"

She nodded.

"I need to get us to the ladder." His words were calm. Much too calm for the current situation, but because of that, she appreciated them all the more.

Safe. She was safe as long as he kept a hold on her. He started to move, and his words suddenly made sense. She dug her fingers into his neck.

"No! I can't swim!"

He smiled, gently rubbing her arm though she clawed at him as if she were a cat tossed down the well. "Yes, I know." He patted her again, speaking to her like she'd always spoken to Joy when she'd been awakened by a bad dream. "I'll swim for the both of us. I just need you to relax and trust me."

She clung to him, afraid to let go. He waited patiently, the two of them bobbing in the water like one of Papa's fishing corks. Finally, logic wormed its way past her panic. She must follow his instructions or remain in the water, which she certainly did not wish to do. She drew a deep breath of salty air and loosened her grip, though she kept a fistful of his sodden shirt.

Jed smiled. "I'm going to turn you so you can float on your back. As long as you relax, you will stay above the water."

Her eyes widened.

"I won't let go. You have my word."

Trembling, she allowed him to turn her, and she did the best she could to stifle her terror and get her body to recline as he gently tilted her. He kept his hand under her back, and her feet leveled up on the surface. Then he wrapped his arm up under her ribs and they began to move. Mercy kept her eyes squeezed shut, praying God would not let her go beneath the surface again.

The water pulled at her as though unwilling to give up its victim as Jed gently maneuvered her through the waves. She opened her eyes when he stopped.

"We're at the ladder. I'm going to need you to climb."

Teeth chattering, she nodded. Above, the sides of the large wooden ship bobbed on the surface of the blue water, entirely unconcerned that it had just coughed her out into the sea like Jonah's whale.

At least she hadn't been swallowed by a mighty fish. The ridiculous thought had her kicking frantically once more, anxious to free herself from the many dangers of the water.

Jed held firm, steadying her as she got her feet beneath her once more. She began to sink, but before the water reached her chin, he guided her hand to the ropes. "Hold here." He gently plucked her other hand from his shirt and drew it up to the coarse fibers. "And here."

She clung to the rope, her hands trembling.

"There are rungs beneath the water. Do you think you can find one with your foot?"

She kicked the limp dress hanging around her feet, feeling nothing but swirling fabric. She kicked out against the swaying side of the ship until her foot caught on something.

"I...I think I have it."

"Good. Now, put your weight there and pull yourself up. I'm right behind you."

Her body felt weighted as she struggled to free herself from the water's hold. Slowly, she pulled herself up until she stood above the ocean. The ship bobbed, the ladder against it swaying. Mercy closed her eyes, her grip so tight the rope dug into her palms.

"You're doing fine. Take another step up."

Jed's words were gentle, and she found herself wanting to do as he asked, even though she feared her body wouldn't cooperate. She managed to let go with one hand and reach for another rung, her feet following behind, rough rope scratching her bare feet. Breathing quickly, she repeated the action until her head rose above the ship railing and more hands reached for her.

She was hauled over the side of the ship in an uncouth manner that would cause any lady to become undone, what with a man beneath her sodden skirts and all, but Mercy was no longer interested in such nonsense. Never had she been so glad to have her feet hit unstable footing.

No sooner had the sailors steadied her than Hezzie was wrapping a blanket around her shoulders. "Come, let's get you out of them soggy clothes."

She cast a look over her shoulder at Jed, who leapt over the railing with ease. His concerned eyes met hers, and he gave her an encouraging smile she could not return. Hezzie steered her down the narrow stairs and to the small chamber she'd only recently escaped. At the moment, however, it seemed more a haven than a confinement.

"You gave us an awful scare!" Hezzie scuttled around the room, her hands fidgeting but not seeming to know what to do. She stopped. "I'll get you another dress from my trunk."

Mercy watched her hurry off, then looked down at the water pooling around her feet. She drew a long breath of sweet air. Tears gathered, and she let them fall down her cheeks and take up residence with the ocean's remnants on her collar.

A moment later, Hezzie scooted back in, her hands full of fabric. "Don't just stand there. Get that wet stuff off."

Her words might have been harsh, but they were delivered with such gentle concern that Mercy once again found herself obeying someone's orders without hesitation. When Hezzie had her dried off and dressed in a too short and a bit too tight faded yellow work dress, she took a scarf and twisted it around Mercy's damp hair.

"There now. That's better." Hezzie wrapped the sodden garments in the blanket and pushed the bundle through the puddle on the floor, then deposited the heap by the door.

Mercy watched her, unable to do anything more than stand there.

"The Lord had you in His hand, sure enough." Hezzie clicked her tongue. "But I was sore afraid you were going to go under out there."

"I'm thankful Jed came for me, or I would have drowned."

Hezzie looked her over for a long moment, then gave a slight nod. "Not what I was expecting, but I'm pleased."

Mercy tilted her head. "You weren't expecting him to jump off the ship to save me? Or...you weren't expecting me to survive but you're glad I did?"

"Hmm?" Hezzie busied herself checking the water barrel, in constant motion in a room that was far too small for endless movement. "No, no." She waved a hand in Mercy's direction. "I mean you weren't the one I'd expected for him, but I do rather like you."

Mercy stared at the woman. Asking for clarification on this woman's comments only seemed to lead to more confusion, so she waited instead to see if Hezzie would explain herself.

"You did well in the water." Hezzie nodded as if that made sense of her previous statement. She looked Mercy over. "I think most people wouldn't have been able to keep a calm head like you did. That's good."

Mercy sat on the edge of the cot, more to get out of the fidgeting woman's way than because she wanted to rest. "I learned as a child that allowing myself to panic only made things worse."

Hezzie stopped moving. "What things?"

The memory wasn't one she cared to remember, but it rose up with such force that she shuddered. "When I was a little girl, none of the house girls liked me. They always lowered their eyes and were polite when my mother was around, but if they ever found me in the big house without her or Faith, it was…different."

"Who is Faith?"

Mercy paused. "My childhood…friend. Ironwood is her house."

Hezzie's eyebrows rose, then understanding colored her eyes. "Ah. White girl?"

Mercy nodded. "We were allowed to play together as children. I foolishly thought that relationship would always be the same."

Hezzie was shaking her head before Mercy had even finished her sentence. "But it wasn't, was it?"

Mercy swallowed and looked away. "Ironwood is different. More different from the rest of the country than I ever realized until I left." She brushed aside thoughts that needed further examination, unable to process all she'd learned of the world outside of Ironwood thus far. "Anyway, that isn't part of the story. One day, two older girls found me on the back porch alone. I'd been writing a story on my slate, which I'd hidden away from the governess."

"You learned under a governess?" Hezzie hurried the three steps it took her to cross the room and sat on the edge of the cot. "You know how to read and write?"

"And do figures and sums. I learned history and geography and enough about the world to want to see it. But what I found wasn't what I had dreamed it would be."

Hezzie grunted. "The world never is."

"The girls took my slate and broke it and then hauled me

off the porch and down the path to the kitchen. I tried to get away, but they were too strong. They threw me in the cellar and locked me down there."

Hezzie waited, watching Mercy closely as she drew a long breath, the confines seeming to shrink in on her again.

"It had to be hours that I was trapped down there in the damp. I tried banging on the door, but no one heard me. The darkness..." She shivered. "I hated being trapped down there. It felt like I couldn't breathe. When I panicked, it was worse. I had to force myself to calm down and remain still, waiting for someone to finally find me."

"But you didn't tell on those two girls, did you?"

She picked at her fingernail. "How did you know?"

"You just don't seem the type."

She wasn't sure how to respond to that. "I never told anyone. Only the cook ever knew I'd been locked down there. But I learned that when things happened, if I panicked, I couldn't think. If I couldn't think, I couldn't escape. I learned to rely on my ability to focus to avoid ever finding myself trapped like that again."

Hezzie considered her a moment, and then nodded. "Feeling trapped and lacking freedom is never a good thing."

Mercy nodded. "That's probably why I wanted to leave Ironwood so much. Because no one would ever let me."

The thoughts of home brought a pang to her chest. Perhaps her parents hadn't been so wrong to want to shelter her after all. "When will the boat dock? I need to send word to my parents." Another thought spiked her alarm. "How long have we been on this boat?"

"This is the second day." Hezzie shrugged. "Supposed to

make a couple of stops. Not sure when." She patted Mercy on the shoulder. "You've got to be plumb tuckered. Why don't you take a good rest?"

She opened her mouth to protest but thought better of it. Hezzie rose and headed for the door, snatching the wet clothes on her way.

Mercy lay on the cot.

Hezzie's words drifted back as she closed the door. "Lord, she sure ain't what I thought you'd send."

Dismissing the cryptic words, Mercy pulled the thin blanket over her and tried to push her dismay about how worried her family must be and troublesome thoughts of the ocean from her mind.

Fourteen

$\mathcal{A}$ more confounding woman he had never seen. Nolan watched Miss Faith Harper square her shoulders and head straight for an establishment that could be called questionable at best. He left the carriage door swinging open, which received a grunt from the driver, and reached out to snag her arm. Such an action was rather unbecoming of a gentleman, but he'd found it necessary with this peculiar lady on more than one occasion.

Faith looked down at where he held her arm, and a look of surprise widened her eyes only to be quickly followed by a downturn of her lips. "Why, sir, do you continually take hold of me in such a manner? I am given to understand that it is not the common way a gentleman escorts a lady."

He withheld a retort about how this particular lady only wanted to be treated as a lady when it suited her. Apparently, their conversation in the carriage had not gained him as much insight into her mannerisms as he'd hoped. "Given your pace and trajectory, I sought to slow you before you entered." He looked down to where he still held her and dropped his hand. "Forgive me."

Faith brushed her hands down her skirt, sudden uncertainness entering her eyes. "I need to find Mercy."

The statement didn't seem in keeping with their current discussion on how a gentleman and lady were to interact, so it took him a moment to catch up with her capriciousness. He glanced up at the swinging sign depicting a pink bird with its head tilted back and wings spread wide. "I understand you are in a hurry to find your friend. But we cannot just dash inside. This is not the kind of place for a lady."

She quirked an eyebrow. "Nor for a *gentleman*, if I've guessed correctly."

Heat shot up his neck, and the vein under his collar pulsed. "It's not a Christian establishment by any means, but I believe entering it will damage my reputation less than it will yours." He tugged at the hem of his jacket. "Therefore, I should be the one to enter and make inquiries."

Faith stared at him, and they found themselves at yet another impasse. This time, however, Nolan refused to budge. He set his feet, giving her the time she needed to come to her senses. There were fewer people on the walks here than there had been uptown, but the few who lingered gave them a wide berth— which Nolan took to be another bad sign. There was no way he was letting her go in there.

The salty sea air tugged at his hair and brought back sudden memories that he'd rather forget. He clenched his hands. Regardless of how unconventional this woman insisted on being, he would not let Mr. Harper's daughter sully her reputation. He should never have let her out of the carriage.

The stubborn set to her jaw tried his patience. It took a hefty amount of willpower to keep his tone conciliatory. "You should wait in the carriage while I inquire inside."

Faith stared at him for another moment with wide eyes, as though she truly expected he would state anything to the contrary. Regardless of her unconventional ways, she was still a lady, and he still a gentleman.

She made a strange noise that, if he didn't know better of a lady, he would consider a snort of derision. "I think not." She turned on her small heel and strode straight for the door, pulling it open without hesitation.

He ground his teeth and hurried after her, calling for the driver to wait on them. The last thing he wanted was to end up stuck in this part of town for any length of time. He caught the door as it swung back on its hinges. He'd barely taken a step across the threshold when he bumped into where Faith had halted.

She stumbled forward but didn't cut him with a retort on his ill manners. Instead, her head was tilted back, and her hand placed at the base of her throat. He followed her gaze around an entry that did not match the rough look of the exterior. Crystal dripped from the ceiling, sending dancing candlelight in shards of radiance across the pink papered walls. Exquisite furniture dotted the wide space, currently unoccupied with waiting patrons, thank heavens. Underfoot, carpeting in the same rich rose as the walls cushioned his feet.

"May I help you?" A smooth female voice had him lifting his gaze past the top of Miss Harper's feathered hat to a polished desk that stood sentry in front of a sweeping staircase.

Nolan cleared his throat and stepped around Faith. Heavy perfume thickened the air, and he felt as though he had to swallow it down in order to speak. The woman behind the counter swept her gaze over him, then turned her lips up into a smile unlike any he'd seen a lady don before. This one seemed almost predatory.

"Hello, sir. Welcome to the Pink Parrot." She placed her hands on the polished desk and leaned forward, the low cut of her gown revealing far more than he desired to see.

He took a quick intake of breath and kept his eyes firmly locked on hers. They were blue of a most striking color, and she hid them periodically behind long sweeps of dark lashes. Her skin was like that of a porcelain doll, likely enhanced by rice powder. Full lips turned up into another smile, their unusual strawberry red snagging his eyes.

Nolan cleared his throat again. "Good afternoon, ma'am. I'm here to inquire about a girl."

Her smile widened and she stepped around the receiving desk. "Of course you are."

He opened his mouth to protest her implication, but words snagged in his throat. The woman wore a gown that nearly matched the tone of her skin, its tight fabric much too thin. Before he could utter a word, she placed an ungloved hand on his arm.

The scent of vanilla and lavender swirled in his senses as she leaned close. "Such a fine looking gentleman deserves the very best treatment." She lowered her voice. "Why, I even think I shall escort you myself."

Escort him? Where?

"Excuse me."

Faith's clipped words snatched him out of his stupor, and he stepped back from the woman who kept a possessive hand on his arm.

Faith narrowed her eyes. "*He* won't be going anywhere."

She glared at him, icy eyes stabbing him with accusations. "Except back outside to wait in the carriage."

He blinked at her as she turned those stabbing eyes back on the proprietress. "Since clearly this is no place for a proper gentleman."

Rather than being riled, the woman laughed as she tossed a long curl hanging over her nearly-bare shoulder. "Why, darling, this is exactly the type of place for a gentleman." She gave him another cat-like smile. "We enjoy the company of Boston's finest gentlemen on a daily basis. And we do our very best to make them feel comfortable here."

Nolan took another step back, the predatory look in her eyes making his chest tighten. He felt anything but comfortable. Perhaps it would be best if he stepped out for fresh air. The cloying perfume must be making his thoughts cloudy.

He looked at Faith, who stood with her arms crossed, clearly furious. He said, "I don't wish to leave you here alone."

"And I do not wish to remain in your company while you become *comfortable* at such an establishment. I do believe in this particular instance, my father would think it best if *you* were the one to wait in the carriage."

He stared at her, at a loss as to how to respond. He could not leave her in such a compromising position, but neither could he dispute the fact that he should not be here. The proprietress made a sound that he could only equate to a purr, and suddenly her hand was on the back of his neck. He jumped and stumbled away from her.

She poked out her lower lip. "As your lady is currently souring the atmosphere, I suppose you'll have to return to visit me later, yes?"

Nolan shook his head and backed toward the door. He grasped the metal and scrambled outside, but not before hearing the woman's laughter and "he'll be back" before the door slammed behind him.

As soon as Nolan disappeared, the woman's features hardened. Gone were the wide eyes and cheery smiles. Instead, she pinned Faith with a glare and stretched her lips into a snarl. "What do you want?"

Flustered, Faith returned the woman's glare with one of her own. "I came here looking for my friend. She's missing."

The woman—she couldn't be called a lady in such attire— turned back to her receiving desk. "And what makes you think your friend is here?"

Something cautioned her to speak carefully, so Faith took a deep breath and tried to get herself to calm. "My friend's name is Mercy. She's a young lady who has never been to a city before. She came here looking for employment but was turned away. With nowhere to go and no family or friends in the area, I'm not sure how she would be able to care for herself."

To her surprise, the woman's features instantly softened. "Oh." She pulled her lip through her teeth. "When did your friend arrive?"

"A few days ago."

The woman shook her head, sending loosened blonde curls swinging against her cheeks. "I'm sorry, we haven't had any new girls in a couple of weeks."

Faith twisted her hands, the impossibility of her task gnawing at her stomach.

The woman brightened. "But perhaps Amanda saw her with the last group." Worry flashed in her eyes, but it was gone so fast that Faith questioned if she had seen it at all. "I'll see if Amanda will speak with you."

"Thank you. I truly appreciate the help."

The woman turned to look up the stairs. "Why don't you wait down here? Only gentleman are allowed upstairs."

The comment set Faith's teeth on edge, but she did her best to offer a smile and another word of thanks. She perched on the edge of an overstuffed settee and watched the woman glide up the stairs.

Really, what had Nolan been thinking? The way he'd looked at that woman...

Faith tossed the thought aside. What had she been expecting? He was a man, after all. Better that she be reminded of the truth of men's nature now before the disturbing tenderness he'd cultivated in her truly took hold. Men were ruled by their appetites.

And apparently this establishment was frequented by men who called themselves gentlemen. But was it any real surprise that even men of standing would make use of such an establishment? Faith ground her teeth until they hurt, thinking about the unfortunate women who were supposed to remain docile and submissive wives at home while their husbands visited with the likes of, well, whatever that coy woman's name was.

A moment later the object of Faith's caustic thoughts descended the stairs with a young woman wrapped in a flamboyant dressing gown. The new girl eyed Faith as she walked, her soft fawn-colored brow wrinkling. She was a striking woman with a tanned complexion and a huge mass of shiny dark curls.

She sat next to Faith on the settee and arranged her gown over her legs.

The other woman gestured to Faith. "Amanda, this lady wants to ask you about her friend." She slipped a delicate silver timepiece from her pocket. "But not long now. We need to get ready for the evening."

Amanda dipped her chin and turned hazel eyes onto Faith, wasting no time with introductions or pleasantries. "What does your friend look like?"

"Mercy is a colored woman with a tawny complexion and raven hair. She's tall and slim." Faith stumbled to think of better descriptions of the friend she'd known all her life, and her voice hitched. "She's full of energy and life. Mercy is never still. Her eyes sparkle when she talks, and she's quick with a compliment."

Amanda pursed her lips and then gave a small shake of her head. "I didn't see anyone like that in the last group."

"What group?"

The girl, for she couldn't have been more than fifteen or sixteen, shifted. "The group I went to see two days ago."

Would she have to mine for answers? "How many girls were in this group you speak of, and why were you there?"

She shrugged. "To see if any of them would fit Miss Clara's specifications. I didn't choose any, and, I'm sorry, but I don't remember any girls that fit your friend's description." She began to rise.

"Wait!" Faith struggled to understand. Were these the missing girls the archbishop spoke of? "Are you sure? What about the other girls? How many were there? Where did they come from?"

Amanda narrowed her eyes. "Why are you here?"

"I told you. I need to find Mercy."

She glanced toward the stairs, as though expecting someone to be there. "But why look for her here?"

"The priest at the church said that he'd heard girls that went missing in the streets were here."

Amanda actually rolled her eyes. "Of course he did."

"I'm sorry, I don't understand."

She sighed. "Look, miss, you seem like a nice lady, and you really do seem worried about your friend." She glanced up the stairs. "So I'll tell you what you probably are not ready to hear about those girls."

Faith swallowed and waited.

"They are not all missing. Most find their way to the groups on their own to find a placement."

"A placement? What kind of placement?"

Amanda ignored her question. "Not many girls get to come to the Pink Parrot. Miss Clara is very particular about her girls." She lifted her chin. "This is a good place. It's clean and fancy, and we are well cared for."

Faith leaned forward, the unease in her stomach growing.

"The gentlemen are usually that—gentlemen. It's rare for any of us to be used roughly. Because of that, Miss Clara is very particular about who she takes." Amanda lifted her perfectly arched eyebrows. "Your friend, she ever been with a man?"

Faith's jaw dropped at such an inappropriate question. She snapped it closed and merely shook her head.

"Miss Clara likes fresh girls the best, because their first night goes for a high price. It would be the same for any of the other madams, or even the traders. Your friend could make a good wage if she is unsullied and pretty enough to draw men's eyes."

Faith's tongue remained glued to her pallet as her ears burned. What would Daddy say to hear such a conversation? Mother, certainly, would be outraged. Faith did her best to gather her wits and took a breath.

"Where might a girl end up if she doesn't come here?"

Amanda shrugged. "Some work on their own or with Madam Rigby down at the docks, or..."

Faith leaned forward. "What?"

"Well." Amanda glanced at the stairs. "I do remember something now. There were these two big men, Irish accent, I think. I only saw them for a moment as I was leaving. One had someone, maybe a girl, slung over his shoulder." She wrinkled her brow. "I didn't see what she looked like, but she could have had dark skin. It was hard to tell."

Faith's stomach fluttered. "Anything else?"

"One of them might have said something about one of the traders, but I can't be sure."

That didn't sound good at all. "What are traders?"

Amanda looked at her with pity. "You really are a sheltered lady, aren't you?" She'd somehow managed to make the words sound like an insult.

"Where do these traders take girls?"

"I'm sorry. I don't know." She rose again. "I need to be going."

The truth of the situation chipped at Faith's heart. Had these girls been forced into a life they never wanted? By poverty or lack of rights or... What else could make a woman turn to such an undesirable profession?

Compassion swelled for this pretty girl who had not been given a fair chance in life. "What about the girls here? Were they stolen from families and taken without their consent?"

Amanda rose and brushed off her skirts and glanced to the stairs again. "I told you. We have it good here." She turned to leave.

Why did the girl keep looking toward the stairs? Faith reached for her. "I can help you. Women have more rights, you know. You don't have to let men treat you this way."

Amanda laughed. "The only men here are the ones we let in, and believe me, here, women have the upper hand."

Faith blinked and lowered her hand. "But...maybe I can help you get out of here and find a more respectable place."

The girl's face hardened. "What makes you think I want to be anywhere else? I'm a mulatto. There's no other place that gives me as good as I've got it here." She turned and looked over her shoulder. "I hope you find your *friend*." She eyed Faith with an icy glare. "That is, of course, if she actually wants a white lady to find her."

With that, she stalked up the stairs before Faith could conjure another word.

Fifteen

ootsteps tromped down the hall, jarring Mercy from her fitful dozing. She rubbed crust from her eyes, wondering how long she'd been resting. A knock pounded on her door, rattling it against the hinges. Mercy lurched to her feet.

Jed's voice penetrated the wood an instant later. "Come above deck!"

Fear twisted through her middle as she flung off the blanket and hurried out. By the time she made it out the door, Jed had disappeared.

Hezzie held on to the railing, slowly making her way up the stairs as though her son's proclamation hadn't stirred any concerns.

Mercy gained her side. "What's happening?"

"Don't know," Hezzie replied. "Reckon we'll find out up there." She nodded toward the opening to the deck.

It took a great deal of Mercy's patience to stay at the woman's side as they made their way above. As soon as they exited the narrow stairwell, however, her senses pricked.

Something had changed. Mercy stepped out onto the ship's deck, and the wind buffeted her face. Men scurried about, gathering rope and dropping sails.

"What's happening?"

Jed grabbed her elbow and put a hand behind his mother's back. "Storm is coming." He guided them through the scurrying sailors. "Captain says we have to make it into the harbor before it hits."

The words sent a shiver down Mercy's spine, and she quickened her steps. They found the captain, a hearty olive-skinned man with the same raven hair as Jed, shouting orders. When they stood in front of him, he looked the women over with a scowl.

"Storm blowing in. Big one."

Mercy lifted her eyes to the horizon. A solid wall of black clouds churned ominously.

The captain turned, listening to something one of the sailors shouted. Then he nodded and spoke to them in English. "Grab hold of something. We're making the turn!" He rushed off, throwing back over his shoulder, "Once we've turned, get below and hold tight."

A thick arm wrapped around her middle as Jed grabbed one woman in each arm and hurried them—thankfully—away from the railing and to the center of the deck. He plopped down on a bench that backed against a raised wall, pulling them down on either side of him and bracing his feet to the floor.

Above her on the raised second deck, the captain shouted.

A single sail made a loud pop, and Mercy turned to bury her face against Jed's shoulder. The last time she'd heard such a sound, the ship had lurched and sent her overboard.

"You're safe." His words brushed over the top of her head. "This time we are prepared, yes?"

She nodded against him, still keeping her eyes squeezed

tight.

"When the storm came, the Lord slept," Hezzie said from Jed's other side, "and the disciples quaked in fear."

Mercy opened her eyes and peered around Jed's wide chest. Why say such a thing in a time like this?

"The Lord, though, he didn't worry. He controls all the waves, you know."

"Yes, Mamá. We know."

Perhaps Hezzie meant for the words to bring comfort, but Mercy found herself clinging all the tighter to a man she didn't even know for fear she would soon tip back into the water. And Hezzie's talk of storms wasn't helping in the least.

The bench tilted underneath her, and the boat gave out a mighty groan. Her fingers dug into Jed's shirt. Something in the back of her mind balked at the familiar way she held on to a stranger, but in her terror she ignored it. She had nothing to fear from Jed.

She didn't know him but she somehow sensed her instincts to be true.

Suddenly, the ship straightened again. Mercy held her breath. The air was quiet, broken only by spits of wind that slapped at the wrap around her hair in sporadic bursts. She loosened her grip, telling herself she had no reason to be embarrassed.

Still, she cast a furtive glance up at Jed. He stared straight ahead, his deep brown eyes scanning the horizon. His jaw line was covered in short bits of stubble she hadn't noticed before. Then he suddenly turned, his face only a breath away from hers. His eyes seemed to darken.

She sucked in a breath.

Suddenly, he was on his feet.

Mercy gulped. She must have embarrassed him with her childish...no worse, her *unseemly*...clinging. Heat crawled up her neck.

Hezzie scrambled after him, putting her hands on her slim waist. "We ain't moving."

Jed craned his head back to look at the sails, which flopped like mighty birds with broken wings.

"I don't know much about sailing," Jed said, "but the wind seems to be coming from a different direction than the way we need it to."

Coming to her feet, Mercy widened her stance in order to be more prepared, should the ship decide to tilt once more. "What does that mean?"

"It means," the captain said, coming to stand by Jed, "that it would take a miracle for us to make it to shore before she smashes into the rocks."

Mercy's stomach tightened, and she gripped the fabric of her dress as though that would help. She looked to Hezzie, but the woman stood with her head bowed and her lips moving. Mercy silently added a prayer of her own, but the good Lord hadn't seemed interested in any of her prayers lately.

Another gust of wind hit, snapping her gown back around her legs. The captain yelled out something in Spanish and then turned to them. "I'd hoped to give you better news, but you best prepare for the worst. Stay below decks. We'll do our best to keep her afloat."

Hezzie gripped Mercy's arm, and they ducked their heads against the steadily increasing wind. The boat lifted and fell in the water, and Mercy's stomach followed suit. She swallowed down bile as they descended the steps. The boat listed to the left. Mercy placed her hand against the wall to brace herself. "What about Jed?"

"He'll do what he can to help the men above."

The idea didn't sit well. He'd said he didn't know much about sailing. What if he went over the edge as she had?

They entered Mercy's room and sat on the bunk in the darkness. Her breath quickened. This wasn't the cellar. She wasn't locked inside. She gripped the chain that connected the edge of the narrow bed to the wall of the ship.

No, this was far worse.

"'And there arose a great storm of wind, and the waves beat into the ship, so that it was now full.'"

Mercy looked at Hezzie, but she had her eyes closed. What was she doing?

"'And He was in the hinder part of the ship, asleep on a pillow. And they awoke Him and said unto him, Master carest thou not that we perish?'"

A shiver went down Mercy's spine, and she gripped the chain tight enough that it dug into her palm.

"'And He arose,'" Hezzie said, her voice gaining strength. "'And He rebuked the wind, and said unto the sea, Peace! Be still!'"

As though in direct contradiction to her pronouncement, the ship lurched, and a heavy pounding beat against the hull. Mercy's stomach roiled, threatening to spill what little it contained.

Hezzie kept her eyes shut and raised her voice above the furious beating of rain. "And the wind ceased! And there was great calm!'" She opened her eyes and looked at Mercy. "And

He said unto them, "Why are ye so fearful? How is it that ye have no faith?'"

Mercy stared at her, the waves sending the boat careening to one side and then the other. "Did you memorize that?" was all she could think to shout over the increasing roar.

"All four gospels."

"How about asking Him to calm the waves now?"

She grinned. "I already did. How about you add a request of your own?"

The ship rocked so far to the side that Mercy slammed into Hezzie. It then jerked back the other direction, sending them tumbling onto the floor. Mercy grabbed Hezzie's hand and tugged her to the wall, wrapping an arm around the old woman's shoulder.

"Go ahead, child," was all she said when they braced their backs against the wall.

The Lord hadn't seemed all that interested in anything Mercy had to say lately, but she bowed her head all the same.

"Out loud," Hezzie prompted. "There's power in words spoken aloud."

Mercy trembled. She dug her nails into the wood beneath her, trying not to slide across the floor as it ruthlessly heaved beneath her. "Lord! Calm the storm." She slid to one side, losing her grip. "Please!"

The boat groaned, and there was a mighty creak. Mercy's eyes widened. "What was that?"

Fear increased the whites around Hezzie's dark eyes. That made Mercy's own panic worse. The ship heaved, sending them tumbling across the floor again. She tried to crawl back toward the bunk, but the floor jerked out from beneath her. She lifted into the air, only to slam down a moment later.

An unholy roar and a splintering *crack* pierced through the roar of the rain. Her head spun. She gathered herself enough to crawl back toward Hezzie, taking the woman's hand.

"Hold on!" Mercy reached for the bunk to gain some stability, and Hezzie did the same.

They gathered their knees beneath them. When they were able to brace themselves against the tossing ship, hope fluttered. If they could hold on until it passed, perhaps they would make it out unscathed.

That hope diminished when dampness crawled up her legs. Her pulse quickened.

No!

The floor was covered with water.

Sixteen

Nolan never should have left her in there alone. He paced the length of ground in front of the hired carriage, gaining a raised eyebrow from the driver. What had he been thinking? He hadn't, and that was the problem. The proprietress had muddled his senses.

Shame crawled down his neck. His father would've been so disappointed to know he'd entered such an establishment. He was still muttering about his foolishness under his breath when the door swung open and Faith stalked out.

She kept her eyes ahead, and he had to scramble toward the carriage in order to get the door open for her in time. She stepped in without his assistance. He entered behind her, closed the door, and then asked for the driver to return them to the hotel. And to Mr. Harper. He wasn't looking forward to that conversation.

They rode in silence for a few moments, but when it seemed Faith had no intentions of offering any information on her own, he prompted, "Did you find out anything?"

Faith kept her head turned toward the window. Had she not heard him? He leaned forward as the carriage swayed into a turn. "Pardon. Did you not hear me?"

"I can hear you perfectly well, Mr. Watson. I merely chose not to answer you."

He ground his teeth. Vexatious woman. Why would she not share any information she'd learned? He sat back against the seat, eyeing her. Why did he care so much about the moods of this contentious creature? She'd done nothing but insult him and disregard his every effort toward her. Now she looked as hot as a hornet. Was she sore he'd taken her advice and gone outside, leaving her alone?

"If you would be so kind as to inform me of the reason behind your current petulance, I would be most obliged." He truly didn't mean for the words to come out as caustic as they had. But, heaven help him, his patience was wearing thin.

She turned his direction and lifted one eyebrow, giving her pinched face an almost amusing expression. He was in no mood to be amused, however, and met her stare with one of his own.

"Surely you jest."

"Jest?" he asked. "I am in no mood for jesting. I ask in earnest."

She sniffed and turned away. He clenched his hands. Petulant indeed.

A moment later, she huffed and glared at him. "I suppose I should not be angered by such lecherous actions, as they have no bearing on me, but I find myself perpetually annoyed by the salacious mannerisms of men."

Nolan let the words wash over him. As they settled, however, the vicious barbs buried beneath his skin. She'd accused him of scurrilous behavior? He clenched his jaw tight, finding his father's practice of considering one's words before releasing a response increasingly difficult. He drew a long breath, then released it slowly.

"Would you care to explain the reason you have chosen to insult me in such a malicious manner?"

Her delicately arched eyebrows lifted nearly to her hairline. "Seriously?"

The carriage swayed and jostled on the cobblestones, and her hat loosened its pins. It started to slide to one side. She ignored it, continuing to stare at him instead.

His gaze traveled down from her incredulous eyes to the rosy splash of heat rising from the base of her throat. "Miss Harper, if you would be so kind as to explain yourself, I would be grateful."

She crossed her arms. "As though making me speak of such things would make them better."

He nearly groaned but held his annoyance to himself. He wouldn't try to get her to speak further for fear anything else she might spout would rid him of any good manners he still had left at his disposal.

They rode in tense silence until the carriage reached the hotel. He opened the door, climbed down, and then held out his hand to assist her.

She ignored it.

Nolan closed the carriage door, then paid the driver for his services. When he finished, he wasn't at all surprised to see that Faith had not waited on him but had stalked forward to the hotel on her own. The doorman was busy talking with an elderly gentleman, but she didn't wait for him, either. She yanked the door open and marched inside.

He followed in behind her, silently rehearsing what he would say to her father to explain why he had allowed his employer's daughter to enter an establishment of ill repute.

He didn't have much time to consider it, however, since Mr. Harper was seated in the lobby, a newssheet spread open on his lap.

"...and I'm pleased to see you are feeling better, Daddy," Faith said as Nolan approached.

Mr. Harper gestured to two wing-backed chairs flanking one of the hotel's twin fireplaces. This time of year, the hearth lay cold, but the cluster of parlor furniture made for a pleasant, if not private, gathering space.

Nolan took a seat and folded his hands in his lap. Mr. Harper slid his gaze between the two of them but said nothing.

Finally, Faith spoke.

"I've found out girls have gone missing around Boston." She shook her head, causing her hat to tilt further to the side and a lock of shiny hair to slide down and rest against her neck.

Mr. Harper nodded for her to continue.

"The Father at Holy Cross pointed us toward an establishment at the docks, but unfortunately...She shook her head. "No, thankfully, we did not find Mercy there."

Mr. Harper shot Nolan a glance, but before he could defend himself, Faith hurried on.

"But we must make haste to the docks. The girl there told me about traders, and then there were some Irish men who had taken a lady that could possibly fit Mercy's description." She fiddled with the trim on her neckline, drawing Nolan's eye to her smooth collarbone as her words tumbled out.

Mr. Harper closed his newssheet and regarded his daughter. "You will not be going to the docks."

"But—"

He held up a hand to stay her response, and to Nolan's surprise, she pressed her lips together and waited for her father to speak again.

"Why don't you go up to your room and freshen up?"

"But Mercy..." Her words died as she took in her father's expression and she dipped her chin. "Yes, sir."

Nolan rose when she did, but she didn't even look at him. He watched her turn toward the stairs, then regained his seat.

"I take it you had trouble with my daughter?"

He shifted, hating to see this man's opinion of him crumble. "My deepest apologies, sir. I should have been more adamant and brought her back here to you. I never should have allowed her to continue her quest into an undesirable location."

To his great surprise, Mr. Harper laughed. "Son, I'm surprised you didn't have to drag her back through those doors"— he nodded to the hotel's entrance—"as it is."

Nolan hesitated, unsure what to say to such a proclamation. Surely he didn't expect Nolan to ever drag a lady anywhere.

Mr. Harper leaned forward. "I fear her mother and I failed Faith in some ways, but the independence we instilled in her isn't one of them. I know she's different than most young ladies, and I'm sure it comes as a shock to you. However, I cannot say I regret allowing her the freedoms I did." He pinned Nolan with a serious gaze. "She merely needs a gentleman who can appreciate her boldness. She would make a good wife for any man who wants a competent partner and helpmeet."

Nolan tugged on his collar.

Mr. Harper slowly folded his newssheet and set it on the side table. "I realize that was far too forward." He smiled. "But I fear you'll need to grow accustomed to such things if you plan to associate with this family for long."

"I let her go into a brothel," he blurted.

Mr. Harper raised his brows. "Did you go in with her?"

"Only as far as the reception area. Then she got angry with me and insisted I wait for her outside. I don't know how far into the establishment she wandered." He hung his head. "I shouldn't have let her oust me. I allowed my own need to escape muddle my better judgment."

Patrons moved through the doorway, and a bluster of wind skirted in leaves with them. The doorman called for a bellboy to find a broom. Nolan watched women duck inside holding their hats. A storm must be coming in. They would have to wait to go to the docks. Faith wouldn't be happy about that.

"Well, that at least explains Faith's mannerisms upon your return."

Nolan looked back to Mr. Harper. "It does?"

"Of course." He laced his fingers. "Let me venture a guess. You both went inside. A woman, likely a bold one, showed a great deal of interest in you. Being a man, of course, she would wish to lure you into spending your money there."

The memory of the proprietress's coquettish smile had him nodding. "Yes. She leaned in far too closely, and her abundance of perfume was making me"—he lifted his shoulders— "muddled."

"I wonder what that appeared like to Faith?"

Had her indignation been toward the woman more than toward himself? The carriage ride would suggest otherwise. "I can understand her annoyance with the proprietress. We were there to ask questions, and she certainly wasn't very friendly to Faith."

Mr. Harper leaned back in his chair and let out a hearty laugh. "Boy, for one so quick with numbers and business, I fear you are rather lacking when it comes to women."

"Sir?"

"My daughter is sore with you because she thinks you were smitten with another woman."

"I…" He frowned. "Oh." Nolan rubbed his temples. "Forgive me, sir, but your daughter is most confusing."

His employer chuckled again. "As are most women, my boy. Though I daresay Faith and her mother may be exceptional cases when it comes to confusing a man." He reached over and patted Nolan's shoulder. "In this instance, however, the reaction is rather common. She's angry because you looked at another woman. To her reasoning, you were interested in someone else, and that didn't sit well."

Nolan pressed his lips together and pondered the preposterous statement. He'd never be interested in spending time in a brothel. "Why would Faith care about the absurd actions of a lady for hire? Miss Harper has made it abundantly clear she's not interested in me in any manner."

Mr. Harper nodded toward the staircase where Faith descended in what could be considered nothing short of splendor. She wore a walking dress, its blue and gold stripes catching the glimmer of the gas lights from above. Her thick hair had been coiled in an intricate fashion, and she'd perched a delicate hat on her head. A small veil swooped down over one eyebrow. How had she affected such a look in so short a time?

Her gaze found his from across the room, and she lifted her chin.

He couldn't take his eyes off her as she glided toward them.

Mr. Harper chuckled. "It would seem your assumptions are mistaken."

Faith darted a glance to her father, who seemed strangely amused, and then back to Nolan, who continued to gape at her. Good. She withheld a smile. It would be a service to remind him what a proper lady looked like. After he'd shamed himself with that nauseating fawning over the woman at the Pink Parrot, he certainly needed it.

His retort that she could act like a lady only when it pleased her nipped at the back of her mind. She pushed it away. And why not? Could she not be a lady who had thoughts in her head and wit on her tongue? Why should a lady have to hide who she was in order to find a man? And why must a man want a lady to be nothing but a bit of vapid, docile fluff for him to display on his arm?

The thought that neither of them fit the descriptions she was trying to force them into rankled, so she pushed it away. What was it about this man that unraveled the carefully constructed air of confidence and assurance she'd worked so hard to compose?

For without the comfort of affected confidence, she was left with something undeniably terrifying. She was merely herself. Timid, weak, and struggling to be anything more than mundane.

The thoughts dissipated as she reached her father. He rose to greet her, pain evident on his face. "Has your knee not improved, Daddy?"

He smoothed his features. "It pains me some, but it's nothing to worry over."

She darted a glance to Nolan, who was still staring at her.

"You look lovely, Miss Harper."

Faith dipped her chin. "Thank you." She turned back to Daddy. "We need to hurry to the wharf. I'd like to make inquiries before it gets dark. Do you think a carriage ride would overtax you?"

Daddy's jaw hardened. "I fought in a war. I don't think riding in a carriage would tax me."

Had she offended him? "Of course." She turned toward the door. "Then let us make haste."

The men followed her, one of them mumbling something under his breath. Her shoes clicked across the floor a bellboy was furiously sweeping. She skirted around him.

The doorman pulled open the door. A gust of wind hit her in the face, bringing in a swirl of leaves and other debris that had the bellboy scurrying with his broom again. Faith placed a hand on her hat. Perhaps her choice of attire wouldn't be a fit for such a blustery day.

But it had gotten a reaction out of Mr. Watson and therefore completed its purpose. She stepped outside and paused. "Why is the sky that color?"

The gray clouds from earlier had changed to a strange orange glow. On the street, people scurried. The chaos tinting the air certainly didn't bode well. Faith readjusted her hat pin. Well, storm or not, they needed to find Mercy. She wouldn't be deterred by a little rain.

Daddy turned back to the doorman. "Where are all the

hackneys?"

"Closing up before the storm, sir. The Signal Corps put up the warning signs for a tropical cyclone." He gave a small bow. "If I may, I suggest your party remain inside."

As though in line with the man's words, the church bells began a rhythmic toll that had nothing to do with the turn of the afternoon's hour. Faith clutched Daddy's arm. "What's happening?"

The doorman ushered them toward the door. "Inside, please, everyone!"

"What is it?" Faith asked as she hurried back over the threshold.

The word he shouted over the wind sent a shiver down her spine.

"Hurricane!"

Seventeen

It was coming for her. Mercy gripped Hezzie's arm, unable to contain the shriek that escaped her throat. Water lapped around her legs as though the ocean sought to devour what it had previously been denied. The ship careened again, sloshing her and Hezzie across the room. She slammed into the wall, and searing pain ripped through her shoulder. She cried out, trying to gain some kind of bearing.

Hezzie grabbed her arm, and they did their best to hold on to one another as the ship sought to heave them out. The water now lapped at her waist, and she struggled to her feet to try to escape it. She didn't stay there long, however, as another vicious wave knocked her feet out from under her.

"This boat is going down!" Hezzie cried. "We have to get out of here."

Cold water pulled at her, confirming what she didn't want to be true. She held Hezzie's hand, and they fought their way to the door, half stumbling, half crawling, until they could finally wrench it open. More water hit them, sending them backward.

Mercy screamed as the water forced her back into the room, the pain in her shoulder protesting as she flailed her arms. The room tilted at an unnatural angle, lifting the door above them.

She felt like one of Joy's lightning bugs trapped in a jar. Except she didn't have wings to help her reach her escape.

"We have to get out!" Hezzie screamed. "Now!"

Mercy launched herself toward the door and held onto the frame, fighting against the current of water that tried to push her back into a watery coffin. With great effort, she pulled herself through the opening, kicking with all her might to get through.

Finally, she scraped her knees over the edge, using the tilt of the wall to her advantage. Bracing against it, she turned and grabbed Hezzie's hand. The woman was stronger than Mercy would have given her credit for, and she was able to scramble through the opening.

They paused for a moment, braced against the tilting wall as the boat rocked back and forth. Mercy tried to steady her breathing and think.

Take stock of the surroundings. Make a plan.

She assessed their only option for escape. No longer a stairway, they now faced a treacherous waterfall. Mercy gritted her teeth and struggled forward, using her fingers to claw her way up the hallway. She leaned forward, trying to keep her footing. But the floor kept sliding beneath her, and her bare feet could not keep traction. Climbing it felt like attempting to mount a hill that was as slick as one of Papa's tabletops. Finally, when she thought her legs could push no more, she gripped the handrail of the staircase.

Mercy clung to it with a scraped palm, her chest heaving. Thankfully, she'd not lost Hezzie. The woman sloshed her way up the hall, then grasped Mercy's waiting hand.

Mercy screamed as pain seared her shoulder, but she pulled Hezzie to the rail despite it. They paused there, breathing hard.

Water steadily flowed down, tangling their skirts around their legs and spraying in their faces.

A shout came from above, nearly indistinguishable over the roar of the water.

Jed shadowed the doorway at the top of the tilted stairwell. In another moment, he'd sloshed down the stairs and gripped her arm. Without a word, he grabbed his mother and tucked her against his side, then held fast to Mercy's hand.

She gripped the rail and followed him as he hefted his mother up the stairs. Mercy's feet slipped, washing them out from under her. Jed grunted, but his grip remained firm, and Mercy was able to get traction once more. What seemed a lifetime later, she emerged from the stairwell into a world worse than the one she'd left behind.

Wind battered the deck where men struggled to hold on to the railings. Angry water crashed against the ship from every direction. It tore down from the sky like arrows. The ocean burst over the edges like serpents from mythology. The wind battered the broken vessel, slinging the water in a vortex around them. She could hardly see Jed, though he stood only an arm's length away from her.

She was going to die.

Jed lowered to his knees to try to crawl beneath the power of the wind and maintain better contact with the shifting deck, and the women followed his lead. He placed Mercy's hand at the hem of his trouser leg, shouting something about holding and following that she barely understood. Hezzie took hold of Jed's other ankle to maintain contact as they slowly began to scoot across the slippery floor.

Mercy kept her head low, unable to see anything but the

tilted, slippery deck beneath her. The wind snatched her hair and swirled it into her face, but she didn't dare spare a hand to pull it from her eyes. Each slide of Jed's leg she followed, slowly making her way wherever he led.

The ship groaned and creaked, releasing an eerie sound that foretold the ship's demise even over the roar of the wind and waves.

Her sole focus was following where Jed's boot slid across the deck. She couldn't think of what would happen when this boat sank. How she would survive in the waves.

She couldn't think about that. One thing at a time.

Forward. One hand. Then the other. The taste of salt on her lips. Her fingers dug into the planks. Hold on. She just had to hold on.

Slowly, methodically, they crawled, until finally Jed stopped. Mercy looked up, the wind beating salt and water into her face that she had to blink away. A hazy shadow, blurred by both the rain and the stinging in her eyes, loomed in front of her without any sense of context.

"Get in!" Jed shouted.

She blinked the moisture away, and the shape took form.

"What?" Her voice was lost on the wind.

Jed banged his hand against a small safety dinghy and shouted again. He wanted her to get into a smaller boat? Was he mad?

She shook her head. That could not be safer than the boat they were on. In a matter of heartbeats inside that thing, she'd be tossed into the mercy of the ocean. And thus far, experience had taught her the water had no grace to spare.

Jed made a rumbling noise she couldn't decipher. In one swift movement, he was on his feet. Before she could protest, he whipped her off the deck and into his arms. She landed in the tiny boat with a thud. Hezzie scrambled in on top of her.

Mercy struggled to get free.

Jed shouted above the roar. "The island isn't far. You can make it!"

"Wait!" Hezzie cried. "Get in with us!"

He shook his head, sodden locks plastered to his face. "I have to help the others!"

Before either of them could say more, Jed loosed two ropes, and the dinghy plummeted. Mercy screamed, her own cry mingling with Hezzie's as they dropped toward the water. The boat landed hard, and water sloshed inside.

Hezzie cried out, but in a moment, they were bobbing too far away from the ship for Jed to hear her pleas. Mercy's stomach heaved, and she had to lean over the side to lose the meager contents of her stomach.

The dinghy lurched across the waves. Mercy and Hezzie were powerless to do anything but hold on. After a time, Hezzie lay in the center of the small hull, shivering. Mercy lowered down beside her, stretching her frame out along the entire length of the boat. The position offered a bit of protection from the wind, but it had the distinctly unfortunate effect of placing her into the gathering water.

The wind whipped over them, trying to loosen them from their succor. She could only pray they wouldn't sink. How far was the island Jed mentioned? Were they even going in the right direction?

There were no answers to her questions. The rain beat down, not allowing her to see more than an arm's length in front of her. If they were to reach any land safely, it would be only by the grace of God.

Eighteen

ebris covered the road, leaving a once-ordered world in chaos. Ignoring Nolan's call, Faith walked out onto the street and pressed her fingers to her lips. The morning's first rays of light revealed evidence of terrors the night had wrought. Water lingered in the street, carrying with it splintered boards, seaweed, and sundry other items that did not belong on the sodden walks.

A child's doll had caught in the spokes of an overturned curricle, one arm dangling toward the cobblestones as though reaching for help.

Tears stung Faith's eyes. What had happened to the girl who would be missing her doll?

Nolan gripped her elbow. "Come, you must get back indoors."

Faith could only stare. After she'd spent a sleepless night huddled in the hotel, the wind had finally ceased its tirade, sputtering now in only fits and starts, petulantly kicking up papers and leaves and shoving them around. She pushed her hair behind her ear. If it looked like this here, how much worse would it be at the water's edge?

"What if Mercy is hurt?"

His arm settled around her shoulders, and the unexpected tenderness broke something deep inside her. She turned into him and buried her face in his lapel. The soft material caressed her cheek, and she breathed deeply. He smelled of aftershave mingled with ocean air and something else she couldn't quite place. It was a strangely pleasant sensation, and she let herself draw another long breath.

He pulled her closer, and the comfort of being wrapped in his arms summoned a torrent of emotions. She let it out, the reassurance of his embrace overriding the shame of public tears. Not that other people had ventured back out onto the streets. Faith and Nolan stood alone, joined only by the restless wind and a few spattering raindrops that lagged behind their brethren.

Nolan gently stroked her arm with his thumb, holding her as she released her worries and frustrations. "We'll find her. I promise to do everything in my power to find her."

Faith sniffled and lifted her head, looking into eyes that were so sincere, words she thought never to speak broke free. "But what if it's too late?"

Nolan bent and kissed her forehead, and tingles shot through her. She clung to his jacket. Was this the feeling that made women forsake their freedoms and bind themselves to a man? Was it for this overwhelming sense of security, protection, and...something else she couldn't quite put her finger on...that they lost themselves? He stared down at her, then reached up and brushed his finger down her cheek.

"No matter what happens, I'll be here for you." He leaned a bit closer. "If you wish it."

In that moment, she could no longer think of such women as ninnies. For who could blame them? To be bound to a man such as this surely meant refuge and stability. A chance to be known—and accepted?—for herself. Just when she thought this feeling would sweep her away, he stepped back.

The warmth of him slipped away, and a startling ache settled on her. She let him lead her back through the doors. Once she stepped inside, however, whatever magic had sparked between them disappeared as quickly as a fabled nymph. The hotel lobby bustled with activity as patrons' curiosity brought them downstairs. Her father and several other men loitered around the reception desk, where they waited for news.

"Heading north…"

"Hull Island Lifesavers are reporting another hit. Don't think it had cargo."

Their voices mingled in snippets of partial sentences and worried tones. It took her a moment of listening at the fringes to fully piece together the news they'd gathered.

A tropical cyclone had neared the east coast, dipping in close enough to shore to sweep the land with the edges of its destruction. Thankfully, from what they had been able to ascertain, the worst of it had remained out in the ocean. Boston had not suffered a direct hit.

Faith thought about the mess outside and wondered how much worse it would have been if they had seen more of the storm than just the outer edge. It was a question she was glad to leave rhetorical.

Nolan tucked her fingers into the crook of his arm as they listened to the men chatter. A couple of the fellows sent curious glances her way, but Nolan simply patted her hand. The mere fact that he understood her need to remain and did not ask her to find a place at the hearth where all the other ladies had gathered further widened a crack in her heart. One that was slowly letting him in.

If she were honest, that little fissure had led to her rather foul mood at the Pink Parrot. She'd not cared for the way that woman had draped herself on Nolan. The very thought set her teeth on edge. Not that she had any right to be angry. She had no claim on him.

Unless she wanted it.

Faith pushed the thought away, more concerned with the irrational jealousy that had overcome her. She'd always rolled her eyes at the way that ladies preened over men at balls, then preceded to verbally attack one another with thinly veiled insults for doing exactly as they themselves had done. She'd always judged such jealousy as unbecoming. And now she had done the same.

She glanced at Nolan, who was intently listening to the conversations she should be paying attention to. To his credit, though he'd stared at the seductive woman, he'd not truly done so with the lecherousness she'd accused him of. Nor had he gazed upon that woman with the appreciation she'd seen in his eyes when she'd entered the lobby in her best walking gown.

A sensation as strange and annoying as her jealousy rose up from her core. What was it? Satisfaction? She'd enjoyed seeing him look at her that way. She'd enjoyed being in his arms. The thoughts swirled through her head and made her chest tighten.

Enough with such foolishness! Shame rose to blanket the other feelings she wasn't yet ready to deal with. She should be thinking about Mercy. Worrying about whether Mercy had been harmed in this storm and figuring out a way to find her.

Not standing here woolgathering about a man when important matters were at hand!

Her emotions firmly in check, Faith turned her attention to the men. Animated, they spouted speculations about what damage had been done and which businesses would be affected. It was a comfort to be standing at Nolan's side, waiting to hear how the rest of Boston had fared.

"Damage along the wharf…"

"A schooner smashed into Shag Rocks," one man said.

"The Hull Lifesavers saw it go down," another replied, "but they couldn't reach it."

The voices increased as the men discussed bits of information. Her father emerged from the crowd, using the cane he so despised. From the determined look on his face, she guessed he'd heard something important. His gaze lingered on where she still clung to Nolan's arm, but not a trace of disapproval swept over his features.

"I've been gathering information from as many places as I can," Daddy said, drawing close to be heard over the din of other hotel guests engaged in their own conversations. "One fellow's briny story may be of some use." He nodded toward a gentleman in a gray suit who stood with his arm propped on the reception desk. "That's Mr. Carron. He manages a shipping company. His men had an interesting report." He looked at Faith.

She clutched the fabric around her middle.

Daddy scratched at his beard. "One of his sailors saw two men fighting at the dock on the portside of their steamer three nights ago." Daddy drew closer, lowering his voice despite the clamor of the men around them. "He paused to watch them, and then he said something very strange happened. Another man approached and picked up something from the shadows. It wasn't until the man crossed under a lamppost that the sailor noticed it was the shape of a woman. Another woman joined him, and the three hurried away from the fighting men. They were seen going up the plank to a schooner not far away."

Faith put her hand to her galloping heart. "Do they know which one?"

Daddy shook his head. "Mr. Carron didn't know. The sailors didn't seem to care to find out such information as they were making"—he glanced at Faith and grimaced as though loathing to say the words—"uh...jests."

Nolan ran a hand through his hair, disheveling it. "How would we know if that woman was Mercy?"

"We wouldn't." He lifted his shoulders. "But given the information Faith uncovered, it could be worth inquiring about."

Faith grabbed Daddy's arm. "It's possible the two fighting men could have been the same two Irish men Amanda saw."

Daddy nodded along as she spoke, then turned to Nolan. "This is where your family connections come in, my boy."

Nolan seemed to pale. "It is, sir?"

"We'll need to speak with your uncle. Perhaps there's some kind of passenger records, or at least some information on the ships in harbor that night."

Nolan shifted his feet. "All of this assuming, of course, that was the same two Irishmen, and those two men had Mercy." He glanced at Faith. "What if it wasn't her?"

Faith's fingers went cold as the rest of Daddy's statement took hold. "Wait. You said she went on a schooner?"

Daddy nodded.

Catching her breath, she scanned the faces of the men until the one whose voice matched the words thrumming in her memory surfaced. Ignoring a startled statement from Nolan, Faith pushed her way through the gentlemen, making them hurriedly bow out of her way.

She rushed up to a portly man in a russet suit. "Excuse me, sir. Did I hear you say something about a schooner hitting rocks?"

The man nodded solemnly. "She hit on the Shag Rocks. Split the hull. Pieces of it are..." He paused, then, as though remembering he was addressing a lady, and his cheeks reddened. "Forgive me, miss. That was more detail than necessary."

"I'd prefer more, if you have it."

"Pardon?" He tilted his head, regarding her curiously.

Daddy introduced himself, shaking the man's hand. The fellow, who introduced himself as Mr. Loden, glanced at Faith again before relaying the information to her father.

"Keeper Bates saw the distress signal. Humane Society would have sent out a lifeboat, but the waves were fierce. They won't be able to go until morning. Last I heard, debris is washing up all over Brewster."

She'd never been more thankful to have Nolan gripping her arm as her knees trembled. Could Mercy have been on that schooner? There had to be dozens of them in the harbor.

One thing was certain. Any boat out on the water in the storm couldn't have fared well.

Nineteen

A piercing noise poked holes in the peaceful darkness surrounding Mercy's consciousness. What was that? Squawking? Mercy groaned as the sound plucked at her senses and beckoned her to shake off the blanket of sleep. She resisted. Tired. So very tired. She drew in a long breath and tasted salt. Where was she? Memories flooded back.

The ship. The storm.

Her eyes shot open. Above her, a slate sky no longer hurled rain. Instead, large white birds dipped down toward a rocky beach, their loud calls fraying her nerves. She turned and found the safety dinghy empty save for her own sodden body. With sore arms, she raised herself up. Ignoring the pain in her shoulder, she got into a sitting position. She'd washed aground on a rocky shore, but it was too dark to see into the distance much farther than a few feet. What time was it?

Blinking back the fog in her brain, she stumbled out of the small vessel. Where was Hezzie?

Waves lapped at her legs. The beach was littered with broken boards, debris she couldn't identify, and....

Oh! Was that a person?

She stumbled forward on wobbly legs. Wind tugged at her

damp skirts, giving her a chill despite the humid air. The trek took more effort than she would have suspected. With each step the seaweed-littered rocks greedily tore at her bare feet as though seeking to deny her forward progress.

Finally, she reached the motionless form of a dark haired man. He laid face down, his shirt flapping in the breeze. Dread squeezed at her stomach, coiling around in the empty confines and churning up bile. She leaned over him, struggling to see in the darkness.

She placed a hand on his back to rouse him, only to find his cold body lifeless. She cried out and turned her eyes to the heavens.

It took several deep breaths before she could rise. Clutching the fabric around her waist, Mercy turned back toward the dinghy, dread increasing her pulse and further clearing her mind. *Where is Hezzie?*

The thought that the woman had tumbled out into the ocean while Mercy had lost her senses had panic rising. She returned to the dinghy and peered down the other end of the beach. No other bodies that she could see. Only broken barrels, bleached wood, and globs of seaweed revealed themselves in the first tinges of light after the stormy night. Where were the others?

Mercy rounded the dinghy, then took another few paces up the beach. The terrifying sound of the waves crashing upon rocks was the only answer to her calls.

She was alone, all alone.

"Hezzie!" She hurried forward, desperation forcing its way through her exhausted frame. "Hezzie!" She shouted. "Jed!"

The wind tugged at her cries and cast them into the crash of the waves.

No response.

Mercy trudged farther down the beach. The shoreline stretched ahead of her, a narrow bit of sandy land flanked by scraggly trees. Not a person in sight. Not even the—

Her toe bumped into something and she recoiled. The soulless eyes of a drowned sailor stared up at her. Mercy screamed and jumped back, placing a hand to her heart.

Lord! Why have you forsaken me?

Drawing a long breath to calm her rattled nerves, she offered up a quick prayer for the man to have entered heaven's gates and then hurried past. What if she was the only one who had survived?

No, it couldn't be. She shouldn't think such horrible thoughts.

Barrels and other items bobbed along the shoreline as the waves battered them around like a cat with a mouse. Mercy plodded on. Hope insisted she would soon find help, even if the shadows and the dead seemed to tell her otherwise.

Any moment now, she would find Hezzie. She'd be frightened, but alive.

And Jed. What had happened to him after he'd put them in the dinghy? She couldn't stand to think that the man who'd fearlessly jumped into the ocean to save her had been taken into its heartless depths.

What if she found his lifeless form on the shore? Tears blurred her vision as she plopped one foot in front of the other, trying to make her way without tripping.

Lord, what have You done? Will You hear none of my prayers?

No answer came, though she hadn't expected one. She'd

once felt His hand on her heart, His gentle spirit speaking into her. But as she'd grown older, that voice had faded. Or she'd stopped noticing it. Now she wondered if He had left her to untangle her messes on her own. Not that she deserved any less. As Mama always said, *if you the one making the mess, then you best be the one cleaning it.*

A shout came from somewhere ahead.

Fear and relief surged with such power, her knees weakened, but she gathered herself with a quick intake of salty air. Mercy hurried along the narrow beach, tripping in her haste. Thankfully, she kept her footing and rounded the end of what must be a small island or peninsula.

Voices!

Mercy gathered what remained of her tattered skirt and half-ran, half-stumbled toward the sound, shouting incoherently.

The form of three shadows took shape, lifting something from the ground. One shouted at the other in Spanish. Mercy hurried forward, her raw throat forcing out a desperate call that scarcely made it to her own ears.

One of the men turned to her. She strained her eyes in the dawning light. Jed!

He waved his arm and started to run toward her. Her elation at seeing him alive stripped away what remained of her sense of propriety, and when she met him she launched herself into his arms.

"*Gracias a Dios!*" He drew her close only for an instant before pushing her back to arm's length and sweeping his gaze down her form. "Are you injured?"

Mercy shook her head. "No. You?"

"No. I swam to shore."

Tears spilled down her cheeks. "Your mother. I...I cannot..."

"She's here." He nodded toward the shadowy forms. One of them cradled what looked like a child in his massive arms.

Mercy's heart wrenched, and she put her fist to her mouth. "I should've taken better care of her. I—"

"Easy, now." His hand tightened on her shoulder. "Mamá is alive."

Relief swept through her, and her knees weakened. Jed kept a tight grip on her arm.

Mercy blinked at him, relief flooding through her heart. "Who else have you found? How many sailors were on board? Couldn't they swim as you did? How many survived?"

Jed slowly shook his head at her questions, his sodden dark locks sweeping his cheeks. He nodded back toward the two sailors and his mother. "I don't know. Many of the men stayed with the ship. The Captain..." He cleared his throat. "The Captain pushed me into the last dinghy and demanded I row for shore and get out of their way. After a time, it grew too dark and the rain to strong. I lost sight of the ship. My dinghy eventually filled with water and sank, but by then the rain had stopped and I could see land. I swam the rest of the way."

Guilt laced his tone, but she couldn't understand why. Did he think he should have stayed with the sailors? What help could he have been?

Mercy wrapped her arms around herself. "I found two sailors on the other side of the beach. They didn't survive." She looked out toward the ocean, a great expanse of ink. How many more of the lively men on the ship had gone down with it, their bodies destined to wash up on the shore or be forever lost?

Jed wrapped his arm around her shoulders as the other two men approached. He spoke to them in Spanish. After a moment of discussion, Mercy let him guide her away from the water's edge, too thankful to be alive to ask any more questions.

Before long, Jed had his mother spread out on a bit of torn sail, and Mercy settled on a weathered log. The clouds had broken, but the scant light of the dreary sunrise could not adequately push back the night's mire. She watched Hezzie's side rise and fall, wondering how much the ordeal had taken out of the woman. It was a wonder it hadn't taken everything from her.

Hezzie was close to her Maker, that was for certain. Mercy should be grateful she'd found herself in the same boat with someone whose prayers probably received a high priority. It was likely the only thing that had kept them alive.

Had Hezzie truly memorized all four gospels? What sort of memory—or dedication—did such a task take? She certainly had a faith unlike any Mercy had ever seen before. Her thoughts bounced randomly from Hezzie to home to the warmth of Jed's arms. Anything to keep her mind occupied.

The hem of the borrowed dress was little more than rags, revealing her calves and ankles to the pink dawn. Mama would be horrified to know men could see her legs exposed.

Mercy listened as the men talked in a language she couldn't understand. But she didn't really need to know the words to know they must be speaking of lost friends, a sunken ship, and plans to survive. Not a one of them cared about her ankles in the light of such circumstances.

What must her parents think now? She placed her chin on her knees. If her heart had nearly burst from worry over people she'd only just met, what manner of pain had Mercy put her family through? Tears coursed through the salt on her cheeks, and she let them fall.

A movement at her side startled her. "Oh! Hezzie You're awake." She swiped the tears away.

The old woman chuckled and settled herself next to Mercy. "So I am."

"Are you well?"

"Of course I am, girl. Here I sit, don't I?"

The smile in the woman's voice was baffling. How could she think to laugh at such a time as this? After a moment, Hezzie leaned close and took Mercy's hand in her weathered one.

"What happened to you, Hezzie? You weren't in the dinghy with me. I'd feared the worst."

"Not sure, child. I remember cold water, and at some point floating. Next thing I knew, I woke up next to you, and now here I am."

"Yes, here we sit," Mercy said, shaking her head. "After a terrible shipwreck others didn't survive." The three passengers taken on board had survived when experienced sailors had not. Why had God let the men of the sea perish in it?

"You know," Hezzie said, "We never know what's going to happen with our lives, or how our end will come. What we think oughtta happen with our days isn't usually what God has planned. But we can't be mad at Him for carrying out the day He'd ordained since the start of time just 'cause it ain't the day our mortal minds expected."

Mercy turned to look at the woman's profile, astonished. She really believed that, didn't she?

To Mercy, the words grated. Sure, she was glad Hezzie could accept such disasters, she really was. It probably made circumstances much easier to bear. But Mercy couldn't do the same. Too much had been lost. Too much pain lodged in her heart for her to laugh in the face of disaster. She remained silent for fear any words she spoke would disrespect her elder.

The men bustled around behind them, doing what, she wasn't certain. Mercy should've helped, but she couldn't seem to raise the gumption or energy to do anything more than stare out into the ocean that separated her from home and all she'd ever known—and loathe it.

"Tell me, child. Are you a Christ-follower?"

What kind of question was that? Mercy shot a sideways glance at Hezzie, whose conversational tone seemed no more out of sorts than if they were sitting on a quiet garden bench having a friendly discussion.

Hezzie waited patiently on a reply.

Finally, Mercy sighed. "I accepted the gift of salvation when I was twelve. After that, I tried everything I could to always be the good daughter, to take care of my sisters, and to help my mother. I tried to be what God wanted me to be."

Where had that come from? A simple *yes* would have been plenty. What was it about this woman that made Mercy divulge more than necessary? Perhaps it arose from exhaustion. She was too out of sorts for unnecessary discussions.

"And what was it that God wanted you to be?"

"I don't know." Mercy curled her toes, trying to remember all the sermons she'd heard over the years. "Obedient?"

"Hmm." Hezzie bobbed her head, her gray-streaked hair matted above her ear. "Is that how you ended up in Boston?"

Mercy ground her teeth. Hezzie's tone held no judgment, but she felt it all the same. No, she'd not been obedient in any sense when she'd run from home to chase a wild dream in Boston. Perhaps all that happened was her punishment for disobeying what she knew her parents wanted. Had she even asked God what He wanted? Mercy picked up a broken shell and rubbed it between her fingers, then flung it out into the churning ocean.

"No." She splayed her fingers, hunting for another shell. "No, I wasn't obedient to anyone when I left. I suppose that's why I'm in a mess."

Hezzie shrugged. "Maybe so."

So much for words of encouragement.

"God sent a storm for Jonah, too, when he was goin' the wrong way."

Mercy ground her teeth, the sudden anger burning within her pushing words out of her mouth. "So I'm to be miserable like Jonah, then? Is that it? Just because I wanted, for once, to do what *I* wanted to do and not what everyone else told me to?"

Hezzie was quiet for a time, the only sounds the fervent talk of the surviving sailors and the rhythmic crash of the waves.

Mercy fought back tears. She didn't want to discuss this. Didn't want to try to decipher the reasons for her choices or what she was running from. Fortunately, Hezzie said no more.

When Hezzie spoke again a few moments later, her words were soft. "What did you follow that brought you to Boston?"

"What?" They'd been quiet for so long that Mercy thought Hezzie had given up on conversation. She rubbed her temples. "What did I follow?"

"Was it God, your own desires, someone's advice...?"

Mercy turned away. "Can we talk about this another time?"

"I'm afraid not." Hezzie stretched her feet out next to Mercy's, then reached down and unlaced her shoes. She pulled them off, dumping water out of each before setting them by her side. "God's telling me that if you don't deal with this now when that strong will of yours is malleable, then it'll soon harden to the point that it'll take breaking before you'll listen."

Mercy stared at Hezzie in the paltry light. "You're telling me that God told you all that?" She scoffed. "You can't be serious."

"He tells me many things."

Mercy narrowed her eyes, something deep within her longing to know what secret Hezzie had for such clear communication. "How?"

"Spend time seeking Him. You'll start to notice His voice more as you read His word. It's still and quiet, and often comes by way of verses I've learned."

Mercy sat back on her hands. Maybe Hezzie was mad, then. The Bible certainly didn't have any verses about Mercy's stubbornness.

"But there are times," Hezzie continued, unperturbed by Mercy's sour mood, "times when it's something different. They ain't so much words I can hear, really, but instead just…something I know all at once." She leaned against Mercy's shoulder. "This is one of those times."

Mercy sighed. "Then what is it He wants from me? Because He hasn't told me anything."

"He hasn't?"

"No." She rubbed rough grains of sand between her fingers. "I've read the Bible. I've heard plenty of sermons. He's never given me any insight like that. No, all He's given me is confinement to a plantation with nothing but monotony and a meaningless life ahead of me."

"And how do you feel about that?"

Emotion surged, burning deep from her center and radiating out through her arms. It had been there for some time, but she'd kept it tamped down. It surfaced now, refusing to be contained. She clenched her hands. "I'm angry."

"I know."

She drew in a breath and held it, then released it slowly. "I'm angry at my parents for keeping me from leaving home. I'm angry at the paper for how they treated me. I'm disgusted at the world for how they degrade people based on their physical appearance." The words gained momentum, bubbling up from deep within, from places she didn't know had festered. Her voice gained strength. "I'm angry at my friend Faith for getting to do all the things I've always wanted when I can't. For being born *white*, and for that giving her the keys to the world."

Hezzie squeezed the hand she still held. "Who else?"

Tears burned again, and Mercy angrily swiped them away. "Myself."

"Why?"

"Because I was so foolish. Because I didn't know anything and I got myself into a terrible mess."

"And?"

Mercy squirmed. Who else was there to be upset at? Her heart pinched, and she knew the answer. "God."

Hezzie nodded. "You're angry with Him because He did things according to His plans and not yours."

Mercy swallowed hard, the pinching deep within her increasing. She pulled her hand away from Hezzie and rubbed at her heart, but the pinching didn't go away.

"So again I ask you, are you a Jesus follower? Or are you a child who's accepted her gift of salvation but refused the gift of Him being your master?"

The words grated across her. "Mama says we no longer have masters. We're free."

"Ah, but a Christ-follower has a Master. No matter if she be a queen or a slip of a girl washed up on a tiny island."

Mercy crossed her legs beneath her, feeling like a child again. "But why? He made me, right?" She barely waited for Hezzie's nod. "So why make me with desires to be more than what everyone says I should be? Why fill me with dreams I can't have?"

"Can't you? Have you given those dreams back to Him, and let Him to do with them as He sees fit?"

Mercy wrapped her arms around her knees again. That wasn't what she wanted. She wanted her dreams to be hers. She wanted to do something important. Be somebody important. She wanted to achieve things on her own and receive respect from the people around her.

She knew she should give her desires over to Him, but honestly, she didn't want to. What if He wanted her to do something she didn't want to do? What if His plan for her was to do nothing more than be another farm wife at Ironwood? A nobody who spent her days doing nothing more than hoeing vegetables and cleaning up after a family. Was it so wrong to want more than that?

"I wonder, Mercy," Hezzie said softly, "If instead of giving the desires of your heart to the One who made you, you instead forged ahead with what you wanted and then got angry when the God of the universe didn't follow along with your plans."

The words seared deep into her heart. That was precisely what she'd done.

Mercy hung her head. "Why is it so hard?"

"Life was never meant to be easy." Hezzie rubbed Mercy's shoulder. "The Book always says *when* troubles come, *when* the waters rise, and *when* the drought arrives. It never says *if*. There will be hardships. Our faith is refined in what we do through the hard times. And it's polished when we faithfully obey each step of the way, no matter what task He asks of us, whether great or humble."

"But I wanted to do something more." Her voice cracked.

"Why? For your glory, or for His?"

She lowered her head. She'd wanted to be somebody. For the world to notice her. All at the sake of those who loved her most.

Forgive me, Lord. You alone deserve the glory.

"He's more interested in your heart. He's not goin' to give you something you desire if He knows it'll take you further from Him. Don't fight against Him on that. Otherwise, you'll look up and realize that maybe you got what you wanted, but you lost what was important along the way."

Tears leaked from her eyes and mingled with the salt and sand caked on her skin.

"I'm not saying you have these desires and will never get to use them," Hezzie said. "What I'm sayin' is that you need to remember that the One who gave them to you has His own plans for them. Even if they aren't what you thought."

"But what if all I ever get to do are the mundane tasks of an ordinary life?"

Hezzie studied her a moment. "What's ordinary?"

She shrugged. "You know. Taking care of a home and a family. Doing nothing more than cleaning up for and taking care of other people."

Hezzie grinned. "Sounds wonderful."

Mercy looked away. Maybe for Hezzie. But would it ever be enough for her? Or would she always long for something more? For a freedom she would never find?

"The kingdom of heaven is so often opposite of what people think. Jesus himself said He came not to be served but to serve. Can you imagine that? The God of all creation, who deserves to have all the glory with all of mankind serving at His feet, served His creation instead."

Mercy squirmed.

"Be careful about pride that says you're too important for what you think are ordinary tasks. Any task you're given is important to Him. And what's important to Him should be important to you."

Mercy nodded slowly. "I understand."

"I hope you'll think hard on it. God's got some important tasks for you. Maybe not what you expect. But if you'll give your dreams to Him, if you'll pour yourself out in each thing He gives you, then you'll serve your Master well. He's a good King and a good Father. He won't desert you."

Even through all her stubbornness, God hadn't ignored her prayers. He'd used Jed to save her from men who meant her harm. He hadn't let her drown when she went overboard, and He'd miraculously kept her alive even when she must have fainted in a tiny boat in the middle of the ocean. Her surviving when sailors hadn't was nothing short of a miracle.

Through each disaster, God had orchestrated circumstances that allowed her to be rescued. Despite all she'd done, He had always been faithful.

Mercy dabbed at the corners of her eyes. "Yes, ma'am. I know."

"Good." Hezzie wrapped an arm around her and gave her a squeeze. "Now that we've gotten that out of the way, how 'bout we get on with the day He gave us?"

"What?"

Hezzie grinned. "Just what I said." She gestured above. "Let's admire the beauty of the sunrise." She gave Mercy a good pat. "And give Him thanks for the miracle that we're still alive."

Twenty

Faith paced the floor of the lobby, waiting to hear more information on the shipwreck. An entire day of waiting in this hotel while men cleared the roads had her nerves in a knot. What if Mercy had been on a boat that had wrecked? What if even now she was washed ashore, alone and barely alive, waiting for rescue? Waiting while Faith was stuck in this hotel?

Faith worked the gloves on her fingers, pacing in front of one of the hotel's two lobby fireplaces. The storm had brought with it a cooler temperature, though she suspected the maids had lit the fireplaces more for the comfort of a cheery hearth than warmth. Men gathered around the other hearth, their voices too jovial for the pall that hung over her heart. Most of the women had retired for the evening, but she didn't want to be in her room if any news finally came.

The thump of Daddy's cane drew her attention. When he reached her, she placed a kiss on his cheek. "Any more news?"

"We likely won't hear anything more until morning. Why don't you get some rest?"

"I'd rather have company."

He considered her a moment then gestured for her to sit. "While we wait, I wonder if I could broach something with you.

I've been wanting to discuss it, though you may find the topic unpleasant."

Faith squirmed. "Like what?"

He was quiet for so long, she wondered if he had changed his mind. Finally, he rubbed the top of his cane and kept his gaze on the empty hearth. "I've been thinking over something, and I cannot figure out where I failed you so completely." The lines around his eyes crinkled as he narrowed them.

"What are you talking about? You haven't failed me in any way."

He straightened and turned to face her. "At first, I thought that, as an independent lady, you turned away suitors because they were not complements to your intellect and uniqueness. But you also seem to be striving to drive away Mr. Watson." Contemplation lined his forehead. "Even though at times you also seem taken with him."

Heat crept up her neck that had nothing to do with the flickering fire. She had been trying to drive Nolan away. It had seemed to be for the best. But now something had...shifted. Thoughts of his arms around her this morning on the street brought the flame in her neck up to blossom on her cheeks. She took a moment, drawing her lower lip through her teeth. "Mr. Watson is admittedly more than I expected him to be. He's kind, thoughtful, and it takes quite a bit to rile him."

"Yet you still try," Daddy said with a chuckle.

"I don't really *try*," Faith said, crossing her arms across her churning middle. "It just happens. I ruffle people."

He put a hand on her shoulder. "There's more to this." His gaze sharpened. "I need to know why you have such a distaste for men."

Faith looked into her father's eyes, a man who had showed her nothing but the deepest affections and care. "I..." She closed her eyes, took a deep breath, and opened them again. He deserved to know, didn't he? "I don't want to marry and become property."

The perplexed look in his eyes, followed by the tightening grip on her shoulder, made her wish she'd kept such a statement to herself. It wasn't that she applied such thoughts to him and Mother. She didn't think he'd made her mother property. But the men of her generation were different. They were frightened by the changes women wanted to make and were coming up with wild ideas about how to keep women *properly at home.*

"Has a man ever hurt you?" His grip tightened on her shoulder.

It took a moment, and then understanding dawned. "No, Daddy." She shifted. "I've not been afflicted in that manner."

Relief washed across him, and he hung his head. "Thank the Lord."

"When I was young, Mother taught me to protect myself from the boys." She straightened her shoulders, after his grip released. "They hated that I was smarter than they, and I quickly learned the thing they hated was precisely the weapon to use against their taunts and cruel words."

"Are you sure that's what your mother meant?"

What else could she have meant? "Men of my generation don't understand me. They can't see why I like the things a lady ought not, and they can't fathom that I want to do more with my life than cater to their every whim."

The muscle in his jaw ticked, much in the same way Nolan's always did. Had she annoyed him? "Is that the way you think I treat your mother?"

"Of course not. You and Mother have a wonderful relationship." She fiddled with her gloves. "It's just, well, I don't expect that to happen for me. I'm not like Mother. I lack her grace, poise, and quiet disposition. I'm quite the opposite, in fact, which is why I tend to rile people. Especially gentlemen."

Daddy's frown deepened.

"Please don't think you've failed me by allowing me to read and think. I'm content to remain unmarried and have the freedom of choice. And I won't be a burden, I promise. I will work and earn my own way."

Her plans for a townhome and living with Mercy seemed so far away now. How had she managed to feel so much older in such a short period of time?

Daddy rubbed his temples. "I've failed rather resoundingly if you equate marriage to slavery."

Daddy's words hung on the air, tangling with the hum of nearby conversations. She shook her head, and a stray curl loosened from the tight knot at her nape. "I never said that."

"Perhaps not in such concise words, but you said it all the same. It isn't any wonder, then, that Nolan is flustered."

She didn't mean to fluster him. He seemed a good man, and her heart undeniably had softened toward him. But he still clung to archaic thinking that wasn't in keeping with the way the times were changing. Remembering that made her try to refocus. "It isn't my intention to annoy him, Daddy."

She brushed away thoughts of the tenderness he'd shown her and the reaction she'd had to it. It had been a mistake. She couldn't let herself be swept away by absurd emotions.

"Oh, but I think it's precisely your intention." Daddy looked at her in that way he had, the look he always used when he knew whatever she'd been trying to hide. "Somehow, you think that if you marry, then you won't have any freedom. For reasons I cannot fathom, you think a husband will rule over you like a lord, and you won't get to do any of the things you enjoy. Because of that, you've made yourself most unpleasant to any gentleman who comes around as a way of either defending yourself from what you perceive will be eventual rejection, or, in the absence of that, eventual slavery."

Her pulse quickened. She hadn't made herself unpleasant on purpose. People had just always found her to be that way. Eventually, she'd accepted it and stopped trying to be someone she wasn't.

Right?

But that's not what Daddy thought. And Daddy knew her like nobody else in the world.

Could he be right?

Had her attempts to maintain an appearance of confidence to hide her insecurities turned into a façade that eventually made her into exactly the termagant they'd claimed her to be? Had she attempted to become someone else in order to have the freedom to be herself? Faith rubbed her temples. What a cruel irony. Who she tried to be, who she wanted to be, and who she was jumbled together in a mass of confusion. Daddy's words had broken something open, an inner weakness she'd tried to hide.

Daddy continued to look at her, forcing her to think through her actions. Had she at some point stopped trying to just be herself and instead begun to purposely sabotage any relationship she might have? Why? Was he right? Was she trying to avoid rejection by telling herself she was actually seeking freedom?

"I wish you'd told me about any young men who were unkind to you," Daddy finally said. "I would have dealt with them."

Faith brushed the free curl away from her eyes, alarmed to find wetness there.

"But you have to understand that a good husband isn't going to treat you like foolish boys from your girlhood. A good husband will give himself up for you, as Christ did for the church, and will protect and honor you."

Hadn't Mercy said something similar? That day at the picnic seemed so long ago.

Speaking of a husband brought Nolan's face to mind. He would make a fortunate lady a good husband someday. A lady who wanted to spend her days tending hearth and home. A lady who didn't say and do things a lady ought not. A lady not so…peculiar.

Faith swallowed hard and lowered her gaze to her lap. Daddy was wrong. Even if Nolan cared for her now, eventually he *would* tire of her. They were too different. She too opinionated. It would be wrong to pin a poor fellow down to a union he would soon grow weary of. Nolan was too good of a man for that.

Still, despite the sound logic, the idea brought a sadness she couldn't dispel. She drew a long breath and released it slowly. "Mr. Watson will make a good business partner for you, Daddy. He's genuine and honest. I believe he'll do well managing your offices in Memphis."

Daddy chuckled. "I thought the same."

Yes, Nolan was a good man. And he deserved a lady who would appreciate all he meant to offer her.

Faith lowered her gaze, hoping Daddy wouldn't notice the troublesome wetness that kept stinging her eyes.

Unfortunately, that lady would never be her.

Nolan stared into the amber liquid in his glass, still not taking a sip. He'd purchased the drink thinking it might relax the tension in his gut but could not bring himself to try it. Brandy could relax a man, he'd heard, but it could also make men do strange things. Perhaps one day he might see how the liquid affected him, but this day, like the few others he'd thought to give it a try, wouldn't be it.

He cut another glance to where Faith and Mr. Harper were engaged in a tense conversation. How had he found himself in this situation? He should be back in Memphis, quietly tending the books and securing lucrative shipping ventures. Instead, he'd been put through a strange series of circumstances that left him feeling frustrated and out of sorts. This was not the job he'd been hired on to do, and he felt out of his depth.

He settled his focus on the carpeting beneath his feet. He should return to his room, but with the commotion going on, he'd instead chosen the useless position of sitting in the corner of the hotel lobby. He should be listening to the other men and their discussions of the storm, but he wearied of the chatter. He could join his employer but sensed he would not be welcome.

So here he sat, neither away from nor a part of anything, trying to untangle unfamiliar emotions that couldn't be logically defined.

He'd not felt this unsure of himself since he'd gone out on his own as a boy of sixteen. Since that time he'd carefully crafted his reputation and had worked hard to gain positions where he could better himself. Managing the Memphis offices for Mr. Harper had made him feel as if he'd finally worked his way into the man he'd wanted to become—a confident man with a knack for business and a promising future.

He'd never expected the looming prospect of facing his uncle, chasing down a missing girl, or unraveling complicated thoughts about an equally complicated woman to be a part of that future. Where did he stand with her? One moment Miss Harper seemed to loathe him, and the next one could almost say she was taken with him. This morning she'd felt natural in his arms, as though she belonged there. Later, she'd stayed at his side as though something solid had formed between them.

But as suddenly as her affections had shifted in his favor, they had turned cold once more. He couldn't make sense of any of it, and the feeling rattled him.

Nolan cast another furtive glance toward the Harpers. The vulnerable look on Faith's face had his chest tightening. He turned away. What was this welling feeling of protectiveness? There was no sense denying he'd developed an affection for the lady that went far deeper than what he'd first proclaimed at the picnic.

That had been interest. And if he were honest, that interest had been rooted in her beauty and her family. Since getting to know her, it had matured into a genuine concern for her well-being, a desire to shield her from any pain, and an appreciation for her wit and spark of life.

And for that, he was in Boston, hoping to find a girl he could only pray wasn't already dead. What would he do with Faith then?

The answer, of course, was simple. Nothing. He would do nothing with her because she wasn't his to console.

Across the lobby, she stared into the fire, tension evident in her shoulders. She drew a long breath, then rose, planted a kiss on her father's cheek, and walked away. Nolan watched her traipse the lobby floor with downcast eyes, and followed her progress up the stairs until she disappeared from his sight.

When his gaze returned to the lobby, Mr. Harper caught Nolan's eye. Nolan nodded to his employer. With the man's gesture, he rose from his seat, left the untouched brandy on a marble side table, and made his way toward the hearth.

Nolan lowered himself into a chair still warm from Faith's body.

Mr. Harper looked back toward the staircase. "She's worried about many things."

Understandable. He was rather worried himself. Nolan laced his fingers. "Sir, what will we do if we find Mercy and...?" He let the sentence trail off, unsure how to properly pose such an indelicate topic.

It took a moment for Mr. Harper to answer. "I'm praying we find her well and whole. Anything else and, well"—he wagged his head—"we'll need plenty of grace to make it through the days ahead."

Nolan nodded.

Suddenly, Mr. Harper reached over and clasped him on the

shoulder. "I've grown rather fond of you, Nolan."

He couldn't help but smile. The man's approval meant more than he cared to admit. "Thank you, sir. I feel the same."

Tension eased from him. Now was a good time to push aside the worries they could do nothing about and focus on things they could control. "Would you like to discuss the purchases I suggested? We haven't had much time to tend to company business, but now seems a good time."

"All things we can address when we return home."

Nolan shifted. "But was not the primary reason for me accompanying you on personal travels so that we could also discuss business that needs attention?"

"Business can wait. The current matters are more pressing."

Nolan remained silent. Mr. Harper was right, of course, but Nolan could hardly be of much use with the current problems.

"Besides…" Mr. Harper studied him. "You know that business was not the primary reason I asked you along."

Right. Family connections. If his relationship with Arnold Watson could even be called such. "I could have sent a letter of introduction to my uncle." It certainly would have been easier. With the storm, they'd not yet been to see the man and Nolan was glad of it.

Mr. Harper's steady gaze held an intensity that Nolan wished to squirm out from under. "I know." He waited as though expecting Nolan to fit the pieces together on his own.

They both knew what he meant. Mr. Harper had also invited Nolan along to escort Faith when his knee bothered him, and to give Nolan the opportunity to spend time with her and further their relationship.

The memory of her in his arms that morning brought a

smile to the corners of his mouth he couldn't hide. It had felt good to hold her, to protect and comfort her.

"Faith has always been her own person," Mr. Harper said, breaking into Nolan's thoughts. "I'll not force her to do anything against her wishes."

The words dashed all pleasant sensations away. What was the man saying?

He reached up and patted Nolan's shoulder. "I must admit, I'd hoped things would be easier."

A heavy feeling dropped into Nolan's stomach. What had Faith and Mr. Harper been talking about earlier? Him?

"I still believe you two could make a good match," Mr. Harper continued, confirming Nolan's thoughts that Faith's conversation with her father had been about him, and it hadn't been in his favor. "But she will need a man with plenty of patience."

Patience. Something he'd once thought he was good at.

Mr. Harper nodded toward the stairs. "I'm going to attempt to find some sleep." He slowly rose, then hesitated. "If I know my daughter well, she's not yet readied herself for the night. She always reads for a time between retiring and preparing for bed. Perhaps a talk would help both of you."

Mr. Harper turned toward the stairs, then turned back and lowered his eyebrows. "In the hall, of course. I'll just be a couple of doors down, should you need me." Then with a tired smile he turned and started for the stairs.

Nolan sat for several moments after Mr. Harper departed, waffling. Finally, he stood, squared his shoulders with resolve, and made a decision. He would not be the timid boy he'd once been. That past was behind him. He held Miss Harper in affection, and therefore the next step was to properly ask her to court.

He topped the stairs, took long strides down the hall, and rapped lightly on room twelve before he could change his mind. Silence followed.

Perhaps she'd already gone to bed. That was probably for the best. They were both tired. This likely wasn't the best time for delicate conversations about what was happening between them. He turned to retire to his own room, where, hopefully, sleep would offer the rest the drink had not.

The door swung open. "Nolan?"

Faith stepped into the hallway, her eyes wide. As her father had predicted, she had not yet begun her nightly preparations for bed. She folded her hands in front of her gown. "You have news?"

News? Oh, right. The shipwreck. "No. We won't hear more until morning."

She stared at him.

He stepped closer and lowered his voice. "I'd like to have a discussion with you, if you don't mind."

She gestured toward her open door. "Very well."

"Here is fine."

Her eyes widened slightly as though she had not recognized the nature of her offer, then her cheeks brightened to a warm pink. "Of course." She blew out a breath. "I would have left the door open."

Her awkward gestures made him smile. It pleased him to see her flustered. Not because she was uncomfortable, but because when she was rattled she somehow seemed more...he searched for the right word. Approachable?

"Of course. I would expect nothing different."

Her shoulders relaxed, and she folded her hands primly in front of her and waited. The vulnerability was gone, and she again wore the smooth and somewhat haughty expression that he had begun to guess was a mask she used to cover her insecurities.

He put his hands in his pockets. How to broach such a topic? He cleared his throat. "As it seems you are a woman who appreciates forthrightness, I will be frank."

Her brow puckered, and she narrowed her gaze. Then she gave a slight nod.

"I'd like to speak to you about my intentions," Nolan began, searching for the right way to ask her to court in the middle of their circumstances.

Did her eyes brighten? Encouraged, he opened his mouth to continue, but she spoke before he had the chance.

"First, let me say I'm thankful for your friendship and appreciate how you help my father." Faith took a breath and seemed to try to straighten her already perfect posture. "I feel I must apologize, however, for this morning. I was…" She looked away. "Not myself." She met his eyes again, and what he saw there lacked any warmth. "I'm afraid I let the stressful situation make me act in an unseemly manner."

She saw their moment as unseemly? The muscle in his jaw tightened.

"What happened this morning shouldn't have. And it can't happen again."

He clenched his fists at his sides, disappointment turning to anger at the bite in her tone. Did she once again accuse him of not acting as a gentleman? Just because he tried to comfort her?

"I never meant to distress you with unwanted attentions."

A small sniffle escaped, but rather than dismiss his words as unfounded, she merely nodded.

"I meant only to comfort you." He waited, but she said nothing. "Forgive me, but my actions this morning were done only with pure intentions."

Were those tears in her eyes? Why? Had she nothing to say?

Faith swallowed, dipping her chin as though it were an effort. "I wouldn't think anything different of you. You're a good man, Nolan, and I hold you in high regard."

Her chin quivered. He watched her closely, unsure if warring emotions caused this dichotomy or mere exhaustion. Her words said one thing, her actions another.

Did she have affections for him after all? And if so, why speak as though their closeness had been a mistake? He leaned forward, about to simply ask and clear the air between them, but she stepped back.

"As I believe we have both come to see, however," Faith said with an edge in her tone that severed any words about to escape his throat, "We would not be a match. Therefore, it would be best we not do anything to further muddle our…friendship."

They stood there for several moments in awkward silence. He thought of, then discarded, several replies, dismissing each one. Having not clearly defined these unfamiliar emotions within him, he couldn't find the words to say exactly what he felt.

Patience, Mr. Harper had said. And friendship was a good start. He offered a smile. "I value your friendship deeply, Miss Harper."

She seemed to relax. "We will likely see a lot of each other if you continue your employment with my father."

When she looked back up at him, her eyes shimmered. Nolan stepped closer. The air between them seemed to crackle, and his chest tightened. Did her eyes say something more than her words?

She stared at him, then blinked rapidly. "Unless, of course, you'd rather not. Which, of course, I would understand given the... uh, frustrations I've caused you."

The small vein in the side of her slender neck pulsed. Was her heart racing? He stared at the curve of her neck a moment, then let his eyes slide up over her lips and finally back to her eyes. What was she talking about?

"Rather not what?"

She looked down, but not before he saw a flash of hurt in her eyes. "See a lot of me in Memphis." Her eyes widened and she hurried on. "As friends, of course."

Nolan resisted the urge to pull her into his arms as he had earlier. But she'd made it clear she wasn't ready for such things. The temptation to kiss her pulled at him so strongly, he stepped back.

His voice came out thick. "I'm always pleased to find myself in your company."

Her eyes brightened. Something flickered between them, further confusing him. She'd just stated she wanted friendship and nothing more, yet the energy between them said otherwise. His chest tightened.

Patience. He best return to his room before he succumbed to the temptation to draw her into his arms and find out what her lips felt like against his.

She gave a weak smile. "I think we should get some rest. Tomorrow is likely to be a trying day."

Nolan could only nod. He watched her turn and glide back into her room, latching the door softly without a single glance back in his direction.

Motionless, he stood in the hall, knowing that for him, rest would be impossible to come by.

Twenty-One

Have a little faith, Faith. She repeated Mercy's words over and over to herself, but they refused to stick. The shipwreck was said to have survivors. That should have been enough. Faith gripped hard on the rail, her stomach heaving with each rise and fall of the ferryboat.

Apparently, this roiling torture was the quickest way to reach the strip of land that curved around the southern bend of Boston harbor. She would just have to deal with it. The small ship beneath her shifted under her feet, not giving Faith even the common courtesy of solid footing. Her stomach contracted, imparting the very unladylike feeling of nausea. And with her being trapped on this floating contraption, she had no way of hiding the infirmity. She tried anyway.

Nolan eyed her from where he'd propped against the railing, apparently unaffected by the way the floor bobbed beneath him. He'd hardly spoken a word to her after his visit to her room last night.

For the best, she reminded herself again.

"This is as steady as one can possibly hope for," Nolan said as though he could read her thoughts. Or at least see the discomfort on her face.

She nodded and tried to smooth her features into the pristine calm a lady should manifest at all times. Even if her insides curdled with sickness and her heart squirmed with worry.

He kept his eyes on the horizon, squinting against a morning that had no right to be this bright.

Faith held her tongue. If these waves were steady, what had it been like for poor Mercy on that ship during the storm? The thought made her shiver. She gripped the railing, willing her stomach to settle.

"Perhaps one of the passengers has some ginger. It'll help."

She didn't look at him. "Help with what?"

Nolan sighed and pushed off the rail. "Suit yourself."

Faith gripped the rail tighter and watched him cross the deck on legs that would benefit any sailor. She must have finally irked him enough, indeed. Nolan had been the most long-suffering gentleman a lady could have asked for, but, true to form, she'd managed to annoy even him to the point of distaste. Or perhaps he'd merely considered her words last night that they would never be a match and agreed. He wasn't being callous, he was just treating her as a friend and not a lady he was pursuing.

Either way, she'd been right. She knew eventually her irksome personality would grate on him. There would be less heartache this way.

She gathered a long breath of salty air and focused on the line where the water met the sky. It was supposed to be a short trip. She could make one short trip across the harbor. She just needed to focus on looking at the impressive steamships and the graceful curve of the schooners' sails. Sunlight glinted off the chopping water, causing it to glitter with specks of diamond and aquamarine.

"What thoughts trouble you, my dear?"

Faith turned to see Daddy standing beside her, checking his silver timepiece. She hadn't heard him approach, not even with the thump of his cane.

"Are you feeling well enough to be walking across this unsteady deck?"

He brushed away her concern. "A little bit of discomfort isn't reason enough to remain in the seating area when my daughter needs me."

Even he saw through her effort to hide the way her stomach roiled. Another failed attempt at retaining a lady's mystery. Why did she even bother? She heaved a sigh. "I'm not used to this much movement beneath me." She lifted her chin. "But as you say, a little discomfort is no reason to complain."

Daddy leaned on the rail next to her and watched the puffs of white smoke drift from the stacks on the incoming steamers and disappear into the pristine sky. "I can fetch you some ginger. They say it helps."

She shook her head. She didn't need help. She would be fine enough on her own.

Just ahead, a small strip of land curved away from the mainland and protruded into the harbor like a curled finger. "Seems we are almost there anyway."

Daddy looked to where the ferryboat neared a dock at the curve of what the locals called the Hull. People bustled about, their movements a flurry of activity.

"Right, then. Let's see what information we can gather."

It was another half hour before their small vessel had docked and the passengers allowed to disembark. Most of the people traveling with them were men who looked as though they made their living from the ocean. No other women were present.

Daddy had them wait until the others had made their exit before escorting her across the shifting gangplank and onto the solid footing of a wooden dock. Seagulls squawked overhead and dipped their feathered bodies toward the water's edge.

It took only a few moments for them to locate a small building with a painted sign that read, "Boston Humane Society." Here, they would find the brave volunteers who risked their lives to aid the unfortunates who found themselves smashed upon the many rocks that guarded Boston Harbor.

A distinguished man with a thick beard and a commanding presence strode across the dock.

"Sir!" Daddy called. "Can you give us news about the survivors of the wreck?"

He snorted. "Which one?"

Faith's mouth went dry. "There was more than one?"

He cut her a glance. "Storm got four, God bless them." He spat on the ground. "Coal schooner drove head-on into Shag Rocks. She broke in two almost immediately. Captain got all the men off his vessel, but…" He let the words dissolve and shook his head. "Sailors from two others swam to the Bruckner Islands, and we picked them up this morning. Got a few more coming in."

Nolan stepped forward. "What of women? Were there any women?"

The man shot another glance at Faith, who clenched her hands, hoping his sense of propriety wouldn't cause him to hold his tongue in the presence of a lady.

"Are you missing family?"

"Yes," Faith said. "Any information would be greatly appreciated."

He rubbed the back of his neck. "Were your people on the Gertrude?"

"We are uncertain," Daddy said.

The man hesitated. "She was returning through Hull Gut. Got engulfed by the cyclone and thrown on her beam ends by a flaw of wind. She sank like a stone before the passengers trapped in the cabin could be pulled free."

Faith put her hand to her throat and fought the sting of tears. Could it have been Mercy?

"A mother's love is something fierce," the man said after a moment.

Faith's eyes snapped to his face. "What?"

He shook his head. "The crew jumped overboard, but the woman went below to find her sleeping children. She tried to save them but all three drowned in the process."

Nolan stepped close to Faith as though sensing the weakening of her knees. "Thank you, sir."

"Joshua James."

"I'm sorry for the loss of this lady to her family," Nolan said, taking Faith by the elbow, "but it would seems she's not the lady we seek."

Faith let some of her weight settle into the comfort of Nolan's hand. His touch buoyed her with a friend's offered comfort. "Mr. James, are there any other women among those you brought in?"

"Afraid not." He looked out past them. "Another lifeboat is coming in. You're welcome to ask 'em."

He hurried around them, heading to the dock. A small boat manned by several young men pulling oars glided into the safety of the shore. Haggard-looking fellows sat huddled inside, but there was no sign of Mercy.

Where had she gone?

Faith struggled to keep herself composed in the swarm of noise and activity, feeling disconnected from all that was happening around her. Daddy made inquiries of several men, and for the majority of the morning they remained near the lifesavers' station until every survivor and every report of the cargo ships had been documented. Information swirled around her, dropping and swooping like the raucous gulls.

No one had seen a colored girl.

She hadn't been brought onto any of their ships.

Each bit of news brought further disappointment. Each squawk of the birds plucked something from her soul until she felt as though there were little of her left. She hadn't the energy to do more than follow her father and Nolan around, losing pieces of her crumbling hope as she went.

Twenty-Two

*I*f things got any worse, then Mercy might as well just give up now. Her stomach growled, taunting her. She bit back her fear and waded another few feet into the surf. Jed couldn't know what he was talking about. How could there be any fish this close to the shore, where the waves beat upon the sand and constantly stole it from underneath her feet?

Jed had found six sailors in addition to Hezzie and Mercy. The captain was unaccounted for. She'd heard they found one other sailor alive, but he'd not made it back up the beach to where Jed planned to camp. The splintered board he'd taken to the side had proved fatal.

A sailor with a broken arm sat a short distance away, staring at the waves with a thin sapling in his good hand. How did Jed expect him to fish in such a condition? But then, every working hand was needed if they were going to survive. They'd spent all day yesterday hoping for rescue. By the time darkness settled, their empty stomachs demanded every person shake off their rattled emotions and focus on survival.

The insect on her hook writhed, and Mercy scrunched her nose. She threw the hook into the water again, wishing no one was counting on her to put something in their aching stomachs.

Down the beach from Carlos, the sailor with the broken arm, Hezzie threw another hook in the water. The rest of the survivors were looking for supplies.

The sailors had determined they'd been battered through Pollock Rip and had washed up somewhere near Nantucket Island in their desperate attempt to reach Newport. At first light this morning, Jed had discovered abandoned shacks scattered with broken oil casks and rusted harpoons. After some discussion, the men had decided they must have washed up on the abandoned whaling outpost on Tuckernuck Island, just west of the much larger island of Nantucket.

For all Mercy knew, it could be the very ends of the earth. The end of the flat earth people had believed in centuries before.

She sighed. Help wasn't likely to arrive anytime soon. Who would come out to an abandoned island? They may as well be the survivors in Robinson Crusoe. A gull landed near her and cocked its head at her fishing line. She scowled at it.

The hearty men searched for any hope off the island and, in the meantime, firewood and supplies. Mercy just hoped they didn't end up colonizing this island like the Swiss Family Robinson.

She tilted her head. Why were adventuring people stuck out on their own often named Robinson? Mercy made a disgusted face at the bird as it cawed at her. Perhaps she should have been named Robinson instead of Carpenter.

Mercy stomped her foot, and the bird flew away. Too bad she couldn't follow the creature into the sky and fly home. She hated standing there in the sun with a makeshift fishing pole hoping for a tug on the line. She should be doing something else. Exploring. Finding supplies. Something.

She'd rather help find a way off the island than toss an insect on a rusty hook in and out of the waves that constantly threatened to wrap the contraption around her feet. How, exactly, had she ended up in such a mess? It seemed like decades ago she'd been dressed in a fine bustle and on her way to make a name for herself in Boston. Now, she stood in a tattered dress with no shoes praying she'd somehow catch a fish in the ocean without first hooking her own toes.

Hezzie had kept insisting God had a plan, but in the two days she'd been on this island, Mercy had yet to fathom what that could be. She needed her own plan. But then, it was outright impossible to make any plans, what with each day manifesting into something she would have never hoped for. How did one exercise any control over her life when life kept messing things up?

The wind tugged at her hair, adding to the mass of frayed tangles it had become. She smirked. Joy wouldn't envy her hair today. She resisted the urge to reach up and smooth it. What would it matter? The salty wind would immediately undo her efforts anyway.

Suddenly, the line jerked and pulled taunt. Mercy yelped and gave it a tug, but it tugged back. She stumbled forward, unwilling to let go of the branch and lose whatever had taken hold of her bait.

"Help!" Mercy grabbed the branch with both hands, trying to plant her feet in the shifting sand. She stumbled again. Whatever monstrosity had the other end of this contraption kept pulling her deeper into the waves. But she wouldn't let go.

The monster lurched, and Mercy lost her footing. She hit

her knees, and water sloshed up over her chest, robbing her of breath. She screamed and pulled back on the line with all of her might.

"Hold on! Don't let go!"

Jed's voice called from somewhere behind her, and Mercy ground her teeth. She wouldn't lose this creature. At least for Jed's sake. The fish thrashed in the water, jumping so high at one point that Mercy could see its shiny silver scales reflecting the sunlight. With waves hitting her in the chest and splashing into her face, Mercy held on tight. The loss of the fish would be one more failure she simply couldn't bear.

"*Maravillosa!*" Jed sloshed through the water and effortlessly took the limb from her aching hands. "You got one!"

She grumbled her thanks and struggled to stand. Not bothering to look back at her prize, Mercy ripped her feet from the sucking sand and trudged out of the water. Reaching the warm, dry sand, she plopped down and wrapped her arms around her middle.

Jed bent over the water, his shining hair glimmering in the perfect sunlight. He raised the large fish with a cheer, and her tension eased. At least she'd managed to hang on long enough for him to claim it. One fish wasn't much, but perhaps it would ease the ache in some of their stomachs.

She couldn't help but return his jubilant smile. "It's a good size, right?"

He lifted the flopping fish, the length of it extending from Jed's hand and down well past his elbow. "A right fine catch, Mercy! Right fine!"

She chuckled. The boyish grin splashed across his face and the way the wind played with the smooth strands of his hair...

Mercy reached up and grabbed the wild mass of hair sticking out all around her head and tried to smother it into a tail at the back of her neck. But she had nothing to secure it with.

Jed's expression changed. She lowered her eyes. After that moment on the ship, she'd been too aware of him. She dropped her hair. A moment later his feet appeared before her, and she looked up at him.

"Mamá may have something you can use to wrap it."

She nodded. "Thanks."

"It's a good fish," he said, digging the toe of his tattered shoe into the sand. "The others will be greatly pleased."

Mercy nodded again.

"Help me clean it?"

He wanted her to clean a fish? With him? She glanced at the ocean. It seemed a better choice than wading back out into the surf. "I must admit I don't have much experience in that area. Papa always cleaned the fish he caught before he brought them in for us to cook."

Jed offered his hand and helped her to her feet. "You miss them, yes?"

"Yes," was all she could manage to say. But how could all of her guilt, worry, and anguish be contained in one small word?

Mercy followed him to a shady portion of the beach, where he knelt down by a flat rock. "Did I tell you why we were in Boston?" He slipped a knife from a sheath at his side, then banged the handle of it down on the head of the fish. It stopped moving.

"No."

"My mother wanted to see the Tremont Temple." He flicked his wrist and slid the knife effortlessly through the bottom of the fish.

"Did she enjoy it?" Something about having a normal conversation while stranded on an abandoned island calmed the churning in her insides. Perhaps that had been his intention.

He nodded, locks of shiny black hair sweeping over his forehead. "Did you know that, as far back as '38, they've had a mixed congregation?" He looked at her expectantly.

"Mixed? You mean like Baptists and Methodists in one service?"

He laughed, and the hearty sound brushed over her like the warm breeze. "No, I mean they allow all races to worship together. Can you imagine such a thing?" His eyes brightened.

She tilted her head. Of course she could. She sat in such a gathering every Sunday. "May I assume you've never seen such a service before?"

He regarded her thoughtfully. "No. Where we live in Georgia, such things are not only frowned upon but outright banned. Mamá and I hope one day to build a church, then maybe even a town, that looks like that—a place where all of God's people can live together in equality and peace."

She stared at him.

After a moment, he shrugged. "I know it sounds foolish. But I believe God is leading me to one day preach at such a church." He returned to slicing the fish.

All her life she'd been told Ironwood was special. But until this moment, until looking into the hope filling Jed's eyes, she'd never truly believed it. "Do you think making a place like that would be difficult?"

He sighed. "Impossible. But with God all things are possible." He paused and looked at her. "But maybe there've been enough years after the war to give it a try."

If he believed it impossible now, then how much harder had it been for her and Faith's parents to do such a thing when they had? What kind of sacrifices had her parents made to create the world she'd grown up in? Suddenly, their sheltering didn't seem quite so detestable.

She shifted in the sand. "So you want to start a place where black families and white families go to church together, learn from the same teachers, and…?"

"Yes." He grinned. "And families of people who look like me, too. A place where people live in communities together, and color doesn't decide their occupations." His voice hardened. "Or divide families."

"Like yours?"

His jaw clenched, and he gave a short jerk of his head. "Mamá saved me from the streets. She's the only mother I've ever known."

The implications of his words settled on her heart. How many looks of distain had he suffered? How many people had not accepted the love of mother and son because they did not look the same? Because Jed looked like the Spanish men while Hezzie was colored?

She crossed her arms. "Then why not just live somewhere where there are no white people? Save yourself the trouble?"

He laid carefully carved meat on the smooth rock. "You think white folks are the only ones who dislike and distrust people who don't look like them?"

Mercy shrugged, even though he wasn't looking at her. Seemed about right.

"I've been ousted by people who look like me, people who

look like Mamá, and people who look like neither of us. It isn't an issue of the skin, but of the heart." He looked at her, and his eyes sparked fire. "Why do they think that all the things that make them different are more important than what makes them the same? Especially in God's church?"

"I don't know." She toyed with her lip. "I grew up in a place similar to what you are describing. My mother was once a slave. But she became friends with the white lady in the big house. Miss Lydia freed all the slaves during the war. I was educated with that white lady's daughter."

A pang constricted her chest. She missed Faith. More, she missed the way things had once been, when they were just two girls who had yet to face injustice and a harsh world. Would their friendship survive all that had happened?

"The people of Ironwood listen to both a black preacher and a white one. They share." She crinkled her brow. "Now that I say it, I realize how odd that sounds."

Jed stared at her for a long moment. Then he laughed. "I should have known. She's always right."

"Who's always right?"

"Mamá. She said…" His words trailed off, and he placed a hand up to his brow to shield his eyes from the sun. He lowered his voice, even though his mother couldn't possibly hear them from this distance. "Well, she says many things." He grinned, his eyes sparkling with something Mercy couldn't place. "She thinks you're special."

Mercy snorted. "Hardly."

Jed regarded her for so long, Mercy fidgeted in the warm sand.

"The way you tear yourself down isn't becoming of a child

of God."

Great. Jed was more like his mother than she'd realized. She waved a hand. "Forget I said it."

He set his knife down and focused his deep brown eyes on her. "Are you displeased with yourself?"

What was it with these people? "That's hardly a proper question to ask of a woman you don't even know."

Unaffected by her sharp words, he merely looked at her. "Are you?"

She flung her arm out toward the ocean. "I'm greatly displeased with where I find myself, yes."

"That isn't what I asked."

She glared at him. "Did you ever think that things would be easier for you if you had been born white?"

Jed grinned. "But I was not."

She huffed. He didn't understand. Why did she always expect people to think as she did?

"I was crafted in just the way the Lord intended me to be, for the purposes He has for me."

What had she expected out of a preacher? "Of course. You're right." She looked back at the fish. "Do you suppose it will be enough for everyone?"

He didn't follow her gaze. Or allow the change of subject. "I don't know what life would have been like if I'd been born a different race or to different circumstances. Perhaps I wouldn't have known hardships in the ways I have. My hardships would have been different, for, rest assured, we all have them. But I believe that the experiences I had work with the abilities and desires I have to prepare me for the plan God has in store."

The man would definitely make a good preacher. "The way

He made me does nothing but keep me from the desires I have."

Jed watched her for a moment, then turned back to his work on the fish. He expertly pulled the scales away from the meat, and then the meat away from the small bones.

Thinking the conversation finished, Mercy turned to walk away.

"Would you tell me more of this church at your home?"

She paused, then turned back to him. Talking to him about Ironwood would be better than tossing more insects into the waves. Or talking about herself. She took a step closer and joined him under the shade of a scraggly tree.

"Ironwood is owned by the Harper family. Before the War between the States, it was a large cotton plantation with about two hundred slaves."

She waited, but he had no reaction to this.

"At some point, the lady of the plantation decided she no longer wanted to own slaves. It had something to do with the uncanny friendship she and my mother share. She set them all free."

He nodded along.

"Mr. Harper returned from fighting for the Confederacy only to have changed his own mind about the people who worked his land. At that time, they set up a system for the people to work the land and earn a wage. Some of them took their freedoms and left, but many stayed."

Mercy thought back to the stories of her childhood, peeling away the layers. "There wasn't much peace in the early days. People hated what the Harpers tried to do. They called them nasty names and on several occasions tried to burn the fields.

Mr. Harper had to start setting out watchmen after one of the young men was hanged because he'd been found walking the road alone."

She sucked in a breath as memories came back to her. Nights with fire and screams. Her mother hiding her daughters' heads in her embrace and singing over the sounds that had erupted in the yard. How had she forgotten these things?

Swiping away a stray tear, she forged on. "Eventually, things settled. Ironwood became more and more isolated. The less they made any attempts at connection with the outside world, the more peaceful things became. We grew most everything we needed and traded among ourselves. We became almost like our own little colony, mostly self-sufficient." Talking about Ironwood, remembering her peaceful childhood had her longing for home. She may never live the quiet life her mother expected, but she could appreciate now all she'd taken for granted.

Jed had laid down his tools and was watching her intently now.

She turned to look out over the expanse of the ocean. "I spent my adolescent years ignoring the world around me. I knew people hated us. I knew why I was never allowed to go to town. But somehow, I turned it all into some kind of fantasy, as if I were a princess trapped in an enchanted castle." She shook her head. "Foolish, I know."

Jed smiled. "We often craft worlds when our own becomes hard to bear."

What stories had he crafted as a child? She opened her mouth to ask, but he spoke first, asking her to continue the story.

"Not much more to tell. Faith stopped attending schooling

in town and the Harpers brought in a governess to continue her lessons. I was allowed to learn with her. I caught on quickly, so in those years between girlhood and womanhood, I focused on learning all I could.

"Eventually, though, it wasn't enough. As we grew older, Faith began to leave home more often, participating in events and parties, going on long trips. I wanted the freedom she had, freedom that would never be mine. I started to realize that my life would be nothing more than always being trapped with nowhere to go. My future would be planned for me."

She glanced at him, realizing he had not asked for her own tale of self-pity but for information about Ironwood. She lifted her shoulders. "Anyway, the Harpers, they are good people who genuinely care for the people who work their lands. They take good care of everyone, and I suspect Mr. Harper still takes many precautions to protect us all. Mostly, my people tend to their own lives and ignore what the world is like outside their boarders."

Jed stroked his chin thoughtfully. "And the church there?"

"We have a colored preacher and a white one who take turns. My father says it's to give equal position to all of God's people, but the only white people who attend chapel with us are the Harpers." She picked at a torn fingernail. "And lately, that hasn't been much. With the success of his company in Memphis, the family is often gone, leaving the land to the management of the overseers and the general concerns of the people to my mother."

Jed lifted his eyebrows. "A woman holds a position of authority?"

He said it with such shock she took a moment to consider.

"I haven't really thought of it, but yes. It's been that way as long as I can remember. My mother manages the daily household duties, tells the house girls what to clean, manages the food supplies for the big house, and then hears the needs and concerns of the workers. She takes those to Miss Lydia, when she is home."

Jed absorbed all of this. "Interesting. But I wonder, is Ironwood as odd as you think it is?"

"It isn't?"

He shrugged. "There are many colored communities that came up after the war. They function much in the same way you described, except they do so without a white family."

"I didn't know that."

"One day," Jed said, "I want to see cities where people of all colors live together. Mostly, though, I have this burning desire to see God's church unified."

"Maybe in the North," Mercy said, though even as the words left her mouth, she doubted them. The North hadn't been nearly as accepting as she'd thought.

"Maybe. Though I don't sense God calling me there." He gave a sheepish grin. "I have this impossible idea that God wants all His children to realize that what makes them different isn't nearly as important as what makes them the same. No matter what people look like, if they love Jesus and let Him lead their life, then they are a part of the body of Christ. Why do they insist on separating themselves based on appearance, status, or preference? I can't help but think such things displease God."

He spoke with such passion that her heart stirred. What he wanted was impossible. People would never put aside their judgments and prejudices to join together. She tilted her head.

Not unless they had a common cause. "It's a beautiful dream."

"You think so?"

What would it be like to help him build a church like that? Mercy stepped closer. What she saw in his eyes caused a catch in her throat. She struggled for words. "I...I hope you make it happen someday."

His smile sent a warm tingle down her spine and an ache in her heart she couldn't ignore.

Twenty-Three

Daddy had that look on his face. The one Faith hated. The one that said she wasn't going to like whatever words would next come out of Daddy's mouth. She held up a hand to forestall them. "No. Don't say it."

He raised his eyebrows.

"Forgive my impertinence, Daddy, but I cannot bear for us to give up. There has to be something else we can do. She has to be out there somewhere."

Daddy and Nolan exchanged a glance, but said nothing. Faith smothered her annoyance. She wasn't oblivious to the dangers and the impossibility of their task. But she couldn't sit here and merely wait. She had to keep looking. She refused to give up and go home. Not yet.

Nolan stared out across the commotion of the dock, where men scuttled to and fro and scavengers set out to see what they could bring back from the sunken cargo. The little muscle in the side of his jaw pulsed, the one that told Faith he was irritated again.

"What should we do now?"

Both men blinked at her in surprise. Daddy tilted his head, clearly astonished she'd turned to Nolan for instruction. She was a little surprised herself. She kept it from her features.

"You're asking me?"

She resisted the urge to cross her arms and settled for adjusting her hat instead. "I would appreciate your perspective."

A small smile turned the corner of his mouth, creating a charming little line on the left side that she'd never noticed before. "I think we should report the case to the police."

Faith rolled her bottom lip through her teeth. Why hadn't they already gone to the authorities? Worse, why hadn't any of them thought of it before now? Perhaps they'd all thought as she had, expecting to find Mercy at the paper. "You're correct. They will know what to do." Perhaps if they had taken this to the police in the first place, or perhaps even hired the Pinkerton Agency, the professionals would've had a better chance of finding Mercy.

She just hoped the delay hadn't made things worse.

Faith brushed her hands down her skirt. "Let's get going then, shall we? No use dallying."

The plan made, they took the next ferry back across the bay, and Faith vowed she would never set foot in a boat again as long as she lived. How could people stand to feel as though they would retch for hours, or even days, on end?

People milled about the dock as though they didn't have any work to do. Perhaps, after such a storm, businesses had given their people time to focus on cleaning up the aftermath.

Faith stepped onto the wooden sidewalk that led into the water and had to skirt three men who did not yield to her presence. They seemed to be doing nothing productive.

Gulls called to one another overhead, perhaps hoping for something to scavenge. Debris peppered the sidewalks as crews of men worked to clear broken limbs, scattered household items, and litter from the road. Fortunately, after Daddy asked a loitering cab driver for directions, they discovered the headquarters for the police wasn't far. They were able to make it there after only a short walk, saving the trouble of taking a carriage over cluttered roads.

Faith passed through the door her father held open for her, surprised to see a large crowd gathered in the lobby. People spoke over one another, clambering for the attention of the lone officer who held a notepad and was furiously scribbling with a pencil nub.

"Do you suppose it's always like this?" Faith asked, craning her neck to see through the crowd.

Daddy rubbed his beard. "Not likely, no. Probably because of the storm."

The thought of waiting here all day to report their case, only to have to wait more for a turn for it to be investigated, sent her insides into an anxious flurry. It was far too crowded, and the heat from the press of so many people caused a lightness in her head Faith didn't care for.

Daddy turned to Nolan. "This will likely take some time. Have you still not heard from your uncle?"

Nolan stiffened. "I haven't contacted him." He shoved his hands in his pockets.

Daddy's eyebrows lifted in surprise. "Why ever not?"

Nolan shifted his feet again, looking more rattled than she'd ever seen him. He'd mentioned his uncle in the carriage ride to the Pink Parrot, and it hadn't been with any affection.

"Forgive me. I haven't had the opportunity."

Daddy eyed Nolan for a moment, then dipped his chin. "I'll

wait here to speak with the police while you call on him. Perhaps Mr. Watson can give us more information on the schooner we're looking for." Daddy raised his voice over the cacophony. "It wasn't one of the ones that wrecked in the harbor, thank the good Lord, but we don't know which ship it was or where she was headed."

Nolan glanced at Faith. "Very well."

Nolan's uncle knew about all the ships in the harbor? And Nolan had said nothing about it? Why wouldn't he have—

A woman bumped into Faith, causing her to stumble forward. The woman mumbled a barely audible apology and kept pushing her way deeper into the lobby. The press of people created a swarm of heat, and her nostrils filled with the unpleasant scent of men who'd spent the day in the sun. She removed her fan from her reticule and snapped it open to cool the air around her face.

Daddy glanced at her, and Nolan followed his gaze.

"Take Faith with you."

Nolan shook his head. "She should stay with you."

Faith slowed her fan. The familiar sour feeling of not being wanted wrapped cold fingers around her stomach. She remained silent. How much worse for it to come from her own father and the man she—

She cut the thought short and squared her shoulders. "I'll wait with Daddy." She fluttered her fan again, her cheeks growing warm.

Both Daddy and Nolan watched her closely.

A large man pushed through the crowd, bumping into Nolan and causing him to have to set his feet wide to maintain balance.

The crush of people was now nearly suffocating, and Faith sucked in a breath. "Though perhaps a bit of fresh air first..."

Nolan took her arm. "You can ride with me and wait in the carriage."

The unease in her stomach from the boat paired with the heat of the room had her feeling too unsettled to argue. She heard Nolan and her father speaking in clipped whispers, but she turned and headed for the door.

Outside, she drew a long breath of salty air and tried to whisk the hot air from her face. A moment later, Nolan joined her. They waited in silence while he hailed a Hansom cab. She averted her eyes as he helped her into the open-air conveyance and settled on the seat without comment.

The driver asked for the address, then told them the trip would be difficult, given the state of the roads. Nolan paid him extra, and, after a brief exchange, the clop of the horse's hooves joined the sounds of the bustling city.

Nolan appeared rather flustered. She ought to question him about this uncle and why Nolan hadn't asked for his help sooner, but the set of his jaw and the fact that he had not wanted her company kept her lips pressed firmly together.

The streets were clogged, and Nolan had to aid the driver in removing debris from the road on two separate occasions. What should have been a short trip from the harbor was proving to be more laborious than she'd imagined.

By the time the cab stopped in front of a neat townhome, Faith was weary of the journey and feeling weak from missing the noon meal. She focused her attention on the residence. The townhouse stood three stories tall with sides that nearly touched those of its neighbors. Red brick with white trim, it appeared cozy. Faith accepted Nolan's hand as he escorted her down from the rig.

She hadn't really wanted to sit in the sun, so she didn't remind him he had wanted her to wait in the cab.

The simple touch of his fingers brought a sensation she could not identify. She didn't have time to contemplate it, however, since as soon as her foot touched the ground he dropped her hand. She tried to place her fingers on his arm, but he moved away from her, tension evident in the set of his jaw and the pulsing vein in his neck. Had she annoyed him so much that he wouldn't even escort her?

True, she had been a bit of a shrew lately. But they had decided to be friends, and she would prove her commitment to the pledge by being as patient with his moods as he had been with hers.

She reached for his arm, took it, and looped her hand snugly around his elbow. When he looked down at her, she gave him a reassuring squeeze and an encouraging smile.

Surprised, Nolan stared at Faith. She offered a placating smile as if he were a child in need of encouragement.

He snapped his gaze to the sky and took a deep breath. Was that how she saw him? He was a man. He was supposed to be protecting *her*.

He tried to smother emotions that had no business ransacking his brain. She wasn't to blame. She couldn't know the effect being here had on him.

He'd hoped to never set foot in Boston again. Even after agreeing to come on this maddening escapade, he'd determined he wouldn't return to this house. Send a message, perhaps, or letter of introduction. Nothing more.

Yet, here he was.

Feet still rooted to the ground and heat rolling inside of him, he tugged on his collar and forced himself to focus on Faith. He offered her a tight smile, and, as gentlemanly as he could, extracted his arm from her. She appeared perplexed, and then the hurt that flashed in her eyes stabbed him. But he had to gather himself to face his uncle, and he couldn't do so with a woman coddling him. Had he known she'd suddenly wish to mother him, he might have been more insistent she stay with Mr. Harper.

Nolan squared his shoulders and stalked toward the door, reminding himself he was a man and no longer a boy who had to cower from his uncle's tirades. Before he could change his mind, he lifted the knocker and pounded it.

A moment later, a different butler than the one from his boyhood opened the door. "Good afternoon, sir. May I help you?"

"I've come to call on my uncle. Is he in residence?"

The butler turned up a bulbous nose. "Is he expecting you, sir?" He glanced behind Nolan at the state of disarray in the streets as though wondering why anyone would choose such a time for a visit.

"He's not. If it were not a matter of grave importance, I would not call so unexpectedly."

The man hesitated, then stepped back from the door.

"Please wait inside while I see if Mr. Watson will receive visitors."

Nolan gestured for Faith to enter. She avoided his gaze and stepped into the room, waiting with eyes downcast.

"May I ask your names?" The butler closed the door behind Nolan, instantly making him feel caged.

"Arnold's nephew, Nolan Watson." He gestured toward Faith. "And this is my employer's daughter, Miss Faith Harper."

The butler nodded and left them standing in the entry, not even offering for them to wait in the comfort of the parlor. That, Nolan knew, wasn't a good sign. The odds of them seeing his uncle were slim. If Arnold didn't want to have visitors, he would let them know it by not allowing them to settle in. Nolan suspected that, if it wouldn't be such a blatant lack of manners, Arnold would leave uninvited guests to wait on the stoop.

The house was just as Nolan remembered it. Polished wood floors, floral paper on the walls. Everything in its perfect and proper place. But just like the owner, the house wore a veneer of polish to hide what crumbled beneath. Nolan took three steps further in, swallowing a burning in his stomach that accompanied the memories. Then he moved two floorboards to his left.

The floor let out a resounding squeak. As he'd suspected, that hadn't been repaired in the nine years of his absence. Arnold spent his money on horses, fancy carriages, and anything else he thought might someday make him fit in with the society crowd. Why he failed to realize after all these years that a snide harbor master would never find acceptance among the rich elite escaped Nolan's understanding.

The butler returned a moment later and gestured toward the parlor, which would hold all of Arnold's best furniture. "If you will kindly wait, Mr. Watson will join you shortly."

A mixture of relief and disappointment warred in his veins as Nolan gestured Faith ahead of him. She settled on the settee and arranged her skirts. Nolan stood by the hearth.

"How long has it been since you've visited?" Her voice splintered the smothering silence.

Not long enough. "Nine years. I left when I was sixteen."

Her eyes filled with pity, and he suddenly regretted what he'd told her about his childhood. He tightened his jaw, the ache in his teeth warning he needed to relax. Unfortunately, such a luxury wasn't possible while standing in Arnold's house.

For the next quarter hour, Faith attempted to maintain polite conversation, but Nolan found himself too distracted to properly keep up his end. The last time he'd been in this parlor, he'd accidently walked in on his uncle and one of the maids in an inappropriate embrace. Arnold had been furious and dealt out his punishment with fists. With a battered body and his few personal belongings, Nolan had left later that day and had never returned.

Faith fell silent and studied the lace gloves covering her hands. He would owe her an apology.

He shifted from one foot to the other. How much longer would Arnold make them wait? A part of him, that cowardly part he couldn't stand, still wanted to bolt. Nolan clenched his fists. He was no longer a skinny boy without defenses! The thought did little to ease his nerves.

Footsteps sounded down the stairs, and a moment later Arnold entered. He stepped in like a king greeting his subjects, dressed in an expensive suit that he must have donned purely for their benefit. His thinning hair had been oiled back from his face, and his mustache had gained some gray since last Nolan saw him.

He gave a bow. "Good afternoon." He looked to Nolan and lifted his eyebrows. "Nephew. What a surprise."

Nolan remained rooted to the hearth. "Arnold. Allow me to introduce you to my employer's daughter, Miss Harper."

Faith rose, and Arnold extended a hand.

"A pleasure to meet you, Mr. Watson," she said as he brushed his lips across her knuckles. He held on a breath too long, and she pulled away. "We apologize for calling upon you unannounced, especially on a day such as this."

"My butler tells me it is a matter of some importance?"

Nolan stepped forward, fighting the tightness in his stomach. "We were hoping you could help us locate a schooner."

Arnold raised bushy eyebrows, further elongating his thin face. "And this is a matter of grave importance?"

"It is." He stared at his uncle for a tense moment.

Finally, Arnold chuckled, clearly enjoying Nolan's discomfort. "I see."

No man in Boston would know more about each ship docked in Boston Harbor than Arnold Watson. A fact he clearly relished.

"And why, if I may ask," Arnold said, drawing out the words, "is finding a certain ship a matter of such importance that you braved the conditions to call upon me without notice?"

The snide look on his uncle's face had all decent words lodging in Nolan's throat.

Faith twisted her hands, cut a glance at him, and then stepped forward. "Please, sir. My dearest friend is missing, and we have reason to believe she was taken onto a schooner."

He sat straighter. "Taken?"

Faith wiggled her lower lip between her teeth, a habit Nolan had noticed she did often of late. "My father heard talk of an unconscious woman being taken onto a ship, and we have reason to fear that lady could have been Mercy. I'm most desperate to find her and bring her to safety, so any information you could supply would be deeply appreciated."

Arnold adjusted his collar. "That seems more like sailors' tales than anything else, I'm afraid."

Of course his uncle would dismiss the claim. He thought anything he wasn't aware of in Boston Harbor could only be fabrication.

"Perhaps you're right," Faith said, her eyes misting. "But just the same, I owe it to her to investigate." She smiled sweetly at Arnold, and Nolan's stomach clenched. "Don't you think?"

Arnold swept an appreciative gaze down her gown that made Nolan's blood boil. Then he smiled.

"Why, of course, dear. I would be delighted to help."

Twenty-Four

How would he tell her the news? Nolan adjusted his cravat and then fiddled with his pressed cuffs as he waited for Faith and Mr. Harper to join him in the lobby. He'd come down early this morning, yet again unable to sleep well, and had received a message from the police.

They had not come across any missing colored girls and did not currently have the resources to dedicate to the search. They suggested he try the church.

Nolan sipped his coffee and stared into the cold hearth. After the cool air following the storm, a wave of heat had deemed the cheery crackle of flames too hot even for hospitality. The discarded ash felt like the hope they had in this search. Much as he hated it, the girl was gone. It was time he head back to Harper Shipping.

The idea both satisfied and disappointed him. His thoughts continued to shift from one thing to another until finally the lobby began to fill with the usual bustle of morning. A short time later, Mr. Harper joined him.

"Good morning, Nolan." He selected a seat and settled down.

Nolan thought to comment on the missing cane but instead

inquired about Mr. Harper's night's rest.

"Better than expected." He leaned forward and clasped his hands. "It's been a trying week. I fear sending another missive home."

They were both silent a moment. Words weren't needed following such a statement. The look on his face was enough to know Mr. Harper dreaded sending disheartening news home to his wife and Mercy's family. The similar feeling regarding his own disappointing news couldn't be denied.

"Sir, I'm afraid we received a message from the police, and, well, they say they haven't seen her." He straightened his cravat. "Nor do they have the manpower to look for her."

Mr. Harper nodded, seeming none too surprised. "I can't say I expected different. They seemed to think my Southern accent meant I was looking for a runaway slave." He spat the words out and shook his head.

The priest had seemed to think the same until he'd seen Faith's distress. The friendship between them had to be strong, indeed. When Nolan had first gone to Ironwood, he'd been rather taken aback. Mr. Harper had explained their odd community to him, but he'd still not been prepared. Never had he expected a girl—no, woman—like Mercy.

That day in the carriage she'd been confident, intelligent, and nothing at all like most of the quiet Negros he'd been around. Those qualities likely got her into trouble with people who decided she'd stepped out of her place.

"What thoughts trouble you?"

Mr. Harper's words brought him out of his contemplations. "I was thinking about when I met Mercy."

Mr. Harper chuckled. "You were taken by surprise."

At Nolan's nod, he continued. "My wife loves Ruth, Mercy's mother, dearly. While I was gone during the war, it was Ruth who helped Lydia through some very dark times. For that, I will always owe her a debt of gratitude. They still share a friendship that defies society's understanding. At times even my own, and I fancy myself a progressive thinker."

Faith's independent and somewhat defiant personality suddenly seemed to make more sense.

Mr. Harper tapped his finger on the arm of the leather chair. "But a man does all sorts of things for the woman he loves."

Which explained why Mr. Harper had come to Boston. And why he'd allowed Faith to join him.

"But what do we do now?"

Mr. Harper opened his mouth, but before he could answer, Faith swept up beside them with the rustle of skirts. Dressed in the sturdy brown traveling gown she'd worn at the train station, she appeared as no-nonsense as her choice of attire.

His lips curved. Even with a stern expression and dowdy hairstyle, her loveliness couldn't be hidden. Though sometimes he suspected she tried to do just that.

Both men rose and offered the normal morning pleasantries. The bustle of patrons and the scent of breakfast wafting from the hotel restaurant did little to hoist the heavy mood surrounding their trio. Faith gave Nolan a bland greeting and sat nearest the hearth, the shadows under her eyes evidencing she'd slept as poorly as he.

"We didn't receive a favorable response from the police," Mr. Harper said as he settled back into his chair once his daughter was seated. "I'm afraid they'll not be much help."

Faith remained stoic. "So that only leaves Mr. Watson,

then." She took a deep breath, then popped up on her feet like a startled cat and headed toward the door as if to leave immediately.

"Faith!" Mr. Harper barked her name, and she whirled around, eyes wide.

"We will not call on anyone before breakfast."

She gaped at him. Was she surprised by her father's stern tone or the fact she hadn't considered the indecent hour?

Her response was mumbled, and Mr. Harper appeared more agitated than Nolan had ever seen him. Given the circumstances, it was understandable.

Breakfast at the hotel restaurant was tense at best. The carriage ride across town to Arnold's office at the harbor wasn't much better. All of Nolan's attempts at conversation had long since dwindled by the time they arrived in front of the wharf building that had seen the wear of wind and wave.

Nolan strode ahead and held the door for the Harpers. They passed him without so much as a nod. Nerves on edge, he followed them into the receiving area.

They were greeted just inside the spacious front room by a young man with greased hair and spectacles, who led down a hall to an office. More spacious than he remembered, though he'd not been in Arnold's offices often.

"Just in here. Mr. Watson has been expecting you."

The words turned Nolan's stomach. He gestured Faith inside the office ahead of him.

"Ah, the lovely Miss Harper. What a pleasure it is to see you again." Arnold's voice reverberated in the office, full of far too much charm and cheer.

Faith seated herself in one of two chairs positioned in front of Arnold's elaborately carved desk without invitation. Only Arnold would have a massive partner's desk for a single person.

He skirted around it, giving Faith a nod as he came to stand on the imported rug along with Nolan and Mr. Harper.

"Arnold," Nolan said, "this is my employer, Mr. Charles Harper." He nodded toward the imperious man who had tainted his boyhood. "Mr. Harper, Arnold Watson."

The men shook hands, and then Mr. Harper took a seat by his daughter while Nolan stood by the door.

Arnold flipped through some papers on his desk, then took a seat and folded his hands. The massive leather chair squeaked beneath him. "I've been looking into this issue as per your request." He waited, as if expecting an outpouring of gratitude, then cleared his throat and continued. "There have been reports of another schooner wreck further south. Nothing has been confirmed, however."

Faith leaned forward, twisting her hands. "Was it from the same storm?"

The desperation in her voice unnerved Nolan, and he glanced at her father. The concern etched on the man's face mirrored his own.

Arnold nodded. "Seems a ship loaded with coal was headed to Savannah and reports taking on two passengers, with a possible third added." He tapped his fingers on the smooth oak. "The Princesa has failed to dock."

"But you say there are no confirmed reports?" Mr. Harper also leaned forward in his chair.

"It appears the Princesa may have gone down in the Pollock Rip and possibly washed up on Nantucket."

Faith jumped to her feet. "Then let's make haste. It has to

be her!"

Arnold smiled, seeming unconcerned by Faith's outburst. "You'll need a steamer. The currents and winds are too fickle, and there are only a few hours a day—on a good day—that you can even reach the islands."

Nolan stepped forward, drawing the attention of the others. "Then we go to Newport. It'll be closer."

Mr. Harper agreed. "I'm sure they'll send out a rescue as they did for the wrecks here and return the survivors to the nearest port."

Nolan waited another few moments as Mr. Harper thanked Arnold, then, blessedly, they stepped out of his office. Arnold shook Mr. Harper's hand and promise he'd send word to the hotel if he received further information.

Despite Arnold's willingness to help and his pleasant nature, Nolan was nonetheless relieved to exit the offices a few moments later. As he hailed a cab and gave the driver their hotel address, a weight lifted from him.

They were leaving Boston.

Twenty-Five

Not again. Mercy clutched the ragged fabric that passed as the remnants of her dress and stared up at the dark clouds.

"Storm coming!"

Mercy whirled around. What reason did Jed have to sound so excited? The waves crashed along the beach, their endless rhythm a grate on her nerves. Jed grinned, apparently oblivious to the foul conditions.

"Come on," he said, "I need your help."

"For what?" She cupped her hand to her mouth to be heard over the wind. "We need to take shelter."

Jed gripped her elbow, his eyes alight. "Our prayers are answered. Come. We must hurry."

"There's a ship?" Mercy clutched his arm. Hope thrummed in her chest.

He paused. "What? No." He tugged on her hand, pulling her along.

She followed him, perplexed. If they weren't getting off this island, then what prayers could have possibly been answered?

The wind whipped at her hair, loosening it from frayed braids and slinging it into her eyes. She blinked against the sting and stumbled along behind Jed, her job of checking the wading pool for trapped fish forgotten.

As they neared the makeshift camp along the beach, men scrambled to tear down the tents they had only yesterday completed.

"What are they doing?" How would they be able to shelter from the storm if they didn't have the tents?

"Come, we need to get them spread out." Jed sprinted to the nearest tent and grabbed a flapping corner from one of the sailors. His name started with an "S" but she could never remember its pronunciation.

The men repositioned the limbs they had used as tent poles and flipped the ship's canvas sails inverted, creating a large bowl.

Finally, understanding sparked. Mercy lifted her tattered hem and scrambled through the sand to Hezzie. "Are we going to catch the water?"

Hezzie grinned. "Sure 'nough. Lord brought an answer to prayer right soon as the last of ours ran out."

Mercy blinked. She hadn't even given any thought to the water they'd been drinking these past days. Where had it come from? Shaking off the thought, she grabbed the edge of the small tent she'd shared with Hezzie last night and shook off the sand.

Thunder rumbled, vibrating in her chest and warning the storm wouldn't wait on them much longer. Her fingers worked quickly, securing the material with rough rope they'd found in the abandoned village.

No sooner had they stepped back from their task than droplets began to spatter across the surface.

"Do you think it will hold?" Mercy eyed the canvas. "What

if the water just seeps through?"

Hezzie shrugged. "It'll be enough."

Mercy looked up at the heavens and couldn't help but laugh. "To think I once longed for an adventure."

Hezzie gestured toward a copse of short, scraggly trees. "And here you have it. Now, let's get out of the weather."

They scrambled under the shrubbery. Mercy wrapped her arms around her knees, praying the storm would deliver rain and not much else. Hezzie leaned out and looked up at the sky, then gave a nod and scrambled out.

"You stay here."

Without waiting for a response, the old woman scuttled out of the meager cover and darted across the sand. Probably looking for Jed.

The wind stirred the sand, kicking it up into the air and batting it around for a moment before dropping it a little further down the beach. The droplets increased, pattering on the leaves overhead. The thunder cracked, and Mercy yelped. She drew herself farther up under the bushes.

Cold water dripped down and fell on her head. She took a deep breath. It was only water. Only a storm. She'd been through countless thunderstorms.

But never from under a bush.

She drew her knees up tighter and rested her chin. Lightning popped out over the water, ripping the sky with a flash of light. Where was Hezzie? If she was out on the beach in the open—

Before she could convince herself otherwise, Mercy hurried out into the pelting rain. "Hezzie!"

She used her hand to shield her eyes, but it did little to stop the water from stinging her face. Where had that woman gone?

Another flash of light erupted. It struck the sand just ahead.

Mercy screamed.

She turned back, but the torrent of rain blurred her vision. Where was the shelter? She couldn't even see the tents! She leaned into the wind and pushed forward, desperate to get away from the open beach.

Her bare feet slogged in the sand, slowing her progress. Another step. Just one more. Now another. Mercy pushed forward, hoping that at any moment the low trees would reappear.

Sudden pain ripped through her foot, and she stumbled, hitting the ground and nearly knocking the breath from her. Rain dripped down her head and ran into her eyes.

Her foot throbbed. Her breath came in gasps.

Strong hands lifted her from the ground. Before she could gather her wits, she was bouncing in Jed's arms as he raced across the sand. She buried her face against his chest and breathed in the scent of rain, salt, and that other something she had come to realize was just him.

A moment later she was scooting under the cover of the brush she'd not been able to find. Jed slid in next to her and wrapped a protective arm around her shoulders. She shivered, and he rubbed his hand down her arm.

Neither of them spoke. The storm blew its fury beyond where they huddled but no longer held the terror it had moments ago.

"Hezzie ran out. I don't know where she went."

Jed kept his eyes forward. "I'm sure she's fine."

How could he say such a thing? But then, Hezzie did seem to have a rather uncanny sense of survival and a complete absence of fear. Whatever she'd run out to do, she'd likely accomplished it by now. Unless it was finding Jed. In that case, she'd failed. Because Jed had found Mercy instead. And his arm was around her.

"You're bleeding!"

As soon as Jed spoke the words, pain flared in her foot. Wincing, she looked down at where crimson coated her toes. "I stepped on something sharp."

"Turn this way." Jed twisted her around until her bare foot rested in his lap. "Let me see."

She held her breath as his fingers gently probed her skin. "I see it." He glanced up at her. "I need you to hold still."

Mercy sucked a quick breath as he grasped something and tugged. Then the pain was gone. He held up a sharp bit of shell for her to see before tossing it aside. She watched him as he sat back on his heels, rain dripping down his ebony hair and onto the sides of cheeks now peppered with black stubble.

"We need to stop the bleeding."

Thunder cracked overhead, but she barely noticed it. Jed grabbed the seam at his left shoulder and tugged, separating the sleeve from his shirt with a quick rip. Her eyes trailed down the bronzed skin of a muscled arm and then followed the strip of linen as he wound it around her foot. He looked up at her, and something in his eyes shifted.

He cleared his throat. "That should do until the storm is over. Then it'll need better tending."

All she could do was stare at him. Her chest tightened as her fingers dug into the sand beneath her. Each breath tasted of salt. Each heartbeat strained toward him. His eyes were luminous, rimmed in black lashes. They drew her in, as irresistible as flames to the moth and just as dangerous.

He pressed his lips together and studied her. The wind and rain begged for attention. The lightning demanded to be heard with thunderous insistence. But she saw only him. His face pushed out the terror of the storm, instead drawing her to come closer and be shielded from its fury.

Slowly, he reached toward her. Sand-dusted fingers pushed back her frayed hair and then lingered on the side of her face. She matched her breathing to his. Slowly in. Out. In.

Then he leaned forward. His face hovered only a breath from hers. She sat, frozen. Heart pounding. He waited. She strained forward, only a fraction, and halved the distance between them.

His eyes eased closed, and he let out a warm breath. Mercy swallowed. What did she do now? If she moved, she would lose this strange yet intoxicating feeling swarming through her. But what did he—?

Lips settled on hers. They were soft, gentle. Her eyes flew wide, then drifted closed. She returned the gentle pressure he gave.

Then it was over.

He sat back and looked at her.

She blinked, too befuddled and too smitten to do anything else.

Then he adjusted to sit next to her once more. He wrapped his arm around her shoulder, pulled her into the safety of his side, and turned to watch the storm.

Faith ignored the guilt tugging at her conscience and stepped into the waiting cab. She'd never deceived her father before, but he wouldn't listen to reason. The enclosed carriage rolled into the street and joined the jostling abundance of Boston.

Her plan made more sense than his. Why waste time waiting for trains and traveling by land farther south, only to once again get on a boat to take them to the island? If no one had sent a rescue by now, then it stood to reason they were in no great hurry to do so. She would not sit around another port city and wait while men debated.

Daddy would forgive her.

Thoughts bounced in her head from one thing to another, never settling still long enough to be considered complete. She'd grown desperate to find Mercy. Daddy said last night Faith was becoming unreasonable. But he didn't understand. She had to find her.

This was her fault.

Had she been a better friend, this would not have happened. But she'd been too concerned with her own aspirations and fluffy ideals to notice what happened in her own home. Ironwood was not what her parents thought. They thought they created a haven of equality, but all they really did was isolate themselves from the world.

No one was truly welcome in, and hardly anyone went out. The majority of the people of Ironwood merely hid themselves away. They didn't seek to make a place of belonging. Ironwood was a place of exclusion.

And she, who'd claimed a friendship more like sisterhood, had thought nothing of the fact that she could leave as she pleased and interact in the world without consequence. For what were a few snide whispers? They couldn't change her or her convictions. No one sought her real harm. Their words could only diminish her if she gave them that power.

But the same wasn't true for the people of Ironwood. For Mercy. They stayed at Ironwood to avoid the pain of mistreatment outside of it. Truth be told, Faith had thought little of the opportunities afforded to her, while at the same time expecting that Mercy should be grateful for a safe place and stay quietly at home.

Faith rested her head against the plush seat as it swayed down the road. What a hypocrite she'd been. Carrying on about women's rights and how they should have the abilities to do something other than be keepers at home, if they so chose, when all along she expected Mercy to be content in the role she had been given.

How did that make her any different than the men who balked against women's suffrage because it "wasn't their place" when all along she had had the same mind about the colored people of Ironwood?

The carriage rolled to a stop, and the driver opened the door. She passed him payment and thanked him with a smile. He drove off, leaving her to her business with Mr. Watson. Hopefully he wouldn't mind an early morning call. This was important, after all.

She rapped gloved knuckles on the door and stepped back to wait. A moment later the butler opened the door and scowled at her.

"Yes?"

Faith kept her tone pleasant despite his rude welcome. "Good morning, sir. I'm here to call upon Mr. Watson."

His nose wrinkled as though she were a bit of rubbish on the stoop. "Very well. I shall inform him of your unexpected presence." He glanced behind her and raised an eyebrow. "Without escort."

Mr. Watson would surely understand her lack of propriety when such an important matter was at hand. Faith moved into the parlor but did not select a seat. She stood by the window, watching the quiet street outside. A few people ambled by, mostly men likely on their way to the morning's business.

"Good morning, Miss Harper."

She turned to find the harbor master dressed in a pressed suit with a bright red cravat. He reached for her, and she offered a gloved hand. He bowed over it, pressing his lips to her knuckles.

"Thank you for seeing me as such an early hour."

He smiled. "My pleasure, dear. How can I be of service?"

Whatever had happened in Nolan's childhood, this fatherly gentleman had been quick to help people in need, and that said a lot about a person. "I won't take up much of your time."

He gestured for her to sit on the settee and then settled himself on it with her. He smelled of hair oil and shaving soap. She must have intruded upon his morning grooming.

"Would you care for some tea or refreshment?" He lounged back and crossed one leg over the other.

"No, thank you." Faith laced her fingers together. "I've come to ask if you know of a steamer heading toward Plymouth or Newport."

"A steamer?"

"I'd like to get to Nantucket Island as quickly as possible, and as you informed us, reaching the shores by sail can prove difficult."

He stroked his chin and watched her. She waited while he thought. After a few moments, he sat forward and placed his elbows on his knees.

"Your father could not find one at the port offices?"

She hadn't thought to ask there. She drew her bottom lip through her teeth. "He prefers to travel by train and wait for further information."

The corners of his lips twisted. "I see. And you do not, I take it?"

"No, sir. I would like to save time by going straight to the island. I'll pay well for any ship willing to take me." Every penny of her stipend, if that was what it took.

He nodded along. He didn't shake off her idea or tell her she was rash. His acceptance gave her courage. She was making the right choice.

She hurried on. "I found some maps and looked at the island. There are smaller ones clustered around the main island. One of them is an abandoned whaling village. If they wrecked that far out, it could be some time before anyone searches there." She held his gaze. "I feel that each day wasted waiting could be disastrous for my friend."

When she finished, she sat back, giving him what she'd come to realize was the time men needed to consider before they spoke. He eyed her, and she could practically see the plans forming behind his eyes.

He would help her. Encouraged, she gave him her sweetest smile. "I do so appreciate your help."

"I'll tell you what." He slapped his hands on his knees and rose. "Why don't you meet me this evening at my office and I will see that you get safely to a steamer?"

That long? "Why can we not go now?"

"It'll take some time for me to make the proper contacts and secure your passage. I'm afraid I'll need the remainder of the day to dedicate to your request, and I don't believe any ships are heading toward Nantucket until tomorrow morning."

Thoughts of her father's disappointment surged to the forefront of her mind, but she pushed them away. She owed it to Mercy to do everything she could. Daddy would forgive her.

She offered Mr. Watson a smile. "Thank you again."

He gestured toward the door and placed his hand on the small of her back to guide her forward. "Come around seven. That should give me time to escort you aboard and see you safely settled for the evening."

"Yes, sir. Thank you again." They exchanged pleasantries, and she exited the front door. Now all she had to do was avoid Nolan and her father for the remainder of the day, and come morning, she would be on her way to rescue Mercy.

Twenty-Six

*M*ercy had never once been disappointed to see a storm end. As the sun peeked through the dark clouds and the rain dissipated, she found herself wishing for more wind and water.

Jed released her, and despite the heat and humid air, she somehow felt colder. He offered a hand and helped her out from underneath the shelter. They stood in the final drops of the heaven's release and surveyed their camp.

The wind had overturned two of the three canvases, but one had held. Jed stepped over strewn limbs and hastened toward it. He turned with a grin as the others ambled out of their various hiding places.

"We collected several inches!" He glanced to the sailors. "*¡Recolectamos varias pulgadas!*"

There was a cheer as the disheveled lot drew around the soaked canvas, but Mercy's stomach sank. The water was good. They needed it. But how long would they have to do this? Waiting on storms for water, struggling to get fish from the turbulent ocean?

The men poured the precious water into various containers they'd found. Portions of coal barrels from the shipwreck, two pots that had washed ashore, and several buckets gathered from the abandoned village.

They spent the remainder of the day working to right the camp again. Mercy threw herself into the labor, hoping it would keep her mind from returning to the moments spent hidden from the storm. She understood it now. That thing, that feeling that caused a woman to want to stay sheltered from the world in the arms of a man she...admired. Yes. Admired. That had to be it.

Or perhaps she was lying to herself. Because she spent the working hours picturing him drawing her into his arms in their kitchen while their children groaned about it. That wasn't just admiration.

Was this what her brother had felt that caused him to renege on his plans to leave Ironwood and settle instead? Had Deborah, her sister by marriage, caused such an unsettling in him that he could no longer imagine going anywhere she wasn't?

"Fine collection we got there."

Hezzie's voice tugged Mercy from her thoughts. "What? Oh." She offered the woman a smile. "The water. Yes."

Mischief danced in the old woman's eyes. "What you thinkin' about so hard?"

"Where did you run off to in the storm?"

Hezzie grinned. "Forgot my shoes."

"So you went to get them in the middle of the storm?"

Mercy looked down at Hezzie's bare feet, and the woman laughed.

"Didn't say I decided to wear them." Her eyes sparked with humor. "How did you fare durin' the storm?"

Heat swarmed in her cheeks. "Fine."

"That what you thinking about so hard over here?"

Mercy tugged the limb she'd been dragging and dropped it into the pile of firewood. "Just wondering when we will get rescued."

"Hmm." Hezzie dropped her armload of twigs. "And here I thought it had something to do with my Jed."

Mercy tried to laugh. "Now why would you think that?"

She quirked an eyebrow. "I've seen how you two look at each other. A mother isn't blind to such things, you know."

Mercy lifted her chin. "I don't know what you're talking about."

Hezzie shook her head. With a sigh she turned and ambled off. Mercy scurried after her.

"Wait."

The old woman turned with a knowing smile Mercy chose to ignore. "How does he look at me?" She hated the neediness of having to ask, but she wanted to know. These things were all new to her, and when they left this island, well...well, she just wanted to know was all.

"He looks at you like he's found something he wasn't expecting to find. A treasure he didn't even know he was hunting for."

Mercy's breath ceased. "Truly?"

"And what do you see in him, child?"

Her eyes drifted to where he slapped a man on the back and offered encouragement. "I see a man of character, honor, and impossible dreams. I see someone who has a special touch on his life, and I believe God will have great plans for him."

Hezzie's face split in a wide grin. "So do I." She nudged Mercy's shoulder with her own. "I knew I liked you for a reason."

Mercy laughed and looked away.

"So what you going to do about it?"

"Pardon?"

Hezzie gestured toward her son. "You two have been brought together, but soon enough it will be time to separate. He has plans to start a church. What do you want?"

Once, that question had been easy. Now, she wasn't sure. "I don't know."

"You don't?" Hezzie crumpled her forehead. "I thought you wanted to make a difference in this world."

"I did. I do." She drew a breath and held it a moment before letting the truth out with it. "But what I really wanted was to be someone important. I wanted people to know my name. I wanted them to admire me. I wanted them to respect me and fawn over my talent."

Hezzie's face softened. "And now?"

"After meeting Jed, I realize how shallow my dreams were." Something welled up in her. "It's not my name that matters. It's the work I feel called to do that matters. My words can make a difference. People only need to see the message, not the writer."

The old woman pulled her into a fierce embrace. "I'm proud of you."

The words seeped into Mercy's heart, tugging at places she hadn't recognized needed attention.

When Hezzie pulled back, her eyes shimmered with tears. "I knew you were special. Lord himself sure enough knows it, seeing as He made you and all." Hezzie grinned and cut a glance over to Jed. "Jed sees it too. I reckon your family and your friends do, too." She squeezed Mercy's shoulders. "How many more you need?"

Mercy let her gaze linger on Jed as he hoisted a limb to secure a tent. His exposed arms were a testament to the care he'd given her foot. She looked down at where he had since cleaned and dressed it, wrapping it tight with the other sleeve.

She didn't need the world to admire her. They didn't know her. They didn't know her heart or her fears and worries. They didn't know the way she recklessly dove into things without thinking or the fact that her heart fluttered with excitement over the printed word. She squared her shoulders.

"So, what you going to do, then?"

Mercy smiled. "I'm going home."

Hezzie nodded.

"And I'm asking you two to come with me."

Hezzie opened her mouth, but the sudden shout of "Ship!" had both women turning toward the ocean.

Jed dropped the canvas and dashed across the sand, waving his arms. Mercy sucked in a breath and followed him, ignoring the sting in her foot as she ran. In a few quick strides, Jed plunged knee-deep into the waves. Mercy paused at the water's edge, anticipation thrumming in her veins.

"You see that?" Hezzie shouted. She grabbed Mercy's arm as she came jerking to a halt from her dash across the sand.

"Someone has come for us!"

Hezzie gripped her arm tightly, and together they watched as the massive steam ship dropped anchor a short distance out. In less than a quarter hour, two small boats were lowered over the side, each filled with men.

"Where did they come from, you think?"

Mercy looked at Hezzie from the corner of her eye. "I don't

suppose it matters much who the ship belongs to, does it? So long as they get us off this island."

Strangely, Hezzie remained quiet. They stood together as the remnants of *The Princesa's* sailors gathered, shouting celebratory phrases she didn't need to understand the language to appreciate. They were rescued!

The boats bobbed along the waves. As the figures drew closer, she began to make out the forms of the men on board.

"Why they need so many on that boat?"

She ignored Hezzie and walked closer to the water's edge. The incoming waves lapped at her toes. She squinted, seeing if she recognized any of the people.

Somewhere inside, she hoped her father had come for her, but all the faces bobbing in the water were white. Papa wouldn't leave Ironwood. Not even to find her. Another step into the water. Mr. Charles, then? Would he be among those who rode the water's surface?

She shook her head. Why would she even expect that? She was a colored woman. The Harpers gave them sanctuary, but they wouldn't be coming to her rescue on a steamship.

Hezzie grabbed Mercy's shoulder, bouncing up on her toes as though that would help her better see across the distance. "What?"

Mercy shook her head. "Nothing."

Hezzie craned her neck. "You know any of those men?"

"No."

Violent emotions crashed inside, turning her stomach to knots that had nothing to do with her lack of food and adequate water. She was desperate to get off this island, and at the same time... Her eyes met Jed's, and something passed between them.

She also wasn't ready to leave.

Nolan paced the hall. Something wasn't right. Faith had been coiled like a snake at breakfast, ready to strike at anything he said. Then she'd gone to her room in a fit of temper and he hadn't seen her since.

He checked his timepiece. Three hours. It didn't seem like her to sit in her room and sulk while the men made plans. His chest tightened.

Surely Faith had *not* gone out somewhere on her own. She wasn't that foolish. He knocked harder.

No answer.

He turned from the door and bounded down the steps. Mr. Harper was waiting in the lobby for him with a scowl.

"Where is she?"

"If she's in her room, she's not answering."

Mr. Harper groaned. "Impetuous girl!" He whirled around and stalked toward the door.

Nolan followed after him and waited as he barked orders at the bellboy to find him a hackney immediately.

When Mr. Harper turned back to Nolan, his face was red. "I should've known better. She hasn't been up there resting. She probably went to the wharf to find a steamship."

The tightness in his chest turned to a souring of his stomach. Nolan kept his tone as even as possible. "I thought our plan was to travel to Newport and seek a ship from there?"

Mr. Harper pointed his cane at Nolan. "That was *our* plan. Faith's was to get on a steamer from here and head straight to Nantucket."

Nolan groaned. "She wouldn't."

Mr. Harper hiked his eyebrows.

"Never mind. You're right. She would."

The hackney arrived in short order, and they headed toward the wharf. But after checking at several agencies and asking after a brazen woman in a brown traveling dress, they were still no closer to finding her.

After the last ticket agent told them he didn't recall seeing her, Nolan removed his hat and wiped the sweat from his brow. "Where else could she have gone?"

Mr. Harper, his mood growing more agitated by the hour, merely let out an irritated growl.

Nolan scanned the busy harbor. Men shouted to one another. Barrels were loaded onto some ships and off others. Gulls dipped in between, trying to steal fish that were meant for human stomachs.

"Perhaps we should visit Arnold, then." He hated to admit it, but Arnold Watson had an ear to the ground and nose to the scent of every movement along the water's edge. "He may know something."

They found him in his office a half hour later, puffing a pipe and scanning his ledgers. He didn't rise. "Mr. Harper, what a surprise." He eyed Nolan. "I didn't expect to see you here."

Mr. Harper towered over Arnold's desk. "My daughter. Have you seen her?"

He sat back, appearing perplexed. "You mean you don't

know?" He tugged a timepiece out of his vest pocket. "How odd. You were supposed to leave an hour ago."

Nolan's stomach dropped. "What?"

Arnold paid Nolan no mind and kept his focus on Mr. Harper. "I do apologize. She came by earlier this morning and said you sent her to secure a steamer to Nantucket." He turned out his palms. "I procured three tickets for her, and she went on her way. I assumed the three of you would be onboard."

A sudden throbbing pounded in the back of Nolan's skull, and he forced his teeth to unclench. Perhaps she'd gone back to the hotel looking for them while they were out looking for her. He opened his mouth to suggest they return, but closed it as soon as realization hit him. If the ship left an hour ago, Faith would have left them here rather than miss the boat.

Mr. Harper clenched his fist. "When is the next boat going out?"

Arnold lifted his eyebrows but didn't comment on the man's harsh tone. He trailed a finger down his ledger and shrugged. "Won't be another until the day after tomorrow."

Nolan ran a hand down his face. Did she not know how dangerous it was to get on a ship on her own?

"Thank you," Mr. Harper barked, then turned on his heel and stalked from the room, the trouble in his knee apparently forgotten.

Twenty-Seven

*F*aith twisted her fingers together as she walked down the darkening sidewalk. Shadows played chase across her path, waxing and waning with each brush of her skirts. She ignored the guilt that had taken up residence in her chest and refused to be swept away with logic.

It made no sense to keep waiting. They needed to *do* something. She quickened her pace, keeping her chin up and her eyes forward even as her skin crawled with looks from men swarming over the wharf like rats scurrying in the cellar.

She rounded a corner and pulled the lace of her collar tightly against her neck. There. Mr. Arnold Watson's offices. Almost there.

Gas lights flickered to life along the water's edge, lighting the path for the men who made their living from the sea to get back to warm beds and cozy homes. Many of them cast her strange glances as she stepped up onto Mr. Watson's front stoop, but none bothered her.

She pulled on the knob, only to find the office locked. Had he forgotten?

Faith slipped a timepiece from her pocket and checked the hour. Three minutes until seven. She knocked firmly on the door, but received no response. Where was Mr. Watson?

A quarter hour later she huffed. Fiddle-faddle. Shaking her head, she stepped away from the large building that had soaked up the scents of salt and brine.

Would there be any cabs for hire nearby? Should she go to Mr. Watson's townhome, or consider the entire plan a waste and return to the hotel? As she stood there debating her options, a noise came from the alleyway by the side of the building.

"Mr. Watson?"

No reply. The wind picked up, catching a discarded newssheet and hurling it out into the road.

Faith heaved a breath. Better she go back to the hotel and explain to Daddy what she'd done. She scanned the road, which had become suddenly vacant. It was too far to walk now. It would soon be dark, and a lady certainly didn't need to be out on the streets alone.

Thoughts of missing girls had her stomach in a knot. What was she to do now? Mr. Watson was supposed to be her escort.

Another sound came from the alley behind her and she had to stifle a yelp. Probably just a cat. The back of her neck tingled and she resisted the urge to bolt.

There was nothing to worry over. Just her imagination and—

Something skittered behind her. She whirled around. Nothing. The alley stood drenched in shadows, as though night had already come to claim the small strip of land. Heartbeat racing, she took a step back.

Cab. She needed to get a cab. Her pulse hammered. This had been a bad idea. Forgetting propriety, Faith hitched up her skirts and turned to run.

A massive shadow reached for her from the darkened alley and Faith screamed. She lurched sideways, losing her footing. Before she could scream again, something solid arrested her fall and then snatched her into a sour embrace.

Nolan smacked his hat against his leg before slamming it back down on his head as the cab slowed at the curb. This wasn't good. Not good at all. He jumped down from the Hansom cab and tossed the driver his fare.

That lying, contemptible fiend! He stalked through the hotel lobby, gaining the curious glances of patrons gathered for evening conversations.

His footsteps pounded heavily on the stairs, then tromped down the hall with the echoes of a man steeped in frustration. He pounded on Mr. Harper's door.

It opened immediately. "Did you find her?"

Nolan glanced past him into the richly appointed room and took note that Mr. Harper's trunks were already packed.

"He lied."

Mr. Harper's eyebrows shot toward his hairline. "Who lied?"

"Arnold."

Gesturing him inside, Mr. Harper stepped back into the room and closed the door. "He lied about what? Faith?"

"There wasn't a steamer leaving out at the time he indicated. Only two schooners left port for southern waters. And there is a steamer leaving in the morning, not the day after."

He let the words sink in a moment, their implications setting on his employer's face in deep furrows and feathered lines around narrowed eyes.

"Why falsify the ship schedules?"

Nolan rubbed the back of his neck. "My uncle is a loathsome man. But I never suspected he would mislead Faith on her quest simply to get back at me."

Mr. Harper clenched his fists. "If Faith didn't leave on a steamer set for Plymouth or Newport, then where is she?"

"I wish I knew." If anything happened to her because Arnold sought to repay Nolan for the talk he'd stirred around Boston by leaving as he had, he didn't think he could forgive himself. They should have never trusted that blackguard.

Mr. Harper paced the floor, the color of his neck deepening with each forceful footfall. "Impetuous girl!"

Nolan cleared his throat. "Sir, if I may, I suggest you take the evening train as planned and head south. I will wait here for her at the hotel and then check the ships leaving in the morning. That way, if she left on the schooner, you can sooner locate her. If she is hiding and waiting for the morning's steamer, then I will intercept her."

The plan made, the two made haste to get Mr. Harper to the train station just in time for the warning whistle.

He slapped a hand on Nolan's shoulder. "Thank you."

"Of course, sir."

Mr. Harper wagged his head. "No, I mean for all of this. It certainly isn't in your job description, and I'm sorry I dragged you into such a messy family affair."

"Sir, I don't—"

"Do your best to find her, hear?"

Nolan nodded. "You have my word."

The porter shouted, and Mr. Harper stalked toward the train, his cane thumping across the platform. Nolan watched the Pullman cars gain momentum with the squeal of wheels upon tracks and then move slowly down the line. Then, he adjusted his cravat and hailed a Hansom cab.

He barely noticed the scenery passing by or the shouts of the driver as they entered traffic heading toward some theatre performance or other nightly entertainment for the rich and unencumbered. Nolan drummed his fingers on his knee. Where would she have gone?

He knew one way to find out.

Arnold Watson.

Mercy wobbled as Jed helped her onto the dock cloaked in darkness. The rough wood felt foreign beneath feet now accustomed to sand. She clung to his arm as insistently as night had chased away the last breaths of the day.

"There, now. We'll find an inn for the night and a good meal, and all will be right." Jed's voice soothed her and, probably, his mother, who held on to his other arm.

After he was sure they wouldn't collapse on the dock, Jed pulled himself free and moved to speak to some men. About all that had occurred, she presumed. But Mercy was too tired to pay it much mind and merely stood with Hezzie on the water's edge and waited.

She was back on the mainland, and that was a start. First, they would find a place to stay and my, wouldn't something other than fish be grand to eat?

Men hurried by, none paying much attention to two colored women huddled together in rags. Was their situation so common that human decency had since been stifled? She wrapped her arms around Hezzie. Where would they get new clothing?

The men who had come on the ship to rescue them hadn't offered anything more than to unload them at the first available dock. What would they do now?

"Mercy!"

Her name mingled with the shouts and bustle of the crowd. She glanced to Jed. Did he need her for something? But he was engrossed in conversation.

"Mercy!" That familiar voice. It couldn't be.

Hezzie looked up at her. "Someone's calling you." The disbelief in her voice thickened the air, and Mercy turned.

Striding through the crowd in an expensive suit and looking as out of place as a cardinal in a flock of sparrows was the one she'd doubted would come for her.

She placed a hand over her heart. "Mr. Charles!"

Her knees buckled, and Hezzie propped her up.

Faith's father wove through the crowd, but before he could reach her, Hezzie stepped in front of her and puffed her chest.

"What you want with this girl?"

Stunned, Mr. Charles jerked to a stop. "Pardon?"

Mercy shook the fog from her head and slid around Hezzie. "Mr. Charles!"

A wide grin split his face, and in an instant she was wrapped in his arms and sobbing into his black jacket. He held her for a moment and then eased her back to arm's length.

"Are you hurt?"

She shook her head.

"What's goin' on here?" Hezzie eyed Mr. Charles with keen suspicion.

Mercy ignored her. "Where's Papa? Did he come?" Even as she asked it, she scanned the crowd milling behind them. "Mama?"

"Home praying you're alive. Faith and I came to find you when we discovered you'd gone to Boston." He lifted his thick eyebrows. "We were afraid you may have gotten into trouble."

The words brought a sense of profound relief that started as a hiccup, then evolved into an irrational giggle, and finally bubbled into a hearty laughter that sought to push all the anxiety from her soul. "Yes, indeed. I'm afraid I found far more trouble than I ever expected." She sobered and looked at the crowd on the dock again. "Where is Faith?"

Mr. Charles's face contorted. "She didn't want to take the train. She was determined to get on the first steamship out of Boston and find you."

"Ah, now I see," Hezzie muttered.

Remembering her manners, Mercy turned. "Mr. Charles, this is Hezzie. She and her son Jed were on the ship with me."

"Is he the one who took you from two men at the dock?" Mr. Charles's voice was hard as flint steel.

"How did you know about that?"

Before he could answer, Jed strode up. Dressed in a stained linen shirt missing two sleeves, he looked every bit the washed up sailor. The two men eyed one another, and Mercy stepped toward Jed.

"Mr. Charles this is Mr. Jedidiah, uh…Jed." How could she have fallen in love with a man and not remember his family name? "Jed, Mr. Charles Harper."

Before Jed could speak, Mr. Charles thrust a finger at him. "Why did you take Mercy?"

Jed pulled his head back. "What?"

Tension thickened in the air, overpowering the noise of the wharf and the scent of fish and brine. Mercy raised her hand to calm them, but the two men puffed out their chests and glared at one another like two cocks about to fight.

Mercy said, "Now, wait a moment—"

"My Jed saved Mercy from some men who had some nasty intentions for her!" Hezzie eyed Mr. Charles, her expression thunderous. "What intentions do *you* have for her?"

Mr. Charles now looked as taken aback as Jed. "Excuse me? I don't have to—"

Mercy held up her hands. "Wait!" Their eyes turned to her. "I can explain!"

She looked at the people who cared for her, each face lined with both worry and suspicion. She couldn't help but smile. "I appreciate everyone's concern over me, but it needn't be directed at one another." She gestured to Mr. Charles. "This is Mr. Charles Harper. He is a very dear friend of my parents and the father of my own dear friend. My father sent him to find me."

Mr. Charles's eyes softened, and he gave her a nod. Any lingering doubts left her. "My father sent him not because he didn't long to come himself, but because he knew that Mr. Charles would stand a far better chance of navigating such a city."

Something like respect flickered in Mr. Charles's eyes, and he inclined his head. She turned her attention to the man who had claimed her heart in far too short of a time.

"Jed saved me from some men who abducted me in Boston. If not for him, I don't know what would have become of me." She shivered despite the humid night. A bug buzzed in her face, drawn to the light of the gas lamp overhead, and she swatted it away.

The two men still eyed one another. Mercy motioned to Hezzie, whose distrust of Mr. Charles clearly had not evaporated. "This is Hezzie, Jed's mother. She cared for me and counseled me, and I will forever be the better for knowing her."

Hezzie suddenly grinned, and the tension broke like shattered ice.

Mr. Charles held out a hand, and Jed grasped it. "We are in your debt, young man."

Mercy breathed a sigh of relief.

"Well, that's all lovely," Hezzie said, "But can we please get off this dock now that we got all that settled? These old bones need a stuffed mattress and a long sleep."

Mercy laughed, and peace settled over her heart.

Twenty-Eight

Something scurried across the floor. Faith drew her knees closer to her chest, praying a rat wouldn't attempt to find her hem and gnaw on her limbs. She drew a shuddering breath and let it slowly back out. How long had she been here?

In the pitch black, it was impossible to tell. She rubbed at the sore places on her cheeks where the gag had been bound tight and squeezed her eyes closed. Doing so did nothing to change the heavy darkness nor erase the feeling still crawling over her skin.

Hands had grabbed her. Touched her. Voices had slithered into her ears, promising horrors and nightmares she would never be able to erase.

She'd found the missing girls. And become one of them.

Tears gathered and slid down her face, and the cold eyes of Amanda at the Pink Parrot returned to her. Was that where she was now? In some place where girls were gathered to be sold? Sold into…what exactly?

One of the women coughed, and another sniffled in the darkness. She didn't know how many there were with her, or where she was, for that matter. They had bound, gagged, and blindfolded her and then loaded her in the back of a wagon and covered her with a sour canvas. A short time later, she'd been removed and tossed into the darkness.

First she'd broken the loose bindings. Then she'd freed her mouth. She'd cried out until her throat was raw. Terror had nearly rendered her senseless when she'd discovered she wasn't alone in the dark. Then dismay had filled her when she'd realized she shared the small, dank place with several other women. Women who had listened to her scream without a word.

Not one of them had told her the crying would be of no use. She'd given up when she could scream no more, then crumbled into the silent despair that already clung to the others. They'd ignored her. She supposed they all knew it was a necessary reaction and one had to discover the uselessness of it for herself. Or perhaps they were simply too terrified or too numb to do anything at all.

Hours. It had to have been hours she'd sat in the dark. Maybe it was days. She didn't know.

Lord, are you there?

How long had it been since she'd prayed? Too long. It seemed wrong to do so now, crying out to God only in desperate need when she'd not spoken to Him in a long time. Why had she stopped? She used to pray all the time. When had she become so engrossed in her own plans and own ideals that she'd turned away from what had been her most important relationship?

Forgive me.

Her throat tightened. She'd acted spoiled and selfish. In her pride she'd insisted on her own way, taken her dearest friend for granted, and snubbed the one man who may have actually cared about her. And worst of all, she'd disregarded the Lord until desperation left her with no other options. She could do nothing on her own now.

I'm sorry, Father. Please forgive me. Please come to our rescue and shield us from the horrors intended for us. Help me find a way to get us out of here. Grant me wisdom.

Faith drew a deep breath of the dank air and forced herself to think. She couldn't let the darkness and the dire nature of her circumstances rob her of the one asset she had on hand. She had to figure out a way to get out of here.

Had to, or she would surely go mad.

"Hello?" She tested her voice in the darkness. It was reedy and thin. No one answered. She spread her arms out, then yelped when her fingers brushed flesh beside her. "Who are you?"

The person stirred and brushed Faith's fingers away. "Nobody. Just like you."

Relief surged despite the woman's caustic tone. "I'm Faith."

Silence.

"What is your name?"

"What does it matter?"

She shifted and scooted down the damp wall, yearning for friendly contact. "It matters because I'll not resign myself to what's happening here. I'll fight it with all I have, and if that fight starts with keeping my sanity by introducing myself, then so be it."

Surprisingly, the woman chuckled. "You've got spunk. But that won't help you none."

She brushed away the chilling words. "What's your name?"

"Cecilia."

Faith leaned her head back against the wall. "How long have you been in here, Cecilia?"

The voice that returned to her was haunted. "Not long enough."

A shiver ran down her spine. "What?"

"Better in here than what waits out there."

Faith refused to let fear overtake her. *Help us, Father.* "What happens out there?"

She could feel the woman move in the darkness. "You truly don't know? Where did you come from?"

"Does everyone know?"

Cecilia barked a laugh. "Anyone with any sense. Ain't but one thing that can happen next."

"Enough, Ce. Leave the girl alone." Another feminine voice from somewhere across the room.

Cecilia mumbled something Faith couldn't decipher.

Faith tried again. "Can anyone tell me what they know of where we are, what happens, and any other details that can be useful?"

"Useful for what?" the voice across the room asked.

"Escape."

There was silence for a moment, then someone groaned. "She sounds like you, Barb."

Silence.

Faith waited, hoping someone would say more.

Finally, the voice Faith assumed belonged to Barb spoke up again. "Ain't no use."

"Why?"

Shuffling. Someone coughed. More shuffling. How many more were in here, listening but not speaking?

"They don't give us any light. Whenever they open the door, it's still always dark. They give us a bucket of water, but no food. No one stays longer than a week or so, as best we can tell, before they are hauled out."

Faith ran her hands down her arms. "Then what?"

"They come in and snatch us," Cecilia snapped. "That's what. Sometimes one. Sometimes a couple. We don't know. We never see who they take." She sighed. "I stay quiet. Hard for them to find me that way."

She let the information settle for a moment. "How do they get in and out without any light?"

It was quiet a moment, then Cecilia spoke, her voice thoughtful. "There's two ruffians, I think. One grabs, one blocks the door."

A flicker of hope sparked. "Where is the door?"

"Don't know."

"How can you not know? Which direction do they come from?"

Cecilia snorted. "By the time you hear the creak of the door, they are already in the middle of us. Girls scramble and they get grabbed. It turns into chaos. Then it's over."

Her stomach sank. Still, they had to know which direction the creaking sound came from. It didn't make any sense not to know anything.

"I never move," Cecilia said. "Don't get up and try to run from them. They haven't grabbed me yet because I don't move."

Faith rubbed her temples. Cecilia probably wouldn't have a sense of time in the darkness, so Faith didn't ask again how long she'd been in here. But her answer of "not long enough" made more sense now.

"But you've had water while you are in here, even if you haven't eaten."

"I know what you're thinking. But that won't help. The bucket comes down somewhere in the middle."

Faith thought a moment. "Down? Like from a rope?"

"I reckon."

She snapped her fingers. "That's it then. We're in a cellar. The water is lowered from a rope from a door in the floor above us, which would be our ceiling."

Cecilia shifted next to her. "What does that matter?"

Her shoulders slumped. "It doesn't."

"I have an idea, if anyone would do it." Barb's voice came softly. "But they're all too afraid."

Hope stirred in her chest. "What idea?"

"Well, it is foolish, I know." Barb hesitated and drew an audible intake of breath. "They come in and grab us. It's too dark for us to see them coming, but when the girls hear the door, they scramble. If we pressed ourselves close to the wall near the door, where I am now, and remain silent and still, we might be able to overpower the one guarding the entrance and get out around him."

Faith pressed her fingers to her lips. Someone knew where the door was. And she already had a plan. A dangerous one, but a plan nonetheless.

Thank you, Lord.

"You think it's foolish, too," Barb said.

"No, actually, I think that's brilliant," Faith said, infusing her words with as much confidence as she could muster. God help them. "We only need to figure out a way to keep the two men occupied while the others escape."

"And who's going to do that?" Cecilia asked, disbelief in her tone.

Faith stood. "I will."

There was a smile in Barb's voice. "Then so will I."

"Then it's settled," Faith said. "But first, I suggest we gather and pray."

Nolan pounded on the door to Arnold's house and scowled at the butler as he opened the door.

"I need to see Arnold."

The man turned up his nose. "He isn't home. Shall I take a message for him?"

"Where is he?"

The butler eyed him. "Not home, sir. As I stated."

Nolan turned on his heel and hailed the hackney driver who had not yet ushered his horse back onto the cobblestones. If Arnold wasn't home, he would try his office on the wharf. If he wasn't there... Well, Nolan didn't know. But he would figure out a way to find Faith, God willing.

The hackney bumped over the cobblestones, jostling his already frayed nerves. He hardly noticed the city around him or the workers that still pushed debris from the corners of the streets after the storm. The air smelled more heavily of salt as the horse clopped onto the street running parallel to the wharf.

Nolan asked the driver to wait for him outside Arnold's

offices. Rocks crunched beneath his feet as he hurried to the door. He found it unlocked and let himself in unannounced. The lights had been extinguished for the night, save one.

His shoes tapped an anxious rhythm across the floor.

"Who's there?" A gravelly voice called from the open doorway on the other side of the empty reception area.

"I'm here to see Arnold Watson."

A man appeared in the doorway, his slight frame haloed by the glow of the lamplight behind him. "It's late. Everyone's gone home. Just came back in to fetch my pipe." He frowned at Nolan as he came to a stop in front of him, then his eyes widened. "Nolan? Is that you?"

Nolan leaned closer, trying to distinguish the man's aged features. "Mr. Peables?"

The elderly man laughed and slapped Nolan on the shoulder. "Sure is good to see you, my boy. It's been, what, ten years?"

"There about, sir."

"You look good. Real good. Grew up to be a fine man, I'm sure."

Warmth radiated in his chest. Mr. Peables worked for Arnold and had always had a kind word and bit of encouragement for an orphaned boy under the thumb of his overbearing uncle. "Thank you, sir. You are looking well yourself."

The man barked a laugh. "No need for polite lies now. I've seen this wrinkled face and bald head a time or two in the looking glass."

Nolan glanced around the darkened offices, worry overpowering politeness. "Is Arnold around?"

"He left hours ago."

Nolan rubbed the back of his neck. Perhaps he'd just missed him at home and should try back there.

"Anything I can help you with?"

Perhaps Mr. Peables had seen something. Nolan explained about Faith, her quest to find her friend, and her foolish plan to take a ship on her own. When he finished the brief overview of the events that had derailed his life, Mr. Peables rubbed the scruffy beard that struggled to cover his chin.

"Mr. Watson sometimes goes out to the storehouse in the evenings. Not sure what he does out there, but then, I don't ask. A man can count his barrels as often as he'd like, I reckon. You might find him there. It's three blocks directly east of here. Can't miss it."

Nolan thanked him and hurried out of the offices. Not wanting to make the driver take him such a short distance and then wait again, Nolan paid him extra for his time and sent him on his way. The night deepened quickly, bringing with it a blanket of stars and the light of a persistent moon that would not be ushered out by the flickering gas lamps.

The third block over, Nolan found the building he was looking for. Shadows dripped from weathered wooden walls that must have needed a coat of paint years ago. What did Arnold do with this place? He'd been dabbling in his own shipping enterprises and would need a place to store goods occasionally, but this seemed like far too large of a space for a one-schooner operation.

A sense of unease snaked its way down his back, and Nolan whispered a quick prayer that the Lord would help him find Faith and protect him if snooping around a darkened storehouse brought about trouble.

A gruff voice splintered the unnerving quiet. Nolan slowed, taking careful steps. He ducked into a shadow at the corner of the building and slowed his breathing.

"Got too many this week. Best take 'em all." The muffled voice, heavily accented, seemed to come from inside the building.

"Good haul this time. Some of 'em are goin' ta fetch a good price," a second voice responded.

Nolan eased around the corner of the building and into a narrow alley. As providence would have it, a door stood propped ajar. He kept his back to the building and sidestepped closer. The men's voices continued, but it seemed the men were moving off. Praying there weren't any more, he slipped through the doorway and into the dark storehouse.

It smelled of dust and disuse, layered with the fading stench of fish. A light bobbed in the back corner and then was extinguished.

He blinked in the darkness, his eyes straining to gain enough light by which to function. There was a creak and a scraping. A door perhaps? Nolan took a blind step toward it, and then another.

A sudden shout, then a curse. Nolan froze.

Screams. Female ones.

Despite the darkness Nolan rushed forward. He tripped on something and hit the ground hard, pain jarring up through his knee and into his hip. Groaning, he struggled to his feet and held his hands out in front of him, moving more cautiously.

Sounds of a scuffle ensued and Nolan pushed forward, drawing into whatever battle occurred.

Women screamed. Men cursed. Shadowy shapes darted

around in a swarm, pouring out of what seemed to be a narrow stairway descending down into the ground. Someone scrambled out of it, arms flailing, and bolted past Nolan.

He needed light!

Another figure darted past, stumbling around in the darkness.

"Go! Go, girls!" There was more scuffling at the bottom of the stairs. "Hurry—" The woman's shout was cut off by a yelp of pain.

Spurred into action, Nolan dove toward the stairs. Light suddenly erupted, washing the scene in revealing horror. Tattered women threw arms over their faces to shield their eyes. A man crouched at the bottom of the stairs, holding one woman by her hair. Another man stood over him, holding up a lamp.

Nolan caught sight of a girl on the stairway. Her brown eyes were wide with fear, and she reminded him of a caged cat. He took a step back and motioned for her to pass. Within seconds, she had bolted past him and up to the floor of the storehouse.

The man with the lamp noticed Nolan and shouted.

The man on the floor released the woman from his grasp and shoved her to the floor, then jumped to his feet. Nolan braced himself.

"Barb! Go!"

Nolan's breath caught. Her voice! "Faith!"

The name had no sooner escaped his lips than the fist of one of the scoundrels busted them open. Nolan stumbled back, tripping on the stairs rising behind him and falling on his back. In an instant, the man was on him.

Nolan twisted to the side and held up an arm to block his face. He swung his left fist and connected with the man's ribs, earning a groan.

He shoved the man backward, causing him to tumble down the stairs and land at the bottom of the stone steps at the foot of the doorway. The man with the lamp looked down at his companion then back up at Nolan.

This man, smaller than the first, appeared more calculating. His eyes narrowed beneath red eyebrows. He glanced at the door behind him and spread his body across the doorway.

"Faith! Are you here?"

There was a startled cry from behind the ruffian.

"Nolan!"

Blood surging, Nolan rushed down the stairs. The man with the lamp shouted and dropped it to the ground. Glass shattered. Flames licked at spilled kerosene. The big man on the floor screamed as fire grabbed his arm. He bolted past Nolan up the stairs, waving his arm as the blaze greedily consumed his sleeve.

Nolan looked back toward the smaller man. He reached behind him. Instinct told Nolan to duck.

A loud crack, and the hiss of a bullet split the air just above where Nolan's head had been. The acrid scent of gunpowder burned his nostrils.

Nolan leapt up and dove forward before the man could get another shot off. He hit the man in the torso, dropping him to the ground. As they struggled to gain the upper hold, heat scorched his legs. He kicked, desperately trying to avoid the consuming flames while not losing his hold on the scoundrel who would pay for any harm he'd cause Faith.

There was a shout, and then a sudden wave of water. It hurled through the air then hit the fire with a satisfying sizzle. He shook his head, trying to keep his wits. Someone had doused the flames! Darkness encroached as most of the fire died.

Nolan wrestled the man to the ground and pinned his writhing shoulders with his knees. He glanced up and saw Faith holding a bucket. The flames sputtered and winked out, leaving them once again in darkness.

The man shouted something foul, and Nolan's fist connected with the profane mouth. The man beneath him fell silent, his body slack.

Someone grabbed his arm and he tensed, then realized the feminine hand on his sleeve belonged to Faith. He laced his fingers with hers and tugged her up the stairs, across the dark storehouse, and out into the fresh night air.

"Are you harmed?" He searched her face in the scant light of the nearby streetlamp.

"No." Her wide eyes stared at him.

He pulled her into his arms, drawing comfort from the tangled mess of hair brushing his cheek. She was safe. Alive. Thank God.

Suddenly she tensed and then pulled away from him, the familiar stubbornness wiping the vulnerability from her face. "We had a plan."

He opened his mouth, but no words escaped. He closed it and tried again. "Are you upset with me for rescuing you?" He could scarcely control the anger heating his words.

She backed away from him as though he were one of the vile captors. Her chin trembled, but she kept her tone cool. "I appreciate you looking for me—"

A scuffling sound at his back had Nolan spinning around, fists raised. Two ragged women stumbled out into the night, their eyes wild. Faith darted past him and rushed to them. He watched the three women embrace. None of them seemed to care he'd come to rescue them.

The night air cooled his wet clothes, but irrational anger heated his chest. What did he have to be upset about? Faith was safe. He'd uncovered what had happened to the missing girls.

And he knew who was behind it all.

They needed to find the authorities. He stepped over and took Faith by the elbow. "We need to go."

She ripped her arm away from him. "What?"

He set his teeth. She'd had an ordeal. Of course she would be emotionally distraught. He couldn't hold her sharp tongue against her. "I said we—"

"I heard you." Her eyes snapped at him. "But I have to—"

"Nobody move!" A voice boomed across the alleyway by the storehouse, followed immediately by the pound of multiple sets of boots. "Police!"

Thank heavens. Nolan stepped forward. The first officer shouted again and leveled a pistol at him. Nolan froze.

The women screamed.

A beefy officer grabbed Nolan by the shoulder. "You're under arrest."

Twenty-Nine

After one had spent time on a deserted island, nothing in the world may ever again be as sweet as the warmth of a cozy fire and the scent of fresh bread and roasted meat. Mercy breathed deeply and looked at the people gathered around the table with her, a full stomach and a sense of contentment making her sleepy.

After their reunion on the dock, Mr. Charles had whisked them to the nearest inn, made sure they were fed, and sent them to rest. Mercy had slept through the night and late into the morning. When she'd finally arisen, it had been to a full noon meal followed by the luxury of a tub and hot water delivered to her room. She'd learned the surviving sailors had already found their way home or to other ships.

Mr. Charles had sent an immediate telegram home and had received a reply this afternoon. Her family knew she was safe. They loved her and eagerly awaited her return home. Faith should arrive tomorrow on a steamship. Mr. Charles had said she must have taken it all the way to Nantucket and would dock in the morning. What a shame she'd finally found where they had shipwrecked, only to discover Mercy had been rescued.

But she was rescued. Faith was on her way. Mercy's family

knew she was alive. Somehow, despite all the terrible choices she'd made, God had kept her in His hand, and had kept her safe. But there would still be consequences for her rash actions. Her pride and selfishness had caused those she loved deep heartache.

Mercy ran her fingers over the work dress Mr. Charles had purchased from the innkeeper's wife. He'd also bought two pairs of sturdy shoes for the women. The dress was far too large, but she wouldn't complain. Hezzie had to belt hers at the waist, and it dragged the floor. It would probably get stepped on like the one Mercy had chosen for her first train ride.

Hezzie sat across from her, listening as Jed and Mr. Charles continued to talk about both Jed's aspirations and the life of the people at Ironwood. Hezzie's gaze met Mercy's, and she smiled, then looked back to the men. Mercy would miss her. Hezzie had spoken wisdom and truth into her life, and such a friend was of great value. But she would miss Jed more. Her heart sank as he spoke of his home in Georgia and his plans to return there. Why had she hoped for anything different?

What had she really thought? That he would leave everything he had been working for and run off with her to Mississippi?

As she contemplated ways she might change his mind, the front door of the cozy little eating area burst open and a young man hurried in, scrambling up to the reception desk with great haste and causing the din of the room to quiet. The innkeeper's wife nodded at his request, then pointed toward the table where Mercy and her friends sat.

The young man brightened, turned their way, and hurried among the patrons still lingering over their roasted pork and boiled potatoes.

He sidled up to the table. "Mr. Charles Harper?"

"Yes?"

The man slapped his hat against his thigh. "I've been looking all over the city for you! You weren't in any of the hotels I was expecting." His gaze slid over the people sharing the table, then returned to Mr. Charles. "I have an urgent message."

He passed a paper to Mr. Charles. He opened it, scanned the contents, and then slammed the paper down on the table.

Jail wasn't exactly what Faith had expected it to be. Perhaps she'd read too many stories of fair maidens thrown into dank dungeons and guarded by fearsome knights with great swords. Still, it wasn't the type of place where she'd wanted to spend the night. She pulled the thin blanket over her and listened to Cecilia and Barb breathing soundly. They had been the three remaining when the police arrived. The others, blessedly, seemed to have escaped.

But poor Nolan. Her throat tightened. She'd been in hysterics. Not thinking straight. Nolan had come to rescue her, but after the terror and those men... She let the thought trail off and shivered. She couldn't remember what she'd said to him, but it hadn't been kind. She'd been so worried about the girls. And then he'd been arrested. She, Cecilia and Barb had been taken into custody for questioning, but Faith didn't see how that was any different than being arrested as well.

Oh, what a terrible mess.

At least the other girls had escaped. She reminded herself of that often, because no amount of logic or explanation had satisfied the officers' questions, and she and the other two women had found themselves here rather than in the comfort of a hotel. But the others had escaped.

Thank you, Lord. Better here than in that cellar. I'm grateful.

They'd taken Nolan to another area. She didn't know where. Warmth pooled in her chest. He'd come for her. How had he even found her? Why had she pushed him away when he had?

Thoughts swirled through her head, and she tried to untangle the mystery of what had occurred.

Cecilia and Barb both had similar stories of how they'd been taken. They had been out on the streets late at night. Apparently, Cecilia had grown too old for the orphanage and had been sent out. Barb had been leaving from a late night working in a wash house by the wharf. Both had been taken in the same fashion as Faith and deposited in the cellar of the storehouse.

And she had a suspicion she knew who was behind it all.

Nolan's fists clenched at his sides as he sat in a hard chair at the police station. How had he not seen it sooner?

He'd known Arnold was a cad, but this? Those girls had been in Arnold's storehouse. Arnold had lied about the ships. Had he lied about Faith coming to see him for passage, or was that the truth and he took her when she'd come? Anger constricted Nolan's chest so tightly he could scarcely breathe.

How dare he!

How dare he take any girls for nefarious purposes? But Faith? Nolan seethed. *His Faith!* When he got his hands on that man...

"Mr. Watson?" The officer who had left him in the small office that held nothing more than a single table and two chairs returned with a mug of steaming coffee. "We have located your employer."

Nolan rose. "I assume he's on his way?"

The officer shrugged, lifting the shoulders of his crisp uniform. "I don't know. All I know is the Pinkerton men were able to locate him per your request and deliver your message."

He took a seat at the table and eyed Nolan as if he hadn't already scrutinized him for several hours.

"Explain to me again why you were in the storehouse."

Nolan withheld a groan and repeated the same story again, to which the officer nodded along.

Finally, he sat back in his chair and stroked his mustache. "I'm inclined to believe you. Based on the information you gave us about what you discovered at the Pink Parrot, we were able to convince one of the employees to admit to recruiting girls at that same storehouse for their establishment. That, along with the confirmed identity of one of the women reported missing, brings me to the conclusion that we have finally discovered the nature of what has been happening to unfortunate women in this town."

Nolan waited, sensing the man had more to say.

He tapped a finger on his mug in thought. "What I can't piece together, however, is how you play a part in this scheme."

Nolan clenched his teeth.

"Your story of searching for a missing Negro girl is rather intriguing, I must admit." He tapped his finger on the table. "I found a report filed by your employer about this same girl. That gives you some credibility. And Miss Harper, well…" He lifted his eyebrows. "She was rather vocal about the situation as well."

"Then why do you continue to keep her in your custody?"

"We have no intention of detaining her once her father arrives to confirm her identity and answer some questions about you."

"Why am I under suspicion? I'm the one who discovered the operation."

"A very intricate operation, we've discovered, run by your own uncle."

A deep noise rumbled from somewhere in Nolan's chest that caused the officer to lift his eyebrows once more, offering a bit of life to an otherwise stoic face.

"I may suffer the unfortunate fate of sharing blood with Arnold Watson, but I assure you, he is no family to me."

"Yet you lived with him as a youth and now work in shipping as he does. How are we to know that you are not planning on expanding the operation by shipping these girls to the South?"

Nolan stared at him. "You can't be serious."

"Until I have all the facts, I'm serious about all possibilities."

Worry chased the lingering weariness from Mercy's body and filled her with the pulse of thrumming anticipation. The carriage jerked along the road at a fast clip, swaying and jostling with the increased speed Mr. Charles insisted upon.

After giving Jed and Hezzie a hasty goodbye, she'd joined Mr. Charles on the trip back to Boston. How in the world had Faith gotten herself into jail? Mercy held onto the side of the door, the night outside too dark to offer any view of the passing land between Plymouth and Boston.

Mr. Harper rode up front with the driver, leaving Mercy time in the plush interior on her own. Time to think, pray, and worry. So much had changed in the time since she'd first left home.

Emotions warred within her. She both longed for and feared the idea of returning to Ironwood. Her parents would use this as proof she should never leave again. But that was living life out of fear, and God had not given her a spirit of fear. She would not cower. This time, if she stayed, it had to be by her own choosing.

She had some ideas. Some plans that she wanted to share with the Harpers and her parents about making changes at Ironwood. They should be living out a vision, not hiding from the world. Perhaps they could create a place where everyone truly belonged. A place of Christian fellowship where race and economics didn't matter and only loving Jesus did. The more she thought on it, the more her heart came alive. Was this the calling that God wanted on her life?

It wasn't what she had planned, but it felt right. She could write articles and send them to papers all over the country, opening people's eyes to the possibilities. Such discriminations should not exist in the body of Christ. It would be a long battle, one she doubted she would live to see won, but she could take up her pen and fight for a vision that perhaps someday would take hold in the hearts of believers and blossom into something beautiful.

And if they could do it in Mississippi, then it could be done anywhere.

Despite her fatigue, hope surged, and there in a jostling carriage on the way to rescue her wayward friend, Mercy finally understood her purpose.

Something rattled, drawing Faith from her fitful dozing. Fear surged through her veins and she bolted upright, taking a moment to orient herself to her surroundings. Right. The holding cell at the police station. The other ladies had been released, but she'd remained.

They'd found Daddy, and he would be coming for her. They wanted him to answer some questions about Nolan and Mr. Arnold Watson. She blinked against the light, holding her arm up over her face. Daddy certainly wouldn't be pleased.

"Miss Harper? Your father is here for you."

She hurried forward and scarcely waited for him to pull open the barred door before slipping out of it. She tried to smooth her hair and straightened her posture. Daddy would be sorely displeased with her. Not only had she caused trouble for herself, but she'd delayed them in the search for Mercy.

But the others were free. The police had discovered what had been happening to the missing girls, and now it could be stopped. She straightened her posture. To think she'd trusted that man! Arnold Watson was a scoundrel of the worst kind. It wasn't charitable of her, but she wished him a long sentence in a dark cell all the same.

She followed the officer out of the holding area that contained three more cells identical to the one she'd been held in and then through a door and down a long hallway.

Faith watched the stained hem of her gown slide over the plank floor of the police station. *The women are free. No more will be taken.* They passed a few officers still on duty this late in the night, but most of them had long since gone home to their families. *Lord, save Mercy, too.*

She'd been foolish, but in His great mercy, God had protected her. Despite her ineptitude, He'd used the circumstance to bring the truth to light. And now she knew what sort of atrocities she would spend the remainder of her life fighting against. There were injustices far graver than voting issues. Horrors that screamed for better rights. For awareness. For laws against places like the Pink Parrot. She'd been designed with a mind for logic. A spirit that longed for fairness. She would use those gifts to—

"Faith!"

At the sound of the voice, Faith jerked her head up. It couldn't be! "Mercy!"

She lunged around the officer and launched herself into her friend's arms, weeping and repeating, "I'm so sorry!" in a jumbled mess of words and sobs that she doubted could even be understood.

Finally Mercy laughed and pushed her back. "What in creation are you blabbering about?"

Faith swiped tears from her eyes. "I'm sorry. It's my fault. I should have been there for you. I wasn't a good friend. I was selfish. I took you for granted. I didn't encourage you and help you, and…" The words tumbled out of her mouth until Mercy shook her head.

"I forgive you." Mercy sighed. "I'm the one who took off without a clue what I needed to know about the real world." She laughed. "Some reporter I would have made."

"Where have you been?" Faith scrutinized her friend. She seemed thin but unharmed.

"Shipwrecked." Her father's voice answered from somewhere to her left.

Faith gasped and turned to Daddy, heat warming in her cheeks. "You found her."

Daddy grabbed Faith and pulled her into a tight embrace. "You're safe."

She nodded against his shoulder, breathing in the scent of comfort that had protected her since childhood. "I'm sorry I deceived you."

He sighed and simply squeezed her tighter. "God is good. You're both alive and relatively unharmed, and I can return you to your mothers whole."

There would be some hard conversations and some growing pains in the future. But they were alive, more experienced, and, by the grace of the good Lord, united once again. They would be different women who returned home than the girls who had left it. And heaven help anyone who thought to stand in their way.

A weight lifted off her chest. Only one thing left to do. She glanced around the station. "Where's Nolan?"

Her father met her gaze, then slowly shook his head.

Thirty

*M*ercy squared her shoulders and spread her hands down the smooth front of her new yellow gown. Drawing in a long breath, she lifted her chin and wrapped her hand around the smooth brass knob to the *Boston Globe*. She pulled the heavy mahogany open and burst through the door in a wave of confidence and bravery she'd not felt weeks ago.

Had it only been that long? Tomorrow they would return home after two days of making sure the abduction ring had come to an end and seeing Mr. Arnold Watson, the man behind it all, safely locked away. Someday soon, she would have quite the article about that. But today she had one last thing to do in Boston before they boarded the train.

Men swiveled their heads from where they sat in their matching desks, a sea of small minds unexpanded by the changing world around them. Someone called to Mercy as she made her way for the grand staircase. She ignored him.

A smooth railing. Her hand trembled over it.

Let them see.

Faith's words swelled in her chest. Her friend. They'd cried their hearts out. They'd fought. They'd reconciled. And in the end, Faith had encouraged Mercy to take this final step. Faith had emboldened her to not tremble. Neither of them would tremble. Not again.

Nor would she be ashamed. Mercy wouldn't let anyone's hateful words define her. She wouldn't let their stares intimidate her.

Mercy took one step. Then another. Men called after her. She marched on. After reaching the top step in a swirl of determination, she stalked up to Mr. Johnson's door. Without knocking, she threw it open.

The hulking man startled, and his face turned red.

Mercy took a breath. Then another. She wouldn't downcast her eyes. She wouldn't let him make less of what God had made her. One step. Then another. She stood over his desk, and his eyes widened.

"Let me tell you who I am."

He sputtered and began to rise.

Mercy slammed her fist down on his desk. "No. Last time you talked. Now, you will listen."

He leaned back in his chair, stunned.

She lifted her chin. There wouldn't be a place for her in a world like this if she didn't make one. And she'd been given everything she needed.

"I am Mercy Carpenter. Daughter of the one King. Child of the Most High." She pointed her finger at him. "He made me a writer. Words stir in my soul. He gave me things to say, and neither you nor anyone else can stifle them."

The man began to shake his head, and she narrowed her eyes.

"You can tear down and deny my ability because of the skin He put me in, but your issue is with the Lord, not with me. I'm sorry for you, Mr. Johnson. You're blind."

A vein pulsed in his neck.

"You cannot break me down. You cannot tell me I won't be good enough. Your words don't matter. I am who I'm meant to be. And mark my words, sir. One day, you'll be sorry you disregarded the soul inside because you didn't care for the package she came in."

Her fingers tingled. Mercy swallowed. She'd done what she came to do. Peace flooded her, and she smiled.

"One day, you'll look around and see that the world has changed, and you were left behind. And then maybe you'll see that the voices you tried to drown were the very ones waving the new flag of freedom."

She turned on her heel. One step. Another.

Behind her, he began to chuckle. "Perhaps you're right."

She paused, smiled over her shoulder, then walked out the door a different woman.

She had to tell him. Faith simply couldn't let Nolan return to Memphis without knowing her heart. She'd let fear rule her for far too long. She scanned the crowded train platform, looking for a handsome man with patient eyes and a generous heart.

Nolan had protected her. Put up with her antics. Come after her when she'd been taken and had never once berated her for her astoundingly foolish actions. And she hadn't told him how her heart had soared to see him come to her rescue. She hadn't fallen into his arms and let him know that his quiet strength and gentle valor had won over her heart.

After Nolan had finally been released, they'd spent two hectic days making preparations to return home. Faith had planned to try to find a quiet moment to talk, but hadn't had the chance. No. Truth be told, she'd hoped he would come to her. But he hadn't. And she'd been too much of a coward to make the first attempt.

Now Nolan would be returning to Memphis thinking her heartless.

The hazy smoke stung her eyes. She blinked away the moisture and kept looking over the crowded platform. Where could he be?

People were staring at her, but she didn't care. She'd told Mercy to be proud of who God had made her to be and to never give in to a spirit of fear.

Now Faith had to take her own advice.

Smoke and steam poured from the train, washing over the platform like a dark wave. She put her hand to her nose. Had he already boarded?

The smoke billowed around her, settling itself on her hickory gown, marring the shine. Gone was the glimmer of the appeal of forging her dreams on her own. She'd been wrong. Because even if she gained accolades and acceptance, independence and respect, wealth and fame, none of it would matter unless she shared it with him.

Porters shouted to one another, and the already scrambling people on the platform increased their scurrying. Multiple people jostled her, but she ignored them. Lifting on her toes, she continued to search.

What would it be like to have someone there to catch her when she fell? To have someone support all her dreams and give her courage as she faced the unknown? To do the same for him, giving herself up to support his aspirations? To help him in all of his endeavors?

If she didn't find him, she might never know. She'd just have to start searching the passenger cars. Nolan must have already boarded.

The shrill whistle pierced the air, warning passengers the train would soon depart.

Her breath hitched. She had to stop him. Had to try. Before she could catch herself, she was running down the platform with tears blurring her vision. She raised her hand.

"Wait!" Her hem snagged and she stumbled. "Please, wait."

The wheels lurched, gained traction, and began to grind down the tracks. With a steady pulse, the train gained speed and pulled from the station.

The breath left her lungs. Too late. He was gone. Her heart pounded, and not only from the exertion of her ridiculous run down the platform. Just like she had foolishly chased after a train she couldn't catch, she'd been stubbornly pursuing the next thing she thought would fill the desire to *be more* and to *do more* and to make herself someone important.

But she had always been *someone* to the God who'd made her. A beloved child. A lady. She pulled herself up. She would go to Memphis. No matter what happened, Nolan would know her heart. Pride and fear would stop her no longer.

Besides, it wasn't as though if he left on a train she would never see him again. She would simply purchase a ticket and follow him. Daddy would understand. Faith gathered her traveling skirt to a near scandalous height and marched toward the ticketing counter. A long line greeted her.

She huffed and took a place at the rear of the line. The white-haired woman in front of her turned with a smile. "Excuse me, dear," the elderly lady said, tapping a tortoise shell fan on her arm. "Do you happen to know if there is a train to New York this morning?"

"No, I'm sorry. I'm hoping to find one to Memphis."

"Oh." The woman lifted the shoulders of her lavender dress. "I suppose I'll simply have to wait to find out when I reach the ticket desk."

Faith nodded.

The older woman continued to look at her. "What takes you to Memphis?" She glanced around and arched a brow. "Alone?"

Alone? She could say the same of this meddlesome stranger who also stood without an escort, but offered a smile instead. "To meet someone."

Her brown eyes brightened and she turned completely around to chat as though they were old friends. "Oh? Someone special?"

Faith swallowed the burning in her throat. "Yes."

The woman glanced behind Faith and then back. She smiled. "A special occasion, then?"

My, but wasn't she the busybody? Faith lifted her eyebrows, but the lady simply blinked and waited for a reply.

"I must tell this person I was wrong." Her voice constricted. "It's quite important."

"Oh?" a deep voice said from behind her. "Wrong about what?"

Faith gasped and spun around. "Nolan!"

He stood with his head cocked to the side, grinning at her. "I didn't think Miss Faith Harper was ever wrong about anything."

Her heart thudded. Providence had once again given her another chance. She couldn't waste this one. She grabbed his arm and yanked him from the line, barely registering the chuckling elderly lady.

Faith stepped into a less crowded corner of the busy platform and held Nolan's gaze despite her racing pulse. "But she is. She's been so terribly wrong for some time now."

"Is that so?" He lifted an eyebrow, mischief playing in his eyes. "You were also wrong about the train times for the Memphis line?"

Faith shook her head, not letting his humor distract her. "I haven't treated you fairly because I was afraid of the feelings I have for you. I was afraid of eventual heartache, and so I pushed you away. I've wronged you, Nolan, and I'm sorry."

He grew serious and something sparked in his eyes. Nolan reached out and placed her fingers in his. "You've never wronged me."

She opened her mouth to protest, but he placed her ungloved fingers gently to his lips and stopped her breath. They tingled from his touch.

"Wounded me, perhaps." His gaze roamed her face. "And if you wronged me, I forgive you. I've wronged you as well." He caressed her cheek, further muddling her senses. "I underestimated you at every turn. You are the most capable person I've ever known."

She tilted her head back, her heart pounding. Fear, hope, and anticipation swirled in her veins, pulsing through every breath. "Oh, Nolan. You are too good to me. Far better than I deserve."

"I've been thinking a great deal, and I've decided to tell you something."

Her breath caught.

"I couldn't think of any greater honor than working by your side." He leaned close. "Supporting your dream and helping you fight for equality by showing the world all they're missing."

Faith worked her lip between her teeth. The insecure girl inside of her begged for confirmation. "But... I'm obnoxious."

"Forthright."

"Opinionated."

"Educated."

The next truth hurt more. "Spoiled."

His eyes twinkled. "A bit, perhaps. But you're improving."

Faith smirked, and the girl she'd been sighed with relief and stepped aside for the woman she'd become. "You know what they'll say about me."

"I don't care what they say." He leaned closer to her, ignoring the whispers around them. "Let them talk until their breaths run out." He laced his fingers with hers.

Faith ignored the impropriety. Ignored the fact that being this close to a man in public would label her loose. She didn't care. "Fight for a new world with me?"

"Anything you wish."

Faith's lips curved, and then she pushed up onto her toes, a breath away from him. "Anything?"

His eyes darkened, and he gave a tiny nod. Emboldened, she looped her hand around the back of his neck and relished his surprised intake of breath.

Then, amid the gasps, she planted her lips to his and let the spectators talk.

Thirty-One

Ironwood Plantation
Oakville, Mississippi
August, 1887

*M*ercy's feet wouldn't be still. Mama leaned against her shoulder and whispered for her to calm down, but they both knew such a thing was futile. Papa leaned past Mama on the church pew and grinned at Mercy.

Something had been up with them. She'd caught them whispering all week. She cut a glance over her shoulder at the people gathered in the chapel patiently waiting on the preacher for services to begin. The past weeks of being home had changed her perspective on this place. It was no longer a prison, but it wasn't what it could be. She'd spent a lot of time talking with her parents and the Harpers about the kind of place Jed had dreamed of. The kind of place Ironwood could be.

The thought of him renewed the ache in her heart. His last letter had spoken of an exciting new opportunity that God had given him. After a lot of prayer, he'd become convinced it was the plan he knew he was meant for.

She was happy for him. Truly she was. But missing him still hurt. She ran her fingers over the folded paper in her lap. It was a copy of the latest article she and Faith had penned about what had happened to the women in Boston and the fate that many had suffered. She would show it to Mr. Charles and seek his opinion before sending it to the post office later in the week.

The *New York Tribune* would be the next place for a rousing article from Mr. Fredrick Mercy. And once there were enough of them, the world would know who Mr. Mercy really was. But in due time.

She settled back against the hard pew. Where was that preacher, anyway? Services were supposed to start at nine. Faith sat next to her, calmly fanning her face and smiling contently. But then, it wouldn't be an inconvenience to wait upon a dallying preacher when one had her new beau at her side. Mercy was too happy for Faith and Nolan to be jealous. Mostly.

The two of them made a handsome pair. And they were excited about the shipping business and all they planned to do. Mercy suspected it wouldn't be long before there was a wedding ceremony and Faith moved to Memphis.

She tried not to let the thought sadden her. God had His plans. And any journey He invited her to go on would always be an adventure. Perhaps not the one she expected, but always the one that would be the best for her.

Mr. Charles stepped up behind the pulpit in the Ironwood chapel and smiled at the crowd. What was going on? When Mr. Charles gestured for his wife to join him, she knew something was happening. Anticipation swirled in her chest. Would they start implementing some of the new ideas? Mercy sat straighter as Miss Lydia gained her husband's side and drew a deep breath.

"People of Ironwood," she said, "years ago we did something together that, at one point, we weren't certain we could do. We made a place of safety and peace in the aftermath of war." She placed her hands on the podium and looked at her daughter and Mercy.

"But we must now take another brave step forward. It's not enough for us to hide away from the world. We must seek to change it. And in order for us to do that, we must first change Ironwood."

The people began to mumble, but Mercy's heart fluttered.

Mr. Charles took his wife's hand. "If we ever hope to see the body of Christ unified across all races, nations, and peoples, then we have to see it start here."

Mercy placed her hand to her heart. Faith wrapped her arm around Mercy's shoulders and cut her a smile that was filled with something Mercy couldn't quite identify. They had made a difference. Convinced their parents to make another new future for Ironwood. Things were moving forward, and a new adventure was beginning. Her heart was nearly full.

"And to that end, we would like to welcome a man who has a vision and a calling we believe will help us take the next steps God has in store for each of us."

Her feet stilled. Her breathing slowed.

It couldn't be. *Dear God, let it be.*

Mercy lurched to her feet, the rest of Mr. Charles's words lost on her ears. She whirled around, anticipation swarming in her veins.

There at the back of the church stood Jed, Hezzie at his side.

Her mouth fell open, and he grinned. Frozen, she watched them walk up the center aisle, gaining whispers and open stares from the people. Papa rose and greeted him as though they had already met, and Hezzie's tiny form disappeared in Mama's hug.

Still, Mercy couldn't move. Couldn't believe it.

He was here.

And had Mr. Charles said…would he be…he was staying? Was he Ironwood's new preacher? Could this be the position he felt called to accept?

Mercy looked at Faith, who only grinned. Nolan tipped his chin, a smirk across his lips.

Hezzie sidled into the pew, then plopped down. She tugged on Mercy's hand as she still stood there dumbfounded. "Sit, girl. Our boy has something to say."

Mercy obeyed, unable to take her eyes off Jed as the Harpers stepped down and Jed took their place. His eyes danced with light.

"I cannot tell you how excited I am to be here at Ironwood."

He looked at Mercy, and then right from the pulpit, gave her a wink. And she knew that as soon as this preacher stopped talking, her new life would begin.

Epilogue

Emily flipped through the final pages of her manuscript, amazed the rest of it had come so quickly despite the sleepless nights. Luke walked softly into her office, pausing to look at their baby daughter in the bassinet.

She cooed when she saw him, and he scooped her up. Emily's heart swelled as she watched her little family, cozy in the home that had held her ancestors. The place that had changed her life and the lives of so many. She offered up another silent prayer of thanks for all she had been given, for the legacy her daughter would now share.

Luke swayed the eight-month-old baby in his arms as his gaze settled on Emily. "I take it you've finished?"

She caressed the pages. "I did." She sat back in her chair, content to tell her husband another piece of the legacy. "Faith and Nolan wed in 1888 and later moved to Memphis, where the Harper Shipping Company thrived until the depression. Faith spoke at many women's rallies and made it her mission to end the trade of women. Mercy and Jed wed only one month after he arrived at Ironwood, and they built a church that eventually served both whites and blacks in the surrounding community."

Luke nodded along, knowing this part was important to her.

She needed to finish out their stories, letting the accomplishments of their lives be spoken in the house that had already seen it all.

"The village at Ironwood remained until eventually, after the Second World War, people began to dissipate and the town was abandoned. Eventually, that part of Ironwood was sold off." She looked at him thoughtfully. "We'll have to do some searching. My great-aunt must have known about the old village. I'd like to find out exactly where it was and what happened to the people after they left."

Luke bounced the baby. "I'm guessing Buford has some information."

He probably did. The lawyer who'd come to find her and bestow her inheritance had shared a love with her great-aunt that Emily was determined to uncover. But that was a chapter of their history for another story.

Luke looked down at the happy little bundle swinging her fists. "What do you think, Miss Lydia Ruth? Shall we go down and see Auntie Dee?"

"She's here?" Emily rose and stepped around the desk.

"Yes. She arrived a few minutes ago and let herself in. She's in the kitchen making biscuits."

Emily laughed and gestured toward the door. "Then we better not keep her waiting."

She placed a kiss on her husband's cheek and then smiled down at her daughter.

The newest mistress of Ironwood.

Historical note

This book took me out of the comfort zone years of research into life during the Civil War created. I found myself spending hours researching the fashions, bustle styles, train travel, cab travel, gas lighting, steam boats, and a number of other things for this story. Although I tried my best to be historically accurate, there may have been things I missed. I hope you'll forgive me.

Jed mentions that he and Hezzie travel to Boston to visit the Tremont Temple. This church is recorded to have hosted a mixed congregation as far back as the 1830s. The other church, the one from which Mercy was taken, is based on the Cathedral of the Holy Cross, located on Washington Street in Boston.

One of the most interesting parts of my research involved the Hull Lifesavers and the shipwrecks in Boston Harbor. This took up the majority of my research hours, and had me quite stuck at one point. There was actually a hurricane in 1887 that swept the Atlantic coast without making landfall. Hurricane six, however, struck in mid-August, rather than late May as I have in the story.

The shipwrecks across Boston Harbor are based on a storm that hit in 1888. Records from the harbor detailed the wrecks that my characters learn about in the story. Joshua James was a famous Hull Lifesaver with the "Storm Warriors" of the United States Life-Saving Services. If you are interested in the story of an incredible hero, his is definitely worth reading.

Tuckernuck Island was a whaling village off the larger island of Nantucket. By the point of the story, it had been abandoned for many years. The Pollock Rip Channel is still a dangerous area for sailboats, and can only be navigated under certain conditions.

Acknowledgments

I don't know that I've ever written a more challenging novel. There are at least 35,000 words of this book that ended up on the cutting block. I just couldn't get it right. Looking back, however, I think that is because God was getting me to where I needed to be to write the story I needed to write. Like my other books, He first uses the characters and their story to speak to my own heart. My prayer, dear reader, is that He now does the same for you. May you find something in Mercy and Faith's story to draw you closer to Him.

I'd like to thank the wonderful members of my Faithful Readers Team. You prayed with me, encouraged me, and helped me think of ways out of plot problems. I treasure you all! Becky, what would I do without you? Without you as my assistant, I don't think I could get anything accomplished.

A special thanks to the beta readers who made this book better. Emily, your insight fixed a problem that had been niggling at me for a while. To my dear MS writer friends, Pam Hillman, Patricia Bradley, and Janet Ferguson, thank you for talking me through burnout and sparking passion for writing again.

Toni Shiloh and Piper Hugley I cannot thank you enough for taking the time to read the early version of this story. Writing a character outside of one's own ethnicity can be daunting. I appreciate you helping me avoid pitfalls. Any missteps remaining in the novel are entirely my fault.

The people of Journey Church, your passion and vision for

a church that looks like our community and a place where people of all backgrounds and races are made to feel like they belong, inspires me. Brandon and Stacy, what you strive to do would certainly make Jed and Mercy proud. Thank you for carrying out your calling.

Mamaw, you read them all. I'm sorry this one didn't make it to you before you no longer could. Summers spent with you mean more to me than you can imagine. I love you.

Jason, thank you for your endless patience with me. A writer's brain can be an odd place. My two monkeys, thank you for understanding when Momma spends hours at the computer dreaming up worlds.

Robin, thank you for your great edits! Your attention to story craft always makes my books better. Any mistakes remaining are totally on me. Jim, thank you for believing in me and my work. It's an encouragement when this road is long and bumpy.

Finally, to my readers. I'm still in awe of you. No story I create is complete without you. Your imagination is what brings words on a page to life. Thank you for your reviews (they mean so much!) your emails, and your company on social media. It's amazing to have so many great friends out there.

Discussion Questions

1) Ironwood Plantation becomes isolated in order to stay safe. Do you think that approach works? Why do you think people often become isolated when the world is difficult?

2) Mercy is determined to do things on her own. Why do you think she hid her offer of employment from everyone?

3) Faith tries to put on a mask to hide her insecurities. Do you think that eventually made things more difficult for her?

4) Mercy struggles with wanting to be someone important. What do you think happens when people let ambitions and the desire to be recognized by others dictate decisions?

5) Mercy realizes that the plans she has for herself and the plans God has for her aren't always the same. Why do you think it was so difficult for her to turn her dreams over to Him?

6) The title for this story has a double meaning. Mercy is physically missing, but there was also a lot of mercy missing from the attitudes of the people around her. Where did you notice this the most?

7) Jed longs for unity in the church, yet even today we find our churches divided based on race, economic class, and preferences. How do you think we can better create unity in the Church within each of our own communities?

Ironwood Plantation Family Saga

The Whistle Walk

Heir of Hope

Under the roof of a grand Mississippi plantation, two women separated by generations will discover the power of redemptive healing and a love that mends the heart.

The Accidental Spy Series
A Trilogy

*C*aptured and
mistaken as a spy,
can she unravel a
conspiracy before
her secrets cost a
man his life?

About the Author

Award winning author of Christian historical novels, Stephenia H. McGee writes stories of faith, hope, and healing set in the Deep South. When she's not twirling around in hoop skirts, reading, or sipping sweet tea on the front porch, she's a homeschool mom of two boys, writer, dreamer, and husband spoiler. Stephenia lives in Mississippi with her sons, handsome hubby, three dogs, and one antisocial cat. Visit her at www.StepheniaMcGee.com for books and updates.

Visit her website at www.StepheniaMcGee.com and be sure to sign up for the newsletter to get sneak peeks, behind the scenes fun, the occasional recipe, and special giveaways.

Facebook: Stephenia H. McGee, Christian Fiction Author

Twitter: @StepheniaHMcGee

Pinterest: Stephenia H. McGee